GALVESTON

Books by P. G. NAGLE

Glorieta Pass

The Guns of Valverde

Galveston

*Red River

*forthcoming

GALVESTON

P. G. Nagle

A TOM DOHERTY ASSOCIATES BOOK
NEW YORK

GALVESTON

Edited by James Frenkel

This book is printed on acid-free paper.

Maps by Chris Krohn

A Forge Book
Published by Tom Doherty Associates, LLC
175 Fifth Avenue
New York, NY 10010

www.tor.com

Forge® is a registered trademark of Tom Doherty Associates, LLC.

Library of Congress Cataloging-in-Publication Data

Nagle, P. G.
    Galvelston / P. G. Nagle.
        p. cm.
    "A Tom Doherty Associates book."
    ISBN 0-312-87614-9
    1. Texas—History—Civil War, 1861–1865—Fiction.   2. Galvelston (Tex.), Battle of,
1863—Fiction.   I. Title.
    PS3564.A354 G35 2002
    813'.54—dc21

                                                                    2002003938

First Edition: August 2002

Printed in the United States of America

0 9 8 7 6 5 4 3 2 1

This one's for Chris:
husband, partner, and best friend.

Acknowledgments

A great many people lent their advice, support, and expertise to the creation of this book. Thanks to Daniel Abraham, Edward T. Cotham, Jr., Ken Dusenberry, Steven C. Gould, Sally Gwylan, Earl W. Hester, Chris Krohn, Lynne Lawlor, Jane Lindskold, Louise Malone, Laura J. Mixon, James L. Moore, Fred Ragsdale, Scott Schermer, Melinda Snodgrass, Chuck Swanberg, and Sage Walker. To my editor, James Frenkel, and my agent, Chris Lotts, thanks as well.

Very special thanks to J. Patrick Kelley and John Kennington without whom the navy scenes would have been sadly wanting, to the staff of the Texas and Galveston History Center at the Rosenberg Library in Galveston (Casey Edward Greene, Shelly Kelly, Anna Peebler) for their enthusiastic research, to David and Dana Whitehorn-Umphres for their generous support of this project, and to Bruce and Marsha Krohn and Madeleine Quillen for their kind understanding.

Heartfelt thanks to Cornell University's Making of America digital library for online access to the Official Records of the armies and navies in the War of the Rebellion, and to the National Oceanographic and Atmospheric Administration and the Library of Congress for online access to historic maps and charts.

Thanks to the Galveston Historical Society, Tall Ship *Elissa*, Texas Seaport Museum, Ashton Villa, Williams House, King's Tavern (Natchez), Natchez Visitors Center, Artillery Company of

8 ✦ ACKNOWLEDGMENTS

New Mexico, New Mexico Territorial Brass Band, Houston Public Library Texas Room and Archives, UNM Center for Southwest Research, and many others, especially the editors and authors of histories and diaries covering the Battle of Galveston.

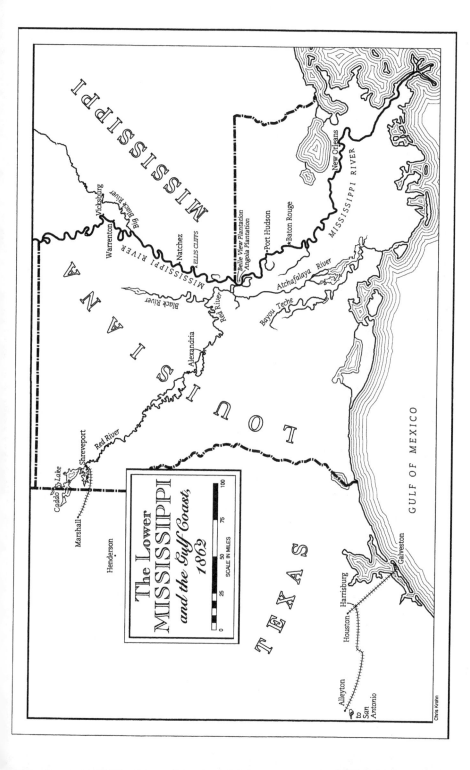

The Lower
MISSISSIPPI
and the Gulf Coast,
1862

SCALE IN MILES

0   25   50   75   100

Chris Krohn

MISSISSIPPI

LOUISIANA

TEXAS

GULF OF MEXICO

New Orleans

MISSISSIPPI RIVER

Baton Rouge

Port Hudson

Angola Plantation

Belle View Plantation

Atchafalaya River

Bayou Teche

ELLIS CLIFFS

Natchez

Warrenton

Vicksburg

Big Black River

MISSISSIPPI RIVER

Black River

Red River

Alexandria

Red River

Shreveport

Caddo Lake

Marshall

Henderson

Galveston

Harrisburg

Houston

Alleyton

to
San
Antonio

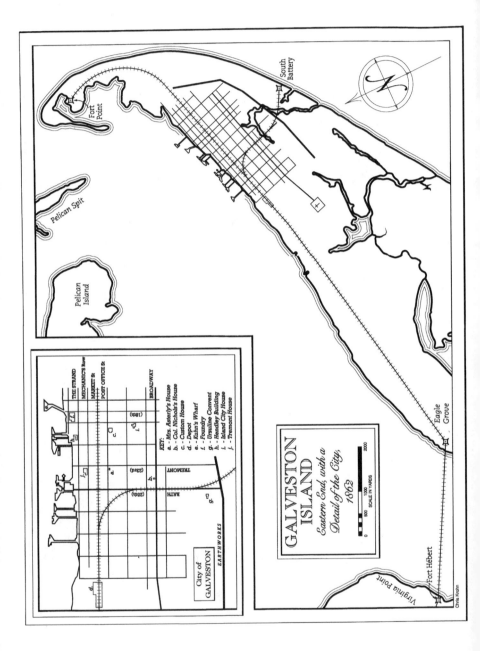

GALVESTON ISLAND
Eastern End, with a
Detail of the City,
1862

SCALE IN YARDS
0 500 1000 2000

City of
GALVESTON

EARTHWORKS

KEY:
a. - Mrs. Asterly's House
b. - Col. Nichols's House
c. - Custom House
d. - Depot
e. - Kuhn's Wharf
f. - Foundry
g. - Ursuline Convent
h. - Handley Building
i. - Island City House
j. - Tremont House

THE STRAND
MECHANIC'S Row
MARKET St
POST OFFICE St
BROADWAY
TREMONT
BATH

(19th)
(23rd)
(25th)

Fort
Point

Pelican Spit

Pelican
Island

South
Battery

Eagle
Grove

Virginia Point

Fort Hébert

Chris Krohn

. . . while we defend our rights with our strong arms and honest hearts, those we meet in battle may also have hearts as brave and honest as our own.

—Albert Miller Lea

1

. . . at last we reached San Antonio, where we were given a good suit of clothes each, furnished with a square meal, and all but the Valverde Battery furloughed for sixty days but subject to be called in at a moment's notice, and we all went home to rest and recruit.

—William L. Davidson, 5th TX Mounted Rifles

Jamie Russell gazed at the low-slung ranch house, almost glad he was not permitted to go toward it. The whitewashed boards of the old porch shimmered under the sun and the big live oak to the west of the house was just beginning to cast a dappled, restless shadow along its side. It seemed not to be real—a mirage, or some kind of trick—not the home he had longed for these many months.

Behind him the men of the Valverde Battery, in advance of the straggling remains of Sibley's Brigade, trudged eastward on the road to San Antonio. They had got some tired old mules to haul the six captured cannon—all the brigade had to show for its toilsome campaign in New Mexico—but except for Jamie and the other officers they were all on foot. On the trail baked dry by the hot July sun the column raised a dust that smelled of memories and caused Jamie's throat to tighten. Cocoa stamped with impatience; she had recognized her home, and clearly wanted to hurry up the lane to the barn. Jamie leaned down to rub the mare's neck.

"Just a little longer, girl," he said softly.

"Would you like to be dismissed, Russell?" he heard Captain Sayers say behind him. Turning in the saddle, Jamie found his new captain watching him with the steady gaze that always made him feel he should straighten his shoulders and sit or stand taller.

"No, sir. I'll come into town with the battery."

Sayers nodded approval and moved on to the head of the column. He was Jamie's age, but had been educated at the military institute in Bastrop, and always carried himself like a general. Or at least, like a colonel anyway. The only general of Jamie's acquaintance was General Sibley, who was more flash than steel. Colonel Green—a hero ever since San Jacinto—or Colonel Reily, or Colonel Scurry even, was more Jamie's idea of what a general should be. Sibley was farther back on the trail, traveling slowly with broken-down horses, and Jamie couldn't help but be glad he was not present.

The column's slow pace gave him plenty of time to muse on this, also to observe the condition of the country he had been away from for most of a year. Things seemed not to have changed much: a new barn on one neighbor's ranch, a new field under cultivation. Children scrambled down to the trail to greet the weary artillerymen, and as they neared town the column collected a sizable escort including friends and family members of those men who came from San Antonio. Jamie's family was not among them; Poppa and Gabe and Emma would all be out with the herds, and he'd known when they passed the ranch that Momma wouldn't come out and make a fuss—she wasn't that sort. It was just as well, for Jamie found his feelings were getting stirred up in a way that was not entirely pleasant. After all the Confederate Army of New Mexico had been through they were coming home at last, and the relief of it was almost painful itself.

The battery came into the Military Plaza from which the army had set out the previous autumn and halted, drawing the guns into line where they were much admired by the crowd of citizens who had turned out. A band was there playing spirited marching tunes, the mayor made a short speech, and with much waving of flags and handkerchiefs and many hurrahs, an eleven-gun salute was fired. The men of the battery were clearly cheered by the warmth of the welcome, though it was all rather too much for Jamie who was wishing to get away and just sleep for a week or two, or stare at the sky for a while and try to believe that he was really home.

At last they were dismissed, and after bidding farewell to Captain Sayers, who admonished him to report at seven sharp the next morning, Jamie turned westward again on the trail toward home. Cocoa needed no urging, and before long they were back at Russell's Ranch, turning in at the lane.

He had dreamed of this moment for so long and had always imagined himself galloping up to the house, but he found he couldn't bear to go any faster than a walk. Cocoa was tired after the long, weary march, though her ears pricked forward and she snuffed at familiar smells. Jamie let her go at her own pace. He sat back, the reins loose in his hand, just gazing at everything: the house, the barn, the well, the corral. That was Smokey in the corral, fatter than ever, and with him an unfamiliar sorrel mule. Smokey neighed a greeting and Cocoa picked up a trot. Jamie sat up straighter in the saddle, his weary bones complaining.

A figure in dusty chaps emerged from the barn and for a moment Jamie wondered if Poppa had hired on a hand. Then the tanned face turned toward him, black eyes piercing in the shade of the hat. It was Emma.

Jamie raised a hand, his throat too dry to call out. Emma stood watching, leaner than he remembered and hard-edged. As he reined Cocoa in by the rail and dismounted, she strode up the steps to the house and flung open the door.

"Jamie's home," she called into the house.

She had won out over Momma's concerns about her work clothes, then. When he'd left she was still changing in the barn and staying out of Momma's sight, with the family pretending she didn't ever wear men's clothes—oh, no. Not Miss Russell. Not Momma's daughter.

She stayed on the porch, watching him approach. He put a hand to his pocket, where he had all her letters to Captain Stephen Martin and the last one Martin had written to her, and the captain's watch, with the portrait of Emma hidden inside the fob. Jamie tried on a smile, hoping his sister would smile back. By the time he reached the steps Gabe came tumbling out the door, followed by Momma, and they both flung themselves on him, hugging and asking questions, Momma crying.

Laughing, Jamie hugged them back. He glanced up and saw Emma going back to the barn. He ignored the stab this gave him, turning instead to Momma.

"Yes, it's me," he said. "Here, where's your handkerchief? Mine are all gone."

"Oh, I have it somewhere," Momma said, feeling about her pockets. "Your father will be so sorry he was not here to greet you, but we shall see him shortly. Oh, how thin you are!" Momma's dark eyes roved his face, and her fingers squeezed his arms over and over. "Come inside, I will get you something to eat."

"Let me tend to Cocoa first."

"Gabriel can do that."

"No, I will. But you can help, Gabe. Here, stand up straight a minute."

Jamie stepped in front of his younger brother and put a hand flat on top of Gabe's head, then swung his arm back till his hand came level with his own chin. "You're going to be taller than me," he said.

Gabe grinned. "I'm taller than Davey Swanson," he boasted.

"What, that bully used to whip you after Sunday school?"

"If not before," Momma said severely. "He has not troubled us lately." She had found her handkerchief at last and stood dabbing it at her eyes.

"I bet not," Jamie said, ruffling Gabe's hair, and thinking Gabe wouldn't let him do it much longer.

"Come inside when you are finished, both of you," Momma said, moving toward the door.

"Go ahead and unsaddle her, Gabe," Jamie said as they stepped off the porch. "I'll go get a brush." He glanced over his shoulder at his brother, who reached Cocoa in five strides of his gangly legs, then he went into the barn.

It was dark, and he paused inside the door. He could have found his way around blindfolded, could have gone straight to the tack room without waiting for his eyes to adjust, but he wanted to soak it in first. Smells of musty hay and dry wood, of horses and oats and home rose up to welcome him. Specks of dust caught fire as they floated through a sunbeam that had squeezed through a crack in the wall up in the loft. The barn was silent; Momma's milk cow would be out grazing, and Poppa must still be out with the herds.

"Emma?" Jamie said softly.

He walked forward, glancing into the stalls, noting a new lantern hanging from one of the hooks. The tack room door was barely ajar. He pulled it open.

Emma was inside, reaching for a bridle. She slung it over her shoulder as he came in.

"Emma, I have some things—"

"Not now," she said curtly. "I have to ride out and check on the beef herd." She pulled her saddle off the tree.

It was late in the day for that, but Jamie didn't question it. "I'll come with you," he said.

"When you just got home? Momma would have kittens."

"Emma, I—"

"No!"

Her eyes blazed in the dimness. Jamie could see well enough now to recognize the look on her face, the look that meant she was through talking. Matt got the same look sometimes. He had worn it on the day he had left for the army.

Emma hefted the saddle and brushed past Jamie on the way out. He let her go. Maybe she would cool down, riding. It helped him sometimes.

Only there was the weight in his gut that he'd carried ever since Martin was killed in the fight at Valverde. Writing to Emma—the hardest letter he had ever written—had eased it some, but it was still there. Maybe it would never go away.

"I miss him, too, Emma," Jamie whispered, though she was long gone. He stood still for a minute, remembering how happy she had been on the night before the brigade's departure, the night Martin had proposed. They had all been happy that night. Maybe that had been the last time.

He became aware that he was staring at the tack room floor. He raised his eyes to the saddle trees, all empty except for Gabe's. As he stood gazing at them, Gabe hurried in and grabbed his saddle and a bridle, catching Jamie's eye with a frowning glance before running out again. Poppa must have ordered him to stay with Emma when she rode out. Jamie couldn't imagine their father allowing her to ride herd by herself, and he could imagine all too well how she must resent it. Poor Gabe.

He looked back at the tack room wall. Six trees empty. Matt's and Daniel's were deep in dust. So was his own, Jamie realized, and brushed his hand along it, as if that mattered. He missed his elder brothers, away serving with their own regiments. It made coming home less delightful than he had hoped. Shaking off that thought, Jamie reached for a brush and headed back outside.

The U.S.S. *Harriet Lane* strained at the hawser, her sidewheels digging into the Mississippi as she tried in vain to drag the mortar schooner *Sidney C. Jones* free of the sandbar on which she had lodged. Acting Master Quincy Wheat watched from the *Lane*'s brass-railed deck with his brother, Nathaniel, who had crossed the peninsula opposite Vicksburg to pay him a visit. Nat was serving as a carpenter aboard the ram *Queen of the West*, flagship of the U.S. Army's river fleet, which lay above Vicksburg, hidden from its batteries by the Mississippi's sharp bend.

Quincy had visited Nat on the *Queen* the previous week, and found her inferior to the *Lane*. She had begun life as a towboat in Cincinnati, and had been converted into a ram by application of heavy oak reinforcements to her bow and a bulwark over her lower deck to protect her machinery. The *Harriet Lane*, by contrast, was a former revenue cutter so handsomely appointed she had won a prize for her designer, and had frequently been used to entertain visiting dignitaries before the war.

Nat's joining the *Queen*'s crew had added army-and-navy differences to the rivalry he and Quincy had indulged since boyhood, though in fact Nat was more a riverboat man than anything else. The rivalry persisted, though, and while the *Harriet Lane* was unquestionably more beautiful than the *Queen*, Quincy could not help hoping that she would succeed at her task while his elder brother was present.

He kept an eye to the river, rubbing at a trickle of sweat that had run down into his collar. He disliked the sultry, sullen Mississippi with her writhing course and her treacherous snags. Though river-bred himself, navy service had taught him to prefer open water, set sails, starlight, and the breath of the sea. The air here was bad. The river's level was dropping with the high heat of July, but the mosquitoes and miasmatic swamps were no better. Already the crew were succumbing to fever, and the men could not be spared. The low water had also made snags and bars an increasing danger, hence the mortar schooner's distress.

Quincy looked up at the *Lane*'s funnel, just aft of the foremast. Smoke chuffed out of it in writhing clouds as the engine drove against the current. It appeared the *Harriet Lane* was not strong enough to pull the *Jones* free. He glanced nervously toward the center of the river, where a certain rippling of the water indicated shallow hazards. If the hawser parted, the *Lane* could shoot out across the channel and be in danger of grounding herself. A detail stood ready to cast loose the anchor if this should occur; still it would be an embarrassment at the very least.

"She won't come off," Nat said behind him.

Quincy threw him an irritated glance, then turned to acknowledge the arrival on deck of Acting Master Frank Becker, his immediate superior. Becker was a South Carolinian, tall and burly with keen eyes and reddish brown side whiskers, rather more like Nathaniel in appearance than Quincy was himself. Nat's years working in their father's boatyard in Cincinnati had given him large shoulders to go with his curling golden hair, while Quincy remained lean, with hair of an undistinguished watery brown and inclined not so much to curl as to appear disordered. Quincy had long deplored this unfair allocation of attractions and sought to make up for it by cultivating a charming manner. The fact that, after his departure for the Naval Academy three years before, Miss Renata Keller had not succumbed to Nat's advances, or for that matter to those of any other of her numerous admirers, gave Quincy cause to hope that he had succeeded.

Becker looked at Nat. "Seen you before, haven't I? You're Wheat's brother?"

Nat nodded, and a wry smile crept onto his face. "Too bad about the schooner. Nasty job getting her off that bar."

Acting Master Robert Gerard joined them, shaking his head and saying, "She's stuck fast." He was from Kentucky, half a year younger than Quincy, junior to him and a bit shorter, with dark hair that clung limply to his head in the heat. "We'll have to leave her behind," he added.

Nat raised an eyebrow at Quincy, who said, "Commander Porter wants the steamers to tow the mortars down to New Orleans as soon as possible."

"What, no more nighttime bombardments?" said Nat, grinning. "We've been growing rather fond of them the last couple of weeks. You fellows put on a good show."

"Waste of ordnance," Becker said. "Without a land assault we'll never take Vicksburg."

Above them on the bridge Lieutenant Lea, the executive officer, called "All ahead a quarter" down the speaking tube to the engine room. A moment later the wheels' swish slowed to a whisper. The tension on the hawser eased, and Quincy sighed, disappointed.

The mortar schooner remained solidly lodged atop the bar, canted a little to one side. Commander Wainwright, the *Lane*'s captain, called off the attempt to remove it and ordered the anchor loosed, and the Lanes who had gone out to the bar disengaged the hawser and began bringing it back aboard.

"I see you have also been filling up your crew with contrabands," Nat said, watching the sailors at work.

"Some of them are free blacks," Quincy said.

"Not that there is much difference," Becker added.

"There is in their eyes."

One of the midshipmen, a lad of seventeen with a face all over freckles, hurried up to Becker, who stepped aside to speak with him. Gerard turned to Nat.

"Do you have many contrabands aboard the *Queen*?"

"They're about all we can get these days," Nat said. He gazed out at the sailors with a critical eye. Quincy knew he mistrusted negroes, as did their father. He was not overly fond of them himself, but necessity had caused the navy to enlist them in ever greater numbers over the past year. Some were slackers, but so too were some of the white men. For the most part, the negroes made good sailors.

"How is Colonel Ellet?" Quincy asked. The commander of the ram fleet had suffered serious injury at the Battle of Memphis in June. Nat had described the battle to Quincy during Quincy's visit to the *Queen*, and had also written him a letter about it, which was somewhere en route between Philadelphia and New Orleans and would reach him eventually.

Nat shook his head. "His leg is very bad. Grows weaker every day. The surgeon is in despair, not to mention Ellet's son." He looked from Quincy to Gerard. "Pray for him, lads."

"We do," Quincy said.

Becker returned. "Commander Wainwright is going to inform Commander Porter that the *Jones* cannot be freed. We'll be leaving shortly after his return." He consulted his timepiece and looked at Nat. "I must prepare for my watch. Good day, Mr. Wheat. I will probably not see you again." He shook Nat's hand, gave a curt nod to Quincy and Gerard, and went below.

Nat looked at Quincy, the humor gone from his face. "Leaving that soon?"

Quincy nodded. "We have to coal yet, and we must get down to the barges before dark. We have no pilot, so we cannot run at night."

"You could pilot her, couldn't you, Quincy?" Nat said, a sly smile curving his lips. "Uncle Charlie taught us the river to Natchez."

"Eight years ago. I believe the river may have altered a trifle since then."

Nat's smile softened. "Well, I'm glad I came to see you," he said, offering his hand. "Sorry you have to go."

Quincy shook it, smiling back. Despite the rivalry, he loved his brother very much.

"At least you've been able to visit each other," Gerard said. "The rest of us poor devils have to wait for mail from home."

"Speaking of which," Nat said to Quincy, "I've a letter from our mother that you haven't read." He withdrew a handful of papers from his pocket, picked one out and offered it. "Father appended his usual request that I stop all this nonsense and come back home to help him build boats."

"He always writes that." Quincy took the letter, noting that among the others was one of a certain shade of pale blue. "You've had a letter from Miss Keller, too, I see."

Nat grinned. "Yes I have, and that one I will not share with you." He returned the papers to his pocket. "Will you be coming back up, do you think?"

"I hope not," Quincy said. "Not that I don't love your company, brother dear, but to be honest I'd rather be out on blockade. At least there we'd have a decent chance of some prize money."

"That's right," said Gerard. "You don't need our help taking potshots at Vicksburg, after all, do you? Send us word when the army's ready to attack them in earnest, and we'll come back up and lend a hand."

With a cheerful wave Gerard left them, stepping closer to the bridge in response to a summons from Mr. Lea. Quincy turned to his brother.

"Anything you'd like me to send you from New Orleans?" he said, knowing there probably wasn't but that Nat would envy him the chance of visiting the Crescent City.

Nat's eyes narrowed and a smile curved up one side of his mouth. "No, thank you," he said. "I've requested leave to visit Cincinnati for a couple of weeks. I'll give Miss Keller your regards."

"Touché," Quincy said, laughing, a hand to the imaginary wound in his heart. "Come on, I'll see you ashore."

"Get up, Smokey!" Emma refrained from kicking the horse, wishing for the thousandth time he was not such a slug. She kept him to a lope though he would clearly have preferred to walk. She had no sympathy for the horse, and no desire to make it easy for Gabe to catch up to her. She could hear Strawberry behind her, the mule's hoofbeats muffled by the sweltering air.

She threw one glance southward to where another bedraggled column of returning soldiers was raising clouds of dust from the trail. Chiding herself, she faced forward and slapped the reins against the saddle to wake Smokey up again. No use looking at them, she thought angrily. No single use whatever. There was no one there she wanted to see.

The wind stung at her eyes and she kept her head low, shielding her face with the wide brim of her slouch hat. Smokey's hooves pounded the grassy hillsides. Here and there a live oak grew, casting spots of shade through which she could ride for a moment's relief from the sun. The herd was a few miles away; she would have to hurry in order to get back for supper. She did not particularly want to hurry back, but she knew Momma would be angry if she was absent from the table on Jamie's first night home.

I should not have been so short with him.

She had not even welcomed him home. A fine sister she was! She blinked in the bright sun, wishing she had behaved better. All she had been able to think of, though, since the moment she had seen him riding up the lane, was the awful news he had sent her.

Dearest Emma. I am so sorry. Stephen is dead.

How had he dared to write her a letter like that? How could he wound her so, and crush her every hope? He had told her Stephen died a hero, trying to make her feel better, she supposed, but she had not wanted him to be a hero. He was a quartermaster, heroics were not his business. They both were quartermasters. He and Jamie should never have been in that fight. He should have come home today.

Emma drew one sobbing gasp, then bit down hard on her sorrow. Smokey had dropped to a walk during her inattention, and she heard the mule slowing to a trot. Gabe had the wit not to come up and talk to her; maybe he knew she'd bite his head off if he tried. She wiped the back of a gloved hand across her cheek and lifted the reins again. No self-pity; she did not need or want pity of any kind. She had work to do.

"Get up, Smokey," she said bitterly, and cracked the reins in the air.

"No, not another bite," Jamie said, leaning back in his chair and patting his stomach, which was stretched to the limit and already beginning to ache. Momma had made his favorite meal, chicken and dumplings, followed by cherry pie, which seemed an enormous extravagance after the campaign fare he was used to. "Supper was wonderful," he added.

Momma's smile expressed her pleasure. "Thank you, Jamie," she said, setting down her silver pie server.

"I can eat another piece," Gabe said, and held out his plate.

Momma gave him a stern look, but picked up the pie server and accepted his plate. It was a celebration, which in the Russell household meant everyone could have as much as they wanted. This was not Momma's usual way, for hers was a saving disposition, but on holidays, birthdays, and Sunday dinners when there was company, she relaxed her rules. Jamie smiled at the thought he was being treated like company. It felt good, and it wouldn't last, which was also good.

"When you are finished, you may clear up," Momma told Gabe, serving him a generous slice of cherry pie.

"I'll do it," Emma said. She stood up and picked up her dinner plate and Poppa's, striding away to the kitchen. She had put on a dress but she still walked like a ranch hand, and her short hair tended to be unruly. She looked awkward, unlike herself. Jamie saw Momma's eyes follow her, then turn to Poppa.

"Well," Poppa said. He did not continue; he had said "Well" several times during the meal, and only once or twice had followed it with a comment about the weather or a bit of news from town. He had settled into looking at Jamie with a slightly surprised expression, as if his son had grown six inches overnight or done something equally unexpected. Jamie was conscious of it, and ignored it, and tried not to let it annoy him.

"Will you be returning to work in town, now that you are home?" Momma asked.

Jamie glanced up at her, smiling in the hope of setting her at ease. "I'll be going in to work with the battery, but Captain Sayers said I could sleep here."

Momma blinked at him as if she did not understand. Really,

she did, Jamie knew. It was only that she had not liked his answer. She had been picturing him back at work in Webber's Mercantile, he supposed. She still disliked the idea that he was a soldier. She and Poppa had convinced themselves that by allowing him to join the Quartermaster Corps they were preserving him from exposure to war's hardships. He had thought so, too, he admitted to himself. How naive of them all.

Now he was home, not a quartermaster anymore but a lieutenant of artillery, still learning his duties and not quite sure what he expected of himself, except that he knew he must honor Martin and the others who had fallen at Valverde by serving the guns they had given their lives to capture. The Valverde Battery was all Sibley's Brigade had left of the dreams that had carried them to New Mexico. He could not turn away from that small success. To do so would be to accept utter defeat.

Emma came back from the kitchen and cleared away more dishes. No one said anything. Gabe was busy gobbling up his pie, and Momma and Poppa seemed to have run out of questions for Jamie. He had answered most of them over supper. Most. The big question still hung over them all like a cloud that would not drop its rain. The big "What happened?" question. The one Jamie least wanted to answer.

So he sat, silently looking from one to the other of his parents. They did not know quite what to make of him, it seemed. He was not the son they expected. Maybe he didn't belong here anymore, he thought, and his stomach clenched down on its unfamiliar burden.

The table was clear; Emma returned a last time and passed straight through to the family room. Jamie heard the front door bang shut. After a moment, he quietly excused himself, and followed.

She was sitting on the steps, but stood up again as Jamie came out. He looked up at the first stars peeping out, hazy in the warm evening. The air was so moist here—he had been in the desert so long he had become accustomed to the dryness. He felt sleepy, but he wanted to talk to Emma before going to bed. He just wasn't quite sure how to start.

"I missed you," he said.

"Well, we all missed you, too."

"When did you cut your hair?"

Emma's face hardened, and she looked away. "Right after I got your letter."

That hurt, and it made him say, "It wasn't my fault." He had not meant to say that.

"I know," Emma said in a low voice. "I know that."

Jamie pressed his lips together, wanting to make sure he said nothing that would hurt her. "I have your letters," he began. "I thought you might want them back."

"M-my letters?" She looked up at him, seeming suddenly younger, and afraid.

"Your letters to Stephen," he said. "He saved them all, and I brought them back for you." He reached into his pocket, but she raised a hand as if to hold him off.

"No," she said, barely above a whisper. "No, I don't want them."

"Well, there is also—"

"Don't," she said in a strangled voice. "I don't want to talk about it."

"Emma, please let me give you these things!"

He had not meant to speak so sharply. They stood still, both of them, shocked into silence. Jamie felt his hands start to tremble and he gripped the watch tightly, not wanting to drop it. He swallowed, and drew a breath. "You can burn the letters if you don't want to read them," he said, his voice low and rough. He held out the packet tied with ribbon—a pink ribbon, one she had worn, he suspected. Emma accepted it, and the three unopened letters that Jamie had collected when the army got back to Mesilla. There was one more, a letter Martin had written to her and never got to mail. Jamie had found it in his pocket after the battle. He held it out to her in one hand and offered the watch with the other.

Emma's letters scattered at their feet; she cupped Martin's letter in both hands as if it were made of glass, and allowed Jamie to place the watch on top of it. The chain spilled into her hands, and without a word she strode away, down the steps, treading on her own letters, out into the night. It was getting dark now, but he didn't need to see her to know she had started to run.

Jamie gazed up at the sky. No moon yet. A tear fought its way out of him and ran down his cheek. He brushed it away, and bent down to pick up the letters Emma had dropped. She wouldn't want them to blow all over—her secret hopes scattered on the ground for anyone to trample—so he picked them up and bundled them all together in the pink ribbon, then turned to go back inside to the family.

2

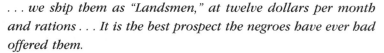

. . . we ship them as "Landsmen," at twelve dollars per month and rations . . . It is the best prospect the negroes have ever had offered them.
　　　—Acting Master Roswell H. Lamson, U. S. Navy

"Would you fill the coffee, Emma dear?"

Emma accepted the empty pot from Momma's hands and went to the kitchen without a word, her skirts hushing against the doorway. She had not felt like talking much this morning, having slept poorly despite going to bed very late. She did not know what the time had been, exactly, but Momma and the boys had already retired when she returned to the house. Only Poppa had waited up for her, giving her a severe look when she came in. He had not scolded, though. A small blessing.

The kitchen was filled with sunshine, and a warm breeze tossed the curtains around the open window. Emma drew it nearly closed, then went to the stove where both kettle and coffee boiler were roiling. She took the coffee off the fire and put in a spoonful of cold water to settle the grounds, then rinsed the coffeepot with hot water from the kettle. She tried to remember how far she had run last night, or in what direction. The whole horrible evening was unclear in her mind. She knew she had been unkind to Jamie but he had not exactly been kind to her either. She had run until she was exhausted, fallen weeping on the ground, then slowly returned to the ranch house, guided by the lights of the windows and on the front porch. She had not gone in but had entered the barn instead and silently lit a lantern to carry into the loft, an awkward climb in her dress but one she had made many a time. There she had opened Stephen's letter with shaking fingers and read it, half-blinded by tears. It was full of inconsequent nothings; all the same things he had written in other letters, with only one addition: "We are likely to have a turn-up tomorrow. Jamie is a trifle nervous but don't worry, I will take care of him. He will be steadier after a taste of fighting."

Emma brushed a threatening tear aside and poured coffee into the pot. She set down the boiler, then straightened up and closed her eyes, taking two deep breaths before she returned to the table.

Poppa lifted his cup and she came around to pour for him, then filled Momma's and Jamie's cups as well before going back to her own place. She glanced up at Gabe, raising the pot, but he shook his head, so she served herself.

"So you went ahead with the mules?" Jamie asked Poppa as Emma sat down.

Poppa nodded. "Cattle prices never recovered after they dropped so bad last year. We were lucky to have that contract with the army."

The contract Stephen got us, Emma thought. From the corner of her eye she saw Jamie glance her way. She picked up a biscuit she wasn't hungry for and set to buttering it.

"The army buys mules, too," Poppa went on.

"And they'll bring a lot more money," Gabe added around a mouthful of biscuit.

"Gabriel," Momma said quietly.

Gabe hung his head, hastily swallowed, and apologized. Emma took a bite of her own biscuit. It tasted like chalk; Momma's tender buttermilk biscuit. She forced herself to swallow it.

"What about the beef herd?" Jamie asked.

"I'm just letting it grow for now. Selling off the scrub stock for hides and tallow, enough to tide us over until the first mules are grown. The beeves are up by the north creek. I wanted to keep them out of the way of your column."

"Why, Poppa!" Jamie assumed an air of dignified offense. "I have no notion what you may be implying. Our army is made of noble men—"

"Pack of coyotes," Poppa said.

"—who would never dream of despoiling loyal Texians of their property."

"If they stood to get caught," Poppa added, and Jamie's mouth widened in a reluctant grin.

"It is a great pity that our soldiers are forced to forage for their meat," Momma observed. "It cannot but lead to the degradation of their morals. I am afraid it has always been so, however, so I shall not say any more about it. Did your father show you Matthew's letter, Jamie?"

"No. Has he been in another fight?"

"Yes, a pretty bad one, at Gaines' Mill," Poppa said. "They lost two hundred out of their regiment, and all the field officers."

"*All?* Matt wasn't hurt, was he?"

The sudden tense note in her brother's voice made Emma look up. Jamie's face looked taut; there were lines in the tanned skin that were certainly new. She watched as they eased while Poppa reassured him, though they never vanished completely. Jamie looked older, she realized. She hadn't noticed it before.

Well, he was older. So were they all. The past year had not been especially kind to the Russells. She had thought she had recovered from the news of Stephen's death, but it seemed she was mistaken. Since Jamie had come home her feelings were all awry and she could not get them back into order. She wondered why it was so hard to behave normally; why every comment made by any of the family pricked at her so; why she resented the dress she had put on in her brother's honor.

A nudge from Gabe made her look up. He was holding out his empty coffee cup. She picked up the pot and filled it for him.

"We have had a letter from your Aunt May as well," Momma said.

Emma glanced up, but Momma was speaking to Jamie. A splash of coffee dripped onto the tablecloth. She set down the pot, frowning as she wiped at the spill with her napkin.

"How is she?" Jamie asked.

"She complains of the heat," Momma said. "She feels a visit to the sea would do her good."

"Wants to go to Galveston," Poppa added. "As if it would be any cooler there."

"The island enjoys more breezes than Houston, perhaps," Momma said. "Sea air has always benefited her constitution. She wants a change most of all, I believe."

Emma took a sip of coffee, keeping her eyes on her plate. She knew what was coming. Already her anger was rising; she wrapped both hands around her cup, as if that would help her control it.

"This may not be the best time for her to go," Jamie said. "The blockade—I mean, Yankee ships could attack anywhere along the coast."

"Your aunt's opinion of the blockade is not very high," Momma said. "The better part of their ships are along the eastern coast. But you make a good point. I will mention it to her in my next letter." She paused, and Emma felt her shoulder muscles tightening.

"She has invited your sister to come for a visit," Momma added.

"To Houston, or Galveston?" Jamie asked, frowning.

"She doesn't seem to have decided," Poppa said.

Emma put down her biscuit. "I won't go," she said.

Everyone's eyes turned to her. "Emmaline," Momma said in much the same tone she had used to Gabe.

"I don't want to go to Houston. I have work to do here."

"Jamie's back now," Poppa said.

Emma raised her gaze to Jamie's face, which wore a startled look. "I—Poppa, I can't stay," he said. "I'm not even on furlough yet—"

"But you will be, won't you? I thought you said the army would have some time off."

"The army, yes, but the battery is just organized—"

"Can't you request a furlough? You're an officer."

"Well, yes, I could—"

"Then you can help here while Emma visits Aunt May," Momma said.

Jamie looked dismayed. He glanced Emma's way, mouth half open as if preparing to speak, but it was taking him too long. He never did stand up to Momma. He would not be any help.

Emma rose and picked up her cup and plate. "I have work to do," she said, and strode into the kitchen. She put her dishes in the basin and went out the back door, not wanting to pass through the dining room again.

The kitchen garden was full of motion: bean plants and Momma's prize tomatoes waving in the breeze. Emma hurried through it and around to the front of the house, where she slipped in and went to her bedroom. Stripping off dress and petticoats, she reached for her work clothes—they had been Daniel's before he left to join Terry's Rangers. She had tried one of Matt's shirts but it had been too big for her. She would owe Dan a new wardrobe, whenever he returned.

She pulled on her boots and strapped her chaps over her trousers. Looking down at her dresser, her gaze fell on Stephen's watch, lying atop the letter she had cried over. Beside them lay her letters to Stephen, packaged again in their ribbon, occupying the farthest corner of the dresser as if trying not to intrude. She frowned and picked up the watch. Inside the fob was a miniature portrait of herself for which she'd willingly paid an extortionate fee to San Antonio's best painter. She looked at it, marveling at the happy smile, the long, dark curls, the blushing cheeks. That girl seemed a million years away from her. Maybe that girl was dead.

She heard Gabe enter his bedroom next door. Probably hustling to get ready for work, so he could keep an eye on her. She knew it would be useless to protest being saddled with her younger brother's escort, but she never went out of her way to wait for him. It was almost a game they played, except that she didn't find it especially amusing.

Closing the fob, she clipped the silver chain to her shirt and stuffed the watch into her pocket. It felt heavy there, an unfamiliar burden. No doubt she would get accustomed to it. She picked up her hat and headed out to work.

Jamie hesitated a second too long while retrieving the rammer, and Captain Sayers chided him for it. "Get away from the muzzle faster," he said.

"Sorry. I was trying to remember which foot to step back with," Jamie said.

"If you cannot remember just get back. Get away from a loaded cannon as fast as you can."

Jamie nodded, rested the rammer against the axle of the gun carriage and took off his hat to wipe his sweating brow. The little mountain howitzer gleamed hot, and the air was thick enough that it seemed to waver. Sayers stood patiently behind the carriage in the gunner's position, his face shaded by a wide-brimmed hat, his trim form looking impossibly cool in the midday, midsummer heat of San Antonio. He had shaved and trimmed his mustache since returning, perhaps even had his hair cut. Jamie had only managed a shave. He would have to ask Momma to cut his hair for him.

No one else was out; they were alone in the yard of the old mission—that famed Alamo that General Sidney Sherman had bid the heroes of San Jacinto to remember—now being used as a depot and presently housing the Valverde Battery in its courtyard. The batterymen were at the stables being drilled on care of horses, and Sayers had taken the time to come help Jamie understand the details of the school of the piece.

"Which foot is it, anyway?" Jamie asked, annoyed with himself.

"The right."

"May I try it again?"

Sayers nodded. It was good of him, Jamie knew, to take the time to drill him in the cannoneers' positions. Jamie had learned a lot while the brigade rested at Franklin and he had drilled his section in the procedure for loading and firing the guns, but directing the actions and performing them oneself were two very different things. He wanted to, indeed he must, be ready to step into any man's position during combat.

He picked up the rammer and rested its end just inside the muzzle, then rammed the imaginary round home and withdrew the rammer in one fluid movement. He stumbled a little but managed to get the implement out and get back behind the carriage wheel in good time.

"Better," Sayers said. "Now, ready!"

Jamie cringed away from the howitzer, looking over his shoulder at the muzzle in order to watch for the flash. "Keep the wheel between your face and the muzzle if you can," Sayers told him, "in case something flies in your direction. And be sure to angle your back toward the muzzle, and be well to the rear of the face. If you are too far forward, the concussion can stop your heart." Jamie nodded and leaned a little farther toward the rear of the gun.

"Good. And on 'fire' you return to post. Care to try number three?"

"I think I remember that pretty well," Jamie said.

"Then try three and four both. That is what you are most likely to have to do on the field, if you lose too many men."

Jamie nodded and replaced the rammer-sponge, trading it for the pouches that held vent prick, thumb stall, lanyard, and primers. He had never handled all these at once, and it proved something of a challenge. Sayers ran him through the drill again and again until he could comfortably manage all the tasks.

"Enough," Jamie said at last. "Let me buy you a beer."

Sayers's smile, rare and fleeting, flashed in the shadow of his hat. They returned the gun to its place in the battery, put away the equipment, and walked over to Menger's next door.

Mr. Menger brewed the best beer in San Antonio, and had recently used his profits to open a modest hostelry of brick in addition to his taproom. The latter was doing brisk business as Sibley's Brigade straggled into town, even though the men had not yet been paid. Jamie and Sayers entered its cool darkness and stepped up to the long, polished oak bar to order their pints.

"Hey, Russell!" called a voice from the back of the room.

Jamie looked around. Still a bit dazzled from the sunlight outdoors, he had to squint to see John Reily grinning and saluting him with a half-empty glass. Next to Reily sat Ellsberry Lane, former adjutant of the 1st, who had recently become the brigade's acting assistant adjutant general. Jamie turned back to the tapster. "Two more," he said, and put coin on the counter to cover the drinks.

Sayers, who had been adjutant of the 2nd regiment and was a former schoolmate of Lane's at Bastrop Military Academy, knew both Lane and Reily well. He helped Jamie carry the beer to the table where the two staffers sat.

Jamie grinned at his friends. "Welcome home!"

"Captain Reily, Lieutenant Lane," Sayers said as he set down two beers. "I believe I ought to wish you many happy returns of the day, Lieutenant."

Jamie glanced at Lane, who smiled. "It was yesterday, actually," Lane said, "but thank you, Captain Sir."

"Happy belated, then." Jamie raised his glass to Lane, then frowned at the ceiling, calculating. "So you have almost exactly a year and a half on me."

Reily, who at twenty-six was himself Jamie's senior by nearly six years, cocked an eye up at Sayers. "Unbend, Joseph, or you'll never be able to sit." He leaned his tall frame back in his chair and finished his beer in one draft before reaching for the new glass. "Saw you out there drilling this poor boy to death," he added.

"At my own request," Jamie said, and took a deep swallow of the rich, brown beer.

"Well, you need it! You handle that sponge like a mop." Reily grinned, giving Jamie a wink. He had teased Jamie ever since he had briefly assisted one of Reily's guns when the Pike's Peakers tried to recapture it during the retreat from New Mexico. Jamie had known nothing of a cannoneer's duties then; he had still been quartermaster. Now Jamie was an artilleryman, and Reily had left the artillery to join his father's staff.

"How's Colonel Reily?" Jamie asked. "Did he enjoy his visit to Mexico?"

"Oh, absolutely. Father loves playing the diplomat, and they received him most courteously, not that it helps us now. He's busy writing placating letters to Richmond at the moment. I predict General Sibley will be called to account for himself."

"Has Sibley crawled into town yet?"

Lane spoke up. "He's a few days out still, traveling with some of Green's regiment. His ambulance mules keep dying."

"Oh, poor general," said Reily in a mocking tone.

"Poor mules," Jamie said.

Lane grinned. Jamie liked them both, but he felt closer to Lane than to Reily. Perhaps it was just that he found Lane less intimidating. Then, too, Jamie and Lane had both been in the heat of things at Glorieta, and Reily had missed that battle, a fact that still rankled with him. Jamie glanced at the scar that ran from Lane's left cheek up into his hair. It was a little less noticeable now.

"Things shaping up at headquarters?" he asked.

"Lord, no," said Lane. "It'll be a mess for weeks. We won't have half an idea of our condition until most of the stragglers get in." He sipped his beer. "How's your family?"

Jamie looked down at the tabletop marred by dozens of carved initials. "Fine," he said. "How's Mollie?"

"She's first rate, thank you," Lane said, grinning like the newlywed he essentially was, though his marriage had taken place months ago, just before the brigade had left for New Mexico. "I want you to meet her."

"How about your sister, Russell?" Reily asked, his voice unusually gentle. "How is she?"

"She's all right." Jamie took another swig of beer.

"Now, Ellsberry," Sayers said, turning to Lane, "can I expect to replace my stock any time soon? We've received a request to display the battery in Austin, but I doubt my poor mules can drag the guns that far."

"I expect you can't," Lane replied with false severity, "especially if you keep calling me by my parents' curse."

"Mea culpa, Señor Lane. A thousand pardons."

"Still no mules." Lane shook his head. "You'll have to do better than that."

Jamie smiled as they haggled, grateful to Sayers for changing the subject. All the officers in the brigade knew of Emma's engagement, of course. Everyone was surely wondering about her now, and Jamie knew she would hate the curious gazes she would get the next time she came into town. He couldn't think of any way to prevent it, except making as little fuss as possible.

"By the way, Owens is back, too," Reily said to Jamie.

"Oh?" Jamie took another deep pull of beer.

"He was over at headquarters this morning. Asked after you."

Jamie gave a fleeting smile. He wasn't terribly fond of Captain Owens, a plantation-bred, old-school Southern gentleman who had also been on Sibley's staff. After Valverde, Owens had pressed Jamie to talk about the battle. Jamie was sure it had been kindly meant, but he hadn't been ready for it.

He looked up at his friends and his captain, joking companionably over their beers. None of them had talked much about

Valverde, except in roundabout ways, ever since it happened. An outsider might think they considered it a victory and no more, but Jamie remembered the way their eyes had turned toward the battleground as they passed west of it, toiling through the mountains on the long march home. For himself, he had felt haunted gazing across the valley toward the ford where Martin and so many others had laid down their lives.

His friends burst into laughter, startling Jamie from his reverie. He smiled, shaking off the cobwebs of gloom, and drained his beer.

Quincy stood on the sweltering deck, holding a handkerchief over his mouth as he watched the crew fill hundred-pound sacks with coal and haul them from the barge across to the *Harriet Lane*. From her deck the line of sweating sailors emptied their burdens down a chute that led into her capacious bunkers. Coal dust filled the air and stuck to everything, dulling the gleaming brightwork and glowing wood of the ship, blackening the sailors' trousers and the rigging. It always took at least a full day to clean the ship after coaling; a filthy, disheartening job that was necessary all too often while they were on the river and unable to use sail. The *Lane*'s engine was greedy; she gobbled a ton of coal an hour under steam, and could store only about six days' worth.

The coal barges had nearly grounded on the way up to the fleet, Quincy had heard. With the water in the river continuing to drop, Commander Porter had openly worried about getting the biggest ships out of the Mississippi if they remained up by Vicksburg much longer. If his fears proved true, *Harriet Lane* and the other light steamers would have the joy of pulling them off of snags and sandbars all the way to the South Pass, where they would no doubt stick again trying to get over the bar at the river's mouth.

Seeking escape from coal and heat both, Quincy went below. The starboard watch had been sent to mess while the port watch kept coaling. It meant a dinner seasoned with coal dust, but there were worse fates.

The wardroom was stuffy and a faint haze hung in the air, but at least the sounds of feet trampling the decks, coal crashing into the bunkers, and men shouting orders were less immediate. The room was large for shipboard, eighteen feet long, though it seemed small when filled with officers, which happened often enough. Quincy's quarters and those of Becker, Gerard, Lieutenant Lea, Mr. Richardson, and Dr. Penrose all opened off it; tiny compartments of precious semiprivacy, shut behind slatted wooden doors with brass fittings. Their appointments and those of the wardroom itself were handsome, like everything aboard the *Lane*. Her maker, William H. Webb, had fitted her out everywhere with fine woods and copious brass ornamentation. This might make the sailors who had to polish it all every day groan, but it also made the *Lane* a pleasant ship on which to live. She had been used for numerous ceremonial occasions before the war, and had once carried no less a dignitary than the Prince of Wales, on a visit to Mount Vernon to place a wreath on the tomb of George Washington.

Becker and Gerard were getting up from the table as Quincy came down. The wardroom steward, a free black named Peter, cleared away their plates.

"Dinner good today?" Quincy asked.

"Excellent," Gerard told him, patting his gut.

"Where'd you get the sweet potatoes?" asked Becker.

"Traded for them," Quincy said. "Some field hands came alongside of us in a skiff, wanting coffee."

"You are a genius, my friend," Becker told him. "And you are covered in dust. Shake yourself off before you come in, old fellow. You'll get it all over our beautiful carpet."

Gerard glanced at the painted oilcloth that protected the wardroom's floor. "Too late," he said. "Come on, let's go get covered in dust ourselves."

"God, I hate coaling," said Becker. "Always takes twice as long as it ought. Those slugs won't go above a snail's pace."

By "those slugs," Quincy knew him to mean the contrabands.

"Well, it is hot," he replied temperately.

"It would make no difference if it were freezing," Becker said. "You can shout until you are blue in the face, and never get them to put their backs into it. They only understand the lash."

Quincy glanced toward the galley, but the steward was not in sight. His eyes met Gerard's, and the other shrugged. "Look on the bright side," Gerard said. "We'll be at Natchez tomorrow."

"Wonderful. A different set of Rebels to stare at."

"And maybe a dispatch ship," Quincy said. "Maybe ice, maybe mail—"

A clatter overhead and a crescendo of angry shouting made them all look up at the skylight. The noise subsided, the trample of feet resumed, and Gerard started up the companionway but retreated when the paymaster, Richardson, came down.

"What was that ruckus above?" Becker demanded.

"One of the men fainted and spilled a sack of coal on the deck," Richardson said, easing his lean figure into a chair at the table.

"He'll be all right, I hope?" Quincy asked.

"Yes. Just overcome by the heat."

"Or felt he wanted a rest," Becker said.

Richardson put up an eyebrow. "I doubt it," he said. "Dr. Penrose is pretty good at spotting shirkers, and his cures are effective discouragements."

Becker shrugged, and followed Gerard up the companionway. Quincy gazed after them for a moment before joining Richardson at the wardroom table. Becker, Quincy, and Gerard had been midshipmen at the Naval Academy when the war broke out, and had been scooped up together with all of their class and thrown into the navy. Hard work and hard study had helped them pass their exams, and earned them promotion as acting masters. In the spring they had participated in the subdual of Forts Jackson and St. Philip below New Orleans and the subsequent capture of that city. Their recent duty had consisted of harassing the Rebel fortifications at Vicksburg. Quincy got along with his classmates, but at times he wondered if Becker, particularly, was a bit unreliable. He seemed quick to anger, especially with the negroes. There was nothing extraordinary in that, Quincy supposed, but it gave him pause.

A rumble from his gut recalled him to the more important matter of dinner. He sat down, exchanging greetings with Richardson. Peter came out of the galley with plates of roasted doves and boiled sweet potatoes, which he set before Quincy and Richardson. The doves were the product of a hunting excursion, a popular pastime with the officers that made Quincy's job a little easier. He had been elected caterer of the Wardroom Mess, which obliged him to collect money from all the officers and spend it on food for their table. He didn't mind doing this, as it gave him reason to get off the ship whenever they were at a friendly port, but the last two weeks in the vicinity of Vicksburg—a decidedly unfriendly port—had taxed his ingenuity. The sweet potatoes had been a stroke of luck.

"Beautiful," Richardson said, digging into his meal. "Thank you, Quincy, and Peter please thank the cook."

Peter smiled slightly as he poured cups of water. It was flat and not very cool, but it was clean, having come from a drain pipe on the boiler safety values. Better than drinking river water in any case.

"Thank you," Quincy said, and began cutting his dove.

As Peter was leaving, a blur of golden fur shot past him into the room and disappeared beneath the table. "Hello, Fitz," said Richardson. "Just now make it up out of the hold?"

Quincy leaned down to look at the ship's cat—a fat yellow tabby—cowering at their feet, ears flat and eyes wide with fright. "Want some, Fitz?" he said, offering him a morsel, but the cat wouldn't move.

"He hates coaling," Richardson said. "Drives him crazy."

"He's not alone," Quincy said, and attacked his dinner before it could get too gritty with coal dust.

Emma allowed Smokey to slow to a walk as they reached the mule herd. The sun was hot, but the breeze cooled her and the shadows of live oaks formed dark pools of shelter. The mares and their mule babies grazed along the creek, lazy in the hot afternoon. Emma spied a foal she hadn't seen before, still shaky on its legs, shadowing a black mare. She nudged Smokey over to them and dismounted.

"Well, hello, there," she said softly, squatting a few feet from the newborn. The mare kept a jealous eye on her, and she was careful to make no sudden moves toward the foal. She took a carrot from her pocket.

"Here's a little something for you, Mama," she said, showing the treat.

The mare's dark nostrils flared; her wary eyes softened and she allowed Emma to approach. Accepting the carrot, she munched while Emma stroked the baby's thick, soft fur. It was a colt, with bright, curious eyes and his coat a crazy patchwork jumble of black and a speckled gray that would soon go white.

"Hey, there, Patches," she said, smiling. She fondled his ears and his nose, which he tolerated pretty well. His questing mouth—pink, toothless gums—found her thumb and pulled eagerly at it. "Go see your mama," Emma told him, and nudged him toward the mare.

She heard Poppa and Gabe riding up behind her and turned to them, smiling. "New colt," she said, as they dismounted.

"Wow, look at him!" Gabe cried, running toward them.

Emma caught him back. "Not so fast, or Mama will kick you to bits!"

"You know better than that, Gabe," Poppa said in a stern voice.

Gabe approached the colt more cautiously, and managed not

to annoy its mother. He ran his hands over the baby's mottled coat.

"He's going to be a pinto! Can I have him to ride, Poppa?"

"You want a mare for a saddle mule," Poppa said. "Horse mules are for packing."

"Oh, I don't care! Please? Pleeease?"

"No reason you can't ride a horse mule," Emma said, "but better wait till he's grown. Might turn out mean."

"He won't be mean. Will you, boy? I'll bring you carrots every day, and you'll be a fine saddle mule."

Emma stood with her father, watching Gabe fondle the colt. Time enough to decide his fate. Likely, since he was from the first crop, he'd have to be sold anyway. Money was tight for the ranch just now, but this crop of mules was promising. Two or four years down the road, things would be much better.

"He is a pretty thing," Emma said. "Must have been sired by that spotted jack."

Poppa nodded. Emma's favorite foal had been sired by the same jack, on an Appaloosa mare. She was a little filly with an amazing coat—soft gray that would eventually go white, with big splashes of darker, roan gray dappled with black Appaloosa leopard spots, mostly over her rump. Emma had fallen in love with her on sight, and named her Raindrops.

"Maybe we should keep one or two of these babies," she said to her father. "Pip is getting old, and Smokey's already ancient."

"Hm. We'll have to see. Is that colt there a bit club-footed?"

"Yes, I was going to point him out to you. Will he grow out of it, do you think?"

They examined the little chestnut colt, and Emma clapped her hands to startle him into running. Poppa frowned.

"Looks a little lame. We'll keep an eye on him. If he doesn't improve we'll have to cut him from the herd." Poppa gave the colt a slap on the rump, which set him capering to his mother. "The mares all look good. We'll move the herd to the rock pond today, and start breeding the mares that have come into heat tomorrow."

"Sure you want to breed on the foal heat? It's only a few weeks difference," Emma said.

"We don't have a day to waste," Poppa said. "Not that it's a fit subject for a young lady to discuss."

"Pooh! If I can help breed mules, I don't see why I can't discuss it. Not a thing unfit about it."

"Your Aunt May would disagree, I expect."

He had said it quietly, but Emma looked up frowning. The care she saw in his face took the fight out of her. Poppa ran a hand through his thinning hair and gave her a rueful smile.

"Your mother is set on it, you know."

Unable to find anything civil to say, Emma held her tongue. She looked away, watching the horses and mules. Some had bedded down for a siesta in the shade of the trees.

"You've never even been outside of San Antonio," Poppa went on. "You might like it."

Emma shook her head, swallowing the threat of tears. "This is my life," she said in a rough voice, gesturing toward the herd. "I don't want anything but this. Can't you understand?"

"I do understand," Poppa said gently. "But your mother is worried about you, Emma. She wants you to have a good future."

"You mean she wants me to have a husband."

"To her, they are the same thing."

Emma sat down under a live oak and hugged her knees. Poppa sat beside her with a grunt and a sigh. They watched Gabe pick up the new mule colt and hold it with all four hooves off the ground. It let out a startled squawk, and when he put it down it stood stock-still, as if thinking about what had just happened.

"I don't want to find a husband," Emma said in a low voice.

Poppa sighed again. "Sugar, I wish things had turned out different. I truly do. But we don't always get what we want."

"I *like* working the ranch. I know Momma doesn't approve, but I don't care."

"Hush. You don't want to hurt your Momma and you know it."

"Well, does she want to hurt me?" Emma turned to him, brushing at her face. "Does she?"

"Of course not." Poppa's concern was furrowed deep in his brow. "She just wants you to see a little more of the world."

"I'm happy right here."

"You don't look all that happy," Gabe said.

Emma looked up to see her younger brother standing right before her. She scrambled to her feet and turned away, leaning against the rough trunk of the oak tree and wiping at her face.

"Go on down and catch that gray mare, Gabe," Poppa said sharply. "She's the only one still hasn't dropped, and I want to take a look at her."

"Yes, sir," Gabe said in a chastened voice. Emma heard his boots thud down the hill as he ran. She pressed a hand to her eyes.

"Emma, I'd like you to think about this," Poppa said gently. "It wouldn't be forever, you know. Just a few weeks. It would please your mother, and it would please Aunt May. You know how kind she was to Susan. It would be a good thing for you to be on her best side."

"I don't care about Aunt May. I never even met her."

"Well, that might be another good reason for you to go."

Emma felt Poppa's hands on her shoulders, and turned to slide into his strong embrace, burying her face in his shirt. "Family is important, Emma," he said. "When times are hard, family is all we can count on."

Emma sighed. She was being unreasonable and she knew it. She feared leaving the ranch, she realized. Actually feared it. The ranch was all she had left, and she didn't want to lose it.

"Besides," Poppa said, rubbing her back. "You might meet a

nice young fellow who wants to ranch cattle and mules. We could use an extra hand, you know."

Emma coughed on a laugh and gave him an accusing glance. He always could make her smile when she didn't want to. She sniffed and wiped at her face. "Speaking of cattle, we'd better go check on the other herd," she said. She picked up her hat, which had fallen off, she wasn't sure when.

Poppa was watching Gabe lead the gray mare slowly up the hill, her belly heavy with foal. "After I've had a look at this mare," he said.

Emma nodded and looked around for Smokey. She spotted him nibbling grass down by the creek, and started off toward him.

"You will think about it, won't you?" Poppa called softly.

Emma felt her hands curling into fists, and made an effort to keep them still. "I'll think about it," she said, without looking back, then strode off to catch her horse.

3

*But what has become of all our men? You left San Antonio eight
months ago with near three thousand men finely dressed, splen-
didly mounted, and elegantly equipped . . . and now in rags
and tatters, foot-sore and weary, you again march—if a reel
and stagger can be called a march—along the streets of San
Antonio with fourteen hundred men, all told.*
 —William L. Davidson, 5th TX Mounted Rifles

Quincy watched Natchez Under-the-Hill grow slowly larger as
the cutter approached the shore. The lower town, a jumble of
warehouses, whorehouses, and saloons that grew like mold
about the river landing, had a bad reputation. From it a road
cut up the steep bluff to Natchez proper where rich mansions
gazed out over the river, although just now these were obscured
from view. Quincy knew they were there, though. He remembered them from years ago, traveling down the river with Nat
and Uncle Charlie, who had been a pilot. He had not been
ashore in Natchez since then, though the Mortar Flotilla had
passed the town some weeks before on the way up to Vicksburg.
At that time Natchez had officially surrendered to the navy, but
there was no occupying force, and the town was not showing a
friendly face to the Union ships.

The cutter's crew pulled steadily. The still air made the sound
of their oars dipping into the river seem overloud. Quincy
glanced at Lieutenant Lea, who was seated in the stern between
him and the coxswain. Lea was a long-boned fellow of twenty-

five, with a quiet demeanor and a sense of honor that Quincy instinctively emulated. He noticed Quincy's gaze, and said, "It seems fairly quiet."

Quincy nodded, scanning the shore. "A few loiterers. Under-the-Hill doesn't really wake up until evening."

A couple of disreputable-looking fellows paused in the street to watch the cutter's approach. A lone, shabby steamer was tied up at the landing, her smokestacks breathing faint wisps. The water being low, the cutter beached rather than tying up beside her. Lea stepped out and Quincy followed him, clambering up the rocky shore.

"Wait here," Lea told the coxswain quietly. "Marks, Kirkson, stay on guard here. The rest come with us."

Quincy glanced toward the *Lane* and the two mortar boats she had in tow, at anchor just out of the channel. Her draft was too deep to permit her to tie up at the landing, so she waited out in the river for the party to execute its errands. Lieutenant Lea was to look for a pilot, a faint hope but one worth exploring. There was not one river pilot in all Porter's flotilla, and though chances of finding one in Natchez were slim, Commander Wain-wright had decided to send Lea ashore. Quincy had asked to come along, hoping to find fresh stores for the Wardroom Mess in the city market, and Lea being unfamiliar with Natchez had readily agreed to his company. The four sailors who climbed out of the cutter to accompany them, armed with muskets and pistols, were a comfort.

Lea stood waiting, his dark, unmarked frock coat proclaiming the sailing-man but showing no naval insignia. Quincy had worn his bad-weather coat, also unmarked and sufficiently worn to make him look at home in Natchez Under-the-Hill.

"Where shall we try?" Lea asked softly as they set out.

"We could look in at the Boar, there," Quincy replied, "but our best chance is likely to be at the King's Tavern, up on the hill."

Lea strolled forward, looking about him as any visitor might do. He gave a slight nod to a man lounging against a shed at the bottom of Silver Street, the lower town's principal road. The man watched them, slowly chewing, and spit a black stream of tobacco juice just as they passed, narrowly missing their shoes. Lea and Quincy continued on as if they had not noticed. Indignation was not a healthy emotion just at present.

The street sloped gently at its foot, becoming steeper as it climbed the bluff. One or two tavern doors stood open to the day, ready to catch early business. A bored-looking mulatto girl in a faded green dress strolled toward them along the boardwalk; she brushed against Quincy as she passed, muttering an obscene invitation. He kept his eyes forward and felt his cheeks grow hot.

The Boar was a two-story brick hotel with a narrow iron balcony along its front on which two seedy women were seated, passing a bottle between them. Their eyes fixed on the men from the *Harriet Lane*, a silent, hungry, vulture-glare that made Quincy hasten inside.

The public room was empty save for one man apparently asleep with his head on a table and a waiter who moved about picking up dirty dishes. When he saw them, he stopped and came toward them.

"Good afternoon," Lieutenant Lea said in a quiet voice. "We are seeking to engage the services of a pilot for the lower river. Are there any such here?"

The waiter glanced at Quincy, then at the armed men behind him. He slowly shook his head.

"Are you certain?" Quincy said. "Perhaps one is staying at the inn—we could wait while you inquire—"

"No pilots," the waiter said.

Lea's lips pressed together. "I see," he said.

"Want dinner? A bed?"

"No, thank you."

The waiter turned his back without ceremony, picked up a tray, and went out through a door at the back of the room. Lea glanced at the sleeping customer, then led the party out of the Boar.

"Goddamn Yankee scum!" a woman's voice drifted down to them as they came out.

Quincy stiffened, but Lea caught his elbow and propelled him forward. Annoyed at himself, Quincy strode up the street. As he regained his temper, he acknowledged a feeling of gratitude for the armed men at their backs.

They passed the last of the saloons and between leafy bushes growing wild and tangled up the hillside. A brisk walk put them atop the bluff in Natchez town, somewhat out of breath. Here handsome houses abounded, whispering of wealth, set behind well-tended gardens and shaded by oaks and pecans. They passed a market where a few vendors plied a desultory trade.

"I would like to stop here before we go back," Quincy said.

Lea nodded. "Let us visit the King's Tavern first."

"It's this way."

Natchez seemed a sleepy town, its curtained windows like drowsy eyes looking out upon the world. In one garden behind an iron fence a young lady was clipping flowers—zinnias, bright pink and orange and yellow—which she was gathering into a bouquet. Quincy paused to admire her, wondering if he might be able to charm her out of a bloom or two. When she looked up he bowed, but she glanced away again quickly and would not acknowledge him.

Turning a corner brought them onto the Natchez Trace, an old trail that eventually led away from the town toward Tennessee. Before steam ruled the rivers, traders from upstream had brought goods down on rafts and many had returned overland with their profits along the Natchez Trace. Such traffic had inevitably attracted robbers, and Quincy knew plenty of dark tales of the Trace, one or two of which he shared with Lea as they walked.

At length they reached a tall, blockish building of brick and wood. The King's Tavern, one of Uncle Charlie's favorite haunts, was brighter and cleaner than the Boar. A flight of steps led to a balcony—much deeper than that at the Boar—at the back of which stood an open door into the tavern. The large beams of the ceiling showed marks and holes from a former life as a ship; all the wood in the place had been salvaged from old boats and rafts to furbish up the brick structure.

The taproom being small, Lea told the sailors to wait on the balcony and went inside with Quincy, where he walked up to the bar and repeated his inquiry. The taverner scratched his head and shrugged. "Ain't a-many pilots round here these days," he said. "Not much traffic."

"Is there anywhere else we might inquire?" Lea asked.

The taverner shook his head. "This here's where they'd come to find work, most likely. I can ask around a bit, if you like. You in town for a day or two?"

"No, an hour or two, only."

"Well, I'll ask the Cap'n over there. He'd know, if anyone would." He nodded toward a large, harried-looking man who was methodically consuming a formidable platter of beef and roasted onions. Captain of the steamer at the dock, Quincy deduced, trying to remember if he'd seen him before. Seated at table with him was a wiry, white-haired fellow whose greasy skin betrayed him as an engineer.

"Will you draw us two beers, first?" said Lea, placing a coin on the bar.

The taverner was pleased to oblige. Quincy and Lea lounged against the bar and observed the patrons. Apart from the steamer captain and his companion, there were only two youths playing checkers and a withered old gentleman smoking a pipe in a rocking chair by the empty fireplace.

"Not very promising," Quincy murmured.

"Mm," Lea agreed, and took a pull at his beer.

Quincy followed suit. The brew was a bit thin, but tasted well enough. A light ale for the warm summer day. Watching the taverner's conversation, he saw the steamer captain shake his head and return his attention to his meal.

"I'm sorry, sir," the taverner said as he returned to his place behind the bar. "There's no word of a pilot to be had anywhere from here to New Orleans."

"Thank you for your trouble," Lea said, passing him another coin. The man hesitated, then accepted it with a nod and a wry grin. Times were uncertain on the Mississippi; one took what one could get.

They lingered, finishing their beer, and Quincy watched with appreciation while the steamboat captain worked his way through his large meal. A waiter took away the empty plate, then shortly reappeared with a whole peach pie, which he set in front of the captain. Quincy, who had not tasted fruit in some days, suddenly found his mouth watering.

"It's time we left," Lea said, placing his empty glass on the bar. Quincy hastily drained his own, and followed Lea out. It seemed even hotter, and the air was thickening as if building up for a storm.

"Thank you for the drink, sir," Quincy said.

"You're welcome."

"I'm sorry your time was wasted."

"Oh, a walk on shore is never a waste. We'll just have to keep anchoring at night, that's all. Now, about the Mess—I count on you to find us something wonderful, Wheat."

The market produced no wonders, but did yield up some onions, a few carrots, two pounds of pecans and a dozen peaches for which Quincy paid too high a price. Lea made no comment at the extravagance. Either he didn't care, or his eye had also been caught by the pie.

They reached Silver Street and started back down the long hill to the river. Rising damp was beginning to coat the street with a film of slick mud, forcing them to go slowly or risk slithering down the hill. Despite the advancing hour Under-the-Hill still seemed quiet—rather too quiet, Quincy thought.

"It was quite different here a few years ago," he said. "There would have been couple of dozen boats at the landing there on any given day."

"Your father must have enjoyed bringing you here," Lea said.

Quincy shook his head. "Not my father. My uncle. Father didn't approve of our going with him."

"Because of Under-the-Hill?" Lea smiled.

"That, and Uncle Charlie's character in general. Father thought him unsteady, but we loved him. He was always ready to look for some fun. Exactly the opposite of my father." Realizing belatedly what he'd said, Quincy glanced up at Lea. "That's not what I meant—"

Lea nodded, laughing softly. "I understand. Fathers can be difficult to talk to at times. I haven't heard from mine but once since the war began." His smile grew wistful. "He's a major in the Confederate army."

Quincy stopped, astonished. "But, why?"

"My father moved to Texas a few years ago. My uncle lives there—he was very strong in favor of secession."

Quincy wanted to know more, but feared to pry. Lea must have read this in his face, for he lifted his shoulders in a slight shrug.

"My father told me I should follow my own conscience when choosing which side to serve. Not that it was difficult—I would never desert my country. But he did say that if I chose to serve the Union we were not likely to meet again except in battle."

Quincy stood appalled. "I am so sorry."

"Don't be. I'm not. We all have hard choices to make."

With a final, ghostly smile, Lea started down the hill again, toward the cutter and the waiting *Lane*. Quincy hastened to follow, thinking he should write to his own father when he next had the time. They were often at odds, and they had never been friends, but at least they were not enemies.

———

Jamie gave the collar of his new shirt a surreptitious tug as he sat listening to Reverend Fletcher's sermon. Momma had made the shirt while he was away, and though he had lost weight on the campaign the collar was a little too tight. The shirt also itched, probably from the starch Momma had ironed into it. Jamie had not had on a nice suit of clothes in over half a year, and it felt strange.

The congregation had no church—construction had been delayed by the war—so they met in the town hall. Jamie looked around at the walls that still boasted recruiting posters for companies in the 4th Texas Mounted Volunteers, his former regiment. Most of those companies were recruiting again, trying to replace the men who had been lost in New Mexico.

He tried to listen to the sermon but his mind kept wandering. He was conscious of Emma sitting rigidly between himself and Momma, of Gabe trying not to squirm between him and Poppa. He was acutely aware that this was the first service—except for burial services—that he had been to in months, and it made him feel both guilty and a little defiant. Churchgoing had not protected him from evil. He was still not satisfied in his mind about the conundrum of having been sent to war with numerous blessings, as if he were an emissary of God almost, only to commit acts that in normal times would have been the height of sin and of crime. He supposed he should speak to a clergyman about it, but he didn't much care for Reverend Fletcher, and anyway he didn't like to talk about that awful day at Valverde. The day Martin had died. The day he had become a murderer.

It was the second man he'd killed—the big Yankee with the bayonet—that haunted him. The first Jamie hardly remembered, some artilleryman who had aimed a pistol his way, and Jamie with shaking hands had given him both barrels of his shotgun. He could practically smell the powder even now. Memories rose around him, unbidden and unwanted: the Yankee—a giant in blue—came out of nowhere and loomed before him, pulled the shotgun right away from him and stabbed at him, nearly getting him. Jamie felt the bayonet's point catch at his jacket, saw his own death in the gleeful eyes of the Yankee. He could smell the man's sweat and his breath tinged with whiskey. He heard the pistol go off before he realized it was in his hand, and the big Yankee looked at him, puzzled-like, right before he fell. Those eyes burned themselves into his mind: surprised, hurt, betrayed, as if the two of them had been playing a game and Jamie had cheated.

Jamie felt his heart, so close to being pierced, thundering inside him, but it was the Yankee's blood and not his own that flowed from the chest wound, running in rivulets over the man's fingers and blending into the dark wool of his coat as he lay there, trying to speak but with blood pouring out of his mouth. The eyes continued to stare up at Jamie, accusing him, still surprised even as the light faded from them. Jamie knew he was watching the departure of the man's soul. He knew the moment the Yankee was dead, by the sudden dullness of his eyes. This man had come nearer to killing Jamie than any other on the field, and it was his death that Jamie carried on his soul. He didn't understand why, but it was so.

He didn't remember very clearly what happened after that. There was more fighting and the Texans pushed the Yankees back from their battery—a glimpse of a bluecoat shoving a lit fuse into a caisson, frozen in the white flash that followed—and then the end of the fight, Yankees dead and dying in the river with their blood swirling away in the muddy water, cheers of victory from the Texans over the captured guns. Finally the gruesome search for Martin on the field of wretched wounded moaning and crying for help or just a sip of water. If Martin had moaned, even once, it might not have been so bad, but Martin was cold when Jamie found him. He remembered how sore his arms were the next day from dragging Martin off the field to the burial trench. He remembered how sticky and cold Martin's blood felt on his hands.

Starting, Jamie came back to himself and looked down at his

hands, which were clean although clenched together so hard the knuckles were turning white. He made himself let go, rubbed his palms along his thighs and then gripped the front edge of the bench, needing to hold onto something.

A rustling and murmuring brought his attention back to the service; the reverend had called for the hymn. Jamie fumbled with the hymnal he was sharing with Gabe, searching for the right page, his eyes blurring up but he choked back the heartache and managed to mouth the words if not actually to sing.

At last the reverend set them free with a final blessing. Jamie stood up at once, impatient to get out of the hall. He brushed past Momma who stopped to visit with Mrs. Webber; saw Poppa buttonhole Major Pyron, who owned a ranch not far from theirs. Gabe had already slipped through the crowd and away with a couple of his buddies. Emma was getting left behind but Jamie didn't care—he had to get outside.

The sun was bright enough it hurt his eyes and made him squint. He had left his hat under the bench. He'd have to go back for it, but not yet. He couldn't go back in that press of people. Instead he walked away, out into the street, with voices chatting around him all cheerful and friendly, making no sense to him.

"Russell! Hey, Russell!"

Blinking as he looked up, Jamie saw Lane waving at him, coming toward him through the throng of departing worshipers. On his arm was a pretty young lady with soft brown curls escaping from beneath her bonnet. She smiled shyly at Jamie as Lane brought her forward.

"Russell, I'd like you to meet my wife, Mollie," Lane said, beaming with pride. "Mollie, this is Jamie Russell, the quartermaster I mentioned to you."

"I'm very pleased to meet you, Mr. Russell," she said, extending her hand. "I have heard so much about you."

Jamie clasped her hand briefly. "How do you do, Mrs. Lane?" He cleared his throat. "You're every bit as pretty as Ells said."

"Thank you." She cast a wry look at her husband and gave a little laugh, then glanced up as Emma joined them.

"You forgot your hat," Emma said to Jamie, handing it to him. Martin's hat once, still with the silver star pin she had given him; Jamie wondered if she remembered. His own hat and star had been lost at Valverde.

"Emma, I'd like you to meet my friend Ellsberry Lane, and Mrs. Lane. My sister, Miss Russell."

"Oh," said Mrs. Lane, a look of pity crossing her face. She replaced it with a smile and offered to shake hands. "How do you do, Miss Russell?"

"How do you do?" Emma said, her eyes glinting in a way that worried Jamie as she shook hands with both of the Lanes.

A moment's awkward silence was broken by Mrs. Lane, who said to Jamie, "My husband has told me about your kindness to him on that dreadful march."

Embarrassed, Jamie only managed a nod and a silent smile. Lane turned to Emma.

"We're all very sorry about Captain Martin," he said.

Emma looked at the ground. The wide brim of her straw hat hid her face. "Thank you," she said, barely above a whisper.

Jamie caught Lane's eye and gave his head a little shake. Lane seemed to understand, but before they could move on another voice chimed in.

"Yes, Martin was a fine fellow," said Val Owens, joining them. "We all miss him."

The hat brim tilted up and Emma shot Jamie a glance like a gathering storm. He gave her an apologetic smile and introduced Captain Owens, who had seen fit to wear his best uniform on this warm Sunday morning, gold braid glinting in knots that climbed halfway up his sleeves. His sandy hair and mustache were brushed into perfect order and he bowed low over the hand Emma offered him. Jamie sensed it didn't please her much, though she was civil.

"Is Sibley in town yet?" Jamie asked Owens, hoping to shift the conversation to a safer topic.

"Not yet," Owens said. "He'll be here in a day or two, along with the 4th. They're moving a little better since the supply train reached them." He turned to Emma, adding, "It was most generous of the townsfolk to send out that train, Miss Russell. I understand you contributed some clothing."

"That was my mother," Emma said, her teeth flashing in a smile that didn't reach her eyes. "Poppa and I slaughtered some bulls."

Owens grinned. "Don't you mean gentleman cows?" he said.

Seeing the flash in Emma's eyes, Jamie hastened to speak. "Have you seen Ochiltree?" he asked Owens. "I heard he was back from Richmond, but I haven't laid eyes on him yet."

They shared headquarters gossip: Pyron was being promoted to lieutenant-colonel, Scurry would likely be made a general, might even get command of the brigade according to Owens, but Jamie doubted it. Both Reily and Green had seniority over Scurry, no matter how fine a commander he was.

Tim Nettles came up to join them, another New Mexico veteran who had transferred to the Valverde Battery when it was formed. He was twenty-four, with smooth black hair, dark eyes, and—since returning to San Antonio—a neatly trimmed mustache. Jamie introduced him to Emma.

"Miss Russell," Nettles said, and bowed. "I am honored."

"Nettles is my counterpart," Jamie explained to his sister. "He's got command of a section in the battery."

"Pretty good for a fellow who left here a private last fall," Lane said, grinning.

"I wouldn't be here at all if it weren't for Russell," Nettles said seriously. "He saved my life."

Emma cast an inquiring glance at Jamie. "You never mentioned this."

"Well, I don't think I did," Jamie said, feeling warmth creep up his neck. "I just gave him a mule, that's all."

"Gave me a mule on a forced march through desert, when I had a leg wound and could barely walk. I would have died." Nettles grinned, a bit crookedly. "I won't forget it."

"Oh, buy me a beer sometime," Jamie said, embarrassed. The thought flitted through his mind that he would have willingly traded Nettles's life for Martin's. He pushed it away.

Nettles had turned to address Emma. "Miss Russell, may I say how sorry—"

"There's Momma!" Emma said suddenly. "Look, she's waving to us, we'd better go. You will excuse us, won't you?" she said, bestowing a glittering smile on the circle of men and Mrs. Lane. Before they had finished their polite responses, she caught Jamie's hand and pulled him away.

Momma was indeed summoning them to the wagon, where Poppa was waiting to drive them home. Gabe was already in the back, gobbling licorice he'd got hold of from somewhere; the stores were closed, so he must have had it from a friend. He grinned at them with blackened teeth.

Jamie handed Emma up to the box seat beside Momma, then climbed in the back with Gabe. This was not the most satisfying Sunday he had ever spent in town. As Poppa woke up Pip and Smokey, Emma turned around and threw him a look by which he knew her feelings matched his own.

Emma couldn't remember ever being so sore and tired, but she was happy with the day's work. She let Smokey set his own pace to follow Pip, Cocoa, and Gabe's mule Strawberry home after taking the mule herd back out to pasture. She and her brothers and Poppa had spent a long, hot, uncomfortable day branding the baby mules—one of those sticky days when the air was like a stifling blanket, unmitigated by cloud, unrelieved by the shade of trees. Even now, getting on toward seven o'clock, the heat was still awful.

She had rinsed her hands before saddling up, but they were still gummed with blood, and the sleeves of her work shirt were spattered up to the elbow. She had insisted on taking her turn at each of the tasks—wrangling, branding, and castrating—which Poppa hadn't let her do for the cattle roundup back in June. But they'd had to hire extra help for the cattle, and today, with Jamie there after getting permission to take a day off from his duties, they had been able to brand all the mule foals by themselves. Emma was proud of that. Even though her head was ringing with fatigue, she smiled.

No one talked as they rode home. Everyone was too tired. They came up on the ranch house from the northwest and rode around to the front, dismounting outside the barn. Emma tossed her reins over the rail and started to undo Smokey's girth, but Poppa touched her shoulder.

"It appears you have a visitor."

Glancing at the house, she saw a horse tied to the rail by the water trough, and a tall figure rising from a chair on the porch. It was Captain Owens.

"He's here for Jamie," she said, but as the words left her mouth she saw the bouquet of flowers in the man's hand. She was suddenly furious; she wanted to cuss, but didn't dare let Poppa hear her, so she just shut her lips tight and finished undoing the girth.

"Shall I talk to him while you go and change?" Poppa said.

"No," Emma said. She pulled her saddle off Smokey's back, but Poppa took it from her.

"Go on, Emma," he said gently. "The man took the trouble to ride out here."

Jamie and Gabe had already gone into the barn with their saddles. Poppa followed them, leaving her no choice but to greet the unwelcome guest. Well, she'd do it, but not like Poppa thought.

He stood waiting on the porch, dressed in his fine uniform again, which must surely have made him uncomfortable on this sultry day. Emma saw his smile fade as he took in her appearance. A look came into his eyes she found hard to decipher. He was staring at her hands, she realized, and fought off an urge to rub them on her shirt. She stopped at the foot of the shallow steps, watching his face with critical interest. He did not seem shocked, which disappointed her. Instead the look in his eyes seemed calculating.

"Evening, Miss Russell," he said, bowing.

"Mr. Owens," Emma said, according him just a nod.

"I made sure you'd be all done with supper by now." He gave a soft laugh.

She glanced toward the barn, but the boys and Poppa were all out of sight. "We've been branding foals," she said.

He nodded understanding. "Jamie told us about how you offered to help on the ranch so he could join up. I think that's mighty generous, Miss Russell, and mighty brave, too."

Emma could not think of a reply. He made it sound like she had made some great sacrifice, instead of doing exactly what she liked. She knew what he was thinking; that she was degrading herself by doing a man's work and wearing a man's clothes. That something must be wrong with any woman who liked such work, so she must not enjoy it. She doubted he could understand, and in fact she didn't especially want him to.

"I brought you these," he said, offering the flowers.

Emma glanced at them. "Thank you," she managed to say. She looked down at her bloodstained hands, then at the door of the house. "You'd better hand them to my mother."

He followed her gaze to where Momma stood just by the door, and she came forward with a smile to accept the bouquet. "I will put them in water while Emma cleans up. Will you to stay to supper, Captain Owens?"

"Oh, no, thank you, I've already had supper."

"You are welcome to stay anyway," Momma said.

He looked back at Emma. "I think maybe I'd better go."

Emma looked away, conscious of Momma's gaze and that Momma would want her to press him to stay. She didn't want him to, though, so she said nothing. She found herself staring at his boots, which looked freshly polished, and glanced down at her own grimy ones.

"Well, it was kind of you to visit," Momma said, "and so kind of you to bring these flowers. They are very pretty, are they not, Emmaline?"

"Yes," Emma said. "They're beautiful. Thank you."

"You're welcome," said Owens, a slow smile curving up one side of his mouth. Emma didn't like the look that had come into his eyes.

She heard footsteps behind her and looked up to see Jamie hurrying toward them from the barn, wiping his hands on his grimy handkerchief. "Owens," he said, glancing from him to Emma. "You're looking spruce."

"You're something of a mess yourself," said Mr. Owens. He tempered it with a grin, "and I imagine you must be starving. I won't keep you." He came down the steps and started toward his horse.

Emma expected Jamie to urge him to stay, but he didn't. They both watched Owens mount, wave a hand in farewell and trot off toward the trail. Jamie turned to her, a trace of a worried frown on his brow. She returned his gaze, trying to read him, trying to decide if he was pushing her, too, like Momma and Poppa.

"I didn't ask him to come," Jamie said after a second.

She felt her throat trying to close. "You tell your friends to keep away from me," she said in a choked voice, and hurried into the house.

4

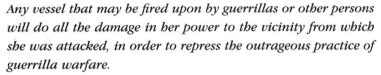

*Any vessel that may be fired upon by guerrillas or other persons
will do all the damage in her power to the vicinity from which
she was attacked, in order to repress the outrageous practice of
guerrilla warfare.*
—General Order of Acting Rear-Admiral Porter, U. S. Navy

Jamie rode into town early on Tuesday. Cocoa whuffed at familiar smells as they crossed the Main Plaza, and made straight for the corral behind Webber's Mercantile, but Jamie guided her to the front instead and left her refreshing herself from the trough while he went in. Smells of old wood and new goods—cloth, leather, foodstuffs—blended into a familiar, faintly musty aroma. Jamie took in a deep breath and strolled over to the candy jars, helping himself to a butterscotch stick while he waited for Mr. Webber to finish his business with a young matron and her two little girls.

Webber's had been Jamie's second home for three years, at first after school and then full-time until he had been invited to join the quartermaster corps as Martin's assistant. He winced at the reminder, and sighed, wondering if he would ever get over feeling tired.

A thin boy in an overlarge apron came out from the back of the store and gave Jamie an inquiring look. With a little shock Jamie realized it was George Willis, younger brother of Miss Celia Willis, for whom Jamie had nursed a secret passion in school. Jamie had a memory of George as a scrubby brat about Gabe's age; now he revised it upward a couple of years. He strolled up to the counter and fished a penny out of his pocket for the candy.

"Hey, George," he said with a friendly nod. "How is your sister?"

"Got married at Christmas," George said. "She moved up to Austin. That's where he came from."

"Oh. Well, please pass along my best wishes."

"Yes, sir. You get five of those for a penny," he said, very serious.

Sir, Jamie thought. *I'm a sir, now.*

He was used to being addressed that way by soldiers, but not by scrubby clerks. He had a sudden, disconcerting image of himself behind Mr. Webber's counter, not much older than George when he first started work. With a slight laugh, he shook his head.

"I'll take licorice, for the rest," he said. "In a bag, please."

George wrapped the candy in a neat, white paper sack, then gave a sharp glance around the store and disappeared into the back again. Mr. Webber was just carrying a parcel outside for his customers, and for a moment Jamie was alone in the store with memories like the butterscotch, mellow on his tongue, gentler than he expected. He knew he had often felt discontented while he was working here, but it really had nothing to do with the store or the Webbers, so only vague, pleasant echoes of a time of simpler obligations and simpler problems remained.

"Jamie!" Mr. Webber smiled as he came back inside. His hair was a little thinner than Jamie remembered, though black still won out over silver. His sleeves were rolled up to the elbows, and his apron protected the usual tidy shirt, vest, and trousers. He strode over to join Jamie at the counter, his hand extended in welcome. "Glad to see you back."

"Thank you, sir," Jamie said around the butterscotch. He took the stick from his mouth and shook hands. "It's good to be back."

"You came through all right, then," said Mr. Webber, retaining his hand with a grip whose firmness surprised Jamie. So did the look in Mr. Webber's eyes—a look of concern, of understanding.

Jamie had to swallow, and he gave a curt nod. "Yes."

Mr. Webber nodded, too, and gave his hand a final squeeze before letting go. "You must have had quite a time getting the army home in all this heat," he said.

"Well, they aren't quite home yet—"

"Near enough as makes no difference."

"—and anyway I resigned as QM."

Mr. Webber paused, gazing at him with a tiny frown, then gestured toward the cracker barrel in the corner where two chairs were set on opposite sides of a checkerboard. "Come and tell me about it," he said.

Jamie checked his watch. He still had half an hour before he had to report to Sayers, so he followed Mr. Webber over, feeling a bit strange at being treated so cordially by a man from whom he was used to take orders. It was because of being in the army, he supposed. Mr. Webber had served in '46 with Kearny's expedition to conquer Santa Fé, and on down into Mexico. He really did understand in a way even Poppa, who had never been in the military, could not. Before long Jamie found himself recounting his troubles more frankly than he had to anyone, even Lane or John Reily. He spoke fleetingly of Martin's death—a wound still too new to bear much attention—and of the subsequent demand on himself as acting quartermaster for the brigade; of the heartbreaking loss of the supply train during the battle at Glorieta, which had ultimately forced the army to retreat from a victory that had almost been in reach; of scraping and scrounging for food and clothing in a country already desolated by war; and of the terrible, grueling march through arid mountains to avoid the Federal forces at Fort Craig. Mr. Webber listened, asked a question now and then, and nodded his understanding and sympathy.

"So you haven't left the army, just the QM job."

Jamie nodded. "I've joined the new battery."

Mr. Webber's brows went up. "The Valverde Battery?"

"Yes." Jamie gave a rueful smile. "They're engraving the names on the cannons right now." He cleared his throat, picking up a checker and turning it over on the board. "The names of the officers who were lost during their capture, I mean. Martin's will be on one of mine."

Mr. Webber sighed and leaned back in his chair. "You know," he said gently, "it wasn't your fault."

"I know." *But I still have to do this.*

They sat silent, their eyes communicating things that could not easily be put into words. Jamie felt unsteady; his emotions were getting all stirred up in a way he had not permitted for some time. It was dangerous, but at the same time it was a relief. And he knew that Mr. Webber understood all this, and somehow that made it easier to bear. There were questions hanging in the back of Jamie's mind to which he had found no answers—riddles of morality and patriotism—dark questions he didn't much like to think about, so mostly he avoided doing so. Someday he would have to decide, he knew. But not today.

The bell on the front door startled him out of his thoughts, and he turned to look at the newcomers—a couple of hands from the Gonzales farm—as Mr. Webber got up to wait on them. Jamie bit off the point he had made on the candy stick, feeling the sharp, fragile sweetness melt on his tongue, then popped the end of the stick in his mouth and crunched it. He got up and looked around for his sack of licorice, saw that he had left it on the counter and went to fetch it.

"I'll be going, I guess," he said to Mr. Webber who was busy assembling some dry goods for the farm hands. "Say hello to Mrs. Webber for me."

"She'll be sorry she missed you," Mr. Webber said. "She's at a meeting of the Ladies' Committee."

"Well, tell her everyone's grateful for the supply wagons."

Mr. Webber smiled. "I will do that." He stacked a half-dozen tins of baking soda on the counter, and paused. "Come visit again, Jamie," he said in a quiet, serious voice.

Jamie picked up his bag of candy and shook hands. "I will. Thanks." He held Mr. Webber's gaze for a moment to be sure he understood how earnestly he meant it, then flashed a smile and went out into the hot day.

A long line of bedraggled men was filing eastward into town along Commerce Street, which connected with the Overland Trail. Jamie instinctively stepped closer to Cocoa, then chided himself. These men might be all too willing to steal a horse under certain circumstances, but not here at home. He searched the weary faces, recognized a couple and knew for certain that it was the 5th arriving at last. Long habit urged him to go to the men with water and food, to find them places to sleep. It was no longer his responsibility, though, and they would certainly be cared for. He stayed in the shade of the porch roof in front of Webber's, watching the straggling column return to the Military Plaza where they had begun so many months ago. No flying banners nor trumpets braying today; their only triumph was in having survived yet another punishing march, this time from Franklin back to San Antonio, through the summer heat without enough water. More than a few had given out along the way, Jamie knew.

He had intended to check at the post office, but he had used up his spare time at Webber's, so he would have to go on the way home. As he mounted up on Cocoa, his attention was caught by a vehicle he recognized. It was an ambulance, black with gilt detail—now badly scratched—on the body and around the windows, whose cloth coverings were tied tight against the blistering sun. Jamie didn't need to see inside to know who rode there; it was Sibley's ambulance, as every man in the army knew.

Some of the anger came boiling back up inside and he sat there, breathing a little fast and staring at the vehicle and trying to decide what exactly had roused his ire. Sibley's promises of glory, now broken in the dust? The general's poor judgment, or his poor health? Upon reflection, he rather thought he pitied Sibley. The army had lost faith in him, and had many harsh things to say about him.

A soldier waved to Jamie, a tall fellow with a thin, patchy beard and a shapeless hat drooping over his eyes. Jamie recognized him from the retreat through the mountains. It made him feel better, made the anger fade away. Whatever became of the army's commander, the men knew who they might count upon, and Jamie was proud to be among that group. He waved back with a smiling nod, then nudged Cocoa forward.

Quincy came up on deck to read in the last of the daylight, and glanced over the rail at the yellow-brown river slithering by. The wheels pushed against the current, driving the *Lane* upstream at a speed of about three knots. Her wake swished like an endless chuckling brook, and through the sound Quincy could hear cicadas whining on the shore.

The *Lane*'s visit to New Orleans had been a disappointment. The crew had not been granted liberty, and spirits had sunk low when they learned they were immediately going back up the Mississippi. Once the ship had delivered its mortar boats and received provisions, along with two dozen new contrabands to replace sick crewmen who had to be sent ashore, she was ordered to steam back up to the mouth of the Red, for the purpose of preventing the Rebels from closing that river.

It was early evening and the port watch had the deck while the starbor'lns lounged in groups, singing or playing at dominoes. Some clustered about the smoking lamp on the forward weather deck, which was the only source of fire from which they were permitted to light tobacco. The new contrabands were fitting in well enough. Quincy had two in his division—a giant of a farm hand who was clumsy and not very clever but was learning to apply his strength to the gun tackle, and a skinny cotton-picker who was nimble enough that Quincy had assigned him to the number two gun crew as a sponger. That made three negroes in his division, counting William, a powder boy. It was a trend he wasn't sure he liked. Becker, who commanded the first division, had been loud in his complaints at having more niggers on deck, and had asked permission to recruit white coal-heavers to fill the gaps in his division instead of the inexperienced contrabands. Lieutenant Lea had refused.

Quincy paused to watch William embroidering white stars on the collar-corners of a blue shirt. The boy's clever needlework was in high demand, and William, who was just fifteen, made good pocket money sewing for the men and even the officers. He was a runaway who had joined up at Hampton Roads, and he had begun to spend a good deal of time in company with the new contrabands. He sat with some of them now. It being the second dog watch, the men were permitted to sing, and the contrabands raised their voices in songs they had brought from their plantations: mournful songs many of them, some hopeful, and one or two joyful. Quincy listened until one of the men sitting beside William glanced up at him.

"That's good work, William," Quincy said to the boy. "Come see me tomorrow, I've got some handkerchiefs I'd like you to mark for me."

"Yes, sir," William said.

Quincy moved on, it being best for the officers not to intrude on the crew during the little free time they had. He found a comfortable spot to lounge against the rail and opened the two-week-old issue of *Harper's Weekly* that he had obtained from an officer aboard a dispatch ship at New Orleans. It contained an article about the Battle of Memphis, which he wanted to compare with Nat's description.

He examined the front page briefly, admiring an illustration of the Rebel rams *Beauregard* (sinking) and *Jeff Thompson* (blowing up) during the battle, with other ships scattered artistically about the river. The article itself proved less than satisfactory. The *Queen of the West* was not mentioned by name though Quincy knew she had been the first to engage the Rebel ships.

Her encounter with the *Beauregard* was described—inaccurately, assuming Nat knew better than the unnamed Memphis reporter what had happened to his own boat—and she was depicted in an illustration, but only at distance off by the Arkansas shore, and labeled "disabled." That she had first struck and sunk the Rebel ram *General Lovell* was nowhere mentioned; the Rebel correspondent attributed the *Lovell*'s demise to a cannon ball. At least the *Queen* would get prize-money for the cotton the *Beauregard* had carried, though it would be shared with every other Federal ship that had been present.

Sighing, Quincy looked toward the shore, which was closer as the *Lane* approached a narrow bend in the river. He wished very much to hear from his brother again. To be denied both the open sea and Nat's company seemed doubly unfair, though he knew he'd been lucky to see Nat at all.

"What have you got there, Wheat?"

The question was friendly, the voice the New York accent of the *Lane*'s captain. Quincy looked up at Commander Wainwright, who stood over him with an arm leaning against the rail and a smile spreading his wide mustache and bushy side-whiskers.

"*Harper's Weekly*," Quincy replied, showing the front of the paper.

"That's not the latest issue, is it?"

"End of June," Quincy said, offering it.

Wainwright took it and scrutinized the engravings on the front page. His eyebrows rose.

"Dear me, a naval battle on the Mississippi. How exciting." His gaze traveled to the lower illustration. " 'Colonel Ellet's ram approaching the City of Memphis—' so this is the *Queen of the West*?"

"Yes, although I can't find her name anywhere in the accompanying articles."

"Hm. Journalists." He leafed through the paper, glancing at the illustrations.

"Would you care to read it, sir?" Quincy asked.

"When you've done with it, yes." Wainwright handed it back. "No need to hurry—I am still reading a stack of New Orleans papers."

"Dull work," Quincy said.

"Oh, not so very. The Orleaners appear to be trying to invent a thousand new insults for our General Butler. They seem to take pride in each original production."

Quincy smiled, and was about to reply when a sudden snapping sound cut through the noises of steam engine and paddle wheel. He turned, scanning the eastern shore for evidence of the cause he suspected. They were entering the bend, where the river was narrower, and had come within rifle range of the shore.

"There," Wainwright said, pointing toward small puffs of smoke dissipating against a drapery of willows. A cloud of small birds rose from the willows farther north, another smoky bloom appeared, and the "crack" of a rifle came as a ball sang over their heads.

"Exceedingly impolite," Wainwright said. He raised his voice to address Becker, on duty on the bridge. "Mr. Becker, beat to quarters. Division commanders fire when ready."

The drum began to roll and sailors leapt up from their amusements to scurry to their places on deck. Dominoes, pipes, banjo, and tambourine all vanished. In moments the deck was transformed, hatches to the berth deck covered by gratings and tarpaulins, division tubs and spare gear put in place.

On Wainwright's order the sailors on watch detailed as sharpshooters fired a volley with muskets, then hastened to their battle stations. Quincy, who commanded the second division, took his position between the broadside guns. The guns were cast loose, and Quincy gave the order to fire the starboard howitzer. The cannon belched smoke and slammed backward, flinging a curtain of canister across the water and into the willows, which suddenly shivered. A second later, through the ringing in his ears, Quincy heard Becker order the first division to fire the forward pivot gun, which had been pointed out its broadside port. Another round flew into the shore.

Quincy saw William carrying up a fresh charge of powder for the Dahlgren, clutching the passing box under his right arm and holding the lid closed with his left. He delivered up the charge, dropped the empty box down the scuttle, and hurried away to collect another round.

Quincy glanced at his new contrabands, who were firing for the first time. The farm hand was handling tackle on the big Dahlgren, his muscles standing out as he helped run the heavy gun out. The cotton-picker seemed all right, too—he manned the sponge capably and stayed out of the gun captain's way.

Three times more the guns spat destruction toward the snipers. The howitzer's crew tended to have their piece ready before the Dahlgren's, and Quincy observed that the new man on the handspike was nimble enough to avoid encumbering his more experienced mates. He paused to scan the willow bank through his glass, but no more puffs of musket smoke were visible. Glancing up at Wainwright on the bridge, he saw the captain raise a hand.

Midshipman Dawes hastened toward Quincy. "Mr. Lea orders you to cease firing, sir," he said, a little out of breath.

Quincy nodded, and Dawes hurried forward to pass the order to Becker. Quincy made his division stand ready. The light was beginning to fade. He could see no movement along the quiet shore. Sounds of machinery and flowing water returned as the ringing faded from his ears.

"Shall I send a party ashore, sir?" he heard Lea ask the captain.

"No," Wainwright answered. "If there were buildings, or even a landing—but they will just vanish into the swamp, if they have not already done so. Secure the guns."

Disappointed, Quincy waited to receive his orders from Lea, then told his men to secure. The guns were restored to waiting readiness, the equipment put away. The best they could hope was that they had managed to hit a sniper or two, but they would probably never know for certain.

Quincy complimented his division, then when the watch below was dismissed he tapped the new contraband on the shoulder. "Good work, sailor," he said. "What's your name?"

"Isaiah," the man said. "Thank you, sir."

"Did you work on a farm, Isaiah?"

"In a cotton press," he said, his voice flat.

Quincy put his hand in his pocket. "Well, you have a good hand."

"Thank you, sir."

"Carry on."

Returning to the deck, Quincy saw Wainwright coming toward him.

"Well done, Wheat," the captain said. "I do hope you haven't ruined that paper."

Quincy followed his gaze to his left-hand pocket, into which he had stuffed the *Harper's* when the action began. He laughed, pulling it out and smoothing it against his thigh, and turned it to the last of the sunlight.

"Green's regiment came into town today," Jamie said.

Emma glanced up to see him handing a plate of cobbler to Gabe, who passed it to Poppa. She had sat uncomfortable through supper, unable to eat much, trying to avoid looking at the pair of letters that lay before Momma's place at table. The one on top was from Daniel; she recognized his handwriting, and would be glad to hear his news. The second looked like Aunt May's pale pink writing paper.

"Is that who it was?" Poppa said. "We saw them on the trail."

"Emma?"

Startled, Emma looked up and took the plate Momma held out to her. She set it before her and fell to gazing at the cream pitcher. If only she could just work the ranch and otherwise stay at home. Not go into town, not receive any visitors. See only the family, and not even them most of the time. She needed time to herself, to think things through, to understand exactly what she had lost and what she still had. Time watching mules or cattle graze, sitting with her back against an oak, listening to birds and insects and regaining her balance. Feeling a sudden threat of tears, she frowned to keep them back. She would not be left alone, she knew. It just would not happen. Jamie had too many kind and well-intentioned friends who knew about her and Stephen. So did the whole family, for that matter. All of San Antonio knew, or nearly so. They would not leave her be.

"Well, shall we see what your brother has to say?" Momma said in a cheery voice.

Emma heard the paper rustle as Momma opened Daniel's letter. She listened in silence to his news. His regiment, Terry's Rangers, was in Chattanooga now and had been placed in a new brigade under command of a Colonel Forrest. Daniel reported that this new commander was considered a risk for disaster by some of the higher-up brass, but that he himself liked the man. He described an energetic, dark-haired Tennessean who was canny despite his lack of formal education. Cautious as ever, Daniel gave Forrest a qualified preliminary approval. They were expecting to move soon, further into Tennessee. He had not heard from Matthew. He concluded the letter with an amusing story of an incident at the Battle of Shiloh. Emma stopped listening after the word "battle."

Love to all and a crinkle of paper; Momma had laid the letter down. Emma glanced at her as she picked up the other.

"Well, now! Here is some news from your Aunt May. Quite a bit of news, it appears," she said, opening the thick packet to reveal three pages filled with Aunt May's elegant handwriting.

" 'Dear Eva and Family, Wonderful news! I have found a most excellent bargain—' Oh, dear!"

Everyone looked up. Momma was gazing at the letter with a

look of dismay; the hand holding the pink pages trembled slightly. She glanced up at Poppa, then took hold of the letter with both hands and continued reading.

" '—a most excellent bargain on a house in Galveston. The owners were anxious to leave the island and Mr. Lawford assisted me by arranging the sale. Even now I am surrounded with boxes, paper, and string, for I set the servants to packing at once and we shall be gone as soon as ever we may.' "

Momma drew a breath and turned the page over. " 'Send Emmaline to me at once for I shall be greatly in need of her assistance and support in settling into my new home. If Jamie can accompany her he will be most welcome, for there are some things, as you know Eva, that only a man may see to. Mr. Lawford of course is willing to assist me in any way, but he is no longer young and I am sure the strong arms of your boy will be needed.' She gives the address. There is more—oh, Earl! I cannot be happy that she has taken this step!"

Poppa frowned. "Lawford generally keeps her out of trouble. He would have prevented it if there was any real danger."

Emma felt this must be true. Mr. Lawford figured strongly in every one of Aunt May's letters; he had been her chief beau for as long as Emma could remember—since shortly after her husband's untimely demise years and years ago, according to Momma—and Emma had often wondered why he didn't marry her.

"But Galveston is on the coast!" Momma said. "Are they not in danger from the blockaders?"

"The island has some sort of defense, I'm sure," Poppa said. He and Jamie exchanged a glance, neither looking very happy.

"Jamie, you must go to Houston and convince her not to move!"

"Now, Eva—"

"Momma, I don't think I can," Jamie said. "We're supposed to take the battery up to Marshall—"

"Can you not get a leave of absence?"

"I don't know. I haven't asked."

"Then you must go, Earl," Momma said, her eyes shining with a desperate sort of gleam.

Poppa shook his head. "Not now. We're short-handed as it is, and those new mules need watching."

"I'll go," Emma said quietly.

Everyone was silent, looking at her in surprise. She lifted her chin. "I'll go and try to talk her into staying. You wanted me to go, didn't you?"

"Of course, Emma, yes," Momma said, in a voice that was nearly calm. "You should visit your aunt. I think—I think she does need your help."

"All right then," Emma said.

"You can't go alone, you're a girl!" Gabe protested.

"Gabriel!" Momma said sharply. "Go and start washing up. You have had enough dessert."

Gabe's face took on the look of a mule about to kick, but he got up and went to the kitchen, taking his half-eaten cobbler with him.

"There is no question of your traveling alone, of course," Momma continued. "Jamie, do you think you might get leave for long enough to escort your sister to Houston?"

Emma looked up at her brother, silently pleading with him to agree. He gazed back at her a minute, then sighed.

"I'll try."

"Thank you," Momma said. She had regained her serenity, and proposed that they remove to the family room while Gabe finished clearing the table. The rest of Aunt May's letter was read, but it contained only rapturous descriptions of her new house, its elegant situation, its comfortable appointments and the benefits to be derived from living near the sea, and a final plea to send her niece and nephew to her immediately. She expected to depart in two weeks' time.

Emma half-listened, a little surprised at herself for agreeing so readily to go. It felt right, though. No one knew her in Houston. No one would take any notice of her, or offer words of sympathy she did not want to hear. Aunt May would be too busy packing and bustling to bother her with such. She would be away from curious, pitying eyes.

She would miss the ranch, but if she were ever to leave for a spell, now was a good time. She had never been away from home before. It felt strange to think about.

After a little while she got up and walked outside. There was no moon yet. She sat on the steps, remembering with a little, sharp pain how Stephen had tried to teach her the constellations, sitting just here. She wiped a tear away and sat a long time, looking up at the stars.

5

The plantations along this portion of the river are among the finest I ever saw. The grounds are laid off beautifully and are well supplied with all the varieties of tropical flowers and fruits. Figs, pomegranates . . . apples, &c are plentiful, though I have not yet come across any oranges or bananas. We are hardly far enough south for them . . .
—Acting Ensign Symmes E. Browne, U. S. Navy

"Captain Sayers?"

Jamie paused beneath the fly outside the captain's tent. He could see Sayers through the open door, seated at his desk, looking up from his paperwork.

"Russell? You're early. Come in."

Jamie entered, removing his hat. The tent was spacious, a ten-foot-square wall tent, set up as living quarters although Sayers, like most of the officers, was staying in San Antonio. Four chairs stood in a line at one side, ready for the battery officers' meeting.

"I was hoping to talk with you before the meeting," Jamie said. "Can you spare a few minutes?"

"Of course." Sayers set his pen in the standish. "Have a seat."

Jamie brought one of the chairs to the desk and sat down. "I'd like to request a furlough. My sister needs an escort to Houston."

Sayers raised his eyebrows. Jamie explained about his family's situation and his mother's hope that he would be able to persuade Aunt May not to move to Galveston.

"I should hope not," said Sayers. "The coast is no longer safe. Not that it was, but this business in Aransas proves it."

Jamie nodded. Sayers referred to information that had reached San Antonio—wild rumors at first, but recently corroborated—of a Yankee yacht that had captured two schooners, a sloop, and nearly a hundred bales of cotton at Aransas Bay the week before.

"I don't see why you couldn't get a furlough," Sayers said. "Have to get the commander's permission of course, but we won't be ready to go up to Marshall for at least another month. Write up a formal request and I'll take it up to headquarters for Colonel Reily to sign."

"Reily? Has Sibley left for Marshall already?"

Sayers shook his head. "He's been called to headquarters, to answer some questions about New Mexico, or so I've heard. The governor is not happy. With good reason," he added, his face becoming grim.

Nettles came in, fanning himself with his hat. "Afternoon, Russell. Captain. Heard about the *Monte Cristo*?"

"Only that she was captured," Jamie said.

"Well, the Yanks won't be getting any prize money for her," Nettles said, grinning as he pulled up a chair. "Some of our patriotic citizens down that way burned her in the bay."

"Burned who?" said John Foster from the door.

"A schooner at Aransas," Nettles told him.

Foster came in and gave Jamie a nod as he joined them. He was the junior of the battery's four lieutenants, in charge of the caissons as well as adjutant's duties. He was about Jamie's age, wore spectacles, and bore the marks of fresh scars from a case of smallpox he'd endured in New Mexico. Officially he and Jamie shared a tent, though he had it to himself while they were near San Antonio and Jamie could sleep at home.

Sayers checked his watch. "Where is Hume?"

"Overseeing a change of guard," Foster said. "The detail was late. He asked me to say he'll be right along."

"Hm. Who is the officer of the guard?" Sayers said.

"Sergeant Hodge, I believe."

"I will have a word with him," Sayers said, pausing to make a note. "Sit down, Mr. Foster. We may as well begin."

Jamie and the others took out their pocket notebooks, ready to record Sayers's orders and instructions. Jamie glanced at the front page of his and saw Martin's inscription—it had been a gift as they left for New Mexico. Caught off guard, he felt his throat tighten. He coughed and rubbed his pocket handkerchief over his face.

Hume came in, apologizing for his tardiness. Jamie was glad of the distraction, for it gave him a chance to compose himself. He began to wonder if something was wrong with him. He should be over it by now, shouldn't he?

"Yes, all right, Mr. Hume," Sayers said. "Now sit down. We will have battery drill on Monday . . ."

"How much do you think all that's worth?" asked Becker, gesturing toward the eastern shore as he joined Quincy on the deck. The *Lane* was steaming past vast fields of cotton—incredibly white, gleaming through the trees fringing the bank—that stretched back deep behind the levee. The land belonged to one Colonel Hawkland, who had furnished useful information to the U.S. Navy, though there were reports of Rebel troops and supplies crossing the river by ferry just below the mouth of the Red River, and the ferry landing happened to lie on the northwest corner of Hawkland's property.

"I can't begin to calculate it," Quincy said, looking out at the endless snowy expanse. "Like fields of gold," he added.

His gut tightened at the thought of the prize money the cotton might have brought them had it been picked and baled, and if they could somehow have captured it all. They had no authority to do so, however, especially here. As far as the navy knew, Hawkland was loyal.

"Commands respect, doesn't it?" Becker said, leaning against the rail to gaze at the cotton. "Europe is hungry for that, why else would they still be on friendly terms with the South? That's power, growing there."

Quincy felt small, all at once. How could the navy, whose few ships were short-handed and blighted with fever, ever hope to prevent the inexorable flow of cotton from such fields to Europe? Not Hawkland's, perhaps, but he was only one of dozens of plantationers along the river.

The mansion now came into view atop a sloping rise, white columns framed by drooping willows and grand-limbed live oaks. Smaller buildings clustered behind it, and a wide drive lined with flowering bushes ran down the hill to join a road running north along the levee. A large, well-kept river landing betokened a prosperous commerce. Two small skiffs lay tied there, but no ferryboat was in sight.

Quincy glanced over his shoulder. Across the river he could now see the mouth of the Red, which poured its rusty waters into the Mississippi's yellow and was quickly swallowed. The Rebels had two gunboats up that river, and the *Lane* was to blockade here, ready to oppose them should they venture out onto the Mississippi. Up at Vicksburg the Confederates had a new and formidable ram, the *Arkansas*, which had embarrassed the army's fleet and terrified the navy. If she were to join forces with the two boats up the Red, there would be trouble indeed.

"Hello," Becker said behind him. "Looks like the old man is coming out to see us."

Quincy turned to see a handsome bay horse trotting down the drive toward the landing. Its rider was gray-haired, but sat straight and tall in the saddle. The captain ordered the anchor dropped, and with a brief flurry of activity the *Harriet Lane* moved out of the channel and stilled her wheels.

Dawes came up to them. "Mr. Wheat, the captain desires you to take the first cutter to shore and invite Colonel Hawkland to come aboard."

"Thank you, Dawes."

When Quincy reached the landing he found the old gentleman waiting beside his horse. Hawkland was spry, though sixty if he was a day. He greeted Quincy warmly, shaking hands with a firm grip that belied the impression of age. His silvered hair was brushed back from a wide brow, and his neatly trimmed whiskers were silver as well. He wore a suit of fine linen with a waistcoat of pale, brocaded silk and boots polished to gleaming. A large diamond pin reposed in his neckcloth, which was tied cravat-fashion, and a single rosebud was pinned to his lapel.

"I cannot say how happy I am to see your ship here," Hawkland said, smiling. "We have been greatly troubled about our safety."

"Commander Wainwright invites you to meet with him aboard ship," Quincy told him.

"Excellent." Hawkland turned to a cluster of black children who had gathered nearby to stare at the *Harriet Lane*. "One of you come here and hold my horse," he called.

Three boys scrambled forward; the tallest elbowed the others out of the way and reached for the reins. Hawkland rubbed his head, smiling, and followed Quincy into the cutter.

"I trust your captain intends to remain here?" Hawkland said.

"I believe this is our station for the time being," Quincy replied.

"Excellent, excellent. I shall rely upon your support. I have been harassed so often I am nearly at my wits' end."

"Harassed? By whom?"

"By these infernal irregulars! Militia, they call themselves, but in fact they are no better than a gang of bandits. They have ordered me to burn my cotton or risk having it burned for me, and they threaten to hang me if I refuse!"

"Why burn it?"

Hawkland chuckled. "Because they don't want me to sell it to *you.*"

The cutter reached the ship, and Hawkland was welcomed aboard by Wainwright and Mr. Lea. Quincy lingered nearby, curious to know more about the plantationer.

"I am most pleased that your ship is here, Captain," said Hawkland. "I hope you will inform me if I may be of any assistance to you during your stay."

"I expect you can," Wainwright said. "We are interested to hear any news of the two gunboats that were here about a week ago."

"The *Webb* and the *Music*." Hawkland nodded. "They are up the Red River. They will be trapped there soon, with the water falling so low. There are any number of steamboats up the Red and the Black as well. They all went there for safety when New Orleans—was liberated."

Wainwright paused for a moment, gazing at his guest with narrowed eyes. "Have you any details about the *Webb* and the *Music?*"

Hawkland nodded. "*Webb* is a sidewheel tug which has been converted to a ram. She is armed with four guns—twelve-pounders, or so I have heard. *Music* is a sidewheeler with two guns. I do not know their size."

"Let us talk more of this," Wainwright said. "Come have a drink with me in my cabin."

Quincy watched them go below, accompanied by Lea. He exchanged a glance with Becker who was standing nearby. "Did Colonel Hawkland serve in the Mexican War, I wonder?"

Becker shrugged. "More like 1812, by the look of him."

"Mm. He's no granny, though."

The ship's bell rang seven peals. "Half an hour to my watch," Quincy said, "and I've got paperwork to finish." With a wave toward Becker, he hurried below.

Jamie and his father dismounted in front of the Vance House, having ridden into town together, Jamie to inquire at headquarters about his furlough, and Poppa to run errands for the ranch. Jamie paused to gaze up at the second-floor window of the office he and Martin had once shared. Around them the street bustled with people, mostly coming and going from the two-story stone house the army had leased from the Vance brothers for its headquarters.

"Stable your horse, Captain?"

Jamie looked at the orderly who had spoken. The soldier's face was familiar—eyes dark and hungry-looking though he had shaved and obviously eaten—and he must have recognized Jamie, who wore no captain's insignia. In fact, he was no longer a captain, having resigned his brevet promotion in order to serve in the Valverde Battery.

"Yes, thanks," Jamie said, handing over Cocoa's reins.

"I'll come in with you," Poppa said, holding out Pip's reins as well.

Mildly surprised, Jamie nodded to the orderly and watched the man walk both horses around the corner of the house, heading for the stables out back. He looked at the building once more and, drawing a breath as if he were about to plunge into cold water, led his father in.

Noise assailed him, a dozen voices at once, issuing from the various open doors down the ground floor hall. He started to work his way back toward the adjutant's office, then heard his name called and turned to see a familiar dapper figure coming down the stairs.

"Colonel Reily!" Jamie stepped forward to shake hands.

"Good to see you, Russell," Reily said, smiling. He looked as if he had never left San Antonio, gray hair and beard neatly trimmed and a crisp-shouldered civilian coat that fit his tall frame to admiration. "I hear the regiment is arriving at last," he said.

"Coming in tomorrow, I believe," Jamie said.

"That is well. I wish you still had the care of us."

Jamie grinned. "Pardon me if I don't. Colonel, may I introduce my father? Earl Russell, Colonel James Reily."

Reily turned a gracious smile on Poppa. "Mr. Russell! A pleasure. Your son is a hero, you know."

Jamie forced a laugh. "Oh, we are all heroes."

"But you brought the army through the mountains," Reily said seriously. He turned to Poppa. "One of my staff saw him riding back along the trail at three one morning, carrying dozens of canteens to the poor fellows who were too weak to make it to water. We would have lost many more than we did if not for your son's efforts."

Poppa's look of surprise made Jamie all the more uncomfortable. "We'd better not keep you," he said to Colonel Reily. "I need to speak to the AAG."

"Good luck to you, then. It is like a hornet's nest in there," the colonel said. "Good day, Mr. Russell," he added as he started toward the street.

Poppa cast Jamie an inquiring glance, which he ignored. Instead he dove into the crowd spilling out of Lane's office, but soon realized the wait would be at least an hour. He knew Poppa had business in town, so he decided to try again later.

Jamie found himself drawing a deep breath of air as they left headquarters. He turned to Poppa. "Do you want your horse?"

"Not yet. Shall we walk a while?"

Poppa looked troubled. Jamie felt uneasy, but said "All right."

They walked in silence. The sun was climbing and the day promised to be sultry. Poppa stopped outside a shop window, and after staring blankly at it for a minute he turned to Jamie.

"You never told us much about New Mexico," he said.

Jamie shifted his weight on his feet. "There isn't much to tell, really."

"Your Colonel Reily seemed to think otherwise." Poppa's voice was softer than usual. "I did not know you had saved lives."

Did you know I had taken them?

Aloud, Jamie said, "A thousand of our men did not come home. They are the ones I think about every day."

"Son—"

"Do you need my help in town?" Jamie said, trying hard to

keep the anger out of his voice. "Because if not—"

"I do, actually. I . . . Let me buy you a drink. I would like to discuss something with you."

Jamie pressed his lips together, but agreed. They walked another block and turned the corner, crossing the street to Menger's. The taproom was quiet, a haven from the hustle outside. Poppa bought two beers and they carried them to a table.

"Jamie," Poppa said, after taking a swallow of beer. "I have decided to hire a hand for the ranch."

Jamie's anger melted. Poppa was truly worried, then. They had so little money to spare this year, it must have been hard to decide they must spend some on hiring help. A stab of guilt went through him. Poppa would not even be thinking such a thing if he had stayed home.

"I want your advice," Poppa went on. "I think I would like to hire—well, a veteran. Someone who needs a temporary job." He raised his eyes to Jamie's, and the look in them caught Jamie so off guard he felt a threat of tears. He could not remember Poppa ever looking to him for advice. He had always been the no-account son, not as tough or as smart as the eldest, not as engaging as the youngest. He found he could not speak, and hid it by drawing deep at his beer.

"That is a fine and generous thought," he said finally in a shaky voice.

Poppa smiled, a little anxious smile that touched Jamie to the heart. "I am glad you approve," he said. "Can you tell me to whom I should speak about it?"

"I'll ask around. I'm sure we can find someone."

"Thank you."

They sipped at their beers in awkward silence. When he had one swallow left, Poppa raised his glass. "I'm proud of you, Jamie," he said, and tossed off the beer.

Jamie bit his lip, his feelings a jumble of pleasure and shame. He should not have been angry at Poppa—how could he have been angry? And he did not deserve Poppa's pride, but he was glad, oh how glad, to have it. He was conscious of the volatility of his feelings; lately any little thing could touch him off into anger, or just as easily into joy, and that worried him some. Afraid of embarrassing himself, he only smiled at Poppa, then finished his beer.

They parted ways, Poppa to pursue his errands, Jamie pausing to buy three cold chicken legs from Menger's chef, which he carried back to headquarters. The crowd outside Lane's office had thinned enough to be entirely contained in the anteroom. He gave a piece of chicken to the orderly on guard at the outer door; the second got him past the clerk and into Lane's office, where he strode blithely past two harassed-looking captains and held out the third chicken leg to Lane, leaning across the heaps of paper on his desk.

"Jamie! My hero!" Lane cried, looking up at him.

"Came to check on my furlough."

"Not yet," Lane said, taking the chicken.

"When can I talk to you?"

Lane made a wry face around a bite of chicken. "Midnight."

"My father wants to hire a temporary hand," Jamie told him. "Someone on disability would do, as long as he can handle ranch work."

"I'll ask the brigade surgeon."

"Fine. Thanks. See you at midnight," Jamie added over his shoulder, grinning as went back out past the indignant crowd in the anteroom.

Quincy frowned at himself in the mirror that hung behind the door of his tiny cabin. His hair flipped up oddly from under his hat on one side, and no amount of combing had served to tame it. What he needed was a haircut, but of course there wasn't time. He, Gerard, Dr. Penrose, and Commander Wainwright were expected to visit at Colonel Hawkland's house at four o'clock, and the cutter would be lowered at precisely a quarter to.

"Drat," Quincy muttered, tugging at the errant lock. Both Gerard and Becker had denied possessing a jar of pommade, and he didn't care to ask Lea. He took off his hat, smoothed his hair again, and carefully replaced it.

A shadow fell on the slats of the door, followed by a knock. "One moment," Quincy said, taking a last anxious glance at the mirror. He stepped back out of the way to open the door. William stood outside.

"Got those kerchiefs done for you, Mr. Wheat," he said.

"Excellent," Quincy said. "Thank you." He reached into his pocket for a couple of coins and handed them to William in exchange for a stack of crisp handkerchiefs, each neatly embroidered with his initials in white. He tucked one into his pocket and put the others in one of the drawers beneath his shoulder-high bunk.

William lingered. "You going up to the big house?"

"Yes, that's right," Quincy said as he brushed a bit of dust from the sleeve of his dress coat.

"Will you watch out for my mama?"

Surprised, Quincy stared at William. "Your mama is there?" he asked, searching the boy's face.

"I don't know," William said. "She might be. She were sold west from Charleston."

"When was that? Do you remember?"

"Two year ago, last May. I run right after that. Follow the drinking gourd, come safe to the free North."

Quincy let out his breath in a sigh. "What is her name?" he asked, though he knew there was little chance that she would be on this particular plantation. He liked William, though, and couldn't bring himself to crush him with the plain truth—that his mother was probably many miles away, if she was even still alive.

"Ruby," William said. "Her name's Ruby."

"I'll look out for her," Quincy said.

William gave him a grateful smile that smote him with guilt.

Quincy told the boy to run along, and hastened up the companionway.

The others were already on deck. As he hurried toward them, Quincy saw the captain replacing his watch in his pocket. They got into the waiting cutter, the captain entering last, and Lieutenant Lea signaled for the boat to be lowered.

This visit was to be ceremonial. Colonel Hawkland had invited all of the *Lane*'s officers to dine with him, which of course could not be done. Commander Wainwright had compromised, bringing three officers with him to partake of a glass of sherry in Hawkland's parlor, while sending a picket detail with a boat howitzer up the Red, to watch for any sign of the Rebel boats.

As the cutter's crew rowed the short distance to the ferry landing Quincy was able to observe the colonel's house more minutely. It was built of two tall stories, each with a deep porch surrounding the house. These were supported by massive white columns, all in the best Greek revival style. Nothing so grand existed in Cincinnati. Indeed, Quincy had not seen a finer house anywhere, even among the dozens of other plantation homes that overlooked the lower Mississippi.

The colonel's carriage drew up at the landing just as they arrived, sent by their host to convey them up the long, immaculate drive to the house. The bushes lining it, Quincy now saw, were roses. Dozens of rosebushes, all red, all blooming furiously. He imagined he could smell them from the landing.

Two negro footmen alighted as the vehicle stopped, to open its door and let down the steps. The *Lane*'s officers climbed in, and a few moments later arrived at the house and walked up the carriage steps to enter the lofty-ceilinged hall.

The floor was of yellow pine, with an intricate marquetry medallion of roses at its center. Two huge crystal chandeliers gleamed with reflected light. At the far end of the hall a large pair of oak doors mirrored the front doors, both sets standing open to allow breezes through.

The butler, an aged negro who moved with stilted deliberation, showed them into a parlor immediately to the right of the entrance. Quincy hung back to admire the hand-painted wallpaper adorning the walls of the hall. The pastoral scenes seemed intended to depict the seasons of the year. He nudged Gerard, drawing his attention to the images.

"Must be from Europe," Gerard whispered. "I saw a set like that once in a packer's house in Porkopolis."

Unable to take vocal exception to this derogatory reference to the city of Cincinnati, Quincy contented himself with treading on Gerard's heel as they entered the parlor.

Colonel Hawkland arose from a gilded chair cushioned in blue velvet. "Welcome, Captain, gentlemen," he said, beaming. "Welcome to Rosehall! Thank you for honoring an old man with your company."

"Thank you for your generous invitation," Wainwright returned, bowing slightly from the waist. "You have met Mr. Wheat. May I present to you Acting Master Robert Gerard, and our ship's surgeon, Dr. Thomas Penrose?"

Quincy took the opportunity to observe the room while the others shook hands. It was square-shaped, at least fourteen feet high, and lavishly furnished with velvet drapes drawn back from tall lace-curtained windows, a thick oriental carpet, ornate sofa and chairs and several large paintings. Over the marble fireplace hung a full-length portrait of a young woman in riding-dress, her hair spilling over her shoulders from beneath a beaver hat; dark eyes looking boldly out of her cream-complected, oval face; and full lips curved in the barest hint of a smile.

"Ah, you are admiring my wife," said Hawkland, stepping up beside him. "That was painted just last year."

"Striking," Quincy said, hoping his surprise was not evident in his face. The lady in the portrait seemed more of an age to be Hawkland's daughter than his wife. "Is it a faithful likeness?"

"It is indeed," Hawkland said, smiling. "We hired the best portraitist in New Orleans."

"Then—you are a fortunate man," Quincy stammered, unable to think of a better compliment.

"I am. I am, though I have not seen her in months. She is in New Orleans. She is my second wife," Hawkland added, raising one eyebrow slightly as if he had deduced Quincy's thoughts. "The first died in childbed, and the infant with her. I was devastated, but then I met my beautiful Marie." He gazed at the portrait, smiling. "We have great hopes of beginning a family, but—"

He left the thought unfinished as a servant brought an ornate silver tray into the room. This man was a mulatto, much younger than the butler. The tray bore a decanter and cordial glasses of fine crystal.

"Please be seated, gentlemen," Hawkland said, resuming his chair and pouring the wine. Quincy perched on the edge of a velvet sofa and accepted a glass. When they all had been served Hawkland raised his glass.

"To the navy, gentlemen! I thank God you are here."

"To the navy," Quincy said with the others. He sipped, and found the sherry to be very fine indeed.

"Is there anything I can provide for you while you are stationed here?" Hawkland asked the captain. "Anything you are running short of?"

"We would be happy to pay fair market value for fresh beef and vegetables," said Dr. Penrose.

"Oh, I have none to spare," Hawkland said, waving a hand. "My slaves have not eaten any sort of meat in some weeks. I do allow them to grow their own poultry and to keep little gardens. You are welcome to buy from them if you will."

Quincy made note of this. Doubtless he would be coming ashore again to supply the Wardroom Mess.

"I had heard that large numbers of cattle were crossing the river here," Wainwright said slowly.

"Yes," Hawkland said, frowning. "The Confederate army has been bringing troops and cattle over on the ferry, and crossing my land with them, curse them! But they are not the worst, it is the guerrillas! They do not care whom they terrorize. They demand money, provisions, transportation, even slaves!"

"I see."

"I tell them I cannot supply them, for I have not been able to sell my cotton. I have last year's cotton yet, which they ordered me twice to burn. I cannot burn my cotton, Captain," Hawkland said in earnest concern. "I must sell it to feed and clothe my poor slaves. Indeed, I am most anxious to know when the river will be safe for commerce again." He looked expectantly at the captain, who stroked his whiskers as if considering his reply.

"There is not much one vessel can do," Wainwright said, "I am afraid we must give our first thought to the gunboats in the Red."

"Oh, I understand, absolutely," said Hawkland. "Your presence here alone is a boon. Do not think me ungrateful. I do hope, though, that more ships will join you?"

"That is our hope as well."

They conversed a while longer, discussing the war and the river. Quincy listened, but had little to contribute. He allowed his gaze to wander back to Mrs. Hawkland's portrait, and found himself sighing, sorry that the lady of the house had not been present. Female company of any variety was a precious commodity with a navy man.

At the end of half an hour the captain rose to take his leave. Quincy and the others stood as well, each shaking hands with their host.

"I hope you will visit again, Mr. Wheat," Hawkland said to Quincy.

"Thank you, sir. I hope I may." He remembered William's request with a pang. "Ah—Colonel Hawkland? Do you—well—"

"Yes?"

"I was wondering if you happened to have a servant named Ruby," Quincy said in a rush, fully conscious of the peculiarity of the question. Past Hawkland's shoulder he saw Wainwright frowning at him, and knew he would be asked for an explanation when they were back aboard the *Lane*.

"Not in the house," Hawkland said with a shrug.

"Have you a Ruby at all?"

Hawkland's smile was faintly disdainful. "My dear fellow, I have over a thousand slaves."

"Of course," Quincy said a bit stiffly. "Never mind."

"If you will give me a description of this Ruby I will send her up to the ship for you. Or something in a similar line."

Quincy could feel the blood rushing into his face. Commander Wainwright came to his rescue.

"That will not be necessary, Colonel," he said, with an amused glance in Quincy's direction. "Thank you again for the sherry."

While Wainwright shook the planter's hand once more, Quincy accepted his hat from a footman, shoved it on his head in a way that he hoped would curb his disobedient locks, and hurried out to the carriage after the others, hoping at that moment that he would never meet Colonel Hawkland again.

6

Some time since Captain Eagle, commanding the frigate Santee, *off Galveston, demanded, under a threat of bombardment and the speedy arrival of land and naval forces, the unconditional surrender of the city of Galveston, batteries, &c. This was refused. Since then nothing has been done by the enemy, and matters remain as they were.*
— P. O. Hébert, Brigadier-General, Provisional Army

Emma realized she was squinting, paused to set down her pen and turn up the wick on the lamp, then rubbed her eyes. It was late, but she was almost finished recording the new mules, and she wanted to get it done tonight.

She thought about making some coffee but decided against it. The others were all in bed asleep and she didn't want to wake them. It would take a good quarter hour to build the kitchen fire back up anyway, and by then she would be finished with the books. She was proud of her accuracy and the neatness of her hand. Poppa had turned the ranch's books over to her almost a year ago, when Daniel had gone to join up.

Emma sat up straight. Yes, it was almost exactly a year, because Dan had left the day after they got the news about Manassas, and that had been July 22nd, and today was the 18th. Even as she thought it, the clock on the mantel began its soft, musical chiming. She glanced at it, saw both hands on twelve, and thought, *No, the 19th.* She wondered where Daniel was now; somewhere in Tennessee. Safe still after a year and several battles. So far all her brothers were safe. All her brothers, but not her fiancé.

"Stop it, Emma," she whispered, and stood up to walk the room a little and rub the stiff muscles at the back of her neck. The skirt of the day dress she had put on for Momma's sake caught at her legs; she was more accustomed to the freedom of trousers now. She returned to the desk, sat down and picked up her pen again. A few more lines, then she wrote, "No. 27, out of sorrel mare Sunshine by brown jack Bill, club-footed, culled."

Emma signed the bottom of the page, closed the ledger and sighed. That had been a difficult choice. All week they had watched the little lame baby, hoping for improvement. Poppa had left the decision up to her, and today she had finally admitted that there was no hope for the poor thing. He could live, but he couldn't work, and they couldn't afford to keep him as a pet, not during this drought year when every mouthful of grass on the range counted. Besides, they were already keeping Patches and Raindrops. So today, while Poppa had gone into town to arrange for his sale for meat, she and Gabe had cut the baby and his mother out of the herd and driven them slowly home. They were in the corral now. Tomorrow, or Monday maybe since tomorrow was Saturday, the buyer would come pick him up. She could already hear him bawling, his mother shrieking, as they were separated forever.

No, that had been a real noise! Emma caught her breath, set the pen in the inkwell and reached out to turn down the lamp, then sat still to listen. Shuffling movement outside, a thud and a stifled curse, then a creak of wood. Someone was on the front porch! She rose and moved to set a hand on Poppa's shotgun leaning in the corner behind the desk. Fear tingled down her arms.

A chorus of voices burst into song outside the window:

"Come all you bold young fellows that have a mind to range,

Into some foreign country your station for to change,
Into some foreign country along with me to go,
We'll lie down on the banks of the San Antonio,
We'll wander through the wild woods
and we'll hunt the buffalo!"

Emma set the gun down again and turned up the lamp, then picked it up and strode toward the door. She could hear Poppa cussing in his room and thumping around, Momma's frightened voice like a hungry kitten's mew. She got to the front door and threw it open, holding the lamp high so its light fell on three laughing men—boys, rather, for they were not acting like men— kneeling on the porch and trying to continue their song. Friends of Jamie's; one was Ellsberry Lane, holding a bouquet of flowers into which a rolled paper was thrust. Another she thought was called Nettles. The third was the tallest; she couldn't remember his name but she knew he was an army friend of her brother's.

A hasty shuffle of stockinged feet made her glance over her shoulder to see Jamie coming to the door, shoving the tail of his nightshirt into his trousers. He gazed in amazement at the spectacle on the porch, and all three would-be serenaders collapsed in laughter.

"I think your friends are drunk," Emma said, offering him the lamp. The look of dismay on his face almost made her laugh. She was hard put to keep a stern expression as she glared down again at Lane. He peeped up at her with such a guilty look that she laughed aloud, then shoved the lamp into Jamie's hand and hurried to her parents' bedroom.

"It's all right, Momma and Poppa," she said through the door. "It's just some of Jamie's friends playing a prank."

Poppa opened the door and looked out. He was still in his nightshirt with his Colt pistol in hand; behind him Momma was sitting up in bed, holding the covers at her neck.

"It's all right," Emma said again. "Go back to sleep, I'll send them away."

Poppa glanced at the porch, saw Jamie talking with the visitors, let out an exasperated sigh and closed the bedroom door. Emma glanced down the hall toward Gabe's room. Likely he'd slept right through it all. She returned to the front door and leaned against the jamb with her arms crossed, enjoying the scene. Jamie had set the lamp on the porch and was lecturing his laughing comrades.

"You mean to tell me you came from headquarters at this hour—"

"It's midnight, isn't it?" said Lane. "I never go back on my word. Besides, I figured you'd want this right away." He thrust the bouquet at Jamie, who took it, frowning down at them in confusion.

Lane seemed to have trouble keeping from bursting into laughter. He said to Jamie, gasping, "It's your furlough!"

Jamie took one look at his friend, yanked the paper from the bouquet and dropped the flowers, which scattered, escaping their ribbon and spilling over the boards and the serenaders' feet. Emma watched her brother hastily read the page, then give a hoot and pull Lane to his feet, pumping his hand and slapping his back. The others got up, too, crowding around Jamie with jokes and more laughter. Emma stepped forward and picked up the lamp, which was in danger of being kicked over.

"Gentlemen," she said, just sharply enough to command their silence. "My parents are trying to sleep. If you will come into the kitchen I will make you some coffee, but you'd better keep quiet or you'll drink it in the barn."

Without waiting, she turned and walked through the dining room to the kitchen, footsteps behind her and a stifled chuckle telling her she was being obeyed. She opened the stove and put a handful of tinder on the dying coals. With a little encouragement the fresh wood caught, and she added two stout sticks and shut the door. Jamie and his friends sat down around the kitchen table and kept talking, quietly enough. A glance at them convinced her that they were not really drunk, only giddy with their own foolishness. She filled the kettle, set it on the stove, and went out to clean up the abandoned flowers from the porch.

After a minute she heard a step behind her. Looking up, she saw Mr. Lane coming to the open front door. He knelt down to help her pick up the scattered bouquet.

"I apologize," he said softly. "We didn't know which window was Jamie's."

"It wouldn't have mattered, with all your caterwauling," Emma whispered, but she softened it with a smile. "You brought good news anyway, so thank you."

"Good news? I suppose so." He paused to pick up some daisies and carefully arrange them with the other flowers in his hand. "I hope you enjoy your visit to Houston, and I hope you can return soon. I don't mean to frighten you, but it is quite vulnerable, you know, with only Galveston between it and the blockaders."

Emma looked up sharply, but he was busy picking up flowers. He gathered the last few and held the bunch out to her. "May I offer these to you?"

At first she was inclined to refuse, but she remembered that Mr. Lane was married, and so could not be flirting with her. He was just being friendly. Be gracious, she told herself.

"Thank you kindly, sir," she said primly, then shot him a mischievous glance. "I am practicing, you see. I'm being sent to Houston to learn how to be a lady."

Lane looked astonished, then laughed. "Completely unnecessary," he said gallantly.

"How right you are," Emma whispered as they both got to their feet and headed back for the kitchen. "Who ever heard of a lady punching cattle?"

A crowd had gathered at the drilling grounds north of the battery's camp. A line of wagons and carriages was parked in among the trees that lined the creek, with families picnicking, children and dogs romping, and a lot of the newly returned infantry sprawled in the shade to watch. Artillery drill tended to draw spectators, but Jamie had not so far seen an audience this large. Then again, this was the first time San Antonio would see the famous Valverde Battery at work.

Jamie rode between the leaders of his two platoons, keeping an eye on the chiefs of the pieces to either side as they marched onto the practice ground in column. Only two pairs of horses were hitched to each vehicle, partly because they were drilling with empty ammunition chests, but also because more horses were still being sought for the teams. When the battery was actually on the march, six horses would be needed to haul each limber and cannon, the same for each caisson. They would have made an even grander spectacle if they had been able to mount all the men and work as horse artillery, but a full battery drill of mounted artillery would be a plenty good show.

Captain Sayers commanded, "Column, halt!" and Jamie and his counterparts repeated the order. The rumble of wheels ceased as the twelve teams halted. A horse snorted, another shook its harness. Otherwise all was still.

Cocoa gave a little whuff of impatience, and Jamie reached down to pat her neck. The waiting crowd had fallen silent. He could see the gleam of field glasses trained on the battery, glinting out from the leaf-dappled shadows of live oaks. He glanced at Sayers, motionless on his gray mare, and the drivers and detachments of cannoneers on foot, all waiting to work.

Sayers at last gave the first order, his voice ringing out clear in the summer air. "Forward into line—left oblique!"

"Section—left oblique!" Jamie cried, and dropped back to ride between the leaders of the caissons.

"March!" called Sayers, and Jamie repeated the command, adding "Guide right!" The guns' teams moved left at an angle, then on his order changed from the oblique to advance straight forward, pulling into line abreast of the first section.

"Section, halt!" Jamie commanded. "Right-dress!" He kept a sharp eye on the guns. His was the odd section—one twelve-pound mountain howitzer, one six-pound field gun—and the detachments occasionally aligned the guns' muzzles rather than the axles of the carriages. To his relief, they did not make this error today, and were in position by the time Sayers commanded "Front!"

A smattering of applause went up from the watching civilians. Jamie kept his eyes on the drivers as Sayers rode into place immediately before him.

The next evolution Sayers called for was a right wheel, which placed the battery in line facing the spectators, to the delight of children who squealed as they scrambled back from the horses. Sayers followed this by commanding the battery to fire to the rear, which meant passing the caissons forward at the trot, then reversing the entire line and unlimbering the guns as if to fire. The crowd cheered heartily as the battery aimed the guns right at them. Jamie saw children capering before the line and had a sudden sickening vision of the battery firing on them: smoke and flame pouring from the muzzles of the guns; canister rounds sending shrouds of musket balls into the crowd who did not really understand what the cannon could do; children swept down to lie bleeding on the ground, shrieking, weeping. He sucked a sharp breath and shook his head. The guns were not loaded. They were not loaded. He swallowed, blinking hard.

Sayers's next order came and Jamie responded, slowly regaining his calm as he oversaw his men. Sayers worked them hard, moving them into column, back into line, marching in oblique and changing fronts. He was apparently pleased enough with their performance to order a more difficult evolution; Jamie had just wiped the sweat from his eyes when the captain called, "Fire to the right! Change front to the rear on the right piece!"

Jamie shouted, "Limber to the rear! Caissons, in rear of your pieces—trot—march!" He stayed in place so his platoons could guide on him, watching as they moved around him. For a moment it all seemed like chaos, then they were wheeling to the left and lining up on the new front.

Horses and men alike were sweating now. Sayers waited for the applause to die down, then ordered the battery into column once more and, to Jamie's relief, marched them forward off the practice ground. The spectators broke into wild cheering. Jamie tried to ignore it, though he felt his neck getting a little warmer. He was proud of his men, and proud of the battery. They had done good work today.

The battery arrived back at the park, the teams were unhitched and put away, and Sayers dismissed them. Jamie dismounted and rubbed Cocoa's sweating neck. Waving away the private who offered to take her, he led her to the creek for a well-deserved drink in the shade of live oaks. He unsaddled her and pulled up a handful of grass to rub her down.

"I'll give you a good brushing when we get home, girl," he murmured. "Promise."

Cocoa stretched her neck around to nip at his hat, and succeeded in knocking it off his head. Jamie hugged her, pretending to scold, then retrieved his hat and brushed it off.

"I remember that pretty mare," said a lazy voice behind him, and Jamie's shoulder muscles tightened. He turned to see Captain Owens—no, Major Owens it appeared, from the star glinting on his collar—coming toward him.

Jamie summoned a smile he didn't feel. "Good afternoon," he said. "I see congratulations are in order."

"I thank you," Owens said, nodding. "And the same to you. You all looked right smart out there."

"Thanks," Jamie said, putting on his hat.

"Smart move, changing to the artillery. You can knock down a whole squad of Yankees at once with those guns," Owens added in a soft, sly tone.

Jamie watched him through narrowed eyes, wondering what he was getting at. He didn't like Owens, had never trusted him.

Unquestionably a Southerner but not a Texan, Owens had resigned from the Federal army to join Sibley's campaign, and
Jamie couldn't help thinking of him as a turncoat. Moreover,
Owens had a way of unsettling his feelings with just a look or a
sly reference to the Valverde fight. He would not leave Jamie
alone about that day, and Jamie resented it.

Owens dug in his pocket and held out a sugar lump to Cocoa,
who gobbled it and grunted for more. Jamie was annoyed, but
held his tongue.

"I hear you are taking your sister to Houston," Owens said,
leaning against the trunk of an oak. "Busy place, Houston. I may
be going there myself. Perhaps I will pay her a call, what do you
think?"

"She is not entertaining callers just now," Jamie told him.

"No? She will soon, I expect. Gal like that, with a lot of spunk
in her, can't keep her still for long."

Jamie turned to face Owens squarely, meeting his gaze, watchful for any implied disrespect to Emma. Owens stroked his mustache, a smile growing slowly on his face.

"Through here for the day?" Owens asked. "I know a little
place you might enjoy. Good mescal, and the señoritas are very
friendly."

"No, thank you." Jamie went back to rubbing at Cocoa's coat
where it had become matted under the saddle.

"You're not shy, are you? Come on, Russell. You might learn
a thing or two. Or is that what you're afraid of?"

Jamie clamped his lips shut. Owens wanted to needle him
into doing something foolish. He took a deep breath, then spoke
as casually as he could.

"I think I know the place you mean. I didn't find it that amusing." He'd been sick, actually, the one time Matt had taken him
there, but he wasn't about to tell Owens that.

"No?" Owens laughed. "I bet your sister would. Hell, she's
more a man than you are!"

Jamie spun around. Owens kept laughing, his teeth glinting

white beneath the sandy mustache. Jamie wanted to smash them in.

Owens saw it, and grinned. "Oho! Maybe you've got some guts after all." He nodded, standing away from the tree. "Come on, then," he taunted.

Jamie stared at him, breathing hard and wanting, really wanting, to hurt him, but his sensible self protested. Owens had powerful friends, Colonel Scurry included. Nothing good could come of rising to his bait.

"You outweigh me and you outrank me," Jamie said in a low, rough voice, "and I'm not as stupid as you appear to think." He glanced at the grass in his hand, saw that he had crushed it, and threw it down. He brushed his hands, watching Owens, whose smile had faded. For a minute they just stared at each other, then Jamie bent down to pick up Cocoa's damp saddle blanket and threw it across her back. She gave a weary sigh that seemed to break the tension.

Owens laughed softly and leaned against the tree once more. Jamie ignored him as he saddled Cocoa and mounted, wincing a little from sore legs. He had not been in the saddle so much in one day since he'd got home. Already he was getting soft, and the trip to Houston would not help, since they were traveling by stage and rail.

He glanced Owens's way as he turned Cocoa toward the camp, but didn't meet his eye. Owens hadn't moved. Jamie started Cocoa forward with a nudge and she walked out into the sun.

"Another day, then," Owens called after him.

Jamie frowned, but didn't bother to reply. Instead he whistled Cocoa to a trot, then a lope, anxious to put distance between himself and Owens.

7

One of the lieutenants pointed them out to me and I trained my gun on them and fired, turning away for I did not wish to see the effect . . . The last shell killed one man and wounded fourteen—so they have told me since. I cannot help crying when I think of them. . . .
—Acting Master Roswell H. Lamson, U. S. Navy

Emma and Gabe stood outside the corral, waiting to see if the spotted jack would cover the sorrel mare. She was just coming into her foal heat, and maybe it was a little too early, or maybe the jack was just tired; they had bred him the day before. He had shown some interest when they'd put him in with Sunshine, but a couple of nips from her had apparently cooled his ardor.

The sound of hoofbeats made Emma look up. Poppa was riding up the lane with Mr. Ferguson, the new hand. He had spent the morning introducing him to the beef herd, and was bringing him back to have dinner with the family.

Emma swallowed, reminding herself to be polite. She had been angry when she learned Poppa had hired on a hand; angry and guilty both. If she hadn't agreed to go to Houston . . . no sense in dwelling on that, though. With her and Jamie both going away, Poppa needed help, and that was a simple fact.

"Bring the jack out and put him away, Gabe," she said.

Gabe went in the corral while she walked forward to greet her father and Mr. Ferguson, who looked younger than she had expected. He was no taller than Emma and was maybe Daniel's age, no more. His neat, dark brown hair and mustache had both obviously just been trimmed. Jamie had told them about him over last night's supper: a former infantrymen, now discharged, who had been a good, reliable soldier. As Emma approached, Ferguson and Poppa dismounted.

"Jack Ferguson, meet my daughter Emma Russell. Emma, this is our new hand."

Ferguson took one startled, searching look at Emma in her work clothes. "How do," he said, his voice deep and quiet.

Emma held her hand out to him and he hesitated, then shook it with his left. She glanced down and realized his right hand was missing the thumb and first finger. Shocked, she froze for a second, still gripping his hand, then released him, feeling herself flush with embarrassment as she met his gaze. He gave a small, tolerant smile and turned to look at Gabe, who was walking toward them with the jack.

"And this is my youngest son, Gabriel," Poppa said. "Say hello to Mr. Ferguson, Gabe."

"Howdy," Ferguson said.

The single word roused Gabe from openmouthed stupor. "You got only three fingers!" he blurted.

"Gabriel!" Emma said. "Please don't mind him, Mr. Ferguson, he says whatever pops into his head."

"Nothing wrong in calling 'em like you see 'em." He brought up his hand to show Gabe. "That's why my friends call me Three-finger Jack."

The skin was red and puckered where the digits had once been, and showed scars from having been stitched. The remaining fingers curled in a bit and looked stiff.

Gabriel stared in fascination. "Does it hurt?"

"Not much, anymore."

"How'd it happen?"

"I'll tell you some time. Right now I think your father has

something to say." Mr. Ferguson looked up at Poppa, who smiled.

"Only this. Who's hungry?"

"Me!" Gabe cried.

"Then hurry up and put that jack away in the barn."

Gabe hastened to obey, and Poppa and Mr. Ferguson left their horses tied to the rail by the trough and started toward the house. Emma found herself walking beside Mr. Ferguson and asked, "Were you wounded in New Mexico?"

He nodded. "At Valverde. I never got any farther than Socorro, that's where they fixed me up. I was paroled and sent to Franklin in time to march home with the regiment. So I missed the fight at Glorieta and that—terrible march through the mountains."

"Jamie wrote to us about it." Emma dropped her gaze to the ground. Jamie had written, but he had not talked about it since he came home. He had not talked much about New Mexico at all. "It sounded like a nightmare."

"It was. Not that I know anything about it; I went down the Camino Real in a wagon."

Emma glanced up at him. His face remained serious, but there was a glint of humor in his eyes. She smiled.

"Welcome to Russell's Ranch, Mr. Ferguson," Momma said, greeting them on the porch. "I trust the family is making you feel at home."

"Yes, ma'am. Mr. Russell's got me all fixed up with a nice cot in the barn, and everything I need to hand."

"Good. Well, dinner is ready, everyone."

They went in and settled around the table for a midday meal of cold beef, beans, fresh bread, and tomatoes from Momma's garden. Emma tried not to stare at Mr. Ferguson's hand as he wove his three fingers around a knife to cut his meat. She kept her eyes on her own plate or on people's faces, and helped Poppa make conversation about the ranch.

"You will meet my son Jamie this evening," he told Mr. Ferguson. "He is in town finishing up some business for the battery."

"I have met Lieutenant Russell, though he may not remember me," Ferguson said. "I watched him drill his section several times, and I saw the battery drill once in Franklin. They were drilling today, in fact." He looked at Momma. "If you ever have the chance to watch the battery drill, ma'am, it will be worth your trouble to go. I've seen whole infantry companies stop their own drilling to watch."

Emma was surprised. "Jamie never told us it would be anything worth seeing."

"He is a modest boy," Momma said. "Thank you for mentioning it, Mr. Ferguson. Perhaps next time we will attend. Now, I hope everyone has room for dessert?"

She had made an apple-spice cake in honor of the new hand. He was duly appreciative, and even accepted a second helping, but he said, "Thank you kindly, Mrs. Russell, and I hope you will not trouble so much about me in the future. No need to set a place for me at your table. A plate of beans in the barn will do for me."

"It is no trouble," Momma said, "and you are welcome at our table, Mr. Ferguson."

"You will settle into whatever suits you," Poppa said. "Tell me what you think of that mare you were riding."

Momma brought out coffee, and they talked about the ranch for a while longer. Finally Poppa rose and declared they should be getting back to work. Momma bid them farewell from the porch and the four of them rode out to the mule herd, which Poppa wanted to show to Ferguson.

"This is where I will be working while you look after the beef," Poppa said. "We are breeding these mares back at the corral, one at a time. I have a half dozen jacks for stud. Right now that's all I have room for."

"You will need a second barn," Ferguson said.

"In time, yes." Poppa looked at Emma. "How many mares left to breed?"

"Just six," Emma said. "I want to breed that Appaloosa to the spotted jack again."

"Emma is our record-keeper, Mr. Ferguson. If you have any questions she can answer them, but you'd better ask today."

"Should I round up that mare?" Ferguson suggested, nodding toward the Appaloosa.

Emma glanced at Poppa, then said, "Yes, do."

Ferguson rode into the herd slowly, freeing up his lariat with his damaged right hand. He approached the Appaloosa mare, who walked, then trotted away. He followed her, matching her gait, which picked up when she realized he was pursuing her. He flung the lariat with his right hand and grabbed the rope with his left, looping it around his saddle horn in a flash and recovering his reins. A moment later he was trotting back with the Appaloosa mare following quietly and Raindrops—loudly protesting this high-handed treatment of her mama—skipping around her flanks.

Emma traded a glance with Poppa, who murmured, "He'll do."

She had not wanted to admit it, but she thought so, too. Mr. Ferguson would certainly do. She was glad, she realized. It would make things so much easier for Poppa while she was away.

She sighed. Momma was packing a trunk for her. She and Jamie had tickets for tomorrow's stage. The time left to her was rushing by, and she felt an urge to get down and hug Raindrops. Instead she held the Appaloosa mare while Poppa and Mr. Ferguson collected the other five she had pointed out to them, all to be taken back for breeding. With the foals following their mothers, the little cavalcade set off back for Russell's Ranch.

Quincy, on duty as officer of the deck, stood on the bridge gazing toward Rosehall. Sunlight was going golden behind him, lighting the water with molten glints, and the mansion gleamed softly within its frame of trees, light spilling from its open doorway and glowing through lace-softened windows. The ribbon of white gravel that was the drive shone in the westering sun. Quincy sighed, wishing he could go ashore to collect a few roses from those splendid bushes. A pressed rose in his next letter would be a pleasant surprise for Miss Keller. He would describe Rosehall for her in minute detail, though perhaps he would not mention Mrs. Hawkland's portrait.

The crew stood at action quarters, as they had done all day, every day until dusk since arriving at this station. Commander Wainwright left nothing to chance; if the Rebels came down the Red he wanted the *Lane* moving and ready to engage as quickly as possible. Thus she kept her steam up while the cooking fires remained out, and the men were sent by mess to get what comfort they could from a supper of cold pork and beans.

The Wardroom fared little better, though Quincy had gone ashore to barter with some of Hawkland's slaves for vegetables. Those he'd met at Belle View had little to spare, and looked so thin and miserable that he hadn't the heart to press them to sell. He would try again in a day or two; Hawkland had suggested he go with the overseer, Mr. Shetland, down to Angola plantation where the slaves did more farming for themselves.

A faint report roused Quincy from these musings. The picket had fired their howitzer! Almost at once the lookout called, "Smoke off the port bow!" and all eyes turned west, toward the mouth of the Red.

Quincy looked at the two midshipmen standing nearby. "Mr. Jewell, up with you, and tell me what you make of it. Mr. Dawes, my respects to the captain and please inform him that there is cannon fire to the west and we are about to slip the anchor cable and move upriver."

"Aye, aye, sir," they said in chorus. Dawes disappeared below. Jewell scrambled up the mainmast shrouds where only a fighting top remained, the upper masts having been left at Pilot Town when the *Lane* had first come up the river.

Quincy stepped to the speaking tube and called down to the engine room, "All ahead a quarter."

There was not time to weigh anchor if they were about to be attacked, and against this possibility a buoy had been attached to the heavy cable so that it might be left where the *Lane* could pick it up later. As the *Lane* started forward, Quincy ordered, "Cast loose the anchor cable."

Three men hastened to cut the lashing that tied the cable end to the foremast, a fourth cut the stopper lashings that held it to rings on the deck, and a fifth prepared to drop the buoy overboard. The cable rattled through the hawsehole and slipped into the water, the buoy following it with a heavy plop.

"All ahead full," Quincy called to the engineer. "Helm, come port ten," he said to the man at the wheel through a speaking trumpet, with an eye to a large sandbar that bulged from the eastern shore ahead.

"Two trails of smoke off the port bow, the first moving fast!" Jewell called from the crow's nest on the mainmast.

Two vessels. They must be the *Webb* and the *Music*. Quincy peered through his glass, trying to spy the smoke. In a moment he saw a black gout rise skyward; the approaching vessels knew they had been sighted, and were laying on coal.

Commander Wainwright came on deck in time to hear Jewell's report. Quincy apprised the captain of the situation and remained beside him on the bridge; until Mr. Lea or Becker arrived he was acting as executive officer. He doubted this would last long enough for him to try his hand at fighting the ship, but even the slim chance of it quickened his blood.

"Center your helm," he ordered the quartermaster at the wheel. "Come starboard ten," he added when they were past the sandbar.

"Mr. Wheat," said the captain, "man the port guns."

"Aye, aye, sir." Quincy took up a speaking trumpet to relay the order to the division commanders. Quarter-gunners stood ready to command his and Becker's divisions; Gerard, at his station near the thirty-pounder Parrot, nodded. If they were to have a fight, which it very much looked like they were, Gerard's stern chaser would probably have the honor of opening the ball, what with the *Lane* chugging upstream as fast as she could.

Quincy heard hasty footsteps and glanced toward the companionway as Lea and Becker arrived on deck. Stifling disappointment, he told the XO their situation and the captain's orders before retiring to assume command of his division. He stared at the mouth of the Red, straining for the first sight of the vessels whose smoke now made a dark smear across the sunset sky. If it was indeed the Rebels, he might yet get off a broadside before the angle became too extreme for his guns to bear.

"Deck ahoy!" cried Jewell from above. "Funnel off the port quarter, and smoke off the port beam!"

The sun was now beginning to sink and the glare blinded Quincy as he tried to distinguish the second smoke trail. The first vessel's smoke now hung in a pall above the cottonwoods. She was perhaps a quarter mile from the confluence. She would be out in mere moments.

Tense silence reigned on deck, then, "There she comes!" Jewell cried, even as a heavy bow appeared from behind the cottonwoods on the western bank. The enemy slunk out of concealment, a sidewheel tug, her bow massively fortified to enable her to ram, the hated banner flying from her stern. The *Webb*, for it had to be she, sped across the bar at the mouth of the Red and turned upriver to pursue the *Lane*.

Every officer's glass was trained on the vessel. Quincy heard Wainwright, above him on the bridge, say, "She is the *Webb*. Mr. Lea, you may fire when ready."

Lea relayed the command through his trumpet, and Gerard's gun fired almost at once. Quincy's guns could not bear but already the *Lane* had begun to pivot—he could feel it.

"Fire as you bear!" he shouted.

Webb answered Gerard's fire with a round from a bow gun—a heavy gun, much heavier than a twelve-pound howitzer—possibly a rifled 32-pounder. Colonel Hawkland must not have known about it. Quincy clenched his teeth, determined not to be daunted. Even if the *Webb* had five guns instead of four, her twelve-pounders could not match the weight of metal in the *Lane*'s broadsides. She was slightly longer than the *Lane*, with a shallower draft and, alas, a more powerful engine. She laid on speed, her heavy bow digging low into the current, and Quincy itched to put a shell into it.

At last the number three gun's captain signaled to fire. The howitzer roared and crashed back on its slides. Quincy peered after the shell as the smoke billowed away. The round had missed. The gun's crew rushed to load again.

Webb's pivot gun fired, a belch of flame, orange in the sunset. The shell fell short and ricocheted upward, striking the *Lane* with a thud that shuddered the deck beneath Quincy's feet. He prayed the shell had gone straight through or was somehow defective, thought for an instant of fire and steam ripping up through the wooden deck, then banished the image. A glance around assured him that his division were all in their places, and seconds passed without an explosion; he drew a deep breath of relief.

The number two gun, the Dahlgren, added its heavy voice to the chorus. The round missed high, crashing into the trees on the western shore. Quincy strode to the gun's captain. "Aim at the waterline!" he shouted over the din, and the man nodded.

William hastened past him to the Dahlgren's breech with his box, heavy with the ten-pound powder charge. He delivered it to the first loader and skipped back out of the way, flashing a grin at Quincy before he disappeared below again for another charge.

Becker's forward pivot fired. The smell of sulphur filled

Quincy's nostrils as all four guns heaved destruction toward the *Webb.* Quincy thought he heard a distant crack that might be a hit. He squinted through his glass at the *Webb,* but saw no sign of damage or unusual activity. She bore straight onward, steaming with all her strength to ram.

Someone was shouting from above, and though Quincy could not make out the words he looked southward and saw the *Music* glide out of the Red. She let off a round from her forward gun; orange-gold, a miss. She was smaller, and had only two guns—six-pounders, if Hawkland was to be believed. Quincy did not dismiss her, but he returned his attention to the *Webb,* by far the more dangerous opponent.

Dawes ran up to Quincy, his freckled face alight with excitement. "Mr. Lea desires you to be ready to man the starboard guns, and to do so when the captain turns the ship downstream."

Quincy nodded, and Dawes dashed away again. William scampered out of his way, fierce concentration on his young face. He was a shadow now, one of many swirling around the guns in their dance of destruction, executed with precision to make the weapons fling death toward the enemy.

The *Webb* closed with speed that was almost too great to be believed and for a moment it looked as if she would succeed in ramming, but at the last moment the *Lane* began her pivot. The current aided her, pulling her bow downstream.

"Man starboard guns!" Quincy cried hoarsely, his throat raw from smoke. His gun crews swarmed across the deck. Quincy hastened to the Dahlgren's captain, and shouted into his ear over the din, "Load with grape!"

Moving on to the howitzer, he saw the rammer already driving home a shell. "Load with canister," he told the gun captain. They would have to fire the shell first, but there would still be time to rake the *Webb*'s deck.

The *Lane,* with the help of the current, swept down past the

Webb. Quincy's number two gun pelted her crew with grape-shot, while the howitzer put its shell right into *Webb*'s heavy bow, where it burst with a dull thud.

A cheer rose on deck. Quincy's triumphant shout joined that of his division, and his heart soared. A ragged, fathom-long hole gaped in the ram's side, above the waterline, but not far above it. She was badly hurt.

"Lively now, we have time to give them another!"

Webb had tried to redirect her ram, but her momentum would not allow her to pivot as fast as the *Lane*. She would still hit, but not well. Quincy braced for the blow, which fell aft of the wheelhouse. The dull crunch made him wince, and as the *Webb* heeled to port, her guns fired.

A loud crack was followed by a snapping, tearing sound. Quincy felt something strike his shoulder. A shower of splinters filled the air, hurtling death across the deck. Someone screamed. Several of the new contrabands cringed against the illusory shelter of the hull.

"Stand to your guns!" Quincy shouted, and though some had wavered, his men resumed their places. The howitzer had fired; the Dahlgren's crew stood waiting for the charge. Quincy saw Isaiah rush up with the passing box. Frowning, he looked round for William.

Behind him, at the foot of the mainmast, a quarter-gunner had just dragged the boy out of the way. William lay bleeding, a jagged splinter lodged in his chest. It looked like it had gone halfway through him.

His gorge rising, Quincy struggled for self-control. Dismay threatened to overcome him; he deflected it and let anger take its place.

The Dahlgren fired, sending grape showering at the *Webb*. Becker's gun fired at the *Music,* and Quincy glanced over in time to see the well-aimed shell strike her amidships. Flame blossomed on her deck. The *Lanes* cheered again. Quincy joined in, but his elation was tempered by awareness of William lying on the deck behind him. With a last glance to confirm that his gun crews were functioning well, he turned to have the boy carried below.

8

---

*Eternal Father, strong to save,/Whose arm hath bound the rest-
less wave. Who bidd'st the mighty ocean deep/Its own appointed
limits keep: Oh, hear us when we cry to Thee/For those in peril
on the sea!*

 —The Navy Hymn ("Eternal Father, Strong to Save"),
    William Whiting

Under a red battle lantern, Quincy stood watching the crew
clean up the effects of the fight. *Music* had started back up the
Red River almost immediately upon being struck, and the *Webb*
had followed her compatriot up the Red. The *Lane* had been
unable to pursue; the *Webb*'s ram had jammed the starboard
rudder, and the shell that had killed William had punched a hole
near her water line. Instead she had limped back to her station
off Belle View to recover her anchor.

Beside several injuries, William and an ordinary seaman from
Quincy's division had both been killed; William by a splinter,
Seaman Iverson by a shell fragment. A round from the *Webb* had
passed through the bulkhead, sending out the sweep of death
that had taken William. One splinter had struck the foremast
with enough force to embed itself two inches into the wood.

Quincy walked to the foot of the mainmast. The puddle of
blood had been mopped up; the deck would be sanded in the
morning. He stood on the spot where William had lain and
looked out over the silent river.

At last the deck was cleared, what could be mended or

cleaned had been seen to, and Commander Wainwright dismissed the watch below. As the sailors retrieved their mattresses and hammocks and slowly dispersed, talking in low voices of the evening's excitement, Quincy sought out his new sponger.

"Isaiah," he said as the negro came away from the rail with his hammock in his arms. "That was quick thinking, to pick up the passing-box. Well done."

Isaiah seemed to be trying to keep his face neutral, but a smile escaped. "Thank you, sir," he said.

Quincy hesitated. "You said you worked at a press?"

"Yes, sir."

"With the machinery?"

"Yes, sir. Steam press. I liked it, that's why when they come lookin' for boys to go in the army I said no. Thought the navy be better." Isaiah glanced toward the *Lane*'s funnel, and added, "Thought maybe someday I could help the engineers."

A couple of sailors brushed against Isaiah on their way below. Quincy beckoned him toward the foremast, out of the way. "Can you read at all?" he asked.

"Numbers. I can tell time." Isaiah's eyes were liquid in the half-dark, brimming with anxious hope.

Quincy tapped a hand against his thigh. "I will speak to Mr. Lea," he said at last. "Perhaps we can organize a class. You and your compatriots should learn how to read at least, if you're going to continue in the navy."

"Thank you, sir."

Quincy nodded and began to move on, but Isaiah said, "Mr. Wheat? Will you teach us?" The dark eyes did not plead, but seemed desperate nonetheless.

Quincy frowned. He had not intended to involve himself with the contrabands. Yet, he thought Isaiah deserved a chance.

"I will talk to Mr. Lea," he said. "Goodnight."

"Thank you, sir," Isaiah called after him.

Quincy glanced toward the stern, where Becker stood chatting with Gerard. He went over to compliment Gerard on the stern chaser's success against the *Music*.

"Did you notice the *Webb*'s full name?" he said. "*William H. Webb*. Odd, isn't it?"

"How so?" said Gerard.

"William H. Webb built the *Lane*."

"Did he?" Gerard smiled, but Becker was silent.

"What's wrong?" Quincy asked him.

Gerard glanced at Quincy with a curious expression, then strolled a little away. Quincy stood waiting for Becker's response.

"You're mighty proud of your new niggers, aren't you?" Becker said in a low voice. In the half-dark, Quincy could see his sneer. "That fellow you were just talking to. Contraband trash."

"He did a good job," Quincy said.

"They're all worthless. You'll learn soon enough."

"Frank—we're all tired. When you're off duty, come and have a drink with me. I've got some port." Quincy waited, surprised at Becker's surliness. "Will you come?"

"You'll be asleep, or you should be," Becker said. His voice sounded somewhat less angry.

"It isn't long before the mid watch, and I have some business to take care of. I'll be awake."

Becker grunted, which Quincy chose to take as assent. He went below to seek out the carpenter's mate, and found Young clearing away his tools from the berth deck, having patched the damage caused by the shell that had passed through. The man looked exhausted, so Quincy said, "Please come to see me in the morning," he said. "We will need coffins—"

"They are already being made," Young said. "We have some blue felt to cover them."

Relieved, Quincy said, "Thank you. The captain asked me to see to it promptly. He wants to leave as soon as possible for New Orleans."

"Got a place to bury them?"

Quincy sighed. "Somewhere ashore." Which meant on a plantation, as all of the land on the river's banks belonged to one plantation or another. "I will have to arrange it in the morning—take a cutter out. . . ."

Colonel Hawkland would be the best to ask, he supposed. He had not even met any of the neighboring plantationers; for all he knew they were away from their holdings, or disloyal, or both.

The ordinary seaman who had died was white, and William was a contraband. Quincy debated whether he should even mention this to Hawkland. Contraband was not a word he cared to use to a slaveholder, however loyal he might be. It meant property. Confiscated property. He had not really thought about it before, but now he realized he disliked the entire meaning of the word. William had been someone's property. Isaiah was someone's property still. No, he did not care for that at all.

Young was watching him, Quincy realized. He gave the carpenter's mate a tired half-smile. "Thank you," he said. "I'll see you in the morning."

Quincy retired to his cabin to fetch his port, lit the oil lamp that hung over the wardroom table, and sat there alone to drink. The first sip startled him, its flavor bursting on his palate. He had forgotten the existence of such things as flavors, it seemed, in the past few hours.

He held the glass up to the lamp, looking through the ruby liquid. Ruby, he thought dully. William had asked him to find Ruby, his mother. He did not think the boy had any other family. He would have to ask Richardson in the morning. They had all retired, now. The ship had become quiet except for the occasional tread of the watch.

Quincy set the glass down and stared at it a moment longer. Becker was not going to join him, he realized. All at once he felt angry, hurt, and remorseful. He drained the glass with two deep swallows and put it away from him, then laid his head in his hands.

Tuesday morning dawned bright and promising warm. Jamie rode in the back of the wagon, sitting on Emma's trunk and keeping an eye on his own valise, while Poppa drove with Emma up beside him wearing Momma's Sunday bonnet. There had been a small skirmish over that, but Momma had insisted that Emma take the hat, and Jamie had settled it by whispering in his sister's ear that it would give Momma a reason to buy herself a new one.

Also in the wagon bed sat a large basket crammed full of food for the journey, including all the leftover biscuits from a gargantuan farewell breakfast. Jamie had kissed Momma and hugged Gabe, but the hardest good-bye had been Cocoa. Maybe it was because he had thought he'd lost her for good back in New Mexico, and it had hurt so much, and had hurt almost as much getting her back. Half an hour ago he had stood in her stall while Poppa and Gabe wrestled Emma's trunk into the wagon, just leaning against her neck, smelling her warm, sweet-grass scent, murmuring to her to be good, he would be back soon. She had nudged him with her muzzle as if to say he should cheer up, and gazed at him calmly with her sweet, dark eyes.

Well, he would be back soon enough. To pass the time driving into town, he thought about how fast he might be able to return. The stage bill promised only three days between San Antonio and Houston with through tickets on the train from Alleyton. Jamie figured he would have to stay at least a day or two, or Aunt May would be offended. Another three days back, so eight days for the whole business. He figured he would spend the rest of his furlough helping Ferguson learn the ropes on the ranch.

He didn't really remember Ferguson, who had been in Green's regiment, but he liked him and was glad Poppa was pleased with him. Lane had produced the disabled man on the brigade surgeon's recommendation, and he was already proving to be a good choice. He had taken up residence in the barn, and when Jamie had gone in last night to say good night to Cocoa, he had found Ferguson sitting up in the tack room with a lantern and a pocket notebook, painfully practicing his letters with his left hand.

Poppa pulled up the wagon as they reached the stage station, the center of a small cyclone to which the Russell family added their mite. The stage driver looked at them as Jamie helped Emma out of the wagon, and said, "Two minutes to six, and we leave with you or without you."

Emma's trunk was quickly strapped onto the coach's roof and Jamie's valise stashed in the already crowded boot. Jamie seized the basket, waited for Emma to finish hugging Poppa, then urged her to the coach and climbed in after her amidst a jumble of voices wishing them well. He shook Poppa's hand out the window and sat back as the coach started off.

Emma had the basket on her lap and was trying in vain to keep it from crowding her neighbor, a sour-looking woman in a black dress and dusty cloak who must have boarded the stage a good while before. Jamie pulled an end of the basket onto his knees, so that it rested across both his and Emma's, and glanced at the three passengers seated across from them. They looked pretty unpromising as jovial companions—all men, one of whom appeared to go with the sour woman as he was seated opposite to her and displayed about the same amount of dust and disgruntlement. Beside him sat a thin, wiry fellow of hardened mien but not advanced years, so tall his hat brushed the coach roof until he took it off and held it on his lap. Last was a towheaded boy a couple of years older than Gabe who seemed to be accompanying the thin fellow. This was confirmed when the boy said, "Something in that basket sure smells good," and the thin man gave him a cuff on the side of his head.

It was just the sort of thing Gabe would have said. Jamie looked at Emma, worried at first but he saw she was thinking the same thing and trying not to laugh. She let out a smile and pulled back the cloth to extract the biscuits, wrapped in a napkin and still warm.

"Pay him no mind," the thin man said. "Acts like he never ate half an hour ago."

"We have plenty," Emma said, unwrapping the biscuits. "Won't you all have some?" She offered them around, and after a wary glance at his companion the boy reached for one.

"Thank you, Miss," he said, and took a huge bite.

The others followed suit, even the dusty woman accepting and melting enough to smile. Jamie took a biscuit, too, though he wasn't hungry. He nibbled at it, and watched Emma befriend the passengers, asking them all where they were bound. She was doing her best to enjoy the journey, it seemed. With a thankful sigh, Jamie relaxed into his seat for the long ride ahead.

Just before noon Quincy informed the bosun's mate that all was in readiness, and the whistle piped "all hands to bury the dead." The *Lane*'s crew assembled on deck to hear Commander Wainwright read from the Episcopal service. Quincy watched the faces of the men as they listened. Seaman Iverson had been popular; his messmates had made a little memorial banner which they draped over his coffin. The smaller burial case was unadorned save for its blue covering. The sun shone brightly, and by the time the captain had finished reading, Quincy was already hot.

The ship's boats were launched to carry the cortege to shore, and Quincy climbed into a cutter with several of the other officers. As they departed, the Parrott was fired and the ship's bell tolled.

"Lost a good man out of your crew, Wheat," Richardson said.

"Two good men," Quincy said. "William will be sorely missed."

"Sad, for a lad that young to be taken," said the paymaster, nodding.

The others murmured agreement, then began talking of Iverson's merits. Quincy met Becker's gaze, then looked away toward the shore, toward Rosehall. It was good that they would be leaving today, Quincy thought. This place was bad for the *Lane*, bad for morale as well as for the crew's health, and bad for his own peace of mind.

At the ferry landing a procession formed, consisting of an honor guard of twelve sailors since the *Lane* had no marines aboard, followed by the two coffins carried by messmates of the deceased, the ship's two drummers, then the boys, sailors, petty officers and lastly the officers, with Commander Wainwright in the rear. Colonel Hawkland had ridden down to meet the cortege, and now handed his horse to a servant and joined the procession, walking beside the captain. He had willingly agreed to have the ship's men buried on his property, and had suggested a site a short distance down the track that led eastward from the landing, separated from the house by a large grove of pecan trees, but within sight of the river. There, beneath an old gnarled oak, the burial crew awaited the procession. Two graves yawned beneath boughs draped in Spanish moss, and wooden markers bearing the names of the deceased leaned against the oak's trunk.

The party assembled around the graves and the coffins were lowered into their places while two sailors with a fiddle and a tin whistle played "Eternal Father." When they had finished, Commander Wainwright stepped forward and read once more from the service.

"Man, that is born of a woman, hath but a short time to live and is full of misery. He cometh up, and is cut down, like a flower; he fleeth as it were a shadow, never continueth in one stay. . . ."

A mosquito whined around Quincy's ears and he brushed a hand at it. From the corner of his eye he saw movement, and turned his head to look. Two horsemen had appeared on the road perhaps half a mile to the east. He could not distinguish their dress, but thought they were white men. As he watched,

Colonel Hawkland directed a long glance toward them, then looked back at the captain, ignoring them. Whoever they were, Hawkland did not seem surprised to see them. Overseers, he supposed. Part of Hawkland's enormous staff.

The captain closed his prayer book and commenced reciting the Lord's Prayer. Quincy joined his voice to the company's. When the prayer was concluded the honor guard fired three rounds from their muskets, and the burial crew came forward to begin covering the bodies while the procession formed up again and moved away to the slow beat of drums. Quincy paused to observe the men wielding the shovels. They were landsmen— unskilled laborers—one white, the others black. They had kept their blouses on despite the heat, perhaps out of respect to their dead comrades. Or perhaps, Quincy thought, because the implications of negroes digging on Hawkland's property inspired them to retain the uniforms that identified them with the *Harriet Lane*.

He looked at the graves, thinking of William, wondering where in all the South mother Ruby might be. That no longer mattered, of course. At least William would have the company of Seaman Iverson. Perhaps his death would be less lonely than his life had been.

Shaking himself free of such dreary thoughts, Quincy hastened to catch up to the procession. Commander Wainwright stood on the road talking quietly with Hawkland, then shook hands and moved toward the landing. Hawkland turned to gaze eastward and his glance fell on Quincy, who stepped forward.

"Thank you again, Colonel Hawkland."

"Of course," Hawkland said. "It's the least I can do. I am sorry for your loss."

"Thank you." Quincy glanced toward the graves and swallowed.

"Did my overseer take you to buy from the slaves at Angola?"

"Not yet," Quincy said. "I was hoping to do so now." He was heartsore and weary, but this might be his last chance for days to get vegetables for the Mess. Onions and potatoes. Eggs, perhaps. His mind did not seem to want to cope with such trivial things.

"Well, you will probably find Mr. Shelton near the slave quarters, back along the road there."

Quincy nodded. "I was wondering—" he began, but stopped from embarrassment.

Hawkland waited patiently. "Yes?"

Quincy smiled weakly. "Would you mind if I cut a few of your roses?"

Hawkland's brows rose. "You are fond of flowers?"

"Yes. Your rosebushes are magnificent," Quincy said, looking up the hill at them. "I just thought . . ." He didn't know what he thought. He was too weary to think. Hawkland must think him an idiot.

"Go right ahead, my boy," Hawkland said gently. "Cut as many as you like."

Quincy looked up, smiling his gratitude. Hawkland gave him a nod, then strode away up the hill toward his house, passing hundreds of roses blooming to either side of the gleaming shell drive. Quincy might fill his arms with them and not diminish the appearance of the garden. Somehow this impressed him more strongly than all other signs of Hawkland's wealth, more than Rosehall itself, more than the fields of cotton that stretched five miles and more downstream. The weight of that wealth seemed palpable, here in the summer heat on the banks of the river. Quincy could not remember ever feeling so insignificant. He shook off the sensation, turning from Rosehall with its wealth of beauty to the road that would take him toward potatoes and onions.

9

I, as Commander-in-Chief of the Army and Navy of the United States, do order and declare that on the first day of January in the year of Our Lord one thousand, eight hundred and sixty-three, all persons held as slaves within any state or states, wherein the Constitutional authority of the United States shall not then be practically recognized, submitted to, and maintained, shall then, thenceforward, and forever, be free.
—First draft Emancipation Proclamation, proposed by
Lincoln to his Cabinet July 22, 1862

At Columbus the mail coach crossed the Colorado River on a ferryboat, giving the passengers a brief respite from the rattling ride as they all disembarked for safety while the coach was being crossed. Emma gave Jamie the basket, which had been considerably lightened with the help of their fellow passengers, and assisted Mrs. Cooley to alight from the coach.

"Thank you, child," Mrs. Cooley said with a smile.

Mrs. Cooley had become much less sour as the miles had passed. Emma had taken pains to draw her out, and now knew much more than she cared to about all the Cooley children and grandchildren, and the impending arrival of the first great-grandchild, for which event the Cooleys were traveling to Clear Lake. Mr. Cooley had mostly kept silent, but his eyes had told Emma of his gratitude, and she was glad to have made their journey a little easier.

Zack, the young boy, pulled at his father's arm. "Hey, Pa, the ferryman says there's a castle! Can we go see it?"

"There ain't no castles in Texas, boy," said Mr. Garson. You been hornswoggled."

"There is, honest! Some crazy old Scotsman built it up north of town, right by the river. It's got a moat and a drawbridge and all, and he throws dances on the roof! Can we go, Pa? Can we?"

"I think there will not be time," Emma said. "Look, the coach is almost across."

"See that there?" said Mr. Garson, pointing at the ferry. "She's right. They'll be back for us right quick."

"Aw, you just don't want me to see it," Zack complained.

Emma came up to him. "I wish we could go see it, Zack. I've never seen a castle. But I also have never seen a railroad. Have you?"

Zack glanced up at her, trying to maintain a sulky mood, but a glimmer of a smile crept onto his face. "No," he said.

"Well, you know, we're going to be riding on one as soon as we get across the river and get to Alleyton."

The smile grew into a grin, and Zack turned to his father. "How far is it to Alleyton, Pa?" he demanded.

"Oh, shouldn't take more'n another two three days," Mr. Garson said, winking at Emma.

"No, sir!" Zack protested. "It's only a few miles, isn't it, Mr. Russell?"

Jamie, who had just fished an apple out of the basket, shrugged. Emma felt a stab of annoyance with him for not playing along, but then he probably thought Zack was sharp enough to recognize that he was being strung along. Jamie had fallen into the habit of treating Zack the way he treated Gabe.

When the ferry returned, Zack appealed to the ferryman, who confirmed that the distance from the far landing to Alleyton was a mere three miles. Accordingly, in less than two hours, the stage deposited its weary and excited passengers at Alleyton, a town so new it smelled of sawn lumber.

The village had sprung up around the western terminus of

the Harrisburg Railroad, on which their through tickets would carry them to Houston that very day. Near the train station were a post office, a hotel, and numerous warehouses. Emma saw a dozen or more freight wagons loaded with cotton leaving the depot, each with A & M TRANSPORT painted on its side in bright red.

"Everything is so big," she murmured to Jamie, feeling a bit daunted. The depot was a long structure built of lumber and painted yellow, much bigger than any of the stage stops they had visited. Passing through it, they stepped out onto a broad platform of wooden planks beyond which the train waited. Emma caught her breath at the sight of the large, black engine hissing a trickle of steam like a sleeping dragon. Behind the engine and nearly as big was an open-topped box filled with coal, and behind that two platform cars, already loaded with boxes, crates, bins, bales, sacks, and all other oddments of goods to be shipped. Last of all was a long car with windows all down its length. Beneath the windows BUFFALO BAYOU, BRAZOS & COLORADO was painted in fancy letters.

Jamie was gazing with narrowed eyes at the freight cars. He glanced at Emma and said, "Go on and get aboard—here's your ticket—I want to look at something." He handed her the basket and was off down the platform.

"Hey, Miss Russell, do you know what the engine's name is?" Zack called, dashing up to her.

"I didn't know it had a name," Emma said, watching her brother walk away.

"Sure does. Can you guess it?"

Emma glanced down at him. "Probably not. Why don't you just tell me?"

"It's 'General Sherman'!" Zack said proudly.

"Oh. Well, that's a fine name."

Zack grinned, and darted off to find another audience for this interesting intelligence. Emma looked at the passenger car, thinking it amazing in size and elegance when compared to the humble mail coach. She walked to the steps that had been set out at the back of the car and accepted the assistance of a conductor in a dark coat and cap who offered to help her ascend.

Inside it was all polished wood and brass fittings, with two rows of double seats separated by a narrow aisle. The Cooleys and Mr. Garson were already seated, as were a number of strangers. Emma selected an empty place and set the basket down beside her. She poked around in it, hunting for another apple.

"I bought a newspaper," Jamie said, joining her. "Look, the *Morning Star*, dated today."

Emma pulled the basket onto her lap to let him sit down. "You ate the last apple."

"I'm sorry—shall I fetch you something? I saw some pies for sale."

"I don't think we have time."

The conductor had stepped down to the platform and was calling, "All aboard!" Mr. Garson opened a window and leaned out to yell at Zack. The boy scrambled aboard just as the whistle blew a loud double-blast.

Emma's heart fluttered a little with the first nudge of motion. The engine began to chuff and the train slowly glided forward, much more smoothly than the rumbling mail coach.

"Let me open the window," Jamie said. "I bet we'll get a nice breeze." He raised the glass and Emma leaned out, watching the station and the town fall away behind them. A handful of children waved from the edge of a field. Emma waved back.

"I feel like a queen," she said.

"Well, you don't look like one," Jamie told her. "You've got a cinder on your cheek. Give me your handkerchief."

Emma submitted to being tidied by her brother. "Isn't it wonderful?" she asked, and Jamie nodded, grinning. "Matt didn't describe it at all," Emma said. "All he talked about was getting kisses from the girls at the stations!"

"Maybe that's all he cared about," Jamie said.

"I wonder how he is. He hasn't written in a while."

"Well, he said they were moving around more. Might be harder to write, and you know how the mails have been bad since May."

Emma nodded. Since New Orleans had fallen, was what Jamie meant. With Federal ships running up and down the Mississippi, communication across the river had become difficult. Even Daniel, who was a much better correspondent than Matt, had not been heard from as often over the summer.

The train gathered more speed as the conductor passed through the car, collecting tickets. Emma admired his ease; she did not think she would be able to walk down the aisle of the moving car. Jamie opened his paper and she looked out the window again, settling in to watch the fields and occasional houses fly past. The gentle swaying of the car and the rumble of the wheels over the track soon made her sleepy. She took off her shawl and bundled it into a cushion, leaning her head upon it as she gazed at the fields spreading green as far as the eye could see, some with gangs of laborers working, most empty and serene.

The train stopped with a jolt, waking her. She blinked, sitting up, and caught her shawl before it could slide out of the window.

"We have to get off," Jamie said, picking up the basket. "We're at the Brazos, and we cross on foot."

Emma rubbed at her neck, which was stiff, and allowed Jamie to help her out of the train. It had stopped a little way back from the riverbank. The tracks ran down a steep cut to cross on a bridge so low that it must often have been covered with water.

"I want to stay and ride the train across!" she heard Zack announce, and a brief altercation ensued in which Mr. Garson emerged the inevitable victor, propelling Zack before him out of the passenger car.

Emma followed Jamie and the rest of the passengers to a place atop the bank with a fine view of the tracks. The train first backed well away from the bank and blew its whistle, then black-gray smoke roared from the smokestack like a volcano as the train accelerated toward the river. Emma felt a little thrill of fright as it speeded forward—much, much faster than it had gone with them aboard—as if it was trying to take off flying.

"Go it, General Sherman!" Zack yelled, waving his arms over his head.

The train plunged down the track to the bridge, rattled across it with a noise like a thousand demons, and ran up the far bank, its momentum carrying it most of the way up the steep incline, the engine groaning with the effort of pulling the laden cars up to the top. At last it halted, and the passengers applauded, then hurried to cross the bridge to reboard the train.

"Not long now," Jamie said as they resumed their seats.

Emma smiled, though she was tired and a little nervous. Not long now and they would be in Houston. Not long until they met Aunt May. She felt self-conscious all at once, and brushed at a cinder that had smudged her sleeve. How strange it all was! She had never been this far from home, never been away at all except once when she was a little girl and Poppa had taken the family to Port Lavaca to look at the sea. That was not far from Aransas, she realized, and felt a sudden tightening in her chest. Lavaca might be vulnerable to the Yankee blockade. It would; of course it would. There might be Yankee ships there even now. The thought took away her excitement, leaving her worried and tired. She wrapped her shawl around herself and closed her eyes, hoping to recover her spirits before she had to meet her aunt.

It was dusk when the *Harriet Lane* docked at last in New Orleans at a wharf crowded with vessels mostly belonging to the U.S. Navy. A constant, thin drizzle served only to make the air muggy as well as hot, and a reddish orange pall hung over the city. Commander Wainwright having granted all off-duty officers permission to go ashore, Quincy, Becker, and Gerard made haste to escape the ship's confines. They were joined on the levee by Becker's younger brother Tom—a quartermaster—and by Paymaster Richardson.

"Shall we have supper together?" Richardson suggested, raising the subject foremost in everyone's thoughts. "I know a neat little establishment in the French market that serves an excellent table d'hote."

"Julius, my friend," Gerard said, "you could no doubt recommend a hog trough in the market that offers better fare than what we have been living on. No offense, Quincy."

"None taken."

"Lead on!" Gerard took the paymaster's arm and made as if to set off through the rain.

"Did someone say supper?"

It was Stone, accompanied by another engineer, Mr. Plunkett. They had plainly made an effort to spruce up, but like all engineers they bore a perpetual aura of grease. "Mind if we join you?" Stone asked.

"No, of course not," Quincy said. He looked for Gerard's group and saw them disappearing into the market. "Better hurry," he said, starting after them.

They caught up just as the party crossed into the butcher's market. Some stalls had closed for the day, but many were still doing brisk business. Awnings cast shadows over the wet street, gutters ran bloodred in the sunset, and a chaotic mix of smells rose to bewilder the senses: raw meat, fish, cooking meat, sewage, spices, coffee. Quincy's gut rumbled. Except for the vegetables he'd acquired at Belle View, his diet had lately consisted of pork and beans. The spirits of the *Lane*'s crew had risen considerably at the prospect of better fare to be obtained in New Orleans, and it was not surprising that by the time the party had reached Richardson's neat little establishment, it had accumulated not only the two engineers but Dr. Penrose and Young, the carpenter's mate.

Monsieur Tujague, the restaurateur, ushered them through the ground floor past smaller parties dining at café tables and a line of men standing at the long, cypress bar. At the back of the room a narrow stair led to a long hallway down which the party proceeded. Passing an open door they heard a burst of laughter, then came to a square room containing a large, round table. Tall, shuttered windows overlooked the market, and a rumble of voices penetrated the wall.

"My apologies, monsieurs," said the owner, nodding toward a closed door beside the fireplace. "There is a large party in the next room, but I trust they will not trouble you."

"Nothing will trouble us, as soon as we get our supper," Gerard said.

The owner bowed himself out, making way for two waiters who were already setting plates of shrimp remoulade on the table. The *Lane*'s officers seated themselves and lost no time getting down to the business of eating.

The first bite of shrimp, fresh and cool with crisp greens and a burst of spice, was like a gift from heaven. Quincy savored his portion, relaxing at last and feeling his spirits rise in anticipation of an hour or more of good company and good food. Following a short discussion between Richardson and Gerard, good wine was added to the program, and the party's mood grew merry.

Quincy was seated near the adjoining door, and while waiting for the soup to arrive he looked it over. It was good, solid wood, paneled and laquered.

"Becker," he said, "look at this door."

Becker turned in his seat. "What about it?"

"Do you see anything unusual?"

"It's a door."

"Yes, but it has no handle," Quincy said.

Becker glanced at it, grunted acknowledgment, and said, "Pass the bread."

Curious, Quincy got out of his seat and fingered the brass plate where the knob should have been. The opening appeared to be blocked; the shaft was there, then, but not the knob. The keyhole below revealed a glimpse of the neighboring room. Unable to resist peeking, Quincy saw a long table covered with the wreckage of a substantial feast and surrounded by naval officers, some of whom he recognized.

"Come away from that, Wheat," Penrose said testily.

"Yes, you are setting us all a bad example," cried Gerard. "You will degenerate our morals!"

"It's our comrades," Quincy said, getting to his feet. "From the *Clifton*, and the *Owasco*, too, I think. I saw Hinks."

A cry of delight met this news. Hinks, an engineer aboard the *Clifton*, was famous amongst the Mortar Flotilla for fierce concentration while on duty and a tendency to outrageous behavior when off. The *Lane* party instantly demanded to see him. The doorknob was sought, but in vain. It was not on the mantel, nor in the hearth, nor on a windowsill. Quincy was about to go down the hall to the other entrance, when Gerard solved the dilemma by shouldering past Becker to the knobless door and pounding on it. It was opened by a stout fellow in a navy officer's frock coat, his napkin tucked into his collar beneath a round, cheery face that was rather red at the moment.

"Gordon Hinks!" cried Gerard, embracing him.

"Robert!" Hinks replied. "Boys, it's Robert and all those rascals from the *Lane*!"

Chaos reigned for the next few minutes as the two parties greeted each other. Quincy cornered Hinks, and demanded to know how he had got the door open.

"Well," Hinks said in a patronizing voice, "First one must locate the handle, then grasp it firmly—"

"There isn't a handle on this side, you great oaf!"

Hinks examined the door, exclaimed at the defect, and pulled the knob out to examine it. He and Quincy tried it on both sides of the door, finding it worked either way. Hinks then inserted the spindle of the knob in his ear, then began to put it up his nose.

"Enough of that," Gerard said impatiently, grabbing the knob and shaking it at Hinks. "What's the news?"

"News? Bah," Hinks responded. "I'm eating." He snatched the knob back and returned to his place at the long table, not to eat but to lead a rousing rendition of "The Constitution and the Guerriere," using the doorknob to conduct. Quincy realized the words had been altered, and now referred to "The Constitution and the Derriere."

"Nestell, get in here," Gerard cried, grabbing at the nearest officer and hauling him into the room. He shut the door and sat his victim down in Quincy's chair. Quincy was acquainted with Nestell, a rather unprepossessing fellow who was the ship's surgeon aboard the *Clifton*.

"Now, give us the news," Gerard said, leaning against the table and folding his arms.

"Some wine?" Nestell said in a mock-pitiful voice.

Gerard seized Quincy's glass and filled it for Nestell, who took a swallow and sighed satisfaction. "Let me see," he said, leaning back in the chair. "The *Sidney C. Jones* was blown up—"

The *Lane*'s officers protested in unison. "After all our efforts!" Gerard said.

"Our efforts didn't get her off the damn bar," Becker said.

"She was in danger of being captured," Nestell said. "The Rebels ran the fleet with a new ram, the *Arkansas*. Have an eye to her, boys—she could give you trouble." He took a sip of wine. "What else? Congress has created several new officer grades."

"Hurrah!" cried Becker, raising his glass. "We'll all be promoted!"

"I doubt it," Nestell said. "They have also transferred the Western Gunboat Fleet to the Navy Department."

"About time," Richardson said, pushing away his plate and reaching for the wine.

"And they have abolished the grog ration."

"What?!" The outcry was instantaneous, and loud enough that Hinks opened the door again to learn what it was about. On being informed, he clutched at his heart, wailed, "My grog! My grog! Alas, poor grog!" and disappeared back into the other room.

Quincy, sitting on the windowsill, pushed the door shut with his foot. He looked up and saw a disconcerted waiter bearing two bowls of soup, and jumped up to relieve the man of one of his burdens. "Thank you," he said, and returned to the windowsill with the bowl, grabbing his spoon from the table along the way.

"You were saying," Gerard prompted Nestell.

"Ah, yes. The grog ration is abolished, effective September first. The sailors will get five cents a day instead."

"They won't like it," Richardson said.

"Of course not," Nestell replied. "There was practically a mutiny on the *Clifton* when the word went around."

"Damned temperance leagues," Becker grumbled.

"There's always been grog in the navy!" said Richardson. "It's an ancient tradition!"

"And one that has always caused problems," Penrose put in, adjusting his spectacles. "We shall be better off without it."

No one could deny this, but no one seemed inclined to praise the good doctor's attitude. Even his fellow-surgeon Nestell spoke with regret about the loss of the custom.

The door burst open again and Hinks intruded, accompanied by two cronies, singing:

"I thought I heard the old man say,
Whisky Johnnie!
'We're throwing all the grog away,'
Whisky for my Johnnie!"

Quincy pushed them back, reached around the door and extracted the knob, then shut it in their faces. He set the knob on the mantel, but Gerard jumped up and snatched it, passing it around the table where it was duly admired by the company.

"Any other news?"

Nestell drained Quincy's glass and set it on the table. "Yes," he said. "Colonel Ellet died on Monday."

The table fell silent. Someone muttered, "Damn."

Quincy thought of his brother, serving on Ellet's flagship *Queen of the West*. Ellet had been the only man of the *Queen*'s complement wounded at Memphis.

"I thought it was a leg wound," Becker said quietly.

"Shattered knee," Nestell said. "He refused amputation."

Quincy put his empty soup plate on the table. Colonel Ellet would be sorely missed. He was a hero, and really a genius. Quincy retrieved his glass and poured wine into it.

"To Colonel Ellet," he said, raising it.

"Colonel Ellet." The company drank, and sat silently musing.

Footsteps thundered in the hall. Quincy looked up to see Hinks running toward them, his cronies in tow and a large knife in his hands.

"You've got our surgeon and you've got our knob!" he roared. "Give them back!"

"You can have him," Gerard said, dragging Nestell out of his chair. "He is taking up space, and Quincy needs his meat."

Hinks stepped aside for Nestell, who sauntered down the hall with a wave of farewell. "The knob!" Hinks shouted, brandishing the knife.

"Knob? What knob?" Quincy said. "Here, let that fellow get past you!" He waved to the waiter who stood behind Hinks, his arms loaded with plates of sliced beef in a fragrant sauce. The waiter edged into the room, guided by Quincy's helpful hands. A second waiter followed with more food, and Quincy whispered in his ear.

"We want our knob!" roared Hinks.

"The knob, the knob!" his cronies chanted.

"Oh, all right," Quincy said. "I left it on the windowsill." He moved toward the open window, reaching for the sill, then cried, "Oh, no!"

"What?" said Hinks.

"I dropped it."

"Aaaah!" Hinks spun round and dashed down the hall, his two companions making haste to follow. Quincy leaned against the windowsill, gazing down. He couldn't see much, but in a moment sounds of a desperate search drifted up from the street below.

"You are lucky you didn't hurt someone," Penrose observed.

"Oh, no chance of that," Quincy said, looking over his shoulder. "It was never in the window."

"You devil," said Richardson, grinning. "What did you do with it?"

"Gave it to the waiter, with instructions to serve it to Hinks à la mode." He glanced out the window again. "That is, if he ever comes back."

"He'll come back," said Stone. "He hasn't finished his dinner."

A mournful cry arose from the street, "Alas, poor knob!"

The men round the table burst into laughter. "Here's to the knob!" Gerard said, raising his glass.

"To the knob!"

Houston was hot and muggy, worse than the worst San Antonio weather. Jamie had taken charge at the train station, leaving Emma to guard the much-depleted basket and his valise while he retrieved her trunk and arranged for transportation into town. Now, riding in a somewhat rundown open carriage, he squinted at a sun that seemed to swim in the heavy, yellow-gray sky. The land here was a flat plain interrupted only by occasional trees and sluggish, meandering bayous. As they came into the city they passed first a warehouse surrounded by bales of cotton, then houses and shops, then tall, brick buildings bustling with commerce. The main street was very wide and paved with crushed shell over which the carriage wheels hissed as they drove farther into town. Jamie looked at Emma, who seemed tired and gazed at Momma's basket instead of looking at the city. She would have plenty of time to see it, he figured, and did not disturb her.

The carriage turned a corner, drove a short distance farther and eased to a stop behind a large cart half-full of furniture. Jamie frowned, looking at a tidy brick house that was being emptied of its contents by three negroes, one burly, two less so. The two were in the act of bringing a sheet-wrapped bundle that looked to be a sofa through the front door, while the burly one, behind them with a crate in his arms, shouted instructions.

"Are you sure this is the right house?" Jamie asked the weather-beaten driver, who had climbed down to unstrap Emma's trunk from the rear of the vehicle.

"Three-seventeen," the man said, jerking his head toward the number on the gatepost of the low picket fence.

Jamie got down, watching the two men try to bestow the sofa safely in the already crowded wagon. The larger one set down his crate and took out a kerchief to mop his brow. With a sinking heart, Jamie approached him.

"Excuse me, can you tell me if this is Mrs. Asterly's house?"

"That's right, but she ain't here no more."

Jamie glanced back at Emma, still sitting in the carriage, starting to look annoyed. "Can you tell me where I might find her?" he asked.

The black man fixed him with a long, cool look. "Wait here," he said, and went into the house, leaving his crate behind. A shout from the wagon drew Jamie's attention; one foot of the sofa was hooked in a large, ornate urn. The two negroes began arguing about whose fault it was. Jamie looked to the house, anxious to get Emma away from here, somewhere inside, out of the heat.

A gentleman in a gray coat and trousers emerged from the house, followed by the burly negro. The gentleman had black side whiskers and waving black hair, both starting to go silver. He was slightly portly but carried it well, and came toward Jamie with a confident stride.

"You must be the Russells," he said, holding out a hand. "We were not expecting to see you here! I am Albert Lawford."

"Mr. Lawford, how do you do?" Jamie said, relieved to hear a familiar name. Lawford's handshake was firm and brisk. "Did my mother's letter not arrive?"

"Oh, yes, but we thought you would join us in Galveston. Everything is at sixes and sevens, as you see. Careful with that, Rupert!"

The large negro, who had just eased the urn off the sofa leg, nodded acknowledgment and set the ornament gently on the ground, then directed the others in bestowing the sofa. Mr. Lawford turned to Jamie with an apologetic smile.

"We are running a little behind our schedule, I fear."

"I'm sorry," Jamie said. "We must be terribly in the way."

"Oh, no, no. Of course not! May—Mrs. Asterly—is all in a fever to see you."

"Where—"

"Say, you want to have them darkies carry this in?" said the carriage driver, pointing to the trunk. "I'm an old man, I can't haul no big baggage around."

"Leave it there, my good man," Lawford said, withdrawing a coin from his pocket, "and drive these young people around to the Capitol Hotel. Suite four," he added, looking at Jamie. The driver accepted the money with a broad grin and a lift of his hat, and started securing the trunk again.

Jamie dug in his pocket. "Here, you shouldn't pay for us—"

"Nonsense. It's nothing, dear boy. Go along to the hotel and tell May I will join you for dinner." Lawford bowed to Emma, adding, "I look forward to making your sister's acquaintance then." Emma managed a smile, and since Lawford was already on his way back to the house, there was nothing for Jamie to do but climb back in the carriage.

"Momma'll just love this," Emma said as they started off.

Jamie sighed. "So much for talking Aunt May out of leaving Houston."

"She's as stubborn as Momma, you know that. Poppa is always saying so."

"Yes, but didn't he also say she would never be packed up in just two weeks?"

"Something must have inspired her," said Emma.

The driver turned the corner, passed another residential street and turned onto a broad avenue. Apart from the shell, none of the streets in the town were paved, and in this damp climate Jamie figured it must become a sea of mud in rainy weather. The carriage pulled up again after just a few minutes, this time in front of a two-story hotel with white wooden pillars. Dormer windows protruded from the pitched roof, and the second story had a balcony all along the front.

Jamie hopped out and helped Emma down. A negro porter stepped forward to take his valise. Jamie hesitated—he had never been waited on by a negro—then gave the bag into his care.

"We're here to visit Mrs. Asterly," he told the man. "Suite four."

"Your name, sah?"

"Oh—Russell. Mr. and Miss Russell."

"Very good, sah. I will have your luggage brought in. Please to follow me."

The porter led them inside and up a stairway of glossy wood, their footsteps hushed by thick, red carpet. Paintings in gilt frames decorated the walls, and sconces of polished brass with glass globes promised brightly lit evenings. Jamie felt bedraggled amidst all this elegance, and glanced at his sister, who was looking pretty tired and windblown.

The stairway ran up the center of the hotel, and at its top a wide hallway branched out on both sides. A large painting of Sam Houston hung at the top of the stairs. Jamie looked at the portrait of the former Texas president and lately deposed governor, then at Emma, who said, "I am surprised they have not taken it down."

"This building was the capitol during the years of the Republic," the porter remarked. "That painting was on display down in the lobby until lately. Please come this way."

Jamie and Emma followed him down the hallway to the left, where he paused outside a door and knocked upon it. A black maidservant opened it.

"Mr. and Miss Russell to see Mrs. Asterly," the porter said.

A small squeal issued from within the room. Maid and bellman both gave way before a rustle of silk, and a vision of mauve and lace appeared in the doorway. The lady was tiny—scarcely up to Jamie's shoulder—with dark hair and bright, restless eyes. A smile broke over her pretty face, suddenly reminding Jamie of Momma.

"Emmaline!" she cried, reaching out her hands.

10

Bow low, Mary, bow low, Martha.
For Jesus come and lock the door. And carry the keys away.
Sail, sail, over yonder. And view the promised land.
For Jesus come and lock the door. And carry the keys away.
　　　　　—"Bow Low, Mary," Negro spiritual

Emma was startled at how petite Aunt May was, how like Momma and how unlike her all at once. She gave her the one hand she had free, which Aunt May clasped and shook, laughing and exclaiming. Finally Emma gave up and dumped the basket at her feet in order to embrace her aunt. As she was a good foot taller than the delicate lady whose hooped skirt filled the doorway, this was a slightly awkward procedure, but Aunt May paid no mind, dropping feather-light kisses on both Emma's cheeks and enwreathing her in violet scent.

"We are sorry to intrude on you like this," Emma began.

"Oh, I will not hear any of that! Yes, Charles, bring up their bags right away, and tell Mr. Eddings to give them the suite next to ours. It is not taken, I believe. Oh, let me look at you!" This last was addressed to Emma, whose hands Aunt May still held as she stood back and gazed rapturously at her niece. Emma admired her in turn, noting the elegant cut of her gown, the richness of the silk, which seemed to change color from lighter to darker with her every movement, and the ethereal lace cap—ornamented with tiny pink roses and pale green ribbons—that scarcely concealed her coiffure. Emma thought she had never seen anyone look so stylish. All at once she was conscious of her own plain traveling dress and shawl. Beside this lovely little butterfly, she felt like a great, clumsy gawk.

"Oh, you are *much* prettier than Susan!" Aunt May exclaimed. "Why did Eva never mention it to me? Come in, come in! Daisy, run tell Charles to bring up a tray of lemonade, will you, dear? Thank you!"

The negro maid slipped out of the room as Aunt May drew Emma toward an elegant sofa upholstered in green silk. Emma saw Jamie pick up the forgotten basket and bring it in, closing the door behind him, which attracted their hostess's attention.

"Oh, and you are Jamie!" Aunt May jumped up again from the sofa and ran to him, offering her hand. "Do forgive me! I have been looking forward so much to seeing your sister, I have quite forgotten myself. You must both call me May, *not* Aunt, if you please! It sounds so dreary. Come, sit!"

She brought Jamie back to join Emma, and he seated himself rather gingerly on a low chair that matched the sofa. All the furniture in the room—a sitting room, with two adjoining doors—was handsome, much finer than either of them was used to. Judging by the various boxes and suitcases Emma saw stacked by the walls, it appeared Aunt May had only recently moved in. She had perhaps been unpacking when they interrupted, for several scarves were strewn across the backs of unoccupied chairs, a scatter of jewelry and gloves covered one small table, and another was buried in crumpled wrapping paper.

"Do excuse the disorder," Aunt May said with a trilling laugh as she followed Emma's gaze. "I wanted to be certain that Daisy had packed my garnet combs. They were a gift from Albert, you know, and I thought they would look so nice with this dress." She turned to Jamie. "Did you see Albert? You must have, for we have only just removed to this hotel, and I have not yet written to tell Eva, so you must have seen him, or you would not have known how to find me."

Jamie, looking somewhat dazed, replied, "Yes, we met Mr. Lawford at your house, and he was kind enough to direct us here."

Aunt May's eyes glittered. "How surprised you must have been! Albert, too, for I know he did not expect you so soon. We thought it would take some time for you to get a furlough."

"I was lucky," Jamie said.

"He has friends in high places," Emma said, glancing sidelong at her brother.

Aunt May seemed delighted, and laughed again. "Well, you shall have even more when we get to Galveston! I know all the best people, though of course they are not all there at present. Such foolishness! People will allow themselves to be frightened by the most trivial things. My dear Emmaline, let me relieve you of that dreadful bonnet." She reached out and untied the ribbons before Emma could protest, saying, "Such a pretty child should never wear such an ugly old thing. Oh! What have you done to your hair?"

Emma gripped her hands in her lap. "I cut it," she said stiffly into the momentary silence, keeping her gaze on the low table before her. She heard Jamie shift in his chair.

"Oh," Aunt May said softly. She reached up to brush a curl back from Emma's cheek, pity in her dark eyes. "Well. I am sure it will grow quickly." She smiled again. "It is just like Eva's. Did she tell you her hair was the envy of our school?"

Emma did not trust herself to speak. She tried to swallow, and was thankful when Jamie said, "No, ma'am. She never talks much about Charleston."

"Never? She was the belle of the town, I assure you! She had all the young beaus at her feet. Oh, thank you, Daisy. Is he bringing the lemonade?"

"Yes, Miz May," said the maid as she came in and closed the door. Emma watched her begin moving about the room, picking up the scatter of scarves and jewelry.

"Daisy is such a gem," Aunt May said. "I do not know what I would do without her, truly. I am so fortunate Mr. Asterly left me good servants."

"Oh," Emma said. She looked again at Daisy, who appeared not to notice the conversation, but continued to tidy the room. Emma glanced at Jamie, who seemed as much at a loss for words as she felt.

He cleared his throat. "Uh, ma'am? Mr. Lawford asked me to tell you he will be joining you—us—for dinner."

"Of course he will. But, yes, we must order dinner for the two of you! Are you quite starving?"

"No, ma'am—"

"Please call me May."

"No, Au—May. Momma put us up a basket—"

"The cherry jam!" Emma said, sitting up.

"I'll get it." Jamie retrieved the basket and brought it to Emma, who extracted two large jars of preserves wrapped up in blue checkered cloth.

"These are for you, from Momma," she said, offering them to Aunt May.

"How sweet!" May's face lit with a smile. "She knows I adore cherries. Tell me, how is she? It has been an age since I last saw her."

Gossiping about Momma was safe, and as they chatted Emma began to relax once more. She was tired and her head ached a little, but the promised lemonade arrived to refresh her. The porter who brought it informed them that while the suite next to Mrs. Asterly's was in fact occupied, that across the hall was not, and the young lady's trunk had been brought there. He handed a brass key to Jamie and bowed himself out of the room.

Emma glanced at Jamie, who was looking at the key, turning it over in his hand. She doubted he had enough money to pay for the hotel; such elegant rooms must be very costly. Remembering the stocking purse of money Momma had pressed into her hands upon her departure, Emma resolved to use some of it for the bill. Momma expected her to spend it on new clothes, but she did not need to be fashionable.

Echoing her thoughts, Jamie said, "Aunt May, I am afraid we did not come prepared—"

"Do not trouble yourself for one minute," she told him firmly. "You are my guests."

"Thank you," Emma began, "but we cannot accept."

"Nonsense. I invited you, and you certainly did not expect to put up in an hotel! It is inconvenient, for which I apologize, but it will only be for a day or two."

"But, it must be expensive—"

"I cannot think of a better use for my money, and fortunately for you," Aunt May said, a teasing note entering her tone, "Mr. Asterly left me very well provided for."

"Do you have a portrait of Mr. Asterly?" Emma asked, allowing herself to be distracted. "I have always wondered what he was like."

"Oh, he was the most delightful man! So kind, and so handsome. I was heartbroken when he died. I truly thought I would die myself." She sighed, and Emma felt a sudden commiserative pang of loneliness for Stephen.

"You don't look to be in any danger of that," Jamie said.

"Dear boy!" said Aunt May, laying her hand on his wrist. She looked at Emma. "I do have a portrait, a very fine miniature, but it is packed away so you shall have to wait to see it. And now," she said, rising from the sofa, "I will set you free. You must be aching to change your clothes, poor dears! And I must lie down for half an hour before I dress for dinner. Emmaline, I will send Daisy to you after she has done my hair."

"That isn't necessary—"

"I suggest you order a hot bath. You will find it refreshing after your long journey." She reached out her hands to Emma, as if to assist her in rising. Emma took them, and submitted to another perfumed embrace.

"Thank you," she said. "You are overwhelming us with kindness."

"It is I who am thankful for your visit," said May, cupping a delicate hand to Emma's face. "We shall have such fun together!" She smiled, kissed Emma's cheek, and retired to the next room in a whisper of silk.

Emma watched Daisy lay the last of the scattered jewelry into a handsome cherry-wood box, which she then tucked under her arm and carried out, following Aunt May without a word or a glance at Emma or Jamie. Emma looked at her brother, who shrugged, stood up, and walked to the outer door. Feeling the weight of miles upon her shoulders, Emma picked up the basket and silently followed him across the hall.

"Twenty cents, and not a penny more," Quincy said. He placed two dimes on the stained wood of the poulterer's table, beside two dead chickens.

The poulterer, a heavyset German with jowls like an old hound, seemed unimpressed. "Plucked and dressed," he said thickly. "Thirty cents."

Annoyed, for he knew he was being cheated, Quincy slapped down another dime, caught up the chickens, and hastened from the market. The *Harriet Lane* would soon leave New Orleans— already her engineers were bringing up steam—so he had no time to dicker. Determined to have fresh meat and vegetables for at least a few more days, Quincy had ventured to the French market, sped on by the urging of his messmates. With chickens grasped by the feet in one hand, a sack of cabbages, carrots, and onions slung over his shoulder, and a small bunch of lilies that had caught his eye stuck through a buttonhole of his coat, he strode back toward the wharf.

The rain had cleared though the sky was still grey, and the day was not yet unpleasantly warm. He was sorry to be leaving the city again so soon, but that was the way of life in the navy. Commander Porter wanted the rest of his mortars, hence the

Lane was to return up the river to Vicksburg at once and tow two more of them down. She would be in the company of two other vessels on the same errand, so it was unlikely that *Webb* and *Music* would venture out of hiding again. Quincy couldn't decide if he was sorry for that or not. River service was certainly exciting—perhaps more exciting than blockading would be, though he missed the open sea—but he had possibly had enough excitement for now.

The docks were crowded, mostly with navy men, though one or two private vessels—a mere shadow of the dozens that would have been there in peacetime—rested among the U.S. ships. Piles of supplies were stacked on the wharves: provisions, ordnance, canvas, waiting to be loaded into the holds of hungry vessels. Quincy saw sacks of mail on the deck of a dispatch boat, and hastened his steps. Perhaps he would have some letters waiting aboard the *Lane*.

Ahead, a small group of civilians stood conversing near the gangplank of a private steamer. Quincy was about to pass them by when a lady in the party half-turned, allowing him a view of her face. He was struck, surprised out of his breath, and he stopped short a few feet away.

"Mrs. Hawkland?"

The young woman turned, inquiry in her dark eyes, a suspicion of a smile upon her lips. She was wearing green, he thought, and a hat with some kind of feathers, but he noticed no more details of her dress. Her face held his attention, lovelier in flesh than on canvas, creamy skin framed by glowing chestnut hair. A single red rosebud pinned to the shoulder of her cloak caught his eye. He felt his heart begin to beat alarmingly fast.

"Do I know you, sir?" she asked in a soft, rich voice.

"No, I . . ."

Acutely aware of his humble burdens, and of the stares of the gentlemen to whom Mrs. Hawkland had been speaking, he decided to put the best face on it and said in a rush, "I recognized you from your portrait at Rosehall."

"Did you?" Mrs. Hawkland looked intrigued, and said to the gentleman beside her, "Will you excuse me for a moment, Mr. Everett?"

Mr. Everett would, though he shot a disapproving glance at Quincy as he turned to converse with the other men. Mrs. Hawkland stepped toward Quincy, saying, "May I walk with you?"

Anywhere.

"Yes," he said, "though I have no wish to disturb you, ma'am."

She began strolling along the wharf in the direction Quincy had been going. He kept pace with her, holding the chickens behind his back so as to keep them away from her dress.

"I am curious," she said. "When were you at Rosehall?"

"Last week," Quincy said. "I—you see, I am in the navy—"

"I gathered that." Her tone was amused, and a glint of matching humor entered her eye.

"—and I met—"

The words, "your husband" would not leave his mouth. Instead he said, "Colonel Hawkland."

"Ah," she said, nodding. The feathers in her hat bobbed slightly. "He must be quite lonely."

"Yes, ma'am. He misses you terribly."

Mrs. Hawkland stopped walking and gazed at Quincy as if trying to weigh him. After a moment she smiled. "May I know your name?"

"It's Wheat," he said. "Quincy Wheat. Acting Master Wheat." He was making a fool of himself. He began to wish he had passed by, or better yet, had never seen her.

"Mr. Wheat," said Mrs. Hawkland, "would you care to take a luncheon with me? I would so like to hear more news of my husband."

Quincy swallowed. "Nothing would please me more, ma'am, but I am afraid I cannot. My ship leaves within the hour."

"Oh." Her smile faded, then returned, now with a hint of sadness. "What ship is that?"

"The *Harriet Lane*, ma'am," he said, feeling his pulse quicken further. "That's her, just there." He gestured with his elbow to where the *Lane* lay.

"Ah, the pretty ship."

Quincy only smiled. It was all he could do to school his face from breaking into a foolish grin.

"Perhaps when you return you will pay me a visit?" she said. "I would be so happy for any news you might give me of my home."

"It would be a pleasure, ma'am, though I cannot say when we might be back."

"I will hope that it is soon," she said, smiling warmly. "Call on me when you are in town again. I live in Chartres Street."

"Thank you," Quincy said. "I shall look forward to giving myself the honor." He made as graceful a bow as he could, barring chickens and onions. Mrs. Hawkland responded with a nod, her eyes holding his gaze from beneath her hat brim, her lips curving slightly. She then turned and strolled back to her party.

Quincy watched her until Mr. Everett's attention was aroused. Turning away, he hastened toward the *Lane*.

"I shall look forward to giving myself the honor," he muttered to himself. "Quincy, you are an idiot!"

Nevertheless, his veins pulsed with an unsettling sensation, like the sense of danger one felt sailing into a storm. He rather liked it, he decided, and broke into a grin as he ran up the gangway to his ship.

Jamie fidgeted as he sorted a pile of miscellaneous papers into stacks of bills, business correspondence, personal correspondence and papers he thought might be discarded. He glanced at each piece only long enough to identify which it was. He didn't like handling Aunt May's papers, but Albert Lawford had asked him to assist, and if May had seen fit to hand her business over to Lawford, he supposed she wouldn't mind her own nephew helping out. He recognized Momma's cream-colored stationery and added the envelope to the personal pile, then stood up to stretch.

Emma was off seeing the wonders of Houston in company with her aunt. He envied her a little. He had not expected to spend his furlough sorting papers. The parlor of Aunt May's house seemed forlorn; it had already been emptied, and the rough-hewn table and two ladder-back chairs they were using had come from the kitchen out back. Jamie sighed as he gazed out the curtainless windows. It was brighter today, less overcast, which meant it would be hotter, no doubt. He glanced at Lawford, who looked cool and sophisticated in his dark gray suit and silk waistcoat. Jamie felt a pang of envy. He rubbed his neck and sat down again.

Mr. Lawford, seated across from him, glanced up and smiled. "It is tiresome, is it not?" he said. "Would you like to take a break for lunch?"

Overhead a sudden thumping of feet and a burst of shouting signaled some hitch in the progress of emptying the bedrooms of furniture. Jamie and Lawford both paused, gazing up at the ceiling. A low, loud voice quelled the outburst, and steady footsteps began again.

"Are those men all—Mrs. Asterly's property?" Jamie asked.

"Only Rupert. The others are mine," Lawford said.

"I didn't know she owned any."

"Asterly liked to spoil her. Daisy is indispensable, of course, and she wanted a butler, though Rupert does much more than that."

Jamie sighed, reaching for another batch of papers. "How long has she let all this pile up?" he asked, gesturing to the two large crates they had yet to sort. Between them they had only gone through one, and Lawford had started working on that the previous day.

"This time, about two years," Lawford said. "She does try to keep up, but she is not very organized. Every so often she asks me to straighten things out."

"She is lucky to have your help," Jamie said, careful not to let his irritation show in his voice.

"I only wish she would let me do more." Lawford straightened a stack of bills of alarming proportions. "She should not have to trouble herself at all over such matters."

"Why don't you ask her to marry you?"

Lawford looked up at him. "I have. Several times. She always puts me off."

Jamie smoothed the folded corner of a butcher's bill. "That was rude of me. I apologize."

"No need," Lawford said calmly. "I am sure your family are all wondering at May's placing so much trust in me. I hope you will believe that she is entirely safe in doing so."

"We don't know much about you," Jamie admitted.

Lawford set down a handful of papers and folded his hands on the table. "I came out with the railroad, a couple of years after Asterly brought May to Houston. Made my fortune in the Texas and New Orleans, went in with the Galveston, Houston and Henderson, then started my own carrier company, A and M Transport. I invested in steam packets, too, but I sold out a few years ago. They will never keep up with the railroads."

"What were you before the railroads?"

"An unsuccessful attorney in Savannah." Lawford gave a rueful smile. "That is a slight exaggeration, but I did want more opportunities than I had in Georgia. Old money reigns there, and my family is nothing significant."

"A and M Transport. Do you have a warehouse in Alleyton?"

"Yes, near the train station."

"I think I saw some of your wagons there. What does A and M stand for?"

"Austin and Matagorda."

"Not Albert and May?"

Lawford looked up, slowly smiling. "Don't mention that to her, if you please."

Despite himself, Jamie smiled back. "Did you start your carrier company before Asterly died?"

Lawford dropped his chin and peered at Jamie over his spectacles. "That is an outrageous question, young man."

"I know. Did you?"

Sighing, Lawford said, "Yes, the year before, but Asterly was already ill. He was a friend, by the way. A good friend."

"And you were kind enough to offer assistance to your good friend's widow."

"I would have done so in any case." Lawford took off his spectacles and began to clean them with his silk handkerchief. "Peter knew I was fond of May. His illness was very hard for her. She thrives on society and entertainments, you see. She finds it difficult to be still."

Jamie could easily understand that. "So you escorted her when Asterly no longer could."

"With his blessing. He wanted her to be happy, and he was glad I was there to protect her from any extravagant folly."

"And you fell in love with her."

Lawford put away his handkerchief and put on his spectacles. "Is it so hard to imagine?" he asked.

"No," Jamie said slowly. "She loves you, too, I think."

"Yes, I believe she does."

"Why won't she marry you, then?"

"Perhaps she is afraid of being widowed a second time."

Jamie gazed at him, musing. "Wouldn't she have the same feelings if you died, whether or not you were married?"

"Probably. I expect that has not occurred to her. She is very innocent in some ways."

Jamie handed him a pile of the questionable papers, and paused to rub his forehead. "My parents expect me to talk her out of moving to Galveston," he said.

Lawford shrugged. "I doubt you will succeed. I couldn't convince her to stay."

"The blockade is a genuine danger."

"I have told her so. She says she is tired of being a mud-turtle." He glanced through the papers Jamie had given him, extracted one page, and dropped the rest into an overflowing dustbin beside him. "I think she is curious, actually. The idea of glimpsing an enemy warship excites her."

"It's no game," Jamie said, more forcefully than he had intended.

Lawford regarded him thoughtfully for a moment. "I am aware of that," he said. "If you can suggest an argument that will change her mind, I am all attention. All of mine have failed."

"You don't mind if I try?"

"By all means. I hope you exceed my expectations." He picked up a paper, looked at it, set it down again. "I am glad you are here, by the way. I must go to Brownsville for a few days to deal with some pressing business. May will want your assistance in my absence."

Jamie frowned. "My furlough runs out soon," he said. "I have to be in Marshall by the eleventh, and my horse is back at home."

Lawford waved a hand in dismissal. "I'll transport your horse," he said. "And I'll give you a ticket to Marshall. I have an interest in the stage line."

"Mr. Lawford—"

"Just get her to Galveston safely." The older man looked up at him, not quite pleading, but entreating. "Please. I have put this matter off for too long. I will be very much in your debt."

Jamie wanted to ask what the pressing business was, but he felt he had pried enough into Lawford's affairs for one morning. He didn't like being pushed, but as Lawford seemed to be motivated by concern for Aunt May, he decided to comply with his wishes. Besides, if Emma was going to Galveston, he wanted to get a look at the place.

"All right," he said, hoping he wouldn't regret it.

Mr. Lawford smiled. "Thank you." He reached a hand across

the table, and Jamie shook it. "Let me buy you lunch," Lawford said. "I know an excellent place."

Jamie glanced at the papers under his hands, and the two crates still mostly full. He nodded, and without another word they both rose, abandoning the chore.

As the cutter approached the ferry landing at Hawkland's plantation, a dozen negro children scampered down to meet it. Its sole passengers were Lea, sent by the captain to seek news from Colonel Hawkland, and Quincy, who had volunteered to visit the burial site and make sure that it remained intact. Wainwright had raised an eyebrow at the request, but had granted it. Quincy thought the captain probably knew his real reason was a desire to see William's grave once more. He carried some of the flowers he had bought in New Orleans—still fresh after two days, for he had kept them in a jar of water in his cabin—to lay upon the grave. He still felt badly about William, and he was trying to understand exactly why.

A man on a sturdy bay horse approached from one of the outbuildings as they landed. Quincy and Lea stepped out of the boat and the children immediately surrounded them, begging for sweets or pennies. Quincy shooed them away as Lea stood waiting for the rider, who proved to be Mr. Shelton, the overseer, a white man younger than Hawkland but looking worn, his face weathered, possibly by a life spent out-of-doors. He reined in beside the landing and said, "What's your business?"

"I am here to see Colonel Hawkland," Lea stated.

"He's down at Angola Plantation. If your business is urgent I can send for him."

"That will not be necessary. Please tell him that I called to pay my respects. Lieutenant Commander Lea, of the *Harriet Lane*."

The rider glanced out at the *Lane*, anchored once more off the bank opposite Rosehall. Looking back at Lea he gave a single nod. "Anything else?"

"This gentleman would like to visit the grave we made a few

days ago." Lea indicated the roadway leading east.

The man glanced that way, then looked at Quincy. For a moment his eyes rested on the flowers, then he shrugged. "Go ahead," he said, and turned his horse back toward the outbuildings.

"Well," Lea said, turning to Quincy with a smile. "I may as well accompany you."

"We could return to the ship if you prefer," Quincy said.

"No. It will not take long, and I could do with a walk."

They set out down the road, passing north of Rosehall. At first the children followed them, but as Quincy and Lea proceeded farther from the buildings, they lost interest and fell away, until the two men were alone on the road. A rail fence separated the road from the plantation beyond the grounds of Rosehall.

"What did you think of Colonel Hawkland, sir?" he asked Lea.

The executive officer shrugged. "I thought him interesting. He has certainly been hospitable."

Quincy raised the flowers to his nose, inhaling their sweet, fading scent. "I met his wife in New Orleans," he said, trying to suppress a grin.

"How did you manage that?"

"I saw her on the wharf, and recognized her from the portrait in Hawkland's parlor."

"Ah, the famous portrait," Lea said. "I'm only sorry I didn't see it. Is she as beautiful as her picture?"

"More beautiful," Quincy said, and the grin escaped.

"Oho. Did you speak to her?"

"A few words, only."

"You dog."

Quincy laughed. He had thought a great deal about Mrs. Hawkland in the last two days. More than was good for him, he suspected. He was tempted to tell Lea about her invitation to visit, but thought that would be bragging. Besides, Lea might decide to prevent it, or to come along.

They reached the little hill where the two graves rested undisturbed beneath their tree, and walked up it together. Dividing his handful of lilies, Quincy left some on each patch of fresh-turned earth, then stood and made a short, silent prayer. Lord, may they be happier in heaven than they were upon this sad earth.

When he turned, he saw that Lea had descended to the road again and stood gazing out toward the river. The *Lane*'s bow was just visible in the space between trees. Quincy joined him and they walked back briskly. When they reached the shore Quincy glanced toward the house.

"Wait for me just a minute?" he asked.

Lea raised an eyebrow but nodded. Quincy strode to the drive and a little way up it, took out his pocketknife, and cut half a dozen roses from two bushes.

"You'd better hope that overseer didn't see you," Lea said, laughing as Quincy joined him on the landing.

Quincy grinned. "I have permission." He climbed in the cutter with his prize, offering a bloom to Lea, who refused.

"You're the flower lover. I suppose all those roses will go out in letters to pretty young girls."

"They will." Quincy inhaled the roses' heady perfume. All but one, he thought to himself.

11

. . . with an atmosphere for salubrity and purity unsurpassed anywhere on the globe, free from the freezing, chilling blasts of a more northern climate during the winter, while the summers are rendered delightful by the cool breezes that sweep over the gulf. All that is desirable in life can be found or produced on this gem of the gulf, if those who come to seek a home but make the proper effort and are contented.

—Charles W. Hayes

It was Monday before the Russells and Mrs. Asterly finally boarded a train for Galveston. Aunt May had hired a private car, sumptuously appointed and furnished with plush chairs, oriental carpets, and a tiny galley to which Daisy repaired at once to make tea. Another, much humbler car had been sent away on Saturday, filled to the brim with furniture and packing crates under the watchful care of Rupert and Mr. Lawford's two slaves. Mr. Lawford had gone away on the same train, to oversee the safe arrival of the furniture; he would then travel to Brownsville. Aunt May had been somewhat listless since his departure, though she had done her best to keep her niece and nephew entertained.

Emma chose a chair by a window on the right side of the car, looking out between red velvet curtains at the station bustling with passengers and railroad men coming and going. Jamie sat beside her. Aunt May disposed herself on a chaise longue, arranging the skirt of her bronze-colored, velvet-trimmed carriage dress, and opened a silk fan.

"Well, at last we are on our way," she said. "My dears, what are you staring at? We are not even moving yet."

"It's only our second train ride," Emma confessed.

"And Alleyton Station is much smaller than this," Jamie added.

"Oh. Well, by all means enjoy yourselves. I dislike traveling, but if one must do it, a well-appointed car is the only tolerable method."

"Do you dislike even trains?" Emma asked.

"Yes, I fear I do. Is that not terrible? Peter was so disappointed in me. He was always certain I would enjoy the next trip, if only he tried harder to make me comfortable."

"What about boats?" Jamie asked.

"If the water is perfectly smooth, then a boat is delightful," Aunt May said, fanning herself, "but if there is any sort of roughness or roll, I become ill."

The engine's shrill whistle signaled departure. Emma noticed Aunt May close her eyes and grip the back of the chaise. She herself felt a little flutter of excitement. They were going to Galveston, the grandest city in all Texas! She had thought she didn't care for such things, but in spite of herself she looked forward to seeing the Island City. Glancing down, she smoothed the sleeve of her dress. It was her second best. The dress she had arrived in, along with two others she had brought, had after long and somewhat heated discussion been passed on to the Methodist Episcopal church, to be given to the poor. ("My dear, I would not even give them to Daisy to wear!" Aunt May had said.) Emma had allowed this, for Momma expected her to buy new clothes, but she had resisted all attempts to discard Momma's best bonnet. She was wearing it now, despite Aunt May's entreaties and offers to lend Emma one of her own very fashionable hats. Emma had not argued, nor explained, but merely put her foot down where the bonnet was concerned. What was good enough for Momma was certainly good enough for her.

The train began to move, and Emma returned her attention to the window. People on the platform stood waving, children jumped up and down in excitement, and one small boy ran alongside the cars for a spell.

Emma looked up at Jamie and said, "Thank you for coming with us."

He looked surprised, then hooded his eyes. "Well, I have to make sure this town is good enough for you."

"I expect the question will rather be whether I'm good enough for the town."

"Nonsense. Miss Russell only moves in the highest circles," he said, putting on an aristocratic air.

Emma widened her eyes at him and shook her head, glancing in Aunt May's direction. Jamie choked on a laugh, and looked out the window again. Aunt May, who was leaning back in the chaise with her fan shading her eyes, did not appear to have heard.

Soon the city was behind them and they were passing fields of cotton, brilliant white under the summer sun. Daisy emerged from the galley, opened the windows a crack to let in the breeze, then served tea and some dainty little cookies. This revived Aunt May's spirits enough that she sat up and chatted happily about taking Emma shopping in Galveston.

"We shall go to Mrs. Maume at once," she said. "She is my favorite dressmaker, and is always up to date on the latest Parisian styles. And Mrs. Brassier's, of course, for hats and gloves."

"Of course," Jamie murmured, and Emma shot him a quelling look.

"And I want to take you to visit the Female Seminary. It is a very fine establishment. Miss Cobb's reputation is excellent—she and her sister have students from everywhere, even Louisiana and Missouri. You might like to consider enrolling in a class or two. The French instructor is reported to be superior."

"I doubt I will be in town long enough to make it worthwhile," Emma said.

"Oh, please do not say that," said Aunt May, pouting prettily. "I am counting on having you with me for a good, long visit. Oh, it is so hot! I cannot wait to reach the ocean."

Emma watched her unfold her fan again and wave it. She did not want to begin an argument, particularly when her aunt was so uncomfortable. Once she saw Aunt May settled into her new home she would be able to return to the subject. Discussing her departure now, when her visit had scarcely begun, would be impolite.

She sat back and watched out the window. The entire journey from Houston to Galveston, a distance of some forty-two miles, would take less than three hours, according to Mr. Lawford. He had spoken with pride of the Galveston, Houston and Henderson Railroad, in which he was an investor. It had been completed a year and a half before, in January of 1861, and had already carried hundreds of passengers and hundreds of thousands of dollars worth of goods between the two cities. The trestle bridge on which the tracks crossed Galveston Bay, he had told her, was the only link between the island and the mainland. Before construction of the railroad, all travel had been conducted by boat. Emma glanced at Aunt May, trying to picture her braving the discomforts of water travel—the only way to reach the island before the bridge was completed—and concluded that the attractions of the city must be great indeed.

Jamie had tried to talk May out of leaving Houston. He had expressed concern about the Federal blockade; May had dismissed it with a wave of her hand. There had been a hullabaloo in the spring which had amounted to exactly nothing, she said. The Yankees had been ineffectual in preventing the gallant blockade runners from leaving Galveston Bay. They would certainly not trouble the citizens of the town. The Galvestonians who had left, including the previous owner of her new home, were panicking fools who would soon regret their decision.

Emma took out her pocket watch and found to her surprise that they had been traveling nearly two hours. The cotton fields were giving way to wild lands, sometimes forested, sometimes marshy. After a few minutes she saw a dozen seagulls playing overhead, and spied a stretch of grayish water. Emma laid a hand against the window. "Is that the gulf?" she asked Jamie.

"The bay, I think. Yes, see, there's an island."

"Is it Galveston?"

"Galveston's bigger. Whoa, we're on the bridge!"

He got up, and they both pressed their faces to the window. Water raced by beneath them; Emma couldn't watch it without feeling a little dizzy. She kept her eyes toward the horizon instead, and was able to discern a brightness that soon resolved into white sand.

"That must be it," Jamie said.

"Must be what?" Aunt May asked sleepily.

Emma came to her. "Did we wake you? Please forgive us. We are crossing the bridge."

Aunt May sat up, searching among the folds of her skirt for her fan. "Good," she said, "then we will soon be in town. Where is Daisy?"

The maid appeared at once from the galley and assisted Aunt May to compose herself while Jamie and Emma continued to stare out the window. The sandy beach grew larger until suddenly they were upon it, turning eastward to race along the island, passing banks of grass, a winding bayou, one or two clumps of trees. Dozens of seagulls wheeled, screeching at the train. The whistle blew, the engine slowed, and houses began to appear, at first widely scattered, then upon definite streets, then clustered together as the train huffed its way to a stop at the foot of the city.

At once all was bustle and hurry; Emma handed Jamie his forgotten book and picked up the little handbag Aunt May had bestowed upon her to use instead of Momma's basket, which had been sent with the furniture. Jamie hastened to fetch a porter to take care of the baggage, and Emma, unable to wait while Daisy collected Aunt May and her possessions, stepped down from the car to the platform.

A breeze caught at her bonnet and she reached up to hold it, though the tug at the ribbons had been gentle. Birds swirled overhead, some raucous, some silent or whistling mournfully. Smells followed one another on the wind: fish, burning coal, horses, the smoke of the locomotive, a wet and green scent that distant memory identified with the ocean, and others she could not identify. Before her stood brick buildings, warehouses close by, taller city structures a street or two away. The sky was hazy, pale blue. Looking back toward the train, she glimpsed water in the space between the cars.

"Emmaline! Come, my darling, your brother has found us a carriage."

Emma hastened to join her aunt and the maid, walking briskly across the platform to a one-horse buggy where Jamie stood waiting. "Aunt May," she said as they climbed in, "won't you please call me Emma? Whenever I hear 'Emmaline' I think I am in trouble."

"Certainly, my dear, you should have mentioned it before. Now, will you call me May in return, and dispense with this tedious 'Aunt'-ing?"

"I'll try. Momma would disapprove very much."

"Dear Eva," said Aunt May, smiling. "Always so correct."

The driver flicked his whip over the ears of the horse, who responded by moving forward at a sleepy walk. Emma gazed curiously at the city. The depot was just inside the town, and she could see that the city's center was farther east. Several wharves ran along the north shore down that way, and tall buildings rose above the town. As they drove eastward along the railroad tracks, which appeared to continue through the town, she saw that the streets were busy, full of citizens going to market, or to work, or just strolling along. Everywhere she saw negroes, more than she had ever seen before, many more than the few she knew of in San Antonio. Even Houston had not seemed to have so many. The women's clothing indicated they were servants; a number of men also looked like domestics, though on the wharves and in the warehouses big laborers sweated as they moved cotton and other goods. Emma realized she was staring at them, and glanced at Daisy. The maid's face was as unrevealing as ever. Emma wondered what she was thinking, if she was glad to be in Galveston, or if she simply did not care.

At last the carriage turned south, drove one more block, then turned and stopped before the corner house, a pretty, two-story wooden building, set back from the street with a garden surrounded by a low iron fence. The house was painted white with blue trim, the front door a pale yellow. A wisteria vine draped along the balcony railing of the second story, and flowers bloomed riotously in the garden.

"Oh, how pretty!" Emma exclaimed.

"It is charming, isn't it?" said Aunt May. "I fell in love with it on sight. Ah, here is Rupert to greet us."

Emma remembered the large black man from the house in Houston. He now came forward and took charge of a portmanteau that Daisy had been carrying, as well as Jamie's valise. He glanced at Emma, then said to her aunt, "Welcome home, Miz May."

"Thank you, Rupert. I trust everything arrived safely?"

Rupert held the gate open, saying, "Yes, ma'am. Them two boys of Mr. Lawford's didn't manage to break a thing."

Aunt May laughed, and went lightly up the four steps to the front porch. Tall windows flanked the double doors, which stood open. May went in, sighing happily, and Daisy followed her up the stairs that filled half of the hall. Emma and Jamie came in after them, rather timidly. The floors were wooden and highly polished. There were no ornaments on the walls, but pairs of pretty oil-lamps flanked the hall and a crystal chandelier hung between the front door and the stairs. Open doorways to either side led into large, high-ceilinged rooms that were presently filled with a jumble of furniture and packing cartons.

"The parlor's not set up just yet," Rupert said. "Bedrooms first."

With that, he began climbing the stairs, and the Russells followed. The upper story proved to be a mirror of the ground floor, with a broad hall from which four doors led to separate bedrooms. A tall, uncurtained window at the front of the hall let in a splash of sunlight. Rupert led Emma and Jamie to the front rooms, setting Jamie's case down by the left-hand door.

"Your baggage being brought with Miz May's, Miss?"

Emma glanced at Jamie. "Yes."

Rupert nodded, and said, "I'll go keep a eye out, bring it up when it comes." He went to the closed door of the room behind Emma's, set Daisy's bag down, then started downstairs.

Emma looked at her brother. "Well, we're here," she said.

Jamie smiled and picked up his valise. Emma turned to her own room. The door handle was made of crystal. She turned it, and the door swung open on a gentle push.

Sunshine poured in through lace curtains over a tall window that went right down to the floor. Drapes of amber-gold were pulled back from this, framing it prettily. The light fell on a canopy bed, wardrobe, armchair, chaise longue, and table, all of carved mahogany, the bed and chairs upholstered in pale gold. A thick oriental carpet in shades of red and gold cushioned her footsteps. Emma put her handbag down on the table and took off her shawl and bonnet, setting them on the bed. She noticed two small tables flanking the bedstead, each bearing a large vase filled with lilies. She smiled, thinking that Aunt May must have ordered the flowers to be put there, and that Rupert had done very well to remember them in the midst of all the fuss and bother of the move.

She stood in the middle of the room, marveling at its size and luxury. It was even larger than her room at the Capitol Hotel had been, and that had been palatial compared to her little bedroom at home. Walking to the window, she threw back the lace and found that she had a clear view of the harbor. It was a sash window, the bottom panel of which was nearly as tall as she. She undid the latch, raised it and stepped straight through onto the balcony.

A large, white steamboat was backing away from a wharf. It blew its whistle—a deep, mournful sound—then slowly turned northward. At another wharf a sleek gray ship with the name *Susanna* painted on its bow was being loaded with cotton. She could just see the train depot off to the west, laborers still swarming around the cars, moving baggage and cargo.

A sound caught her attention and she turned to see Jamie stepping out of his own window. He smiled and joined her at the balcony railing. "Like it?" he asked.

"It will do, I suppose," she said airily, then abandoned the pose with a chuckle. "My goodness, I never dreamed of being in such a place!"

"God bless Aunt May," Jamie murmured.

Emma had to agree. How strange it was to remember her resistance to visiting her pretty, charming aunt. She had been afraid of the unknown, perhaps, or felt constrained by loyalty to the ranch. She wondered how Poppa and Gabe and Mr. Ferguson were getting along without her, and felt a pang of guilt at being here when things were so hard back at home. Never mind, she decided. She would not stay away long. She was here because Momma and Poppa wished it, and she would pay all the attention to Aunt May that duty required.

"Is that a blockade runner, do you think?" she asked, pointing to the *Susanna*.

Jamie's face grew serious as he looked at the ship. "Could be. I don't know much about them. They do paint them gray like that, I heard." He turned to her, looking worried. "Emma, maybe you should come back to San Antonio with me."

Emma frowned. "We just got here! Aunt May would be terribly hurt."

"This island isn't safe," he said, shaking his head. "I don't want—"

A tapping noise behind them made them turn. Daisy stood at the center window, gesturing for them to come in. Emma looked up at Jamie, who had already turned to go back in through his bedroom. She met him and Daisy in the hall.

"Miz May would like you both to accompany her to the Tremont House for luncheon," Daisy said. "She will be ready in ten minutes."

"Thank you," Emma told her.

Daisy nodded, then returned to May's room. Emma looked at Jamie, wondering if he wanted to continue their conversation, but he just said, "I'd better go comb my hair," and went into his bedroom. He had retreated behind his wall again, the wall he had put around himself since New Mexico. A memory of Stephen came to her—of the letters he'd written, always with a word of kindness or concern about Jamie—and she felt her throat tighten with sudden tears. She looked out the hall window, blinking at the brightness of the sun. It seemed a little harsher, less magically beautiful than it had a few moments before.

"Emma Russell, don't you dare fall into a gloom," she whispered. "Not when you're being treated like a princess." Lifting her chin, she went into her own room to tidy herself for luncheon.

Army headquarters was the last place Jamie ever thought he would seek diversion, but after a day and a half spent assisting Aunt May it seemed like a haven. He had discharged numerous minor errands and then visited an employment agency to summon to the house what seemed like a battalion of candidates for the position of cook, who were even now being interviewed in May's parlor. He had not the manhood to face it, he freely admitted, and Emma had let him off with only a minor scold and a command to be on time for lunch.

He strolled north from May's house to the Strand, a wide street that ran along the bay side of the island and was home to the business district, with which—thanks to May's errands—he was becoming quite familiar. An inquiry after the whereabouts of army headquarters led him to a warehouse a little way down the Strand. It was more like an armory than, for example, district headquarters in San Antonio, but Jamie knew that the fact they had a building at all was a boon.

Jamie approached a table that had been set up in the front of the warehouse and identified himself to the assistant adjutant seated behind it. "I was wondering if anyone might be available to show me around the island's defenses," he said.

"I can inquire," said the adjutant. "If you will give me your address in town—"

"I don't need a guide, if that's too much trouble. I just want to look around."

"Look around what?" said a voice behind him.

Jamie turned to see a tall, dark-haired man in a crisp gray uniform, a colonel's three stars on its collar. His instinct was to salute in spite of being indoors, for the colonel looked like the no-nonsense type. Instead he squared his shoulders and gave a short nod.

"Good morning, Colonel. I was hoping to get a look at the island's fortifications. I'm here on leave, and want to assure myself of my family's safety."

"And you are?"

"Lieutenant James Russell, sir. Valverde Battery."

The colonel's eyebrows rose. "Oh, the trophy battery. Lot of fuss over that."

Jamie just gazed at him, not having anything to say in response to what might be construed as an insult. The colonel seemed to relent a bit and offered a hand.

"Joseph Cook," he said. "I'm in command of the defenses, such as they are. You are welcome to visit them, Lieutenant. As regards your family's safety, I make no promises other than to do the best I can with what I have."

"That sounds all too familiar," Jamie said, shaking hands.

Cook's stern face relaxed into a smile. "So you're not fresh from school."

Jamie smiled back. "Not quite."

"I'm on my way out to the South Battery now," Cook said. "If you care to come along you may join me."

"I'd be honored," Jamie said. "I'm afraid I don't have a horse. . . ."

"It's not too long a walk," Cook said, and led him outside and down to Bath Avenue, where he turned south. They crossed the railroad tracks and followed a spur southward. In a few blocks they had left the city behind, passing between low, sandy hills to which clung tussocks of grass. Jamie smelled the sea more strongly now.

"Have you been in command here long?" he asked.

"Just this month. Colonel Debray was commanding, but he's gone up to Houston to take charge of the subdistrict."

Jamie glanced up, surprised. "Debray? I went to his school in San Antonio."

"Did you? I'll warrant he was a good instructor."

"That he was." Jamie smiled. He would have to stop by De-bray's headquarters on the way back through Houston.

They reached the South Battery, a fortification shaped like a shallow U with a point in the long side that faced the gulf. It was situated on a slight rise some thirty yards back from a white, sandy beach. Jamie saw waves curling and heard them slap against the sand. He wanted to kick off his boots and run out into the water; instead he followed the colonel into the work.

Two platforms supported mounted ten-pounder rifles—in less than ideal condition—that looked out toward the gulf through embrasures. Jamie kept his opinion of the guns to himself, and noted that the men on duty appeared well prepared at least, though the store of ordnance on hand was less than he would have ordered. There were embrasures for more guns, and Colonel Cook climbed to look out one of these, inviting Jamie to join him. The gulf lay before them, and the battery was high enough to allow good views northward of the city and eastward of the entrance to the Galveston Bay. Jamie gazed at these, at the guns, and back at the gulf.

"Two guns only?" he said softly.

"They are better than what we had here a year ago," said Colonel Cook. "The Federals sent a sloop out to fire on us, and the guns we had then were badly outranged. We couldn't reach her, but she sent a cannonball up Broadway."

"How many guns do you have altogether?" Jamie asked.

Four on the island. You will have passed Fort Hébert coming in, there are three more there."

"I saw them."

"We will have guns also at Eagle Grove, at Pelican Island out in the harbor, and at Fort Point. Some were removed to the mainland earlier."

Jamie ran a hand along the packed sand of the fieldwork. Grains moved beneath his touch. "Are you planning more defensive works?"

"Oh, yes. We have plans in abundance. Just not the means to execute them."

Jamie frowned, gazing out to sea with the breeze stirring his hair. "My battery is going to Marshall. I will visit headquarters there and suggest that they send Galveston more guns," he said.

"Do that," said Cook, smoothing his mustache. "Tell the big dogs to use some of that cotton money to send us some powder and lead, while you're at it."

Jamie returned Cook's frank gaze, knowing the colonel was sizing him up. At last Cook said, "Will you be sending your family back to the mainland now?"

Jamie grimaced. "I tried to persuade them not to come in the first place."

"Keep trying," Cook said. He looked out at the gulf. "The blockade is being tightened. Had a sea-captain come demand our surrender back in May. He promised the navy would be along in a few days to close our harbor. It was all gum, they never made an appearance, but I think they will come. It is only a matter of time."

Cook walked over to the detachment of the right gun and

spoke to its chief, who signaled to one of the men. The soldier followed Cook back to where Jamie stood.

"Pettis here will take you around to the other fieldworks," the colonel said.

Jamie nodded. "Thank you, Colonel. I will not take up too much of his time."

Pettis, who had arrived grinning like a child suddenly offered a visit to the fair, did not allow this comment to dampen his mood. Cook said farewell and started back toward the city, while Pettis led Jamie eastward along the beach. This was flat, of course; Galveston Island was essentially a glorified sandbar roughly thirty miles long by two and a half wide. Private Pettis led Jamie around the curve of its eastern end to Fort Point, a small fieldwork with a single 10-inch gun aimed out across the entrance to Galveston Bay. Across this Jamie could see the thin line of the far shore, its only landmark a lighthouse. To the northwest in the bay a short distance away was a grassy sandbar Pettis called Pelican Spit, and beyond it the larger mass of Pelican Island, where a handful of dark muzzles protruded from a sandy work to threaten vessels entering the harbor. These, Pettis informed Jamie, were Quaker guns—logs carved and painted to look like cannon—which was disappointing news. Galveston's wharves were visible to the west, jutting out into the harbor from the north side of the island. The one gun at Fort Point seemed a feeble defense indeed.

He looked at Pettis. "You from around here, Private?"

"Yes, sir. Born and raised a Galvestonian," the man said with pride.

"You have family on the island?"

"My mother and sisters. Father's passed on, and my brother's off serving in Virginia."

Jamie stopped short of asking if Pettis was worried about his family. The private was young, maybe seventeen or eighteen, and the Yankee schooner's cannonball down Broadway was probably the only combat he'd seen. A cold feeling ran down Jamie's arms. Not only was the island scantily fortified, the men defending it probably hadn't the least notion of what they were up against.

He put that thought aside for the moment, and summoned up a smile. "Well, let's have a look at Eagle Grove."

12

We are gratified to see that the troops in Galveston are still regularly drilled . . . and at all times in readiness to meet any attack that might be made on the city. Colonel Cook, who is now in command there, is one of the most vigilant and active, as well as popular, officers in this department.
—Mr. Willard Richardson, *Galveston News*

"Now this," said Mrs. Maume as her assistant displayed a gown for Emma's approval, "is the very latest in seaside fashions, direct from Paris. White piqué of course, with Zouave jacket and vest, gauntlet sleeves. The trimming is mohair braid of the highest quality, and the red accents are silk."

"Very elegant," Aunt May said, smiling. "What do you think, Emma?"

Emma thought that a white dress covered in rows upon rows of black braid, to say nothing of the red silk, was a bit excessive for her taste. Not wishing to offend Mrs. Maume, she said, "I think I might be too tall to wear it becomingly. I am such a scarecrow."

Mrs. Maume gave her a patient smile and signaled her assistant, a pretty young brunette, to remove the dress. Very early in their meeting, the dressmaker had expressed her regret that Emma was too tall (or "statuesque," as she put it) to be able to try on any of the made-up gowns. Aunt May had said that it was just as well, for the only way to buy dresses that truly fit was to have them made for one.

"Please tell me, Mrs. Maume," Emma said, "what makes your dress change color?"

Mrs. Maume moved her skirt, causing it to shimmer from mulberry to black in its shadows. "It is shot silk, Miss Russell," she said. "A new fabric, and very fashionable indeed. The warp thread and the weft are different colors. I made a handsome gown of it for your aunt, in shades of mauve."

"Yes, I have seen it," Emma said. "It's a beautiful dress."

The assistant brought forward a walking dress of violet plaid lined with apple-green satin. Even Aunt May agreed that Emma would not appear to advantage in such a startling garment. The dress quickly vanished, to be replaced by a gown with a skirt so full that Mrs. Maume had to help display it. It was enhanced by five flounces, and covered with embroidered roses.

"This is a pretty dress on any figure," Mrs. Maume declared. "Note the quilled ribbon above each flounce and trimming the body. We have a grenadine shawl of deep green that complements this dress quite nicely. Giselle, bring the shawl, please."

Giselle hastened away, and Emma glanced at Aunt May, who was fanning herself. May nodded toward the rose-covered dress. "Do you like it, dearest?"

"I think it would look lovely on *you*," Emma said.

Giselle, returning to the room in time to overhear this, hesitated in confusion, the grenadine shawl in her hands. Emma smiled to reassure her.

"Silly child," said Aunt May furling her fan and rapping Emma's fingers with it. "I am much too old for such a dress!" She appeared pleased nonetheless.

"I like what Giselle is wearing," Emma said, looking up at Mrs. Maume. "I'm afraid I am a creature of simple tastes."

"The Garibaldi shirt?" said Mrs. Maume, pouncing on the first word of genuine approval Emma had voiced. "It is very fashionable indeed! It was 'le dernier cri' in Paris this spring. Not yet passé—I think we need not worry about that for the rest of the season at least." She draped the profusion of roses over a chair and took the shawl away from Giselle, directing the girl to turn around so Emma could see her attire.

"Too severe for you, dearest," Aunt May protested. "Why, it looks just like a man's shirt, nothing more!"

"A Zouave jacket would offset the severity," Mrs. Maume said in a soothing tone, "and I do believe that Miss Russell would look very well in a simple, elegant style."

Emma nodded, liking the shirt of striped cotton, the plain dark skirt, even the narrow ribbon tied in a bow beneath Giselle's collar. She resolved to put up with a Zouave jacket if necessary, if Aunt May could be persuaded to let her dress in this style.

"I think I would like an ensemble like that one," she said, nodding.

Mrs. Maume was all accommodation. The rose garden was sent away and samples of fabric brought out instead: cambric, cotton, merino; plain colors, narrow stripes, and tiny prints. Aunt May protested as Emma compared a pale blue-striped muslin with a soft gray flannel.

"Dearest, it is all very well for the morning, or for country-walking I suppose, but I absolutely promised Eva you would have a promenade dress!"

Emma haggled, but at last was forced to yield and order a Zouave jacket and matching skirt to accompany one of three Garibaldi shirts. She selected gray flannel and, rejecting Mrs. Maume's suggestion of red trim, instead gave her carte blanche to adorn the jacket in the excellent black mohair braid. The colors were the same she had used to make Matthew's uniform the previous summer. She smiled softly, but kept this thought to herself.

By this time she was beginning to be hungry, but Aunt May would not hear of leaving until Emma had ordered an evening gown. A protest that her budget could not bear the cost was swept away; the dress was to be May's gift.

"I must be allowed to show you off, dearest," she said, coaxing. "What do you think of the Satin de Mai?"

More dresses were brought out, fashion plates referred to, and at last they agreed on a gown of lobelia blue embroidered with lilies in the same color. Emma had only to submit to being measured by Mrs. Maume and Giselle, then she bid the dressmaker and a considerable portion of the money Momma had given her adieu, and retired with Aunt May to the Tremont House, where they were to meet Jamie for luncheon.

"I hoped that the Garibaldi shirts would be less expensive," Emma confessed as they were seated at a table by a long gallery of windows overlooking the street.

"Well, they are in fashion," Aunt May said. "They are all the rage, though I am sure I do not know why."

"I like clothes that are easy to wear," Emma said, refusing to be drawn into an argument. She wondered what May would think of her work clothes at home. Had Momma ever mentioned them to May in a letter? She doubted it—Momma probably wanted as few people as possible to know about her daughter's peculiar habits.

A brisk waiter brought them lemonade and they spent a pleasant quarter-hour watching the comings and goings outside the windows on Mechanic's Row. Emma marveled aloud at the crowds of people passing by.

"My dear, this is not crowded at all!" May exclaimed. "Why, the city is positively dead, still. Usually there are at least twice as many people out and about. It will get better, though, as more people return home. Soon we shall see some liveliness!"

Emma, watching the hubbub outside, said, "I cannot imagine it much more lively."

"Well, you have grown up in the countryside," May said. "You have never seen a true city. Even Galveston is quite small when compared with New Orleans, or any of the larger cities."

Like New York? Like Philadelphia? May never spoke of such

places, Emma had noticed, though she certainly had been to them.

Jamie's voice interrupted her musings. "Please forgive me, Aunt May. I'm afraid I am late." Emma looked up to see her brother proffering a bouquet of daisies to their aunt.

"Naughty boy," May said. "You should apologize to Emma, it is she who has been kept waiting for her luncheon, and I know she is hungry."

Jamie turned to Emma, a gleam in his eye, and knelt before her, holding up the flowers. "Please forgive me, Sister dear," he said.

Emma took the bouquet away from him and plunked it into his water goblet. "Sit down. I can't eat pretty speeches."

Not appearing very humbled, Jamie took his place. "Did you pass a pleasant morning?" he asked.

"Oh, delightful," Aunt May said. "So many pretty gowns! Emma is unused to sophisticated clothing, and has chosen to dress rather plainly, but even so I think you will like what you see when her dresses are made up."

Emma saw a hint of curiosity in the look Jamie directed at her. "At least it's over with," she said.

"Yes, now we can devote the afternoon to the milliner's," said May gaily. "I just know we shall find the perfect hats to show off your pretty face!"

Emma overcame the urge to wrench her pretty face up in a scowl. She was rescued by the waiter, who took their order for luncheon and promised the speedy appearance of sage soup and fresh bread to appease their hunger.

"How was your morning?" Emma asked Jamie.

He did not answer at once. She looked up to find him gazing toward the window, a crease of concern on his forehead. He noticed her watching him and gave a rueful smile. "It was— enlightening."

"Did you go all the way to Virginia Point?" asked Aunt May.

"Yes, the engineer was kind enough to let me off, but I had to walk back. It's why I'm late."

"Dear boy, you must be exhausted! Why, it must be three miles!"

"Four or more, counting the bridge," Jamie said.

Emma thought of the horrible march he had made through the mountains in New Mexico, without Cocoa, without food, often without water. A four-mile stroll along the island would be nothing by comparison.

"I did not know one could walk on the bridge," Emma said.

"They put a floor on it this May, when the city was evacuated," Jamie told her. "They wanted to move cattle to the mainland."

Emma looked at him in surprise. "The city was evacuated?"

"It was voluntary," Aunt May said, sounding annoyed. "Everyone panicked, and ran to Houston without knowing what they would do for food or shelter. They created havoc in town for *weeks*. It was the stupidest thing. But they have finally come to their senses, and are returning."

Jamie's expression told Emma he had a rather different opinion, but he did not seem anxious to discuss the matter with their aunt. Emma ventured to change the subject.

"Are the fortifications in good order?" she asked.

Jamie looked from her to Aunt May. "They could be better," he said. "I confess I would be happier if you were in Houston."

"Houston is past," May said, waving a hand. "The house is sold. It is over and done with."

Jamie regarded her in silence for a moment, then appeared to make a decision. "May, please believe me," he said, low and urgent, "this island is almost indefensible. It has a few earthworks and a few guns, no navy, not much in the way of troops. It could possibly be held with double or triple the resources, but right now it is vulnerable."

"People are returning," May said. "The men will come back to defend their homes. You will see."

"I won't be here to see. That is another reason I am anxious for your safety."

May bestowed a warm smile upon him. "Dear boy, how sweet! You need not worry, however. Rupert can stand up to any threat, and Albert will be here soon."

The waiter arrived, and Jamie didn't pursue the discussion. Emma tasted her soup, found it savory and good, and ignored all else for a few minutes. Aunt May chattered about the friends she would soon meet again and the parties they would attend. Jamie ate in silence.

Emma set down her spoon and said, "The blockaders don't seem very effective so far."

"They are growing more so every week," Jamie said. "I have talked with Colonel Cook, who has seen the changes ever since New Orleans fell."

"Blockaders," Aunt May said with scorn. "Let them come. They will never close our harbor."

Jamie frowned. "Aunt May, I don't think you realize the seriousness of the situation—"

"You must think I know nothing of military matters," said May. "Indeed, you are mistaken. I am very well acquainted with General Sherman—"

"General Sherman?" Emma said, laughing. "Oh, forgive me! It's just that—wasn't General Sherman the name of our locomotive from Alleyton?" she asked Jamie.

"Yes," said Aunt May, breaking into a smile. "That locomotive was the first in Texas, and was named for General Sidney Sherman, who helped build the railroad. He is a dear friend of Albert's and mine."

The waiter reappeared with plates of chicken salad. Jamie sat back in his chair, waiting thin-lipped for the man to leave. Emma was troubled by his frown; he seemed cross, and that was unlike him, except that recently he had been moody. Watching him, she felt she didn't know him anymore, then wondered if she had ever really known him very well. He was quiet, much more like Daniel than like herself or Matt. She and Matt were the hotheads in the family. Like Poppa, she had tended to discount Jamie. She began to feel that had been a mistake.

The rest of the meal passed peaceably, the subjects of conversation being confined to the climate of the island, Jamie's description of the wildlife he had seen during his walk, and May's effusive anticipation of a second round of shopping for Emma. Jamie escorted them to Bath Avenue and down it the few blocks to Mrs. Brassier's establishment, then wished them a pleasant time and would have left at once had not Emma caught his arm.

"Jamie, would you—would you take me for a walk tomorrow? I would like to see that creek you mentioned."

He gave her a small smile. "Of course. I'd be glad to." The smile grew as he glanced toward the milliner waiting in the open door of her shop. "Don't become *too* fashionable," he murmured, then bowed and was gone.

Emma turned to face Mrs. Brassier and her aunt. Courage, she reminded herself, and squaring her shoulders, smiled and went into the shop.

Quincy stood before the mahogany door of a trim brick house on Chartres Street, wondering if he was mad. Luck had kept the *Harriet Lane* in New Orleans for a day. Tomorrow she would strike for Pensacola; this afternoon he was at liberty to enjoy himself. He had headed for the market while Becker and Gerard went into the Vieux Carre, excusing himself from joining them on the grounds that he wanted to stock up for the Wardroom Mess. He had shopped, but had purchased no groceries, and had soon left the market for the better part of town. Pushing feelings of guilt to the back of his mind, he reached for the knocker and rapped it thrice against the dark wood.

A servant answered, took Quincy's name and asked him to wait in the hall. He stood near the door, admiring a painting of a spaniel and fidgeting with the small bouquet of roses he had bought in the vegetable market. Perhaps that had not been a good idea. Perhaps he should leave them in the hall, or perhaps he should leave altogether.

"Mr. Wheat?"

Quincy looked up at the sound of Mrs. Hawkland's voice. She came toward him, dressed in dark blue silk, her face glowing above a high collar edged in narrow lace. He made a belated bow, and offered her the flowers.

"I saw them in the market, and they reminded me of the fine rosebushes along the drive at Rosehall."

"Thank you! How kind of you," she said, accepting the flowers and pausing to smell them. "I am very fond of roses. Colonel Hawkland built Rosehall for me, you know."

"I did not know," Quincy said, thinking that the house must not be very old.

Mrs. Hawkland handed the flowers to the servant, saying, "Thank you, Jean. Would you bring some sherry to the parlor?"

Quincy followed her to this room, a cosy apartment furnished in dark wood and red velvet. Gauze curtains filtered the light from two tall windows outside which the passersby in the street appeared as ghostly shadows. His hostess invited him to sit on the sofa, taking a low-backed chair for herself.

"You are very kind to visit me," she said. "Have you been back to Rosehall?"

"Not to the house, ma'am, though we were in the vicinity. I did not see Colonel Hawkland. He chanced to be at Angola when we called."

"He likes to keep an eye on his foremen," she said. "It is just as well, for this spring he found one of them to be communicating with the militia. He let him go at once, of course." She glanced up at him, smiling. "Well, tell me all about my home."

Quincy did his best to gratify her. As he was describing the colonel's generosity in allowing the navy to make a burial on his property, Jean came in bearing a tray with two glasses, a decanter, and Quincy's roses, now reposing in an elegant crystal vase. He set the tray on a low table before his mistress, served the wine, and withdrew.

"My husband must like you," she said. "When the first Federal ship visited our property, I am afraid things were not as cordial."

"I am sorry to hear that."

She waved a hand. "Everything was so unsettled. The neighbors all feared their crops would be burned. They have since come to realize that the navy does not prey upon them nearly so much as the guerrillas."

"Has your husband written to you of the guerrillas?"

"Yes, he is very upset by them. They have no respect for property, but merely take what they want."

"Has he been much troubled by them lately?"

She looked at him, a slow smile growing on her shapely lips. "Mr. Wheat, I should think you would be better able to inform me on that point."

Quincy looked at the glass in his hands. "Forgive me. I must seem overinquisitive."

"No." She continued to smile at him for a moment, then set down her glass and extracted a rose from the vase. "Would you help me pin this to my dress? I have some pins here." She handed him the flower and stood, producing a paper of pins from a pocket in her skirt. Sitting down beside him, she asked, "Have you a knife to cut the stem?"

Quincy, whose heart had begun to thump rather fast, nodded and took out his pocketknife. He shortened the stem to two inches and offered it back to her.

"Thank you," she said. "Will you hold it steady while I pin it? Yes, just there."

Leaning close, his fingers pressing against the silk of her dress, brushing the soft skin beneath, Quincy felt rather dizzy. He strove to breathe steadily, and hoped she couldn't sense his nervousness. He should not be here, doing this, he should not, he thought over and over. At the same time he felt an elation he would not have traded for anything.

"There. Thank you," said Mrs. Hawkland, bending her head to smell the rose. Her hair brushed Quincy's hand as he withdrew it. He laid it on his knee and watched her, admiring the curve of her neck. He was seated rather close to her now, he thought. He ought to move away. He stayed.

"Mr. Wheat, I have been wondering—perhaps you can advise me?" Her eyes were very dark, a brown richer than coffee, warmer than caramel.

"Upon what matter?" he asked.

She gave a small smile. "You see, we are very short of funds. We do not have enough to keep our slaves fed and clothed properly."

Quincy nodded, remembering Colonel Hawkland's similar complaint. The thought vanished as he realized he could smell the rose pinned to her shoulder.

"If I could sell some of my cotton," she continued, "it would alleviate their distress. Is there any way for me to get permission to do so?"

"Ah—you would have to apply to the department commander. General Butler, I'm afraid."

She pouted prettily. "The Beast? How dreadful. Still, if I must, I will go to him. I cannot let my poor people starve. Do you think you could write a note of introduction for me?"

"The general will not know my name," Quincy said.

"But perhaps if you wrote, and explained our distress, he would be more inclined to take pity on me?"

Quincy thought that if General Butler were anything like himself, he would be inclined to do whatever Mrs. Hawkland wished. He tried to think of any reason why he should not write a note for her. As long as he stated the mere facts as he knew them, being Colonel Hawkland's declaration of his people's distress and his courtesy toward the *Lane*'s officers, there could be nothing wrong about it.

"I would be happy to write, if you think a note from me would be of any use."

The smile that lit her face was ample reward. "Thank you!" she said. "I know it will be of use. Let me find you some paper."

She rose and walked to a desk in one corner of the room. Quincy watched her, admiring her every movement as she found writing paper, pen, and inkwell, and brought them back to him. She set them on the table and picked up the tray to make room for him to write.

Feeling a bit foolish, he took up the pen and drew the paper toward him. Such a note would, of course, bear more weight if signed by Lieutenant Commander Lea or Commander Wainwright rather than a mere acting master. Somehow, he could not bring himself to suggest it. Perhaps the captain and XO would be irritated by such a request. Perhaps he was reluctant to let them know he had visited Mrs. Hawkland. Blushing, he bent to write. He did not address the note to General Butler. Instead he simply wrote his description of the Hawklands' exigency and signed it, giving the date and "New Orleans" as the location.

Mrs. Hawkland accepted the page from him and read it over. "Thank you!" she said, looking up with a smile. "I know this will help us. Thank you for your kindness." She folded the page and tucked it into her pocket, then sat beside him once more. "Allow me to repay you with dinner. Can you stay?"

"I'm afraid not," Quincy said, wishing it were not true. He pulled out his pocket watch. It read a quarter after five, which gave him a start. "I go on watch at six. I must leave now, in fact."

"Oh," said Mrs. Hawkland, crestfallen. "Perhaps tomorrow evening?"

For one moment Quincy contemplated writing his resignation on Mrs. Hawkland's pressed letter paper. He gave her a rueful smile, shaking his head, not trusting himself to speak.

"I see," she said sadly. "Well, next time you are in town, then."

"I shall call on you as soon as I may," Quincy said. He stood up, returning the watch to his pocket, and she walked with him to the front door.

"Thank you again for the roses," she said, extending her hand.

"Thank you for entertaining me," Quincy replied. He took her small hand in his and bent over it, daring to brush his lips against her soft skin. She smelled of roses, a sweet scent, not overpowering, but heady. He released her and straightened, to find her smiling at him.

"Come soon," she said, soft and low.

She opened the door and Quincy went out, turning to look at her as she pulled it shut. A last glimpse of warm brown eyes, a soft click, and he was locked out. He turned his back on the door, inhaling a deep breath. He felt as giddy as if he'd drunk a whole bottle of wine, instead of a dainty glassful. Running a hand over his face, he recalled his claim of shopping, and turned hasty steps toward the market to acquire proof in the form of vegetables and fresh meat.

Emma strolled barefoot through soft, white sand, her shoes and stockings in one hand, the other catching up the skirt of her second-best dress, which Aunt May had proclaimed suitable for hiking out of doors. She wore a wide-brimmed straw hat she had bought at Mrs. Brassier's "for working in the garden," also dismissed as dispensable by her aunt. She did not really need its protection; the sky was clouded over, a pearly gray that almost exactly matched the color of the Gulf of Mexico's restless waters. A light breeze blew in from the gulf, cooling her. Though it was August, with the water and air constantly stirring the heat was made much more tolerable than it would have been had they been inland.

Jamie walked beside her, keeping his own counsel. She had hoped he would talk to her, but so far they had walked mostly in silence.

"There it is," Jamie said, nodding toward a stand of tall grass ahead of them. "That's the edge of the bayou. There's another on the bay side, and when the water is high they run together."

"Does it have a name?"

"I expect so. I don't know it."

The tallest grass was taller than Emma. It grew in large clumps that seemed formidable obstructions, but Jamie led her around them to the edge of a marshy tidal creek. A flock of birds, bright pink with long, spatulate beaks, were feeding in the shallow water.

"Those are the exact color of the feathers on a hat Aunt May tried to get me to buy," Emma whispered. "I thought they were dyed!"

"Spoonbills," Jamie whispered back. "I saw a lot of them yesterday."

She followed him between clumps of low-lying grass and thorny brambles that clung to the sand, walking southward toward the gulf. Soon they passed away from the tall grass and Emma saw that they were nearer the seashore. She stood watching the sluggish creek, fat little minnows darting among gently waving water plants. Jamie pointed at a tall, blue-gray bird with long legs and long feathers, standing just within a patch of reeds.

"Heron?" Emma asked.

"Let me guess—May wanted you to buy a hat with those feathers as well."

Emma chuckled, nodding. She had actually been tempted by the long, graceful feathers, but having seen the living bird she was now glad she had not bought the hat.

"It is pretty here," she said as they walked on toward the beach. "The climate is better than Houston's, you must admit."

"I never denied that. It just isn't safe." He stopped and looked straight at her for the first time that morning. The frown that lately seemed always to be on his brow deepened, and he said in a choked voice, "Go home soon, Emma."

She was torn between concern at the trouble in his voice and annoyance that he should dictate to her. Annoyance won. She said, "I am able to look after myself."

"You don't know what you're talking about!" He strode a few steps toward the surf, then spun around and came back. "Emma, if the Yankees come here—anything could happen," he said, his voice low and angry. "*Anything*. Do you understand?"

"Surely they would respect civilian—"

"You can't count on that!"

"But there are rules—"

"*No!* You are wrong, there are *no rules*!" He was shouting, and the look on his face frightened Emma. He gripped her shoulders; his hands were shaking. She had never seen him like this.

"Try to believe that I know more about this than you do," he said, not as loud but unsteadily. "If there is fighting, you do *not* want to be here!"

"Jamie," Emma whispered. "Jamie, what's wrong? What's happened to you?"

His face bunched up in a scowl and he flung away from her, running down the beach back toward town. Emma followed a few strides, then turned her ankle in the sand and fell in an ungainly heap, her dress billowing about her. "Jamie," she called. *"Jamie!"*

Surely he would not leave her here alone. Panic gripped her; she scrambled to her feet. She could see Jamie, well down the beach, still running. She ran after him, but her skirts and the soft sand hampered her progress. She realized she could not catch him, stopped and flung her shoes down in disgust. Angry tears threatened; she slapped them away. She *could* look after herself. He was being unreasonable. She had always looked after herself. Hadn't she worked the ranch for the better part of the year?

Always with Gabe along, or Poppa. They never left her alone, not out on the range. They were always watching over her. It annoyed her but she had tolerated it, and for the same reason that she'd now panicked when Jamie left her; deep inside she knew that a woman alone was not safe. A young woman, like herself, an easy target. What means had she to defend herself? None. Poppa had taught her to shoot, but she had no weapon here. Did Jamie want her to bring a gun into Aunt May's house?

With a cry of frustration, she bent to pick up her shoes and stockings, then sat in the sand to put them on. Her hat had fallen back and the ribbon was choking her. She pulled it off and threw it at the waves. The breeze snatched it and blew it back; it fell in dry sand, a pitiful statement of her meager strength. She finished tying her shoes and got up. She wanted to leave the hat behind, just by way of doing something to appease her anger, but she knew Momma would think it wasteful and May would be pleased it was gone. She trudged over to get it, picked it up by the ribbon, and started after Jamie.

After a moment she realized he was walking back toward her. Relief gave way quickly to anger; she took it out on the beach in long strides, returning to a more ladylike pace only when they neared each other. He stopped a few feet away, and she stood waiting.

"I'm sorry," he said, gazing at her feet. "I apologize." His voice was calm now, if a bit stiff.

Some of her anger drained away. "Jamie—"

"I don't want to discuss it," he said. "Are you ready to go back?"

"Don't you dare order me around, James Russell," she said in a low, angry voice. "I am not one of your soldiers!"

He met her eyes then, and the look in them was something she'd never seen. Cold, bitter cold, and at the same time afire with hidden rage. "Don't worry," he said in a flat voice. "I won't be here to annoy you much longer."

Something was wrong, terribly wrong. Emma sought for something to say. She could think of nothing, though. She was frightened and felt like running until he looked away, out toward the ocean, releasing her from that dreadful gaze. She could see a muscle standing out in his tanned neck, and thought for the first time that her brother might be capable of hurting her. No, she did not know this Jamie. She didn't know him at all.

She drew herself up and took a breath, trying to regain her composure. Jamie seemed to have forgotten she was there. Maybe he wished she was not. She started back toward the city; he fell into step beside her and they walked, silent and uncomfortable, back to Galveston.

13

For Death is a simple thing/And he go from door to door
And he knock down some, and he cripple up some/And
he leave some here to pray.
— "Lord, Remember Me," Negro spiritual

The beach was ripped open by blossoms of red and yellow fire.
It was night, and in the darkness Jamie ran in sand that grabbed
at his feet, weighed down his legs, dragging him slower and
slower. Around him the ground was flung up by shells explod-
ing, raining sand and shrapnel down upon him, choking him
with smoke but he couldn't stop, he had to get to May's house
and get her and Emma to safety. Ahead darkness poured across
the sand—water—no, not water, a river of men. Yankees, black
in the darkness, faceless, flowing across the island, cutting him
off. He stopped running, helpless now as he stood watching the
mass of men flood the street, break down the door, fill the
house and run up the stairs.

Sitting up, he knew he had cried out. Sheets were tangled
around his legs and his nightshirt was skewed round his waist.
He sat for a moment, staring at the splash of moonlight that fell
across the floor from the open window. A faint breeze stirred
the lace curtain. Still breathing hard, he flung the bedsheet away
and got up.

His bedroom door was open to the hall, to let the gulf breezes
through from the windows at the back of the house. He walked
to his own window, where moonlight slanted from the west

along the street below, casting deep shadows in the porches and doorsills of genteel homes. The moon was the only source of light; the gasworks had been shut off during the evacuation two months before, and the town remained in darkness. Aunt May had shrugged away the inconvenience, saying she was accustomed to the light of lamps and candles, for Houston did not yet have a gasworks. To Jamie, it was another sign of just how insecure the city was.

He pushed aside the lace curtains and stepped out onto the balcony, from where he could see the quarter-moon yellowing in the west—gone stale, soon to vanish and leave Galveston in complete darkness. The bay was so close. He saw a lit lantern hanging in the rigging of a docked ship. Too close, too vulnerable. He frowned, gripping the balcony's handrail beneath the wisteria leaves, the white paint cool and slick against his palm.

Not much left of his furlough; soon he would have to report to the battery at Marshall. He would stop a day in Houston, tell Debray how dire was the situation in Galveston—but Debray knew. He'd been in charge here. If he could have helped Galveston, he would already have done so.

General Hébert, the department commander back in San Antonio, must know how things stood. Surely everything that could be done was being done. There were only so many guns and men available to defend the coast, after all. More troops were desperately needed for the defense of Richmond. Jamie's own battery was bound there eventually, as was Sibley's Brigade.

Unless they were diverted. He wondered if Reily and Green would support a redirection of their regiments to Galveston. He would mention it, suggest it, to them if to no one else. But first he would talk to Debray.

He wished he could convince Emma to leave now, but the look she had thrown at him on the beach was one he knew well. When she got in that mood there was no moving her, and it just about drove him crazy. She wasn't stupid but she could be stubborn as anything, and sometimes dug in her heels just for the sake of having her own way. If he pushed her too hard she would do it now, stay in Galveston longer for every word he spoke urging her to go.

He sighed, leaning away from the railing, stretching his arms out as he slowly sat on the balcony and gazed at the town between the posts and the vines. Emma thought he was over-reacting, but he knew he was not. Houston lay less than fifty miles inland, connected to the island by rail and by water. Put an army there and one could strike at San Antonio and at the capital. Galveston would be the perfect staging ground for an invasion of Texas.

What was wrong, she had asked. What was wrong with him?

Jamie pondered that, staring at the pale light bobbing aboard the ship in the harbor. What *was* wrong?

He knew one thing at least. He did not like who he had become; what he had become: a killer, a murderer. He didn't see how it could be other than a sin, no matter how dirty a Yankee was at the other end of the barrel.

But it wasn't one of the seven deadly sins, was it? He ran over them in his mind. No, just to kill did not seem to be a mortal sin, it was more the reason for the killing that was likely to jeopardize the soul. Anger, for instance. Simple anger, a cardinal sin. How many times in his life had he been guilty of that? A cough of laughter escaped him. There must be more to it than that, or everyone walking was doomed.

Maybe it had to do with *how* angry one was. Maybe killing in a just cause was not sinful. But whose cause was truly just, when both sides claimed God's patronage, and did that really matter to the souls of the men doing the killing? Causes brought men to battlefields, but they had little to do with what actually happened there.

Executioners received special absolution from blame for the killings they did. Not so the soldier.

He remembered the face of the man he had killed. It terrified him even now—the surprise, disbelief, shock—the last human thoughts before he became merely meat. Who had that man been?

Jamie gnawed at the back of his thumb. He had left the supposed safety of the quartermaster corps for the front line. In command of a section, he now had the power to kill dozens of men at once. He liked his work; he liked Sayers, he enjoyed drilling his men, working with the horses and keeping an eye out for their safety and health. Liking these things, he ought to be ready and willing to fulfill his duty. He ought to be ready to kill. If he was not, why did he like them?

His hands slid to his bare feet, and he rubbed at his toes. Perhaps he liked the artillery because it wasn't his finger on the trigger.

That made no sense, though. He would be just as responsible for the destructive power of his guns, regardless of whose hands pulled the lanyards. It should make no difference. But it did. Was he a coward, then? Was he hiding behind the men in his section? Shoving his sins onto their shoulders? Distanced from the horror by the chain of command?

He would not truly know until he took his guns into a fight. Cold flooded his limbs at the thought. Glimpses of horses and men screaming in terror and agony. He got up abruptly, pushing the thoughts away. They would only bring him more nightmares.

The moon had sunk, now. Galveston was all shadow. Even the lantern at the dock was gone—no, it was there, moving out into the harbor, almost too small to see. Jamie watched it grow smaller, wink a few times, then glide eastward, making for the channel. Another blockade runner, slipping out to sea. Another reason for the Yankees to come to Galveston.

Pensacola proved to be an excellent harbor, and the *Harriet Lane*'s crew began improving in health from the day of her arrival. A supply of fresh provisions did much toward this, but the location was also considerably healthier than the Mississippi's fever-breeding swamps.

Fresh sea breezes blew through the ship, cheering the sailors who were busy scrubbing every nook and cranny. Ships, being wooden, were apt to harbor bad smells that even constant vigilance could not eradicate completely. Quincy had his division at work, holystoning the berth deck, and the carpenter's mate had been filling the bilge with clean water and pumping it out daily.

While some of the machinery at the Pensacola shipyards had been destroyed by the Rebels as they had abandoned the place and retreated inland, much was intact, and plenty of materials were left. Copper and iron in abundance remained in the storehouses, and that had apparently clinched Commander Farragut's decision to make Pensacola his base of operations. That and the fact that his ships could lie in the calm waters of a harbor while they resupplied, instead of bouncing on the open sea. Farragut had already had the coal-hoisting machine, which saved hours and spared the coal-heavers back-breaking labor, moved here from Ship Island.

Becker came down from above. "First dog watch coming up. Your men finished?"

"Almost," Quincy told him.

"We've got a mail, came by the *Relief*. You've got letters."

"Thank you," Quincy said, trying to ignore the sudden heat in his veins. Had the *Relief* stopped at New Orleans? "I hope you had letters, too," he said.

"One from my mother," said Becker. "I'm saving it. It's thick. She rambles, bless her."

At four exactly Quincy sent his division to put away the holystones and bring out their mess chests, while he retired to the wardroom. Opening the narrow, slatted door to his cabin, he saw two letters lying on his bunk and snatched them up at once. One was from his brother, the other written in a feminine hand that gave his heart an odd lurch, even as he recognized the blue paper. It was from Miss Keller. Never before had he been disappointed to receive a letter from her. He cast both letters upon the bunk and pressed a hand to his forehead, then picked them up again and took them out to the wardroom table.

Gerard was there, working his way through a plate of fresh beef and boiled vegetables. Quincy sat across from him and opened the letter from Nathaniel. It was the one he'd been expecting for so long, written before Colonel Ellet's death, filled with descriptions of the Battle of Memphis and concern for the colonel's suffering. Quincy folded it up again and tucked it in his pocket, then picked up Miss Keller's letter.

The wardroom steward set a plate of food before him. Quincy took a bite of boiled cabbage and opened the letter. A pressed daisy fell out of it; he could smell a trace of its pungence.

Lea sat down beside Gerard and exchanged greetings with them both. "Letter from home?" he said, smiling.

Quincy nodded. Miss Keller wrote of Cincinnati, of their church choir, of meeting with the ladies of the town to knit socks for soldiers. She wrote of rumors that a gang of Confederate guerrillas, led by one John Hunt Morgan, were bent on making trouble in Kentucky. She wrote that she had visited his parents, found them in good health, and been asked by them to convey greetings and assurances that he would soon get a letter from them. His father was building a new gunboat for the navy, had been approached about building monitors but did not have the necessary machinery. Lastly she wrote of the dullness of town with so many young men away in service, and closed with the wish that Quincy and Nathaniel might both return home for a visit by Christmas.

Such a letter would ordinarily have been a treasure to him. He folded it carefully and put it away. He would read it again later, as he always did.

"No bad news, I hope?" said Lea, watching him.

"No, no. Just the usual chat." Quincy began eating, devoting his attention to the rare treat of carrots, onions, and fresh beef. He felt something warm brush his legs.

"Hello, Fitz," he said, looking down. The cat's gold eyes were wide and expectant. Quincy dangled a bit of gristle over his nose, and Fitz took it daintily in his teeth, then gulped it down whole.

"Well, I got bad news," Gerard said, getting up. "My sister thinks it would be amusing to volunteer on a hospital ship. I've got to write and disabuse her, only I'm out of paper."

"I have some," Quincy said.

Gerard shook his head. "I'll get it from Richardson. I want to buy some thread as well. If you'll excuse me," he said, nodding to Lea.

Quincy watched him go, then glanced at Lea, who had finished his meal and taken out a pencil and an old watch bill on which he was scribbling changes. The *Lane* had dropped off more sick in New Orleans and picked up more contrabands to replace them.

Peter came in to take their plates, asking if they wanted more. Quincy shook his head. When he was gone, he said, "Mr. Lea, may I ask you something?"

Lea looked up, gray eyes inquiring. "Certainly," he said.

Quincy found it hard to hold his gaze. He looked down at the tabletop, rubbed a finger over a scar from someone's knife. "I have done something that—that I thought perfectly right at the time, but now I am uncertain about it."

Lea put down his pencil and folded his hands atop the watch bill. "Yes?"

"I visited Mrs. Hawkland in New Orleans."

"Oh. Was she well?"

"Quite well, yes." Quincy felt a blush beginning to creep up his neck. "She asked me to write a note for her, saying she and her husband should be allowed to sell cotton in order to feed their slaves," he said in a rush.

Lea's brows rose. "And did you?"

"Yes. I didn't see that it could do any harm."

He gazed anxiously at Lea. A glint of amusement came into the XO's eyes.

"I don't see that it can, either, though it might occasion remark."

Quincy swallowed, now thoroughly discomfited. He must have been mad to visit her—a Southerner, however loyal, and a married woman—as he had done. In secret, no less. What a fool he had been.

"She must be very charming," Lea said softly.

"Yes," Quincy said. He sat up straighter. "Have I been disloyal?"

Lea appeared to ponder this for a moment, then smiled. "I don't think so. Unwise, perhaps, but it does not constitute disloyalty. Unless," he added with a nod toward the pressed flower lying on the table, "you refer to your fair correspondent."

Quincy looked down at the daisy and picked it up, aware that this thought had been niggling at the back of his mind. His fingers caressed the faded petals, and he thought of the less faded rose that lay in his breast pocket. Miss Keller was all sweetness, all innocence, all good. Mrs. Hawkland made his blood run hot.

"I would not trouble myself about it overmuch, if I were you," Lea said, picking up his pencil again. "Chance encounters are a part of navy life. Though perhaps you should think carefully before doing any more favors for the lady."

Quincy nodded, sighing. "Yes. Thank you, sir." He felt restless all at once. He got up, pushed in his chair and went to the companionway. He glanced back at Lea, who nodded and returned to his paperwork. Quincy hastened up to the deck, where he hoped the fresh air would help clear his head.

The train stood ready to leave for Houston, wisps of steam curling from its smokestack. The day was hot and windless, making Jamie uncomfortable in his coat and hat. In his pocket were his ticket and a letter granting him passage on the stage to Marshall, sent by Mr. Lawford under cover of a brief note stating that they were a gift of thanks, and refusal to use them would deal a mortal wound to the giver's pride. Jamie detected a note of irony in this statement, and liked Lawford the better for it. He conceded that to carry through his intention of refusing Lawford's help in getting to Marshall would be churlish. Cocoa had already been sent there in the tender care of A and M Transport, so he might as well allow himself to be transported as well.

Aunt May and Emma had come with him to the station, driven by Rupert in May's newly purchased buggy. The stout old horse between the shafts was not swift, but steady enough.

Jamie set his valise down on the platform and hugged his aunt, careful not to crush her dress—a confection of white trimmed with red ribbon. She wore a matching bonnet adorned with lace and bunches of cherries. He kissed her good-bye, then turned to his sister.

Emma looked neat and graceful in her new clothes, a blue-and-white striped shirt tucked into the waist of a black skirt. Her hat was stylish, small and made of straw with not a feather, flower, or cherry but only a black ribbon to trim it. A matching ribbon was tied in a small bow at her collar. She hung back a little, and glanced warily at him.

They had not talked since their visit to the beach, except for one strained dinner conversation of which May had borne most of the burden. Jamie was sorry he'd allowed himself to get upset with Emma, but that did not change his opinion that she was unwise to stay here. Now was not the time to raise the subject, however. He took an awkward step toward her, brushed a kiss against her cheek, and said, "Bye, Em."

"Good-bye," she said, a small smile wavering on her lips. "Give Cocoa a hug for me."

"I will. You look wonderful," he added as he picked up his valise.

"Write to us, Jamie dear," said Aunt May. "We shall miss you so! I will tell Eva all you have done for us."

"Which is not much," he said with a rueful smile. "Here comes the conductor. Good-bye. Be careful!"

Their farewells followed him into the car, where he found a window seat from which he could see them. They waited on the platform until the train began to move, waving their kerchiefs. He opened the window and waved back until they were out of sight, then sat back with a sigh.

Leaving Galveston brought no relief. Only when he learned that Emma was home again would he be easier in his mind. He hoped Aunt May would be persuaded to leave as well, but at least he didn't have to worry too much about her. She had Lawford to look after her.

The train rolled smartly along. Jamie changed seats to peer at Fort Hébert as they passed onto the mainland from the bridge. The fort was yet another earthwork, this one rather larger than the rest, and boasting more cannon. He could just see the guns from the window, and the rows of tents where troops were camped. The area, Virginia Point, was flat and somewhat marshy, with tough grasses growing in the sand and not much else. There being little else to look at, he settled himself to sleep and succeeded in passing most of the journey in slumber.

In Houston he went in search of accommodation, passing up the Capitol Hotel for a more modest establishment that was better suited to his means. Here he left his valise and obtained directions to army headquarters, to which he set out without delay.

It was late Friday afternoon and the usual bustle prevailed, clerks and staff officers hurrying to finish the week's business. Jamie managed to get past the first line of defense, but was stopped by an acting assistant adjutant's clerk whose desk barred the way to the inner offices. The clerk was an eddy of calm in the maelstrom, a tall, thin, Roman-nosed fellow who steadily took page after page of correspondence from a stack of daunting proportions, marking each with a note and setting it into one of several piles.

"I'd like to see Colonel Debray," Jamie told him after making his way to the front of the line and identifying himself.

"I can schedule an appointment for you on Tuesday." The clerk didn't pause in his work, or even look up.

"I'm only in town for tonight. Is there any way I could see him today? Just for a minute. I was a student of his in San Antonio."

"You and half the soldiers in Texas," said the clerk, unimpressed. "I can get him a message if you like."

Jamie gave it up, and stepped aside to scribble a note on a page torn from his pocket notebook. He thought he should condense his concerns into one or two straightforward sentences, a task more difficult than might have been supposed. "Dear Colonel, send more guns and troops to Galveston now" seemed abrupt. He frowned, gnawing the end of his pencil.

"Well, well. Look what's washed up on our shore."

Jamie glanced up, knowing before he did who had spoken. "Major Owens," he said, his heart sinking as he stood to shake the hand offered him by the major.

14

In many instances, their return has been rendered necessary pecuniarily, as they can live at their own houses at less expense than elsewhere. We therefore found a large portion of the families once more at their homes in the Island City, and others are returning almost daily, so that the city no longer presents the deserted appearance that has made it so desolate during the past summer.

  —Mr. Willard Richardson, *Galveston News*

"Howdy, Russell," Owens said, grinning. "On your way home from your furlough?"

"On my way to Marshall, actually," Jamie told him. "The battery is ordered there."

"And from there to Richmond? You'll have fun getting across the Mississippi." Owens opened a cigar box on the clerk's desk. It was empty, and he glared at the clerk, who seemed not to notice him. He shut the box with a snap. "You got plans for the evening?" he said to Jamie. "I know a little place that serves a neat dinner."

"Well, I—"

"Or maybe you've set up a discreet rendevous," Owens said with a lewd chuckle.

"No," Jamie said, annoyed.

"Good! Got a couple of things to ask you about, we can talk over dinner. I'm just on my way now, if you're ready."

Jamie sighed. "Give me a minute." He leaned against the wall, scrawled a few lines, then handed his note to the Roman-nosed clerk. It wasn't inspired, but he doubted he'd have much influence over Colonel Debray in any case. It was true that he'd been a student at Debray's academy in San Antonio, up until the war had begun and Debray had closed it to go into the military, but he wasn't sure how well the Frenchman would remember him. At least he had tried, he thought, stifling a sigh.

He followed Owens out of the building and up to Travis Street, turning toward the Buffalo Bayou and the older part of town. Jamie was annoyed at himself for agreeing to go with Owens. He disliked the man, but it would be awkward to back out now, and it was never a good idea to offend a superior officer.

The tavern Owens took him to was small and rather dingy. Situated on a soggy bit of ground near the bayou, it smelled of dampness and decay. This did not enhance Jamie's appetite, but since he had eaten nothing since breakfast he still welcomed the platter of sliced beef and mashed turnips set before him by the taverner's wife. The food was surprisingly good, as was the beer Owens ordered for them both. They had the place to themselves, and Jamie suspected it was somewhat early in the evening for the tavern's usual clientele.

"Care for some entertainment tonight?" Owens said. "There is plenty to do in Houston. Couple of good cock-pits, or a dog fight if you prefer."

"No, thanks," Jamie said.

"Well, there's cards or dice, too, if that's your game. Or I can arrange for some feminine companionship."

Jamie gazed at him, exerting himself to keep his expression pleasant. Why, he wondered, was Owens bent on entertaining him? Ever since Valverde, the man had taken every opportunity to obtrude upon his life in a way Jamie neither wanted nor sought.

"Thank you anyway," Jamie said, "but I've got to make an early start tomorrow."

"Suit yourself. But I know a pretty little piece that would take right good care of you. Might be just what you need."

Jamie cut a bite of meat and chewed it in silence. Owens made quite a habit of telling him what he needed. He realized he was no longer hungry, and pushed the plate away. He took a swallow of beer and watched Owens mop up the gravy on his own plate with a bit of bread.

"Haven't seen your sister in town, Russell," Owens said.

"She isn't here," Jamie told him. "What brought you to Houston, by the way?"

"Working for Scurry. He's getting his promotion to General, and I'm representing him here. He's on sick leave at the moment. Looks like he may get command of old Sibley's brigade."

"Give him my congratulations."

"I will do that," Owens said. He poured more beer for them both from an earthenware pitcher. "So, has your sister gone home?"

"No. She's visiting family."

"Visiting family?" Owens gave him a skeptical look. Jamie saw no reason to enlighten him further.

"Visiting family," Owens repeated, musing. He finished the beer in his glass and refilled it. "You know, where I come from, that phrase has a particular meaning. A young lady who is visiting family is usually with some relations who live quite out of the way. She might be expected to stay away—oh, three months or more."

Jamie narrowed his eyes, unsure what Owens was getting at, but sensing that he would not like it. He watched Owens drink a third of his beer at one swallow and wipe his sandy mustache with the back of his hand.

"And then," Owens continued, "when she comes home, she has with her a dear little baby that someone abandoned on the church doorstep, or perhaps it belonged to a poor, starving couple that couldn't keep it, and she out of the goodness of her heart has decided to take it in." Owens's eyes glinted at Jamie over the rim of his glass. "That's what visiting family means back at home."

Jamie met his gaze, feeling his gut sink. "Well, that's not what it means out here," he said, his voice stony. "Out here it means what it sounds like."

"That so?" Owens said, smiling as he stroked the ends of his mustache. "Where is this family your sister's visiting?"

Jamie's hands clenched into fists beneath the table. Owens was trying to goad him into revealing where Emma was. Well, it wouldn't work, however many veiled insults the major chose to cast. Jamie sat back in his chair, deliberately relaxing his hands and laying them atop his knees.

"I don't believe she would want me to tell you," he said.

"No?" Owens said. "Well, you're probably right. I do know how very afflicted she was by Captain Martin's demise, but of course it is too late for her to be visiting family on his account. That would mean she must have found some other fellow to keep her company in his absence—"

Jamie stood up abruptly, his chair scraping on the plank floor. "That's a filthy lie," he said, his voice hoarse with loathing. He swallowed, and in a clearer tone added, "I suggest you take it back."

"You going to make me, boy?" Owens drawled. His grin was sinister in the half-dark of the tavern. After a second he laughed, a low chuckle that said more than words could about his contempt.

Something snapped inside Jamie and he struck without warning, knocking Owens sideways out of his chair and nearly falling on top of him. Owens rose up with a swing that caught Jamie on the chin and lit up his head like a muzzle-flash. He stumbled back, tripping over the chair, and could not get his balance before Owens was on top of him, grappling, trying to get an arm around his neck.

Somewhere a woman was shouting but Jamie had no time for her; Owens was trying to strangle him. He managed to duck his chin enough to protect his neck, and jabbed his elbow into Owens's gut a few times. Owens shifted, loosening his grip a little and Jamie bit down hard on his arm, tasting the wool of the sleeve, feeling the line of gold braid against his tongue. Owens let out a startled oath and broke away, then backhanded Jamie so hard it knocked him down and sent white spots flashing in his head. Before he could get up Owens kicked him twice, hard, in the gut.

Pain rolled through him in waves. His ears were ringing, dimming the angry woman's voice, the hasty footsteps, the slamming door. Jamie tried once to move, but it made him so nauseated he stopped and just closed his eyes, waiting for whatever the ending would be.

Emma ambled along the Strand with her aunt, dutifully dressed for the promenade in her Zouave jacket ensemble. Aunt May wore a pale yellow dress embroidered with morning glories and a lace shawl with long fringe, and carried a Chinese parasol to protect her complexion from the sun. Daisy followed a few steps behind them with a small wicker basket for marketing. Emma addressed one or two remarks to the slave, which she answered in brief, discouraging syllables. Aunt May did not speak to Daisy except when giving her instructions, and Emma soon gave up the attempt to be friendly, as it appeared neither Daisy not her aunt welcomed it. Instead she listened to Aunt May chatter and let her gaze wander between the buildings, glimpses of the nearby wharves, and the other people out walking in downtown Galveston. Their dawdling pace enabled her to take in her surroundings in detail. She noted, for example, a small, boxy cupola atop the Hendley Building, which at three stories of stout brick was the tallest building in town. The view from the cupola must take in the entire city, she thought. How she longed to go up and see, but when she suggested it, Aunt May declined.

"It looks like the merest shack, dear. I doubt it would be comfortable."

"We needn't stay long," Emma said, coaxing. "Don't you want to see the whole island at once?"

"No, I cannot say that I do. You are seeing the best parts of it from right here on the ground. Oh, good afternoon, Mrs. Dinwiddie! What a pleasure to see you. May I introduce my niece, Miss Russell?"

Civilities duly exchanged with Mrs. Dinwiddie, who reminded Emma ever so slightly of a stuffed pigeon, they passed on. Emma paused to look into a shop window filled with souvenirs made out of seashells.

"May we walk out to the gulf this afternoon?" she asked. "I do so love to look at the ocean."

"That would be delightful, but not today, I fear," Aunt May said, idly twirling her parasol. "I have arranged for Mr. Strythe to come at two and give you a music lesson. You met him the other day, remember? Our neighbor to the east?"

"Yes," Emma said without enthusiasm as they walked on. "I still do not see why I must take music lessons. I can't sing a note. Even the pastor has asked me not to join the choir."

"I promised dear Eva that you would acquire a little polish, love, and since the Female Seminary has *closed*," said May, a note of annoyance entering her voice, "and the Miss Cobbs have sent all their students *home*, I must fall back upon private tutors. Do not worry, my dear. Mr. Strythe is highly accomplished."

"I don't doubt it," Emma said, watching two young girls pass down the far side of the street with their mother. Their clothes were plain, but clean and neat. The taller of the girls carried a basket from which peeped a spotted kitten.

"Do not smile at inferior persons, Emma dear. You may give them a civil nod if you wish."

Surprised, Emma looked at her aunt. "How do you know they are inferior? Perhaps they are only poor."

"It is nearly always the same thing," said Aunt May.

Emma stopped, incredulous. Aunt May continued a few steps

before noting her absence. "What is it, dear?" she said, turning around and tilting her head at a pretty angle.

"I think I will write to my mother this afternoon," Emma said slowly. "It is time I thought of returning home."

"Nonsense," May protested. "Why, we have only just settled in!"

"My help is needed on the ranch."

"But I need you here, dear! Your mother understands that. I cannot let you go before Albert returns."

"You are moved in now," Emma said. "And you will soon have plenty of company, if I may judge by all the people to whom you have introduced me this morning."

"Yes, but—oh, dear!" Aunt May handed her parasol to Daisy, who held it so as to shade her while she reached out both hands to Emma. "I was keeping it a surprise, but—well, Emma, I am planning a party in your honor. On September sixth, when the moon is full. You must stay until then!"

Emma resumed walking, keeping her hands clasped inside the wide sleeves of her jacket. She was annoyed, but she was also acutely aware of the generosity Aunt May had shown her. Her mother would urge her to stay, she knew.

"I wish you would add a feather or two to that hat, dear," May said lightly, walking beside her. "It makes your face look so severe! A flower, or perhaps some grapes—"

"I don't want my hat to look like my marketing basket," Emma said gruffly. She lengthened her stride, her instinct to escape overruling the knowledge that her diminutive aunt would be forced almost to run to keep up. She frowned at the ground before her feet, in consequence of which she did not see two gentlemen approaching until she had nearly collided with one of them.

"Oh, I beg your pardon!" she said to the tall man before her. He reached out a hand to steady her and the corners of his eyes crinkled in a smile. He was some few years older than Aunt May, she thought, though still handsome, with large, dark eyes and a long, straight nose.

"We did not see you coming, I fear," he said kindly. "You see, we have just stepped out of doors."

"That's kind of you, but I fear it was my fault," Emma said. "I was not minding where I walked."

"You must forgive my niece, General," Aunt May said, catching up to them. "She has a great deal of energy!"

"Mrs. Asterly!" cried the gentleman, breaking into a smile. "How delightful of you to visit, and how brave of you to come in these trying times."

"Fiddle," May declared. "I don't believe the Yankee blockade will amount to a thing. Daisy, my fan please." She paused to cool herself, then added, "Furthermore, I am not visiting, I am now a resident."

For a second the gentleman looked concerned, then his smile broadened and he bowed over May's hand. "You multiply my delight, dear lady," he said.

"Thank you," May said, favoring him with a coy look from beneath her hat brim. "Will you allow me to present my niece Miss Russell? Emma, this is General Sidney Sherman."

"General Sherman? Oh!" Emma hastened to curtsey as the general bowed. She glanced up at him as she rose. "I have ridden in a train drawn by your locomotive."

"Have you indeed?" he said, smiling again. "I hope it served you well. Please allow me to introduce my son, Lieutenant Sidney Sherman."

The younger gentleman, who had been hanging back, now stepped forward and bowed to Aunt May, then took the hand Emma offered with a shy smile. He was very like his father, though his features were finer and his eyes did not slope quite as much at the outside corners. He wore the gray uniform trimmed in red that Emma knew designated artillery service.

"How do you do?" she said, returning his smile. "My brother is in the artillery also."

"Is he?" said the younger Sherman in a quiet, firm voice. "Is his hair a bit lighter than yours? For if so I think I met him last week. He came round looking over all our defenses."

"Such as they are," put in General Sherman.

"Yes, that must have been him," Emma said. "He is very concerned for our safety."

"Rightly so, I fear," said the lieutenant.

"Pooh," said Aunt May. "General Sherman, I have just been telling my niece she is to have a party next month. You and your son will attend it, I hope?"

The two men exchanged a glance. "We are at your bidding, ma'am," said the general, placing a hand over his heart and bowing from the waist. "But why only a party? Surely such a lovely young lady deserves no less than a ball."

"Silly man," said Aunt May, furling her fan and playfully rapping him with it. "My house does not have a ballroom, nor parlors big enough for dancing."

"Then you must have it at my hotel," said General Sherman. "I will lend you the ballroom for the evening."

"General! Oh, no, you must be joking," said Aunt May, her face lit with pleasure as she shook her head. "That is far too generous."

"Not at all," he said. "I am afraid there is little use for the place otherwise. Galveston has been so dull this summer. But a ball would be just the thing to liven us up." He looked at Emma, eyes twinkling. "You do not mind, do you, Miss Russell?"

Emma, who had only danced at husking bees and the like, had been feeling increasing alarm throughout the discussion. She could not bring herself to hurt General Sherman's feelings, though, and she was conscious of having behaved badly toward her aunt. Thus she mustered a smile, dropped a tiny curtsey, and said, "It sounds delightful."

Aunt May rewarded her with a kiss on the cheek, which she had to stand on tiptoe to deliver. Nothing would do but that General Sherman must join them for luncheon to assist Aunt

May with plans for the ball. The general cheerfully abandoned his intended business for this pursuit, and Emma found herself escorted by Lieutenant Sherman while Aunt May, bubbling with schemes, leaned on the general's arm ahead of them. Emma glanced back at Daisy, who followed patiently, her face unreadable. She began to find the maid's silent omnipresence unnerving.

"I hope it will not be a great inconvenience," Emma ventured to say to her escort.

The younger Sherman smiled. "Father likes this sort of thing, and he's right, the summer has been very—dismal."

"Do you think the danger is real? Ought we not to be planning parties?"

A slight crease marred his brow. "If you are to remain on the island, I don't suppose it matters much whether there are parties or not. And, yes, the danger is real."

Emma accepted this with a nod. "I see," she said.

"Do not be afraid," he added. "We will have warning, if the Federals come. We should be able to get you to the mainland before anything unpleasant happens."

"Thank you," Emma said. She walked on, listening to Aunt May's happy chatter and thinking that she owed Jamie an apology.

The stage reached Marshall shortly after five o'clock, and Jamie stepped down with relief. Between his bruises and the jolting of the coach, he had passed an interminable and amazingly uncomfortable journey. More than once he had wished that the Galveston, Houston and Henderson Railroad had already been built out to Henderson, instead of just to Houston. It would have enabled him to make most of the trip by rail.

He had not seen Owens again, nor had he thought it wise to present himself to Debray with a plum-colored lump on his jaw. He had come to consciousness with the taverner's wife holding a wet bar-rag to his face. She had helped him to a chair, then demanded he pay for the meal he and Owens had eaten. Not being up to further arguments, Jamie had given her a dollar and stumbled to his hotel to collapse.

He spent the stage journey trying to remember exactly why he had committed the really idiotic mistake of attacking Owens. The insult to Emma had only been part of it; ordinarily words didn't bother him, but Owens's persistence had made him suspect that the major might not stop at vulgar talk. It was clear Owens didn't respect Emma, and Jamie couldn't help worrying it was because he had seen her at the ranch in her work clothes, and come to the conclusion that she genuinely did not deserve respect.

Jamie's face burned at that thought. He couldn't bear to have anyone think his sister was loose. Miserably stubborn and wilful, yes, but she *was* respectable. Jamie was absolutely certain of that.

He consulted his watch and decided not to seek out the battery's camp right away. He was not due to report until morning, so he might as well enjoy his last evening of freedom. He would get something to eat in town, maybe write home. He had spent much of the journey thinking about Emma, and felt he should tell their parents of his concerns. He did not want to frighten Momma, of course, but to avoid mentioning his fears about Galveston would be to imply that he felt complacent about Emma's remaining there, and that wasn't true. Whether he would mention Owens was a different question.

As he stood by the coach's boot waiting to claim his valise, a voice near him said, "Lieutenant Russell? Message for Lieutenant Russell."

"Here," Jamie said, reaching into his pocket for a coin. The messenger, a clerk from the stage office, handed him a folded note and accepted the penny with a nod of thanks.

The note proved to be from Mr. Lawford. Brief as usual, it merely informed him that Lawford had booked a hotel room for him and hoped for the pleasure of his company at dinner.

Cheered by the prospect of one last night in a comfortable bed, Jamie tucked the note into his pocket and, after collecting his valise, proceeded to the hotel on Marshall's main square.

The town was handsome, its wide streets and lush trees giving it a sense of grace that Jamie had not noted in Houston. A white-pillared county courthouse faced the square in which a central garden rioted with flowers. Other fine buildings, public and private, bespoke a successful commerce. There was a rail station not far away from the stage stop—terminus of a track that ran eastward to Caddo Lake and served as a connection to Shreveport.

Lawford had selected the finest hotel in town, of course. Jamie fought down an impulse to decline this fresh bit of lavish hospitality, and inquired at the front desk for his key. It would be all too easy, he knew, to grow accustomed to the thick carpeting, polished wood, and fine appointments of such places. His room was luxurious, and he was sorely tempted to lie down at once on the large featherbed. Instead he sent for hot water, took out his hairbrush and razor, and commenced repairing his appearance as best he could.

He had just finished dressing when a knock fell on the door. Going to open it, he found Mr. Lawford outside, wearing an elegant suit of dark green broadcloth and a slate-colored waistcoat.

"Good evening," said Lawford, shaking hands. "I asked to be notified of your arrival. Why, what happened?" he added, peering at Jamie's chin.

"I got stupid," Jamie said. "Please come in."

"Actually, if you are ready for dinner, I came to collect you. You haven't dined, have you?"

"No, I came straight here."

Lawford smiled. "Good. The chef here is the best in town. I have another guest, if you do not mind—a business associate."

"Not at all," Jamie said, picking up his key from a table by the bed. "Lead on."

The dining room was a long, elegant gallery with high ceilings supported by white Doric columns, walls papered in light peach, and pale gold drapes to the windows. Sculpted carpets in matching tones of white and gold covered the floor. Chandeliers set all this lightness aglow, making Jamie think of where he would most likely take his dinner the next day—in a tent—with a smile.

"Ah," Lawford said as the maitre d'hotel led them toward a table where a solitary lady sat. "My guest is ahead of us. Lieutenant Russell, may I introduce you to Mrs. Hawkland?"

15

None but those who have experienced it can know the excitement of a chase at sea—a sailor's pride in his vessel, his desire of coming up with the enemy, the exhilaration of the motion, the dashing of the waves, and the quick skill required to take advantage of every favorable circumstance of wind and wave; all combine to make it as intensely exciting to those deeply interested as any thing can be.

—Lieutenant Roswell H. Lamson, U. S. Navy

Jamie had not expected to be dining with a lady. He recovered himself enough to bow, feeling a flush of embarrassment over his battered condition, but she showed only the slightest flicker of reaction before greeting him with a welcoming smile.

"How do you do, Lieutenant?" she said in a sweet voice, holding out a hand. Jamie took it briefly in his, bowed over it, and released it.

"He does pretty well for having just got off the stage, I would say," Lawford declared, seating himself. "Was it a miserable ride?"

"I don't know what you mean, sir," Jamie replied in a voice of indignation as he took his own place. "Why, the A and M Stage Line runs only the most modern coaches!"

"Sycophant," Lawford said cheerfully. "I will wager you hated every mile."

"Not more than every other mile," Jamie protested, then grinned and added, "Finish your railroad."

"Oh, we will some day. Just now we have other concerns," Lawford said, glancing at Mrs. Hawkland.

The waiter arrived with soup, and Jamie, mindful of Momma's discipline, waited for Mrs. Hawkland to begin before attacking his own portion. He was very hungry and at first made little contribution to the others' polite conversation, but he stole a glance or two at Mrs. Hawkland.

She was about Susan's age he thought, but where his elder sister might be called good-looking at best, Mrs. Hawkland was enchanting. Her auburn hair gleamed in the candlelight, spilling over her shoulders from a coronet of rosebuds. Her burgundy dress, he knew from his unwilling education at Aunt May's hands, was of the latest fashion and undoubtedly expensive. It also revealed an alluring expanse of white shoulders. Her eyes, big and dark, gazed frankly at Jamie when she caught him looking at her. He returned his attention to his plate, not wishing to be thought rude. From the corner of his eye he thought he saw her smile.

By the time the soup was replaced with roasted chicken and a bottle of chilled champagne, the edge was off his hunger and he made an effort to attend to the conversation.

"Are there still Federal boats at your plantations?" Lawford asked Mrs. Hawkland.

"Not at present," she replied. "They went down to Baton Rouge for the fight, and have not yet returned."

"But you expect they will."

She nodded. Jamie had heard about the conflict at Baton Rouge a few days before, during which the Confederate navy had lost the *Arkansas*, one of its best vessels. He would have to get hold of a newspaper and read about it.

"Then they will block you from crossing more cotton," Lawford said, frowning.

"I have made a request, which I believe will be granted, for a permit to sell cotton," said Mrs. Hawkland, cutting a small bite of chicken.

"To Northern interests in New Orleans, no doubt," said Lawford in disgust.

"Yes," she agreed, a languid smile on her lips, "and with that in hand, and some papers betokening such a transaction, we should be able to satisfy any inquiries regarding the loading of cotton at our landing."

"Ah." Lawford smiled. "Very good. How soon may I send a steamer?"

"Wait for word from me," said the lady. "I must first secure the permit. We do not want to arouse suspicions that my husband and I are anything but loyal."

Lawford glanced up at Jamie, and explained, "The Hawklands have cotton to sell. We get the best price for it by bringing it up the Red River and taking it to Mexico."

"Oh," Jamie said. "I see."

"Not merely the best price, Mr. Lawford," said Mrs. Hawkland. "Did you not say we could trade cotton directly for arms?"

"Yes, I am negotiating a deal of that nature," Lawford said.

"What sort of arms?" Jamie asked, his interest caught.

"Rifles and powder from France," Lawford told him. "The army has a pressing need for them, as I understand it."

"Yes," Jamie nodded. "Our brigade was forced to sell their weapons to the Mexicans for food on the way home from New Mexico."

"Well, we should soon be able to re-equip them," said Mrs. Hawkland, smiling.

"That's very good of you," Jamie said, looking thoughtfully at her.

She tilted her head, and a curl of hair brushed the strand of tiny pearls at her neck. "You seem surprised," she said.

"I am wondering what inspired you to go to so much trouble," Jamie answered.

She gazed at him, a slow smile curving her pretty mouth. "We are patriots, Mr. Russell." She picked up her wineglass and sipped.

"Always agreeable to combine patriotism with profit," Jamie said softly.

She pierced him with a sharp look, then laughed. "True enough. Your friend is perceptive, Mr. Lawford."

"He is jaded by service as a quartermaster," Lawford replied. "May I fill your glass?"

"Please."

The conversation revolved to more general topics, and Jamie upheld his part in it through roast lamb and claret, wilted greens, and peach tart. Coffee and brandy were served together, the gentlemen electing at Mrs. Hawkland's request to remain with her while they sipped their liquor.

Jamie liked her, he decided. She was certainly motivated by self-interest, but she need not have gone to the additional trouble and risk of arranging a trade for arms. No doubt the transaction would increase her profit dramatically. Still, it would be a godsend to the army, if things went as Lawford had planned.

At length Mrs. Hawkland rose to take leave of her host, and Jamie and Lawford stood to bid her farewell. "Thank you for the excellent dinner, Mr. Lawford," she said, offering him her hand.

"A pleasure, ma'am, as always."

"And thank you for introducing me to Lieutenant Russell," she added, drawing a pair of lace gloves through her fingers as she gazed at Jamie. "I would say that I hoped to see you again, Mr. Russell, but I fear I am leaving tomorrow."

"A sad loss to Marshall's society," Jamie said, imitating Lawford's bow.

She smiled, her eyes dancing with amusement. "Perhaps I'll return," she said softly.

She turned to allow Mr. Lawford to drape her shawl about her shoulders, and one of the gloves slipped from her hand. Jamie picked it up.

"Thank you," she said, her fingertips brushing his as she accepted it. She smiled once more, dropped a slight curtsey, and moved away. Jamie watched her go, the elegant, expensive gown gliding over the pale carpet.

"Another brandy?" Lawford asked.

"Thank you, no," Jamie said, glancing at him. "I should walk round to the camp and let them know I've arrived."

"I'll come outside with you," Lawford said. He reached into his pocket for a silver cigar case which he opened and offered to Jamie, who shook his head.

They walked through the hotel's lobby and through the front doors open to the warm evening. Gaslight illuminated the square. Lawford paused on the steps to trim his cigar with a pair of silver clippers and light it with a lucifer from a matching silver case. The aroma was fragrant. Finest Havana, Jamie knew from having handed out multitudes of such cigars during his tenure as quartermaster. Tobacco oiled many wheels.

"Your horse is doing well," Lawford said, stepping into the street to cross to the center of the square. "Pretty little mare. I looked in on her when I arrived."

"Thank you, sir," Jamie said, going along. "Thank you for bringing her out. You've been more than generous."

"It was nothing," Lawford said. "How is May?"

Jamie caught himself frowning and made an effort to smile. "Well enough. She'd like you to be there, of course."

"I would prefer it, too," Lawford said. "Alas, I have obligations that will keep me away a little longer."

Jamie nodded, then glanced sidelong at Lawford. "Mrs. Hawkland is an interesting woman. Is her husband not traveling with her?"

"He remains at their plantation, keeping an eye on the river. It is strategically located, you see."

"Ah." Jamie nodded. "Not many ladies would be so active in . . ."

"Blockade running?" Lawford supplied.

"I thought that involved ships."

"It does, eventually. Foreign ships, out of Mexico. That, I am sure you have guessed, is why I traveled to Brownsville recently."

"Isn't it risky?"

"Yes, but worthwhile. In more ways than one."

Jamie looked at him, wondering if he meant the profitability, or service to the Confederacy, or something else. Lawford smiled.

"I am leaving tomorrow as well," Lawford said, stopping beside a park bench. "Taking a shipment of cattle to Shreveport. I hope to see you again when I return."

"I expect I'll be here," Jamie said. "Come watch the battery at drill, if you can."

"That I shall."

They shook hands and parted genially. Jamie mused over the evening as he started toward the battery's camp outside of town. Interesting that Lawford had involved himself in trading with foreign powers. He wondered if Aunt May knew about it, then decided she probably did not. It was the sort of thing Lawford would not want her to trouble her head about.

He glanced over his shoulder at Lawford, who sat peacefully smoking on the bench. Maybe he was just tired and irritable, but he also found it in him to wonder if Aunt May had met Mrs. Hawkland.

Quincy lay on his bunk, trying to get a few hours' sleep before his next watch. The bunk, situated atop the cupboards in his quarters, was level with the tiny port which was open to catch whatever breeze might favor them. The night was still hot, though, and not even the gentle pitch and roll of the ship could lull him. The *Lane* was on blockade now, cruising outside Mobile Bay as part of the offshore squadron, so at least they were on the open sea and away from the unhealthy climate of the Mississippi. The crew was mostly well at last, though Dr. Penrose was keeping a sharp watch over them. He had told the officers to be on the lookout for any sign of jaundice, as he had just received word that the supply ship *Rhode Island*, which had provisioned the *Lane* a week before, might have brought yellow fever from Key West. Of the myriad scourges the navy was subject to, yellow jack struck more fear into the hearts of sailors than most. It was fast, virulent, and painful. It had raged in New Orleans in 1858, killing thousands.

Quincy had his own fever to cope with; a fever of the mind. Thoughts of Mrs. Hawkland distracted him day and night. It was as if she were an addiction, and he was like a drunkard locked away from his wine, or like the poor crew would be in a few days when their grog was discontinued. He was not in love with her, he thought, yet he could not stop thinking about her, and he was conscious of an irrational hope that the *Lane* would be sent back to New Orleans. He had relived his visit to Chartres Street over and over, imagining himself staying to dinner, behaving in a manner that he knew was despicable, throwing honor to the winds and reveling in wicked licentiousness.

It was useless; sleep eluded him. He eased himself off the bunk and stood leaning against the cupboards. There was no moon, but his eyes were adjusted to the feeble starlight. Catching sight of himself in the mirror on the wall beside the door, he saw a dim, shadowy, shirtless form with disheveled hair. He took his shirt down from its peg and put it on, then shrugged into his coat, put on shoes and went up on deck.

They were cruising westward on a broad reach with a light wind on the starboard quarter. The *Lane* was robed in all her plain sail, and her wheels moved slowly, a small amount of steam being kept on to keep them from being dead weight and slowing her.

The captain was up, talking softly with Becker on the bridge. Wainwright nodded to Quincy to join them.

"Couldn't sleep?" he asked.

Quincy nodded. "It's stuffy below."

They stood watching over the ship, listening to the creak of the rigging and the gentle sounds of the water. The quartermaster on duty, Becker's younger brother Tom, came up and said, "Five bells, sir."

Becker nodded and summoned the master's mate to cast the log and find the *Lane*'s speed. Quincy stayed out of the way, leaning against the railing to enjoy the night air and the ship's gentle motion. Standing there under a sky peppered with stars, he felt a gradual increase of ease. Life was simpler on the open sea, if only because one had fewer opportunities to get into trouble. He smiled at himself in the darkness.

"Deck ahoy!" cried a voice from the maintopmast crosstree. "Ship two cables off the starboard quarter!"

Quincy felt for his glass, then remembered he had emptied his pockets upon going to bed. He squinted into the darkness, trying to spot the vessel. Their nearest consorts were *Susquehanna*, cruising miles to the east of the *Lane*, and the *Kennebec* to the west. The low, lithe shape he imagined he saw to the northeast had no discernable masts, and so could be neither.

Becker came up beside him, night glass in hand. "Can you see her?" Quincy asked.

Becker looked through the glass. "Aaah . . . there! She rides low."

"What do you make of her, Mr. Becker?" said Commander Wainwright behind them.

"She's almost certainly a runner, sir," Becker said.

"Very good. I relieve you of the deck, Mr. Becker. Please prepare to take charge of your division. Mr. Wheat, the same if you please. Mr. Ray, call all hands to come about. Quartermaster Becker, send up a rocket in the direction of the runner, and continue to do so at two-minute intervals."

"Aye, aye, sir," said Tom.

Quincy dashed below to collect his glass and watch as the *Lane* came alive with running feet. By the time he returned to his station, the ship was turning, men were in the rigging furling the main's large square sails, which given the wind's direction and the blockade runner's course would impede their progress.

The drum began beating to quarters, and Quincy urged his division to hurry to their places.

Lea joined the captain on the bridge just as the first rocket went up. Quincy averted his eyes from the brightness so as not to be blinded, then peered through his glass toward the dim form of the vessel off the port bow. She was moving fast, striking off to the southeast now; she must have seen the *Lane*'s change of course. She was stretching her lead as the *Lane* struggled to complete her evolution. The other ship was long and trim, and had no sidewheels. She must be a screw steamer. Quincy's heart skipped as thick, oily smoke started to belch from her stack. He could see sparks amidst the smoke from her funnels as she laid on steam.

"Mr. Stone, all ahead full," Lea called down to the engineer. "Mr. Becker, fire as you bear. Coordinate your fire with the rocket, firing during its illumination. Mr. Ray, send fire buckets aloft."

"Aye, aye, sir!" Becker called from the forward pivot gun.

"Lord, she can run!" Quincy said aloud in admiration. The next moment the *Lane* heeled to starboard as the men sheeted home the sails.

Quincy turned his attention to his division. They were ready; all he could do was wait for orders to fire on the fleeing ship, of which there was little likelihood with the runner now just off the starboard bow. Her dash upon discovery had placed her too far for the howitzer to reach her, and farther than he liked for the Dahlgren. Hard to judge in the dark, but he thought she was more than a mile away, though the *Lane* might close the distance now that she had completed her turn.

Lea barked at Tom Becker at the wheel, "Steer small, man!"

Silence and darkness, broken only by the hiss of the wheels, the singing of the rigging, or the creak of a yard, reigned on deck. Quincy raised his glass, hope already fading. The other ship was almost impossible to see now, appearing farther away and edging toward the south. She was faster. She was outrunning them. A vile oily taste was in his mouth and the smoke stung his eyes as he squinted into the growing gloom. He hoped that the man at the crosstree could see over its pall. A glance around the horizon yielded no glimpse of a friendly vessel to aid in the pursuit. He closed his glass with a snap and pocketed it. A well-pitched shell might slow the runner and allow them to overtake her, but he realized that now it was a matter more of luck than skill.

A hail of "Which way does she bear?" was answered with, "Lost sight of her, sir."

Quincy noticed that the pall of the smoke was lightening and shortly thereafter they broke from the gloom. The runner was no longer in sight. She'd given them the slip. The order to secure from quarters came a few minutes later, and he passed it along to his division.

Disappointment washed across the faces of his men as they secured their cannon. A possible prize lost, a blockade runner slipped through their grasp. It wounded their pride as well as their hopes for prize money, but no amount of hope could force more speed out of their ship. She had her limits.

The captain gave orders for the men on watch to return to their places, and dismissed the watch below to their hammocks. The *Lane* kept up speed, but would not do so for long. At top speed she gobbled a ton of coal an hour, and she had already been cruising for several days. If some chance did not bring the enemy vessel within reach in a few hours, the chase would be abandoned.

Quincy checked the time: it was three-forty, twenty minutes until he had the watch. No point in trying to sleep. He went forward to find Becker, waiting until he had seen his division disperse. Becker's face was a scowl.

"Think we'll still see her when it's light?" Quincy asked.

"Not a chance on this earth." Becker moved past him toward the bow and snapped an order at a sailor who still stood gazing forward.

Quincy strolled back toward the bridge. He heard Wainwright talking quietly to Lea. A moment later Lea went forward, to find Becker, Quincy supposed, and Wainwright retired below. With a sigh, Quincy leaned against the rail and stared up at the sky. Stars winked at him through the rigging and around the sails. The night's peace had closed around the deck again, but it brought no satisfaction.

"Now, what of the music, Mrs. Asterly?" said General Sherman. "Does your friend Strythe wish to organize it, or shall I try for the military band?"

Emma glanced up from the vase of flowers she was attempting to sketch. The general had come for luncheon and was now ensconced on the parlor sofa with Aunt May, busy with plans for the ball. Emma welcomed his visits as he never failed to cheer her aunt. He pandered to May more shamelessly even than Mr. Lawford, and she glowed with pleasure at each pretty compliment or little gift he bestowed on her. Emma was all the more grateful since learning that the general did not presently reside on the island but was living with his family at San Jacinto, and only came down to visit his son, or to attend to matters requiring his attention at the Island City Hotel.

"Mr. Strythe does not think he can assemble enough creditable musicians for an orchestra," May said, drawing her shawl about herself.

"Then the band it must be," said the general. "I will speak to Sergeant Harris."

"Do you mean the band that plays concerts on the square?" Emma asked.

"The very same," said the general.

"They are quite good," Emma said, pausing to examine her drawing at arm's length. She was not happy with the results. Her honeysuckles looked more like a collection of frayed toothpicks, and the clematis blossoms just looked like flat blobs.

Stealing a glance at Aunt May, who was looking over a list of dance music with the general, she turned the page of her sketchbook and started over.

"That breeze is making me chill," May complained.

"Shall I close the window?" Emma offered, setting down her pencil.

"Daisy can do that, dear. Do not interrupt your work."

"I don't mind," Emma said, getting up. She stepped over to the window and shut it, though to her the breeze seemed rather warm.

"You are certain we will have enough ice, General?" May asked. "I inquired after having a sculpture made, and was informed that the icehouse is empty."

"Yes, it was all taken away last spring, during the evacuation," said the general. "Do not worry, I have ice brought down on the train every week for the hotel, and I will order an extra shipment for the ball."

"Good," May said. "Emma, ring the bell while you are up. I could do with some more tea."

Emma did so, then knelt beside her aunt and took her hand, concerned. "You are not getting feverish, are you, Au—are you, May?"

"No, no, dear. Go back to your sketch," she told Emma. "I am better now."

Emma returned to her chair, but was no sooner there than she heard a knock upon the front door. She happily set aside her drawing and waited while Rupert answered the summons. In a moment he brought two visitors to the parlor.

"Lieutenant Sherman and Mr. Vale to see you, ma'am," Rupert said in his deep, quiet voice.

"How delightful! Thank you, Rupert," said Aunt May, putting down her fan. "Come in, gentlemen, come in!"

"Good afternoon, Mrs. Asterly," said the younger Sherman. "I hope you don't mind my bringing a friend. He wanted to meet Miss Russell."

His friend, a young man with large hands and good features, dressed in civilian clothes, cast a glance Emma's way. She gave him a polite smile.

"Not at all," May replied. "How do you do, Mr. Vale? Are you in the military as well?"

"No, ma'am," he said, bending over the hand she offered. "That is—I am in the Home Guard. My father works for Mr. Hendley, and I keep accounts in his office."

"Oh!" Emma cried. "Can you take us up to the cupola on top of his building?"

"Certainly, if that is your wish," said Mr. Vale, smiling. "I spend a fair amount of time up there myself."

"Keeping accounts?" asked May with a laugh.

"Keeping watch for enemy ships," he returned.

"Really?" May picked up her fan and waved it.

"He is one of the JOLOs," said Lieutenant Sherman.

"That doesn't explain a thing to them, son," said his father. "They have only been here a few weeks."

"Do explain it, Mr. Vale," said Aunt May. "Please be seated," she added, waving them to chairs.

"Thank you," he said, taking a place between Emma and the sofa. "The JOLOs have been keeping watch over the bay since the war began," he said. "We take shifts in the cupola on top of Mr. Hendley's building."

"And can you see the whole island from there?" Emma asked.

"Nearly. The western end is not easy to see, but there is not much there. We have a good view of the gulf," he added, glancing at Aunt May.

"Oh, I would love to see it!" Emma said.

"You would be welcome. We have had ladies to visit several times." He looked at Emma with a wavering smile. "They have been very helpful in maintaining our line of supply."

"Line of supply?" Emma said. "Goodness, how long are your shifts?"

"Don't let him hornswoggle you," Lieutenant Sherman said.

"When he says 'supply' he means pies and cakes."

"And lemonade," said Vale, breaking into a grin. "That's vitally necessary."

Emma narrowed her eyes. "I see. So the JOLOs require a bribe."

"For you, Miss Russell, no," said Mr. Vale with belated gallantry.

"What does JOLO mean, anyway?" demanded Aunt May.

"Jolly Order of Look Outs," said Vale and Lieutenant Sherman in chorus, and Emma laughed.

"Some of the fellows are a bit—well, salty," said Mr. Vale. "Most are mariners from Mr. Hendley's shipping business. Let me know when you wish to visit, and I will make sure I am there."

"I am not sure this is an appropriate venture for a young lady," said Aunt May.

"Oh, there is no harm in it, dear Mrs. Asterly," said General Sherman. "Sidney will go along to take care of her if you are concerned."

Emma saw a look of exasperation flit across the lieutenant's face, then he glanced at her and gave an apologetic smile, saying, "I would have to arrange it when I am off duty."

"I don't mind," Emma said. She liked the lieutenant; he was kind, rather quiet, but when he spoke he showed good sense, and he never put himself forward. He never exerted himself to captivate her, or to draw her attention to himself, as most other young men of her acquaintance tried to do. As a result, she felt safe in his company, something she had not felt with a man outside her family since Stephen.

With a shock, Emma realized she had not thought of Stephen in some time. A wave of guilt washed through her. She had not believed she would ever forget him, and yet how easily she had been drawn away! He had been killed only six months ago; she had known about it only since May. Yet she had all but forgotten him, distracted by new clothes and plans for a stupid ball. She did not even like dancing! All her grief returned in a rush, coupled with a feeling that she had been faithless. She knew she had not, but her emotions were not subject to rational thinking, and she could not help feeling oppressed.

"Emma, dear, are you daydreaming?" said Aunt May. "Mr. Vale has asked you a question."

Emma looked up from her sketchbook, at which she must have been staring. "I beg your pardon, I—I was distracted." Suddenly she felt unable to be still, and stood up. "I really must prepare for my music lesson."

She picked up her pencil and sketchbook with clumsy fingers, glanced at Lieutenant Sherman and tried to assuage his evident concern with a smile. "Thank you for visiting," she said to him, and turned to his friend. "It was a pleasure to meet you, Mr. Vale."

"Emma—"

"Good afternoon, General," she added, and received an understanding smile from him as she made a hasty curtsey.

She hurried from the parlor before Aunt May could demand an explanation. Her heart was so full of emotion it seemed to burn. She ran up the stairs to her room, cast herself on the bed, and only then allowed herself the luxury of tears.

16

During three nights in the week . . . the military band assembles
upon an elevated platform, erected in the center of the spacious
public square, and discourses most excellent music with a very
large variety of musical instruments that can be heard all over
the city . . . Indeed, notwithstanding their misfortunes, the peo-
ple of Galveston have many sources of enjoyment left in their
city.

—Mr. Willard Richardson, *Galveston News*

The day of the ball arrived all too soon for Emma, who between
hasty dancing lessons and last-minute errands for her aunt was
beginning to feel overwhelmed. Her spirits remained low,
though she tried to conceal this from Aunt May. She had begun
to dream of Stephen again, sad dreams she couldn't remember
well upon waking. She had written to Momma expressing her
hope of coming home soon after the ball, but had as yet received
no reply.

After dinner she yielded to May's insistence and went to her
room to lie down. Sleep would not come; instead she lay on the
chaise longue, thinking about the approaching evening, the new
friends she would see, and how much more she would have
enjoyed it if Stephen were there. Galveston was a charming city,
but it did not assuage her loneliness. Lately she had taken to
escaping for long walks to the beach, looking out over the gulf.
She took a friend along when she could, Daisy or Rupert when
no friend would come.

A quiet knock on the door preceded Daisy's entrance. Emma sat up on the chaise longue where she had been resting.

"I am here to dress your hair, Miss," Daisy said.

"Oh. All right."

Emma rose, pulling her wrapper around her, and moved to the dressing table. She sat gazing at herself in the mirror while Daisy brushed out her hair. It had grown nearly to her shoulders now, and lay in soft, dark waves. When she had first cut it, it had curled wildly around her face, exactly like Matt's. She remembered Momma's distress upon finding her in her bedroom, Jamie's letter in her lap and shocks of hair scattered on the floor around her feet. The bitterness she had felt then was gone now; only numbness remained.

She did not even have a picture of Stephen. She was beginning to forget what he looked like. It was nearly a year since she had last seen him. He had proposed to her on the eve of the brigade's departure for New Mexico, and had not had time to have a picture made for her. She had gone to a portraitist for the watch-fob miniature of herself, and mailed it to Stephen for Christmas.

Looking in the mirror, she saw herself older, less vital, with hollow eyes and a mouth that lay in a sad, flat line. The face was pretty, she supposed, and the neck about which the maid's dark hands moved was long, if more tanned than May liked. Emma glanced up at Daisy's face, ghostlike in the mirror, and wondered if she also bore the weight of past sadness.

"Daisy?" she said.

The maid's eyes met hers in the silvered glass, and her hands hesitated. Emma licked her lips.

"Do you like Mrs. Asterly?" she asked.

Daisy looked away, finished twisting a lock of Emma's hair into a pretty curl and secured it with a comb tipped with sapphires, May's gift to Emma on the occasion of the ball. Pausing briefly, eyes still downcast, she said in a low voice, "She don't beat me, she give me good clothes and enough to eat, and she don't have a husband or a son to come trouble me."

Sharp dark eyes met Emma's briefly in the mirror, a glance that told more than the maid's words had done—of poverty, hardship, and most of all, fear. Daisy picked up the brush and resumed arranging Emma's hair. Emma watched her, stunned into the realization that her own woes were perhaps not as terrible as she had thought.

Jamie sat on a camp stool in front of the tent he shared with Lieutenant Foster, watching the evening sky darken over the treetops surrounding the camp. The military camp was in a good location, on level ground with good water nearby. The battery park had been laid out with the guard tent nearest the road. The cannon, caissons, and battery wagons stood in neat lines behind it; then the harness, the horses at their picket ropes, and the soldiers' tents. Ten yards separated the tents from the mess kitchens, with another ten yards between the kitchens and the two tents that housed Jamie and the other subalterns. Ten yards farther was Captain Sayers's tent, and behind it the officers' kitchen. Jamie had not lived in this arrangement before, but he had laid out enough camps to appreciate the orderliness of the battery's encampment. Best of all, he had arrived after the camp was made, and not had to do any of the work or planning himself.

He stepped out from under the tent fly to scan the sky for stars, but saw few. It was early yet, and the air was hazy with dampness. This part of Texas was much wetter than the hill country around San Antonio, and flatter, with great, dense forests of maple, hickory, oak, and other leafy trees interspersed with pine and cedar. Near the lakes there were cypress swamps and innumerable bayous. He had been out fishing a couple of times with Nettles and Hume, who commanded the battery's other sections, and gone hunting once with Mr. Lawford before he had left for Galveston.

Jamie turned and strained his ears, thinking he had heard

hoofbeats. Foster had ridden into town after supper to check for mail, the stage having been expected that day. The chore was part of Foster's staff duties for the battery.

Yes, that was a horse he had heard. Jamie went into the tent to move the coffeepot toward the center of the stove. By the time he came back outside, John was tramping toward him with a mailbag slung over his shoulder.

"Coffee's on," Jamie said, holding open the tent door. "One or two?"

"One, but it's stuffed full," John replied. "Thanks," he added, coming inside and dumping the heavy mailbag onto the table he and Jamie shared as a desk.

"Want help sorting?" Jamie asked.

John pushed his spectacles up on his nose. "Sure," he said, sitting down and unbuckling the bag's leather straps. Letters spilled onto the table, and he and Jamie began sorting the enlisted men's mail by platoon and separating the officers' letters into individual piles. Captain Sayers had the most correspondence, much of it from department headquarters in San Antonio.

"Here's one for you," Foster said, handing him a thick letter from Momma. Jamie tucked it in his pocket and continued sorting. He glanced up at Foster, thinking it was too bad about the smallpox scars, because otherwise the fellow had a pleasant face. A lot of the boys had been sick with smallpox during the New Mexico Campaign. Jamie wondered if Foster had caught it on the way up the Rio Grande or on the way home.

"You transferred from Green's regiment, didn't you?" Jamie asked him.

Foster nodded. "K Company. I was a sergeant."

"Were you at Valverde?" Jamie asked softly.

"Yes."

Jamie picked up a handful of letters and sorted them. Laying the last on its stack, he rubbed at a crick in his neck, then looked at his tentmate again.

"Did you kill anyone?" he asked.

Foster glanced up at him. "I don't know. I fired at some Yankees, but I didn't see whether they fell. Mostly I was trying to keep my men together."

Jamie nodded and went back to sorting, thinking how pleasant it must be not to know. Halfway through another batch of letters he found one addressed to himself, from Colonel Debray. Surprised, he said, "I'll be damned."

"What?"

"Sorry, just a letter I wasn't expecting."

Foster glanced at the address. "You know Debray?"

"Yes. I went to his academy in San Antonio."

"He studied at St. Cyr, didn't he? Did he teach you tactics?"

"History and mathematics," Jamie said, and pocketed the letter.

When the sorting was finished he offered to help distribute, but Foster declined. "It won't take me long," he said, picking up officers' stacks. "Go ahead and enjoy your letters."

Jamie poured himself some coffee and retired to his cot, opening Debray's letter first. Evidently the colonel did remember him. The note was short, congenial, and candid with regard to the situation in Galveston. Yes, Debray was aware of the potential threat. Yes, more guns and troops were being sought for Galveston, but at the same time Richmond was pressuring the governor for more forces from Texas. Debray concluded with an invitation to Jamie to transfer to his staff.

"You look thunderstruck," Foster commented, returning for the enlisted men's mail. He began to place each stack back in the mailbag, keeping them in order to facilitate handing them to the sergeants.

"Debray's offered me a staff job," Jamie said.

"Thought you were tired of pushing paper."

"I am. I won't take it, but it's good of him to offer."

"Hm."

Jamie got up to refill his coffee. He gestured with the pot in an offer to pour some for Foster.

"Save me some," Foster said. "I'll be back soon." He slung the mailbag over his shoulder and started out, but paused in the doorway. "If you took that staff job you'd probably get promoted."

Jamie shrugged. "I know what captain feels like."

"Don't you want to advance?"

Jamie took a sip of coffee, scalding his tongue. He set the cup down on the table. "I want to do my part. I don't care about advancement."

Foster grinned. "Well, I do. If you go, I'll get your section."

Jamie laughed, and Foster tossed him a mock salute before going out with the mail. Picking up his coffee cup and sipping carefully, Jamie returned to his bed to read Momma's letter.

"This is Dr. Hurlbut, my dear," said Aunt May. "He is one of Galveston's most prominent physicians. Doctor, this is my niece, Miss Russell."

Emma curtsied for perhaps the hundredth time, and offered her hand. "How do you do?"

Dr. Hurlbut bowed. "I have anticipated this meeting with great pleasure, Miss Russell. It is an honor to meet you."

Emma smiled and thanked him, then turned toward the next guest as the doctor moved into the ballroom.

The Island City Hotel, while neither the largest nor best-known hotel in Galveston, was nevertheless the most festive on this evening. The ballroom was filled with candlelight, flowers, and the murmur of happy voices. Emma, dressed in her blue evening gown, stood beside her aunt at the doorway greeting the guests as they arrived. While there were not as many as May would have liked, the island being somewhat thin of company, there were enough to fill the ballroom with colorful gowns, elegant evening dress, and dashing uniforms. The military band, resplendent in their heavily braided jackets, played popular tunes from a platform at the far end of the ballroom. A long table down the side was spread with lavish comestibles, the centerpiece being a huge block of ice which had been carved into the shape of an urn, filled with dozens of fresh oysters and slices of lemons.

Mr. Lawford was present, having returned to Galveston a few days previously. He had brought Emma a gift—a pretty little fan of embroidered blue silk on ivory sticks—which now dangled from a ribbon on her wrist. He stood a little way apart, chatting with General Sherman who had coaxed his wife and two of their daughters to come down to Galveston for the occasion. Mrs. Menard, their eldest daughter, had declined to come but had sent Emma a charming basket of flowers and a polite letter expressing her hope that they might meet in calmer times. Colonel Cook had also declined the invitation, but most of the privileged class who remained in the city were in attendance, including the British and French consuls, Mr. Lynn and Mr. Theron. May was already preening herself on the ball's success, chattering happily with each arriving guest, laughing and fluttering her fan as she stood beneath a glittering chandelier. Emma smiled, shook hands, tried to commit to memory the names of new people her aunt introduced, and secretly wished for the evening to be over.

At last, with a loud flourish, the band struck up the first dance of the evening, a grand march for which Lieutenant Sherman had solicited the favor of Emma's company. She saw him approaching through the crowded room, and turned to her aunt.

"May I go now?" she said, smiling her sweetest smile.

"Yes, of course, dear," May said, touching her cheek with a hand encased in a silk crocheted mitten. "How pretty you look! I will wait a little longer for the latecomers. Go and enjoy yourself!"

Lieutenant Sherman presented himself with a bow, offered Emma his arm, and led her onto the floor. She was a little nervous of her steps yet, though she had taken lessons for three weeks and had been pronounced competent even for the waltz by both Mrs. Schneider and Mr. Strythe, the latter of whom had given generously of his time as an accompanist. Dancing in a ballroom full of elegant Galvestonians was different than dancing around the parlor with Mrs. Schneider, but Emma trusted she would manage. Fortunately, the Grand March was an easy dance, being little more than a promenade with a few variations.

"You look enchanting this evening," said her partner. "I think I neglected to mention that to you earlier."

She glanced up at him and smiled. "Thank you. You look very well yourself." She paused, minding her steps as they changed direction, then said, "Is that a new uniform?" She nodded toward his crisp gray jacket, its sleeves ornamented with loops of gold braid.

"Dress uniform," he said. "I haven't had much occasion to wear it."

"Well, it is very smart," Emma told him, and won a smile in response. "I am glad you could join us this evening," she added.

"My father would never have tolerated my absence," he said, his eyes laughing.

"He has been so very generous," Emma said. "I cannot begin to thank him."

"Your adorning his ballroom is thanks enough," said Lieutenant Sherman. "He is enjoying himself immensely. Your aunt has spared no expense."

"No," Emma agreed. "I think she is having more fun than I am. Oh, that is not what I meant!" She felt herself coloring, even as her partner laughed. "I meant, she is having *even* more fun."

"Don't hide your true feelings from a friend, Miss Russell," he said, guiding her distracted steps through a movement of the dance. He lowered his voice and leaned close to her ear. "I suspect you, like I, would enjoy a quiet evening at home more than this sort of affair."

Emma threw him a laughing look. "I *do* beg your pardon," she said.

He smiled. "No need."

Emma smiled back. She was grateful for the lieutenant's presence. He seemed to understand her better than most.

The dance ended, and the ballroom filled with applause and chatter. Lieutenant Sherman returned Emma to Mrs. Asterly's side and offered to fetch them both some champagne punch.

"Yes, thank you, dear boy," May said. "Although I would prefer coffee." She pulled her shawl around her, smiling at Emma. "You looked delightful dancing, love."

"I hope to see *you* dancing before the evening is over," Emma said.

"Oh, you shall! I must have one waltz, though in general I no longer dance." She glanced over her shoulder at Mr. Lawford as she spoke, and he hastened to join them.

"You looked beautiful on the floor, Miss Russell," he said. "I hope you have saved a dance for this ancient."

"She must dance with all the young gentlemen first," May declared.

"Then I shall have to be content to watch," said Mr. Lawford with a feigned sigh.

"Don't be silly," Emma told him. "Of course I will dance with you!"

Lieutenant Sherman returned with the punch and coffee, and Emma had time to enjoy only a few sips before Mr. Theron appeared to claim her for a reel. Emma took to the floor in a whirl of music with a succession of Galveston's best and brightest young men. She doggedly saved a schottische for Mr. Lawford, who rewarded her by guiding her through the swift dance with a practiced skill that left her breathless.

"What an excellent dancer you are," she said, curtseying to him as the music concluded. "I felt as if we were dancing on clouds!"

"I have had many years to learn," he replied, his eyes glinting at her. "Let me restore you to May. I see that she is trying to catch your attention."

Aunt May, who had moved away from the door and was now

holding court from a sofa near the refreshment table, was indeed waving at her in apparent excitement. When Emma came near she saw a gentleman sitting beside her, resplendent in a gray uniform covered with gold braid, a plumed hat under his arm. His hair and mustache were sandy-colored, and he looked vaguely familiar.

"See who has come to visit you, Emma dear?" May said, as the officer rose and bowed.

Emma frowned, uncertain. "Mr.—Owens?"

He smiled, white teeth flashing beneath the mustache. "That's right, I knew you'd remember. I served with your brother."

"It is *Major* Owens, my dear," said her aunt.

"Oh, yes." Emma gave him a friendly smile. "How good of you to come."

"I must apologize for attending uninvited," he said with a courtly bow to Aunt May. "When I heard there was to be a ball in Miss Russell's honor, I simply couldn't keep away."

"He came all the way from headquarters at Houston," May said, smiling with pleasure.

Emma could think of nothing to say, so she smiled also. The musicians gave the signal for the next dance, and she glanced toward the floor, looking for her partner.

"May I have the honor?" Major Owens said, setting his hat on the sofa and offering Emma his arm.

"Go ahead, dear, I'll explain to Mr. Vale," said Aunt May.

Thus Emma found herself escorted to the floor by Major Owens, quite possibly the handsomest man in the room, with the strains of a waltz commencing. She felt nervous, being uncertain of the steps and a bit shy of her unexpected partner, but he proved himself as capable of guiding her as Mr. Lawford had been, if perhaps not quite so gentle. She was expected to make conversation, she knew, so once she was comfortable with the rhythm of the dance, she glanced up at him and said, "Have you seen my brother recently?"

The major's smile widened. "Yes, we had dinner together when he passed through town."

"Oh." This should have reassured her, but somehow it did not. She remained ill at ease, though she could not have said why.

"You look exquisite, Miss Russell," he said after a moment. "Town life agrees with you. I might not have known you, you are so changed since I saw you in San Antonio."

Emma, not knowing what else to reply, said, "Thank you."

"I am glad to see you are recovered from your disappointment. All your friends will agree, I am sure."

She swallowed, staring at the major's shoulder, trying to think of something pleasant to say. Another couple danced rather too near them, and he drew her out of their way by pulling her closer. She became aware of his scent, an exotic blend of spices that stung at her throat.

"A lovely young thing like yourself should not be alone," he murmured into her ear.

"I am not alone," she said. "My aunt is very kind to me."

"Ah, yes. But, family is not the same," he said, his hand tightening on her waist.

Emma glanced toward the sofa, but it was now empty. Searching the dance floor, she spied Aunt May waltzing with Mr. Lawford, looking giddy with happiness. Emma did not wish to spoil her enjoyment, so she tolerated the major's liberties.

"I don't suppose I have to tell you that I find you mighty attractive," he drawled.

"I don't suppose you would have to tell that to anyone in the room," Emma said, leaning away from him.

He smiled. "I like a gal with a bit of spunk. Tell me, Miss Russell—"

"Aunt May!"

Emma tried to pull free, but Major Owens's grip tightened. She looked past his shoulder to where she had last seen her aunt, then turned an angry frown on him.

"Let me go!" she demanded, and broke away, twisting her hand from his and running across the dance floor.

A babel of voices arose; the music faltered to a stop. May lay in a heap of lace and silk on the polished wood floor of the ballroom. She had fainted, it appeared. Mr. Lawford, kneeling beside her, lifted her in his arms and began patting her cheek. Emma joined him and fanned her with the blue silk fan.

"Aunt May? Can you hear me?"

"She's very warm," Mr. Lawford said, worried eyes glancing at Emma.

"Someone please fetch some ice!" Emma called.

Lieutenant Sherman appeared at her side almost as she spoke, and gave her a handkerchief into which he had twisted some ice shavings from the buffet. Emma applied it to May's forehead.

"Let us move her to the sofa," the lieutenant said, offering to pick up her feet, but Mr. Lawford lifted May without assistance and carried her off the dance floor. Emma and the lieutenant followed and were joined by Dr. Hurlbut, who took May's wrist in a gentle grasp and felt her face and throat. He murmured a few words to Mr. Lawford, who nodded and at once left the room.

Emma looked at Dr. Hurlbut. "Will she be all right?"

"She is in a high fever," he said. "She needs immediate rest and quiet. Lawford has gone to fetch her carriage."

Emma glanced over her shoulder at the roomful of people, many of whom had gathered around the sofa. She saw General Sherman approaching, and reached out a hand to him, accepting his assistance to rise.

"I don't—I ought to go with her, but—" Emma looked at the crowded ballroom, her dazed eyes seeing faces whose names she could not recall.

"You will go with her, of course," said the general, quiet and firm. "I will make your apologies."

Emma gripped his hand. "Thank you," she said. "Oh, after all you have done—thank you so much!"

Mr. Lawford had returned with May's cloak. He draped it over her and deftly picked her up.

"Go with them, Sidney," the general said to his son.

Emma turned to find the lieutenant beside her, and gratefully took the arm he offered. With a last glance at the ballroom, she hurried out after Lawford and May.

17

You will proceed down the coast of Texas with the other vessels, keeping a good lookout for vessels running the blockade, and whenever you think you can enter the sounds on the coast and destroy the temporary defenses, you will do so and gain the command of the inland navigation. Galveston appears to be the port most likely for you to be able to enter, if the forts are not too formidable.

—Order of Rear-Admiral Farragut, U.S. Navy, to Commander Renshaw, U. S. Navy, commanding Mortar Flotilla

"It is not yellow fever," Dr. Hurlbut said, coming into the parlor.

Emma breathed a sigh of relief. "Thank goodness." She glanced at Lieutenant Sherman, who sat in one of the velvet-covered chairs, an empty coffee cup on the table beside him.

"Do you know what sort of fever it is?" Mr. Lawford asked.

"I cannot tell as yet," said Dr. Hurlbut. "I will have to observe her for the next few days. I will return in the morning."

"Should I sit up with her?" Emma asked.

"That will not be necessary. She is resting well now, and her maid is with her. You should try to get some sleep."

Emma and the others rose as the doctor moved to go. "Thank you, Dr. Hurlbut," she said.

"You are welcome, Miss Russell. Do not be overly concerned. Mrs. Asterly should recover."

Mr. Lawford escorted him to the door, asking a quiet question. Emma looked around the parlor at the coffee tray and scattered cups, coats cast over furniture, velvet drapes closing out the night. Lieutenant Sherman took a step toward her.

"I should go, too," he said. "Father will be glad to know it is not a contagious complaint."

"We don't know that," Emma said unhappily.

"Well, we know it is not the worst." He gave a small smile, eyes filled with gentle concern. "Is there anything I can do for you? Anything you'd like me to bring?"

"No, thank you. We will be all right," Emma said, giving him her hand. He wrapped both of his around it.

"I'm on duty tomorrow, but I will try to come by for a short visit."

She should tell him not to trouble himself, Emma thought. Instead she smiled, and said, "Thank you. It was so kind of you to come."

"Call on me for anything," he said, releasing her hand. "Just send a message to the Custom House, and it will find me."

Emma saw him to the door and watched him stride down the path to the street. Mr. Lawford had gone upstairs, no doubt to see for himself how May was doing. She returned to the parlor to find Rupert collecting the coffee cups.

"Daisy is sitting up with my aunt?" she asked him.

Rupert nodded. "I'll be taking turns with her."

"Wake me if you need my help," Emma said.

He directed a thoughtful look at her, then nodded. "Good night, Miss."

"Good night. Thank you, Rupert," she called after him as he carried the tray out the back door to the kitchen.

Emma picked up her cloak, folding the dark satin over her arm. She stood still in the center of the parlor, frowning over the evening's events. Mr. Lawford came down the stairs and joined her.

"She's resting well," he said in a quiet voice. "The doctor left some laudanum for her."

"I feel so badly," Emma told him. "She made herself ill fussing over me, over the arrangements for that stupid ball!"

"No, no," said Mr. Lawford. "She enjoyed every minute of it. Do not blame yourself. She has never been robust."

Emma looked up at him, saw his face was strained with worry. "Maybe you should get some sleep," she said.

The look he cast her told her clearly how useless he thought the attempt would be. She sighed, doubtful that she would be able to sleep either.

Mr. Lawford picked up his coat. "I should try, I suppose," he said. "Our alternative is to sit here and stare at each other all night, which would make us quite useless tomorrow."

Emma smiled. "I'm glad you're here," she said as they went up the stairs. She paused in the upper hall, while he moved toward the room that had been Jamie's and was presently his. "Good night, Mr. Lawford."

He turned, his face softened. "Good night," he said. "Sleep well."

Emma glanced down the hall toward her aunt's room, candlelight shining softly under the door. With a sigh, she went into her own room, determined at least to try.

Ship Island was little more than a stretch of white sand with a clump of pine trees at the east end and a half-built fort at the west. The *Harriet Lane* had come there for coal preliminary to joining Commander Renshaw's expedition down the Texas coast. Renshaw's ship, the *Westfield*, was at Ship Island also, as were the *Clifton* and *Owasco*, all waiting their turn to coal from the several barges stationed there. The expedition was ordered to proceed down the coast and destroy as many of the enemy's temporary defenses as they could reach, which would be a pleasant break from the tedium of blockading. Quincy had not sailed that way before; he was curious to get a look at Galveston, a city reported to be nearly as fine as New Orleans.

By the time the first watch began, Quincy was so tired of the coal dust that he was willing to brave the island's notorious sand midges for a breath of clear air. Having secured the captain's permission to go ashore, he, Becker, and Gerard ventured across the barge to the wharf and thence to the island's pale sands.

Though the sun had set, the sky was still fairly bright, and Quincy didn't bother to light the lantern he had brought. They walked past the fort, which housed a few companies of long-suffering infantry, and continued south to the gulf shore where they sat on the sand and gazed out at the sea.

"Should have brought wood for a fire," Becker said.

Gerard dug a fish head out of the sand. "We could use these."

"Oh, all right. You go ahead and collect about two hundred of them, that should do for a start."

Not dignifying this with an answer, Gerard tossed the fish head away, leaned back on his elbows and sighed. "Think we'll catch any prizes in Texas?"

"I hope so," said Quincy, waving away a midge, then resting his chin on his knees. "This last month has been wasted."

"Well, we've got a pretty tight grip on Mobile," Becker said, "and since New Orleans fell the runners are landing farther west, so I hear."

"Kittredge did well at Corpus Christi," Gerard said, nodding.

"Until the Rebels caught him," Becker grumbled.

Quincy made no comment. Watching the waves in the fading light, he thought dreamily of catching a prize ship, perhaps even being assigned to sail it home, with a prize crew under him and a hold full of Rebel cotton to add to their gains.

Rebel cotton made him think of Mrs. Hawkland, and of New Orleans. The *Lane* would not stop there; she was taking on all the supplies she needed here, and would be able to cruise the coast for two or three months—more, if a supply ship visited. It was better that way. Mrs. Hawkland was too distracting. He was better off away from her. Perhaps tonight he would answer Miss Keller's letter.

"Hallo, who's that?" Gerard said, sitting up.

Trudging footsteps sounded in the sand. Quincy turned to

see a large form lumbering toward them. As he watched, it became recognizable.

"Hinks!" Becker called. "Well met, friend!"

Hinks stopped and huffed a couple of times, then in an ominous voice said, "There was a ship," and sat down in the sand beside them.

"None of that," Becker said. "You only get one of us, if you've a long, boring tale to spin."

Hinks drew a deep breath, flung out a hand, and said, "The ice was here, the ice was there, the ice was all around—"

Gerard interrupted, saying, "That goddamned ice was everywhere, at fifty cents a pound!"

Quincy laughed, and Hinks, attempting to stare haughtily at Gerard, instead dissolved in giggles and flopped backward on the sand. "Unfeeling bastards," he cried to the sky. "I walked all the way out here to bring you important news."

"What news?" Becker demanded. "If it's about Antietam, we've already heard."

"No," Hinks gasped, struggling to sit up. Quincy offered a hand and helped haul him upright. "No," he repeated. "It isn't military news. It's political news."

"Bah," Gerard said. "Keep it."

"No, it's important," Hinks insisted, and Quincy heard a note of seriousness in his voice.

"What is it, Gordon?" he asked.

Hinks took a couple of breaths before replying. "Lincoln's going to free the slaves."

Stunned silence met this announcement. Quincy's jaw slowly dropped, and he inhaled a deep breath.

"I hope you are joking," said Becker.

Hinks shook his head. "All the slaves in the Rebel states. He's going to set them free the first of January."

"My God," Quincy said.

"He can't do that. He can't *do* that!" Becker yelled, getting up. "This is a war for *union*, not emancipation!"

"Frank—"

"God damn it!" Becker started off down the beach. Quincy
and the others scrambled to their feet and hurried to catch up
to him. Quincy got there first, and laid a hand on his arm.

"Frank—"

"Leave me alone!"

Quincy got in front of Becker, forcing him to stop. "I don't
like it either," he said. "But just ranting won't do any good. We
must decide what to do."

"Do?" Becker said, low and angry. "What can we do? The president hath spoken!"

Quincy had no answer. He stared at his shipmate, unhappy,
beginning to feel resentful. They should not have to deal with
this—it was not their problem.

"You can resign," Hinks put in. He was out of breath, still,
from running after them. He took out a handkerchief and
mopped at his brow.

"Resign?" Gerard said, aghast.

"They're all talking about it on the *Clifton*," Hinks said. "Most
everyone feels as you do, Frank. It is just a question of loyalty."

"We have sworn to serve the navy," Quincy said slowly.

"But not to fight for niggers," countered Becker. "We're not
enlisted, we can resign! Gordon, how many of the *Clifton*'s officers are leaving?"

"No one yet," Hinks replied. "It is under discussion."

"And if we all resign," Quincy said quietly, "what will happen?"

They all paused, then Gerard said, "The blockade will fail."

Quincy carried the thought to its conclusion. "If the blockade
fails, it's only a matter of time before the Rebels get foreign
recognition. They will win."

They stood still, the rushing of water onto the beach filling
the silence. It was falling dark, and Quincy could no longer see
his friends' faces well. He wished for his lantern, forgotten in
the sand.

"Listen," he said, "this is bad, but we still have a duty. Never mind politics. We have a duty to the flag."

Gerard nodded. "Commander Wainwright deserves our loyalty," he said.

"Yes," Quincy agreed. "We've got to stick with it, Frank. For the Union."

Becker was silent for a moment, then muttered, "Hell."

Quincy watched him, unable to read his expression but informed by the sag of his shoulders. "Come on," he said. "We'd better get back."

"We can talk more about it," Gerard said, reaching an arm toward Becker's shoulders. Becker shrugged him off and strode away westward, back toward the ship.

Quincy looked at Gerard. "We should let the others know."

They waited for Hinks to catch up with them. "Thank you for telling us," Quincy said to him. "Would you mind not mentioning . . . ?"

"Who me?" Hinks said. "I just came out here looking to shoot an albatross."

"I think you've done it," Quincy muttered, glancing at Becker's receding form.

"You didn't say how you felt about emancipation, Wheat," Hinks said.

Quincy didn't reply. Slogging through the yielding sand, he felt he was against it. Slavery was not the issue over which they had gone to war. He tended to share his father's opinion, that if left alone slavery was on the way to dying out, and in any case, it was none of their business. The damned negroes could fend for themselves.

Quincy stopped, frowning as he thought of Isaiah. The man showed promise. Suddenly conscious of his own power over the contraband, Quincy realized how much even his grudging support had meant to Isaiah, had inspired him to work harder and to hope. If he'd been under Becker's command, he might have despaired by now.

"I think," he said slowly, "that the slaves should be free, or should be allowed to earn their freedom." He stooped to retrieve his lantern. Ahead, Becker was well on his way to the wharf.

"But this is not the time to decide that," he added, looking at Gerard, who seemed as perturbed as he was. "We're at war for the Union. This just complicates everything."

"It does that," Hinks agreed, plodding along beside them as they started toward their ships once more. "It most certainly does that."

Two weeks after the ball, Aunt May came downstairs to the sitting-room, or rather was carried down and tenderly laid on a chaise longue by Mr. Lawford. The room, being at the front of the house across from the parlor, was filled with sunlight, and Emma hastened to draw the lace curtains closed to soften its effect.

"Thank you, dearest," May told her in a thin voice.

The fever, which Dr. Hurlbut had never been able to identify, had finally abated, leaving May weak and querulous. Her graduation to the parlor was greeted with relief by Emma, who viewed it as a sign of her ultimate recovery. She had offered again to share the task of nursing her aunt, but Dr. Hurlbut had declared the fever not to be dangerous, and deemed it sufficient for Daisy to sleep on a cot at the foot of May's bed. Emma had therefore taken upon herself the task of entertaining the invalid while she was awake, which had been no small endeavor. She had been fortunate in the assistance of General Sherman, who had arrived the morning after the ball in a carriage filled with all the flowers from the ballroom, and of May's many friends, who had hastened to visit once the doctor had declared the fever not to be contagious.

The flowers had now faded and been removed from May's bedroom, and replacements provided by Mr. Lawford in the form of a double armful of yellow and white chrysanthemums.

Emma had placed a selection of these into a large Chinese bowl for the sitting room.

"How pretty!" May said as Daisy arranged her dressing-gown of lace, gauze, and multitudinous pink ribbons becomingly about her feet. "Do bring them closer so that I may see them."

Emma carried the bowl to a little table beside the chaise. She glanced down at her aunt, who still looked rather pale. "Are you warm enough? Shall I fetch your shawl?"

"I am quite comfortable, thank you, Emma dear. Do not trouble yourself. How nice it is to be downstairs! Will you bring in some coffee, Daisy? Thank you."

Emma retired to an armchair and picked up her embroidery. She was not much better at this than at drawing—although she was a good seamstress, the skill of making pictures eluded her—but she had traced a design for a pocket-handkerchief border from a ladies' magazine and was managing to follow it fairly well. It gave her something to do with her hands while sitting with her aunt.

Mr. Lawford looked at his watch. "If you are quite comfortable, May, I will go to the post office," he said.

Emma cast him a grateful look. She was anxious for news of her brother Matthew, whose regiment had been involved in both Second Manassas and the expedition into Maryland that had culminated in the disastrous battle at Sharpsburg. There had been no news from him since July, but that was not unusual. He was a poor correspondent.

"Yes, do," May told him. "I am perfectly at ease. Do go and see if there are any letters."

Emma pretended to be absorbed in her stitching and watched from the corner of her eye as Mr. Lawford plucked a bloom from the bowl for May, clasped the hand she raised to take it and bent to kiss her forehead. "I'll be back shortly," he said, and Emma glanced up at him with a smile as he left.

"Oh, la," sighed May, twirling the flower. "What a bore it is to be unwell. I do wish you would not feel obliged to sit with me every second, dear. You should be out visiting your friends."

Emma, knowing that May grew restless when she was away for more than a few minutes, said, "I have been out for a walk every day while you were napping. Yesterday we saw a kestrel near the bayou."

"Were you out with Lieutenant Sherman?"

"No, with the Misses Carter."

"Oh. I do wish the young men were more attentive to you."

"They are almost all in the service," Emma replied, pulling her silk through the cloth. "They spend their days drilling, or on guard duty. Oh, drat! I've tangled it again." She turned over her embroidery hoop and began to pick at the knot with her needle. "Don't worry, they are very attentive when they are off duty. Lieutenant Sherman has been here several times, only you were sleeping."

"Do ask him to dinner, Emma. He has been so kind."

"I will ask him when you are ready to be hostess," Emma said. "Otherwise it would be improper."

"Eva raised you too strictly," May complained.

"Well, she tried to," Emma said, smiling. "I don't know that she succeeded."

May picked up a magazine, flipped through its pages, and tossed it aside. "Has that handsome major called?" she asked.

"Major Owens? No. I expect he went back to Houston."

"He was quite charming, I thought."

Emma deemed it prudent to keep her thoughts on this subject to herself. She succeeded in untangling her embroidery silk, and drew it through the cloth.

"It would be something indeed if you were to marry a major!"

Emma counted silently to ten as she set another stitch. "I think that is very unlikely," she said.

"He seemed quite taken with you."

"You know how bad-tempered I am. I will be lucky to attach a butcher's assistant."

"Rubbish!" cried May. "Why you have any number of admirers," she said, and proceeded to catalogue them, which was what Emma had hoped for. By the time May had finished expostulating, the major was, for the moment, forgotten.

"Well," Emma said when she paused, "with all those admirers I think I must forswear marriage and devote myself to a life of dissipation."

"Now you are being nonsensical," May told her. "I know you don't care, but I truly did hope to find you a good alliance." Her voice broke on the word, and her face crumpled in tears.

"May!" Emma cast aside her needlework and hurried to her aunt's side. Kneeling beside the chaise, she took May's frail hand in hers. "I was only joshing, you know that! Don't be unhappy with me, please."

"I don't believe one of those boys has proposed to you," May said, sniffling. "You would have told me, wouldn't you?"

"Of course I would, and no, they haven't. I have not encouraged them." Emma collected both her aunt's hands into hers. "Dear May, please understand. I—am not ready," she said, feeling her own tears threatening. "It's too soon."

May looked down at her, dark eyes large in her wasted face. "Poor child," she said. "Oh, when I see you look like that, it makes me think of when dear Mr. Asterly died!"

Emma glanced down, struggling to master her feelings. When she could command a smile, she looked up again. "Come home with me," she said. "Come to San Antonio! You can match me up with all the young men there—" she paused while May gave a gurgling laugh, then added, "and Momma would love to see you."

"Oh," May said, searching for her handkerchief. "Oh, I can't bear to think of moving again, even if I were well."

Emma retrieved the lacy kerchief from May's sleeve, and gently dried her aunt's cheeks. "When you are well, you shall not move, but you shall escort me home, please. Mr. Lawford will lend us his traveling carriage."

"Devious creature! You have already enlisted him!"

Emma grinned. "I have. Am I not dreadful? You should wash your hands of me."

"As if I would think of such a thing!"

Daisy, coming in with the coffee tray, paused while Emma got to her feet and out of the way. The maid set the heavy tray on the table before Emma's chair, gave her one flat glance, and departed.

"I don't like the way Daisy is behaving," May said fretfully when she had gone. "Her manner is becoming insolent."

"She has been working very hard while you were ill," Emma said as she poured the coffee. Privately, she thought the news of Lincoln's brash announcement had affected Daisy's behavior, but she did not want to make her aunt feel less secure by discussing the subject. It would be difficult for any slave allegedly freed by the United States to escape his position in Galveston, so far from the border. Indeed, many of the planters along the Mississippi had sent their slaves into Texas to keep them away from the Yankees. For herself, she still felt strange sometimes being waited on by Rupert, or by Daisy with her icy silence. It was a peculiar arrangement, she felt, and not a comfortable one.

She should set aside politics, she thought, and devote herself to the effort of cheering her aunt. "Here you are," she said, handing May a cup of coffee. "Have I ever told you about my little mule filly, Raindrops?"

All was quiet on the deck of the *Harriet Lane*, save for the sound of the men working. The ship lay with the others of Renshaw's expedition, just off Bolivar Point. It was not quite six, and Quincy watched the morning sunlight slant onto the deck while the men laboriously holystoned its wooden surface. It was Saturday, usually make-and-mend day, but he had the feeling the afternoon would not see the men plying their needles. An hour since, a courier had delivered a message to the captain from

Commander Renshaw, and Wainwright had ordered the crew to weigh anchor and run up a white flag. Something was happening.

Becker approached him. "Lea wants you," he said with a nod of his head toward the bridge, where the XO and the captain stood in conference. Quincy hastened to report there, and waited while the two senior officers finished a low-voiced conversation. Commander Wainwright folded up a paper and put it in his coat pocket, then took out his glass and turned it toward the entrance to Galveston Bay.

"Mr. Wheat," Lea said, acknowledging his presence. "You will prepare the second cutter for deployment. We are about to enter the bay, after which you and I have an errand to run."

"Aye, aye, sir," Quincy said.

"Bring a flag of truce with you," Lea added. "The sailmaker should have one prepared."

Quincy gave a nod. "Aye, sir."

Lea nodded back, dismissing him. Quincy turned away and hastened to make the cutter ready for lowering. This done, he fetched a flag, and with the white silk in hand he returned to the deck just in time to watch as the *Lane* crossed the bar into Galveston Bay.

18

At 6 o'clock on Saturday morning the Harriet Lane was sent over
the bar with a flag of truce to communicate with the military
authorities and demand the surrender of the forts, giving them
one hour to decide.
—report of Commander Renshaw, U. S. Navy,
commanding U.S.S. Westfield

Emma was awakened by thunder. It took her a moment to realize that it had been the firing of a cannon. Startled, she sat up
and listened, but heard no more. It was early, but curiosity kept
her from going back to sleep. She got up, put on her wrapper
and opened her window, stepping out onto the veranda. The
morning air was pleasantly cool and a little damp. Down on the
street she saw a woman with a basket over her arm, pausing on
her way to market, looking eastward. Following her gaze, Emma
saw a ship just inside the entrance to the harbor. It was unfamiliar, larger than the *Susanna* or the *Fox*, which had both fre-
quented Galveston's wharves since her arrival. She noticed a
puff of smoke drifting up from Fort Point on the fishhook-
shaped east end of the island. She assumed it was from the
cannon Jamie had told her was there. There were more ships
out in the gulf. Looking back at the vessel in the harbor, she
saw that it flew two flags: one white, one the flag of the United
States.

She drew a sharp little breath, cold flooding her limbs. A
sound behind her made her jump; it was Mr. Lawford, stepping
through his window in his dressing gown.

"It's a Yankee ship," she told him.

He came to the railing to look, then said, "Go back inside. Stay with your aunt. I'll go find out what's happening."

Emma rubbed her arms, which were suddenly covered with gooseflesh. With a last glance at the enemy ship, she went into the house to dress.

Quincy stood with Lea on the beachhead, keeping a watchful eye in all directions while they awaited the arrival of the Rebel commander. The *Lane* lay at anchor just inside the bar, where she had stopped when the Rebel cannon had fired across her bow. The cutter waited on the narrow beach, its white flag flickering in the occasional breeze. Grass and brambles covered the ground between them and the earthwork fort that stood atop a slight rise a little distance from the shore, with a small wooden barracks nearby. The gun that had fired—possibly a Columbiad—protruded from the fort.

Lea took out his watch. "Twenty minutes. They should have been able to find their commander by now. The town is not that far away."

"Perhaps he was at breakfast," Quincy suggested.

Lea glanced up at the fort with narrowed eyes. "I will give him ten minutes more," he said.

Quincy paced a short way along the beach. There were little wildflowers blooming amongst the brambles—tiny sparks of yellow amidst the dark green and thorny black—but he did not try to collect any of them. This was too dignified an occasion for flower-gathering. He did not know what Lea's instructions were, but the *Lane* would not have entered the bay without serious intent to control it. This was not just blockading a little harbor inlet where smugglers might hide. Galveston was a city—the most prominent port between New Orleans and Veracruz—and full of Southern citizens and business interests.

The sound of a horse arriving at the fort made Quincy look up. A moment later a man came striding down the hill toward them. He was tall and lean, dark-haired and dark-whiskered, and wore a Confederate uniform. Quincy had not seen one up close since the surrender of New Orleans, back in the spring.

The Rebel officer stopped before Lea. "I am Colonel Cook," he said.

Lea nodded greeting. "Lieutenant-Commander Lea. My captain has a message for the town's authorities from the commander of the fleet." He gestured toward the ships in the gulf. "He requests that you send an appropriate official to him to receive this communication."

Cook gazed at the fleet, eyes narrowed against the morning sun. "I do not have a boat here," he said. "I will have to send the messenger out from town."

"That will be satisfactory," Lea told him.

An exchange of stiff bows, and the officer strode away again. Lea looked at Quincy. "Back to the ship," he said, and they returned to the cutter.

Aboard the *Lane*, Quincy oversaw the stowage of the boat, cast an eye over his division, and gazed toward the island. The men stood at their action stations, silent and tense.

Minutes passed, stretching to hours. The afternoon watch began, and still no boat was seen. The captain and Lea stood on the bridge watching the city. Quincy stood at the rail, staring at the bay for any sign of the requested messenger. Gerard joined him. "This is maddening," he said. "The captain's working into a rage."

"What, our gentleman Wainwright?" Quincy asked.

Gerard gave a wry grin. "What did the Rebel commander say?" he asked.

"Nothing much. He was polite," Quincy told him, "though he and Lea looked a bit like bulldogs squaring off."

"Look!" Gerard said, pointing, and at the same time the lookout in the crow's nest called out a warning. A sailboat was visible, bearing a white flag, beating its way out from the harbor.

"Now we'll see something," Quincy said.

The boat seemed to have difficulty making progress toward the *Lane*'s position. After half an hour it appeared to have moved very little. After an hour, Wainwright ordered the anchor weighed and the *Lane* retreated across the bar to the gulf.

Wainwright ordered out a cutter, and sailed in it himself to the *Westfield*. Quincy watched the captain's boat move away, and glanced back at the tiny white speck of the Rebel sailboat, still bobbing in the bay. Another hour passed; the first dog watch was approaching, when Gerard came up to Quincy and pointed out a flurry of activity around the *Westfield*.

"Cutter's returning," he said.

Quincy saw this was true, and that other boats tied to the *Westfield* were dispersing to their ships. Whatever conference Renshaw had been holding was at an end.

The cutter had returned, but the captain had not. He had sent a message for Mr. Lea, who soon ordered the anchor weighed. The *Lane* made for the harbor again, this time in company with the *Westfield*, *Clifton*, and *Owasco* with the mortar schooner *Henry Janes* in tow.

"Supper in Galveston tonight, boys," Gerard said, joining Quincy at the rail. "Who'll bet a dollar?"

"No bet," Becker said.

"We are an impressive cortege," Quincy murmured. "I wonder how the Rebels will respond?"

He was answered by a shot from the shore battery, aimed at the *Westfield* which was in the lead of the fleet. The three acting masters split up, hastening to their battle stations in anticipation of the XO's command, which came in short order. Sailors leapt to their places to the sound of the drum beating to action quarters.

"Mr. Wheat, Mr. Becker, commence firing when ready," Lea called as he strode down the deck. "Disable that gun. You know where it is," he added to Quincy.

"Aye, aye, sir!" Quincy said, glad to be doing something at last.

Emma and Aunt May occupied the downstairs sitting room, over which silent tension reigned. May had been carried down by Rupert, and the ladies had taken their breakfast and luncheon there, served on a tray. Mr. Lawford had not yet returned. As the day wore on, Mr. Strythe had come from next door to sit with them, and every now and then he would make some idle remark as if trying to begin a conversation. As if normal conversation were possible under the circumstances.

Emma glanced at her music tutor over her embroidery hoop, trying to decide why he had not been pressed into the military service by the bayonet-gangs that had been scouring the town. He was not forty, she thought, but he was admittedly light of frame, with receding hair and eyesight poor enough to require his wearing spectacles. Perhaps he had been passed over for these reasons, or perhaps he had highly placed friends who had made him exempt from conscription. Regardless, his presence was a comfort to May, she believed, and so she was glad of it.

"Miss Russell," he now said, "I see that your piano is closed. I do hope you have been practicing your exercises."

It took patience, but Emma found a civil reply. "I am much better at the guitar," she said. "I wish you will give me another lesson on that."

"But, dearest," said May from her couch, "a young lady should know how to play the piano."

"I do not have a piano at home, so much good it will do me, but I will make you a bargain." She turned to Mr. Strythe. "If I promise to practice the piano for half an hour each day, will you teach me more upon the guitar?"

Before he could answer, the sound of a cannon was heard. The first explosion brought Emma to her feet; the second sent her running for the stairs.

"Emma!" cried Aunt May. "Do not go up there!"

"I'll be right back," Emma called down the stairs. She hastened up them, skirts grabbed in both hands in a most unladylike fashion. Reaching the upper hall, she went directly to the center window and opened it, going out onto the balcony.

No longer one ship, but four had now entered the harbor, one towing a smaller boat. They were all firing at Fort Point, whose single gun was firing back. Even as she arrived, a shell exploded right over the fort, and a moment later Emma saw men running toward the city, abandoning their gun. She felt a tightness in her chest as she watched.

"Miss Russell?" called Mr. Strythe from downstairs.

Annoyed, Emma did not answer at once. The flash and smoke of the ships' guns held her transfixed, but they soon fell silent. Something was burning at Fort Point; she could see the flames rising. The ships were approaching the harbor proper, and would soon be opposite the town. From there they could, at any time, fire directly into the city. Emma felt a chill, and returned to the hall, closing the window behind her.

"Miss Russell?" came Mr. Strythe's anxious voice from below. Walking to the rail, she saw him peering up from the foot of the stairs.

"Mrs. Asterly wishes you will come down," he said.

"I am coming," Emma said. With a last glance at the window she began to descend, deciding exactly how much of what she had seen to share with her excitable aunt.

The *Westfield* had got off the first shot, and Quincy's division ploughed a shell into the earthwork, but it was a shell from the *Owasco*, bursting right over the gun, that sent the Rebels scattering. The muzzles visible on a small island to the northwest were silent.

"They must be Quakers," Quincy said to Lea, who had come to stand beside him.

Lea nodded. "They appear to be abandoning the fort. They've fired the barracks. Hah, there's a signal from the *Westfield*." Lea signaled to cease firing.

The sailboat had hastily retreated when the firing began;

now it resumed its progress toward the fleet. Quincy and the others watched it approach the *Westfield*. Before it arrived a second shore battery, closer to the city, opened fire on the flagship.

"Two guns," Quincy said to himself. The half-dozen rounds they fired fell short of the ship by fifty yards, then they ceased the futile attempt and the harbor fell still. The sailboat at last reached the flagship and its occupants were taken aboard.

Quincy glanced toward the bridge, where Lea stood observing the events. Very shortly he issued the order to secure from battle stations. When all was as it should be, Quincy ventured to approach the bridge.

"Is Renshaw demanding Galveston's surrender?" he asked Lea.

"I presume so," said the XO. "They don't seem to have much in the way of defense."

Looking at the abandoned fort and the silent shore battery, Quincy had to agree. Too bad, he thought, one did not get prize money for the capture of a city.

"They have stopped firing," Emma said. "I want to go and see what is happening."

"No, no, please stay here with me!" cried Aunt May, reaching a hand up to detain Emma. She was agitated, and in order to calm her, Emma spoke in a cool, gentle voice.

"There is no danger now, May. I only want to go up and look to see if those ships are still in the harbor."

"I agree with Mrs. Asterly," put in Mr. Strythe. "You should not expose yourself."

Emma cast him an annoyed glance, then ignored him. "I won't stay more than a minute, I promise—"

The sound of the front door opening interrupted her. A moment later Mr. Lawford walked in.

"Albert!" cried Aunt May, struggling to rise from her chaise. "Oh, Albert, I have been so worried!"

"What, has Emma let you work yourself into a state?" he said, gently obliging her to sit down again. "All is well." He glanced at Emma, who knew from the sharpness of the look that he had more to tell, but did not wish to share it with Aunt May.

"Mr. Lawford, I am curious about the ships," Emma said. "Are they still in the bay?"

"Yes."

"Will you go with me up to the balcony to look at them? May is afraid I will be unsafe."

"Oh, I doubt that. The intruders are entertaining an envoy from the city, so there should be no more firing. I will go with you, if you wish."

Emma led him upstairs and out onto the veranda. The ships were still there. They had stopped moving now, and lay between Pelican Spit and the city. Emma turned to Mr. Lawford, her eyebrows raised.

"The men who went out were officers under Cook," he said gravely. "As I understand it, their mission is to negotiate a truce to allow time for the evacuation of the city."

"Evacuation?" Emma said. "So they plan to surrender without a fight?" She was both relieved and angered, and could not tell which feeling was stronger.

"There must be thirty or more guns on those ships," Mr. Lawford said, waving a hand toward the bay. "Our defenses cannot compete with that. All that would happen is that innocent people would be hurt." He frowned. "We must get you and your aunt out of the city."

Emma nodded. "I can be ready in half an hour," she said.

"We may not be able to take much with us—"

"Miss Russell!" shouted Mr. Strythe from the house.

"A moment!" Emma called back to him through the window.

"Miss Russell, please, you must come at once! Mr. Lawford?"

His voice held a note of panic. Emma and Mr. Lawford exchanged a glance, then hastened inside and down the stairs, finding Mr. Strythe more than halfway up them.

"She stood up! She wanted to go to the window," he said excitedly. "That is all! She just stood up!"

Emma hurried down the last few steps and ran into the parlor with Mr. Lawford close behind. She expected to see May in a faint on her chaise. She did not expect to see her covered in blood.

By the second dog watch, Quincy knew there would be no more action that day. The men on watch stood tensely on deck, eyes fixed on the city or on the small boats that went back and forth from the *Westfield* now and then. Those off duty went about the business of getting their dinner and spoke in subdued tones of the day's events. Galveston would surrender and that was all very well, but it meant only glory, no money. The Lanes seemed all to agree that it would be better to be out on blockade, with a chance of catching a prize, than sitting in this harbor.

Quincy retired to the wardroom, where he found Becker, Gerard, Richardson, and Penrose at the table.

"See if you can get us some oysters while we are here, will you, Wheat?" said Richardson.

"Oh, yes," Quincy said, taking his seat. "I will go ashore to get them, and bring back a case of yellow fever for you as well."

"Is there fever on the island?" Penrose said sharply.

"That's what the Rebels told Renshaw, according to Mr. Lea."

"Then we don't want to go ashore. I will recommend to the captain that no liberty be granted."

"The crew will praise you for that," Gerard grumbled.

"How long do you think we will be here?" Quincy said.

No one had an opinion. With a sigh, Quincy turned his attention to his dinner.

Emma and Mr. Lawford sat in the parlor watching the daylight fade. On discovering May's distress they had stanched the bleeding of her nose, carried her up to her room, and summoned the doctor to attend her. Mr. Strythe, who was badly shaken, had been thanked for his help and sent home. The cook had prepared a supper for which neither Emma nor Mr. Lawford could summon much appetite, and Daisy had cleared it away again when they abandoned the dining room. Now she came into the parlor to light the candles, and Emma watched her move silently around the room. She had been helpful since Aunt May's collapse, had already cleaned up the blood in the sitting room, and now directed a glance at Emma that almost seemed apologetic.

The sound of footsteps on the stairs brought Emma out of her chair, followed closely by Mr. Lawford. Dr. Hurlbut came into the parlor just as Daisy was leaving.

"She is resting quietly," he said. "The bleeding has stopped."

"Can you tell us what happened?" Emma asked.

The doctor sighed. "A blood vessel in her nasal passage burst. She appears to be very susceptible to hemorrhage. I have taken a sample of her blood to examine."

"Will she be all right?"

He directed a sober look at her, as if calculating her ability to receive unpleasant news. "I cannot say as yet. I must consult my library. She is very weak at present."

"Can we take her to Houston?" Mr. Lawford asked.

A slight frown crossed Dr. Hurlbut's brow. "I would not move her now. The bleeding could easily start again."

A cold feeling settled in the pit of Emma's stomach. "So she is seriously ill?"

"I cannot give you an answer at present, Miss Russell. I will return in the morning." He pressed her hand. "Good night. Do try to get some rest."

Emma sank into her chair while Mr. Lawford saw the doctor out. When he returned, she looked up at him. He was a bit pale, she thought. He resumed his seat on the sofa and leaned his head on one hand, frowning at the floor. Emma got up, stepped to the bell-rope and pulled it, then sat down again. In a moment Rupert appeared.

"Would you bring the sherry, please?" she said to him.

"Yes, Miss."

Mr. Lawford glanced at her between his fingers, and sat up. Resting his elbows on his knees, he clasped his hands between them.

"What shall we do?" Emma asked. "Shall we try to move her tomorrow?"

"The doctor will say she is not strong enough. Fifty miles rattling in a rail car—" He shook his head.

"And she detests it so."

"I am afraid she must stay, for now."

Emma raised her eyes to his. "Then I will stay, too."

"That is generous," he said slowly, "but not necessary. I know you have been wishing to go home, and your family will want you in safety."

"My mother would not wish me to leave while her sister is ill," Emma said. "I will stay."

Mr. Lawford's frown softened, and he smiled. "God bless you," he said.

Emma smiled back. She was frightened, deep inside, but she saw her duty clear before her. Aunt May deserved her loyalty. She would stay.

19

Galveston, October 4, 1862, 10 o'clock P.M. *The Commander of the Federal Naval fleet having granted four days' time to remove the women and children from the City, Notice is hereby given to the citizens, that they may avail themselves of the opportunity of leaving. The Railroad cars will be kept running constantly, and for those persons, who are unable to pay their transportation, it will be furnished to them . . .*
—J. J Cook, Col. Comd'g.

The next morning Mr. Lawford ventured forth again to learn the news. Emma watched him go from the doorstep. The streets were busy with people who would ordinarily have gone to church, it being Sunday, but now they were hurrying about with expressions of worry, or driving carts or carriages loaded with furniture. The sky was overcast, as if to reflect the city's mood of gloom.

Dr. Hurlbut arrived to visit Aunt May, and spent considerable time with her. Emma, coming upstairs to the balcony, heard them talking in low voices. She went outside to view the bay, where little had changed. The ships still stood in the harbor, but the activity in the streets increased with the waning of the morning.

Shortly before noon Mr. Lawford returned, and Emma hurried downstairs to meet him. He had brought with him a copy of a notice—hastily printed, by the evidence of random italicized letters—that had been issued late the previous evening by Colonel

Cook. It informed the citizens of Galveston that the Federal fleet had granted them four days to evacuate the city, that the railroad cars would run continuously, and that persons unable to pay for their transportation would have it furnished them by the quartermaster. A meeting was announced, to be held Monday morning, at which the situation would be further explained to the citizenry.

Holding the page in her hands, Emma suddenly felt the shock of what was happening. The town was melting away around them, leaving them stranded on an island that, while beautiful, could not sustain them without support from the mainland. She looked up at Mr. Lawford.

"Four days."

"Yes," he said. "I have arranged to sell the horse and carriage."

"But we might need them!" Emma said.

"The Federals will only confiscate them," he said. "Better to have the money to lay in some food and supplies."

Emma swallowed, then nodded. "I do not think Aunt May will be well enough to leave in four days."

"What did Dr. Hurlbut say?"

"He has been with my aunt all the morning," Emma told him.

"I would like to speak with him," Mr. Lawford said, starting for the stairs. He stopped at their foot, seeing that Dr. Hurlbut was coming down.

"I am glad to see you, Lawford," the doctor said, his hand on the bannister. "I wish to speak with you. Will you excuse us, Miss Russell?"

Emma stood her ground in the doorway of the parlor. "If it concerns my aunt I would like to be present. I am her nearest relation in town."

The doctor cast a questioning glance at Mr. Lawford, who nodded. "Well, then," he said, "we may as well all sit down." They moved into the parlor, the doctor and Mr. Lawford taking chairs, leaving Emma the sofa.

"Mrs. Asterly's condition is serious," said Dr. Hurlbut in a quiet voice. "I consulted my references yesterday evening, and examined a sample of her blood. While I cannot be certain, I believe she may suffer from leukemia. A form of cancer, Miss Russell," he added in response to Emma's frown. "It afflicts the blood. Very little is known about it as yet, and I am afraid I have not previously seen a case."

"Can it be treated?" Mr. Lawford asked.

"There is no cure," said the doctor. "She can be made more comfortable . . . she will continue to be fragile."

"She is dying, you mean," Emma said. She sat very straight on the sofa, her hands clasped in her lap. She was glad to notice that they were not shaking. "How long?"

The doctor sighed. "Three or four months."

Mr. Lawford got up abruptly and went to the window. Emma glanced after him, then returned her attention to the doctor. "Will you give us instructions for how best to care for her?"

"Yes, of course. And I can prescribe some medicines to make her more comfortable. I will write it all out for you."

"Thank you," Emma said.

The doctor rose, and made a slight bow. "If you will excuse me now, I have other business to attend to. I will visit again this evening and bring you some laudanum."

"Of course," Emma said, rising to show him to the door. In the hall she took her stocking-purse out of her pocket. "Let me pay you for your time—"

"Do not trouble yourself, Miss Russell," the doctor said, reaching out a hand to stay her. "Mr. Lawford settled with me handsomely last night. I only wish I had better news for you," he said, his voice dropping nearly to a whisper.

She nodded, unable to speak, and let him out, closing the door softly after him. Turning her back to it, she realized her jaw was trembling, and put a hand over her mouth to stop her teeth chattering.

Dear God, she thought. *Oh, dear God.*

———

"Galveston is *what*?" Jamie said, dropping the buckle he had been polishing.

"Been surrendered," said Foster from his cot. "The stage driver mentioned it. There's a story in here—"

"Give me that," Jamie demanded, striding across the tent to snatch the newspaper from his tentmate's hands.

"Hey, be careful with that! It's the captain's!"

"I'll take it to him," Jamie said, holding him off with one hand as he searched the front page for the story. He found it, and a frown deepened on his brow as he read of the Federal fleet's arrival and the military withdrawal from the island. "Four days to evacuate, from the fifth—tomorrow is the last day. Damn!"

Foster sat up. "What's the matter? It's bad news, yes, but—"

"My sister is there," Jamie said, striving to keep his voice low. He folded the paper and started for the tent door.

"Hey, I haven't finished reading that!"

"I'll buy you another," Jamie said over his shoulder.

The moon was full, so he was in no danger of tripping over tent ropes. He strode to the captain's tent and stopped outside.

"Captain Sayers? It's Russell."

"Come in," Sayers said from within.

Jamie entered and found the captain in a chair by his stove, reading some correspondence. Jamie handed him the newspaper and pointed out the story about Galveston. He had not taken time to think out what he wished to say, but he felt he could not wait.

"My sister is in Galveston, sir. I wish to go to her assistance."

"Is she without friends?" Sayers asked coolly.

"No, but—" Jamie drew a breath. "Sir, we are not going to be called into action immediately. As I understand it, we are awaiting the muster of General Sibley's brigade."

"That is correct," said the captain.

"The general just arrived," Jamie said. "It will take weeks for the regiments to assemble here." He took Debray's letter from his pocket and handed it to Sayers. After waiting a moment for the captain to read it, he said, "I do not wish to leave the battery. Would it be possible for me to be detached to serve Colonel Debray temporarily, just until we receive orders?"

Sayers tapped a finger on his desk and gazed at the letter. "You have just been on furlough."

"I am not asking for furlough, sir," Jamie said.

"Not so hasty, James. I am considering the reaction of Nettles and Hume. They have not had time off, you know."

Jamie bit the inside of his lip, and waited silently. Sayers read through the letter again, then picked up the newspaper.

"It will not take me long," Jamie said quietly. "A few days only, just time to get my sister home."

"Have you considered that she may already be on her way?"

Jamie had no answer. He knew only that if he waited here, doing nothing, while Emma might be in danger, he would very likely go mad. Certainly Momma would never forgive him, if anything happened to her daughter.

"Please, sir," he said. "Please. I'll return as soon as I can."

Sayers held his gaze for a moment, the clear eyes seeming to weigh him. "Sit down, James," he said, indicating a camp chair. Jamie pulled it up to the desk. Sayers handed Debray's letter back to him, then folded his hands atop his correspondence.

"I am concerned about you," he said.

Jamie's shoulders stiffened. "Have I been derelict in performance of my duty?" he asked.

"No, no. Rather, I am concerned about—your frame of mind." Sayers looked down at the papers beneath his hands. "You seem lately to be struggling. I understand your concerns about your family. Have you had news of your brothers?"

"From Daniel, yes. Not from Matthew, since Sharpsburg. But it's early yet. He isn't a good correspondent."

"Hm." Sayers rubbed at his chin, showing stubble this late in the evening. "I will write to Debray," he said at last. "But, James, if we are ordered to move, and we very likely will be, I must call you back."

Jamie felt relief, so heavy it seemed his heart would drop out of him. "Thank you."

"Leave me word where to reach you."

"Yes. Houston headquarters. There is a telegraph nearby."

"Come to me in the morning, before assembly."

"Yes, sir. Thank you, sir." Jamie got up to leave.

"And James—"

"Yes?"

"Get it resolved this time," said Sayers. The words were softened by a hint of kindness in his tone.

"I will," Jamie said, nodding at his captain. "Thank you."

Galveston was in chaos. Emma had ceased looking out from the balcony, for the view did not change. The Federal ships remained where they were. Citizens scrambled through the streets, westward to the train depot. Mr. Lawford had been there and reported utter confusion: women and children with their belongings crowded on the platforms awaiting the trains; desperate pleas for a cart, a wagon, any sort of transportation.

On Monday Dr. Hurlbut had been shot and killed as he returned to his carriage after placing his wife and children on the cars. The soldier who shot him had been aiming at an officer trying to arrest him for rowdiness, and only that officer's quick response had prevented the crowd from lynching the fellow on the spot. Emma and Mr. Lawford had learned about the doctor's death at the market, where they had gone that morning with the carriage for a load of food and supplies before handing the vehicle over to its new owner.

Since then, Emma had gone to the market several more times on foot, taking Rupert with her and returning with all they could carry. The selection was already dwindling: they bought dried beans and corn, molasses, rice. Little flour could be found. Fish were still plentiful, but vegetables were worth their weight in gold. Emma bought them anyway; money was not a concern.

She bought a milk goat and laying hens from a departing neighbor, and set Rupert to building a coop.

By Wednesday morning the town was quieter, though there were still crowds of people waiting at the depot for transportation to the mainland. Not everyone had left; as Emma and Rupert picked over the few open stalls in the market that morning, she saw a number of others laying in supplies. They seemed mostly to be poor or middle-class folk. Some looked quite cheerful—Unionists, she supposed—while others wore expressions of haunted worry. Those might be the wives of soldiers, left behind on the island when the military withdrew, or perhaps they were people who simply had no refuge to run to. Houston had been overwhelmed with refugees from the first evacuation in May, Emma knew. It must be even worse now.

Returning to the house with heavy baskets, Emma and Rupert were met at the door by Daisy. "That cook's gone and left," she told them. "Gone for Houston, she said."

Emma set her baskets down in the hallway and pressed her hands to her eyes. "Can you cook, Daisy?" she asked.

"I can boil things," Daisy replied. "I never learned fancy cooking."

Emma sighed. "All right. I will help you."

"Miss?" said Rupert in his gentle voice, "I know a little cooking. We can get things done together, Daisy and me."

"Thank you, Rupert," Emma said, "but first I want you to make sure the chickens and the goat are safe. We don't want them stolen."

"No, ma'am. I'll carry these things back to the kitchen and then go finish fixing up that shed."

"Thank you."

Emma picked up one of her baskets and Daisy took the other. As they followed Rupert out back to the small building that housed the kitchen, Emma asked, "Has Mr. Lawford returned?"

"Not yet," Daisy replied.

He had gone to Dr. Hurlbut's funeral, at the cemetery on the

western edge of the town. Likely he had remained, talking, trying to get more news.

"Have we any eggs this morning?"

"No, Miss," Daisy said. "Hens still ain't settled. We just have
three eggs left from the market."

"All right," Emma said. "Bring one out, and I will show you
how to make a fritter."

An hour later Emma carried a tray up to her aunt's room and
knocked softly on the door. May's voice bid her feebly to come
in.

"Are you feeling better?" Emma asked as she entered. "Can
you eat a little luncheon?"

"Oh, I am not hungry," May said from the bed.

"Just a bite or two. Won't you try for me? I've brought you
some fresh milk, too."

"Dear child. You should not fuss so."

Emma set the tray on the bedside table and looked at her
aunt. May was pale, and looked tired despite having spent the
last three days in bed. She had not been told about her illness;
Dr. Hurlbut had told her only that it was a weakness of the
blood, he had informed Emma and Mr. Lawford, and they had
decided not to discuss it further with her in her present state.

"Shall I help you sit up, love?" Emma asked.

"Yes, all right. I will have some of the milk."

Emma piled pillows against the headboard and gently lifted
her aunt, who seemed to weigh no more than a child. May
pressed her fingers to her temple; Emma saw that they were
shaking.

"Are you all right?"

"My head aches," May said. "Where are the drops Dr. Hurlbut
left for me?"

"Right here," Emma said, reaching past the tray for the little
bottle of laudanum. "Let me pour you some water to take them
in."

"Thank you, dearest," May said. "You are too good to me. Is the doctor coming today?"

Emma paused to add three drops of laudanum to the glass of water. "He is gone," she said. "He went to the depot with his family the other day." She handed the glass to her aunt, praying that May would not ask anything more about Dr. Hurlbut. She would have to find another physician, she realized. Perhaps Mr. Lawford would know of one.

She coaxed May to drink most of the milk and eat three bites of fritter, and stayed with her until the drops made her drowsy. Adjusting the pillows to let her sleep comfortably, she allowed herself a sad smile at the frail woman in the bed, then took away the tray and quietly left the room.

Daisy met her in the downstairs hall. "I'll take that, Miss," she said. "You need to eat something. I just made up another of those fritters, still hot. I'll bring it in for you."

"Thank you, Daisy," Emma said, relinquishing the tray. Her own head had begun to ache, she realized. "Bring it to the parlor please, and could you make some coffee?"

"Yes, Miss."

Emma looked after her, wondering what had changed her mood. She seemed anxious to be helpful, now. Perhaps the uncertainty about what would happen in the city had made her cautious. Perhaps she feared that, like the carriage, she would be sold, possibly to a less agreeable household.

Discarding such ponderings, Emma retired to the parlor where she sank wearily onto the sofa. Daisy brought the fritter and she picked at it, not really hungry. She made herself eat it though. They could not afford waste.

After Daisy had taken her plate away she sat gazing at nothing, wondering gloomily what the future might hold. The light coming in through the window seemed dull. Everything was dreary now. There would be no more parties, no more visits, no more gaiety. Everything May had come to Galveston for was now gone, except the sea breezes. Insubstantial things. What good were they?

The sound of the front door opening intruded upon her brooding. She looked up as Mr. Lawford came in to join her, his face set in lines of worry.

"How is she?" he asked quietly.

"Sleeping. She ate a little and drank some milk."

Mr. Lawford nodded, then drew a chair next to the sofa and sat down. "I have come to a decision," he said, then hesitated. Emma watched him fidget with a ring on his right hand.

"I have decided to go to the mainland," he said at last.

Emma was astonished. She opened her mouth, then closed it, waiting for him to explain himself.

"I have given it a great deal of thought," he said, looking at her from beneath knit brows. "I believe I can do more good away from the island than on it. You know at that meeting on Monday Mr. Potter said we should all go where we can render most effective service to our country—well, I believe I can serve better there than here."

And what of us? Emma thought. *What of May?* She felt the first stirrings of anger, but waited.

"There is talk of organizing a force to recapture the island," he continued. "I have—business interests that may be of help. In fact, if I remain it is possible that I might be arrested by the Federals."

"Because of those interests?" Emma asked.

"Yes."

"I see."

He looked up at her, unhappiness etched in his face, and said, "I am not abandoning you. I will return, only I feel I should look into assisting the resistance, and—and I cannot bear to watch. . . ."

His face crumpled, and he got up to walk a few steps away. Emma's anger withered. She rose and followed him, placing a hand on his arm.

"I cannot look at her without—I fear I will betray the truth to her," he said in a broken voice.

"It's all right," Emma told him.

He ran a frantic hand through his hair, disordering it, and drew a deep breath. Turning to her, he said, "I am sorry I am not stronger for you."

Emma swallowed. "You are strong enough," she said.

"You are too forgiving," he said with a rueful smile.

"You must not know me if you can say that." Emma found his hand and squeezed it. "You know, for some time now I have thought of you as my uncle. I wish it were so."

"Thank you," he said, pleasure showing in his face. "I wish so, too. I will ask her again, when I can see her with composure, but now—"

"Now you have other things to do. I understand. I wish you success."

"You are a gem, Emma," he said softly. "May was absolutely right."

Emma smiled, and blinked away the sudden threat of tears. "Can you do one thing for us before you go?" she asked. "Can you find another doctor for my aunt? If there are any left in the city."

"Of course." He glanced at the window, where the afternoon light was yellowing. "I had better go and do that at once. The truce expires at ten tonight."

"Shall I have Rupert pack your things?"

"Yes, thank you. I will return and have supper with you before I go." He took her hands in his, squeezing them tightly. "Do not worry. Rupert will look after you. The Federals do not appear to have any intention of harming the city."

Emma nodded. "May I send some letters with you? I should let my family know—"

"Yes, of course." He let go her hands and moved toward the door. "I will return soon," he said.

Emma smiled after him. When the door had closed she stood

still for a moment, numb from all the week's alarums. The ranch seemed very far away now, and Momma and Poppa and Gabe like fading memories. Taking herself in hand, she went to the desk in the sitting room and sat down to write to them.

Mid-morning on October 9, the day after the truce expired, Quincy stood on the deck of the *Harriet Lane* as she lay at the foot of one of Galveston's several wharves. The *Westfield, Clifton*, and *Owasco* settled at other wharves, each commanding a principal street of the city. Uniformed men stood at the head of each wharf. Looking at them through his glass, Quincy decided they were firemen. They made no move toward the ships.

After waiting a good while for a representative of the city to approach, the *Westfield* fired three shots toward the west end of the island. This seemed to wake Galveston up, for shortly afterward a delegation appeared and was taken aboard the flagship. They remained there just under an hour, during which time Quincy watched a small crowd of curious Galvestonians, many of them children, gather behind the fire brigade. The *Westfield*'s boat returned her guests to the shore, following which orders came to the *Lane* to land Commander Wainwright and a party of sailors on the wharf for the purpose of raising the United States flag over the city.

Quincy sought out Commander Lea. "Sir, I'd like to volunteer to go with the color-guard," he said.

A corner of Lea's mouth twitched. "Curiosity?"

"Yes, sir, and—" Quincy tried and failed to stifle a grin. "Incipient madness due to enforced inactivity," he said.

"That's life in the navy, friend," said Lea, shaking his head. "Sorry, Gerard was before you. Don't worry, we'll likely be getting shore leave."

"Shall we? What about the yellow fever?"

Lea glanced toward the city. "That danger appears to have been exaggerated," he said. "According to their mayor pro tempore, there have not been many cases of fever this summer. It appears the Rebels wished us to think there was a danger so that we would not care to land in force."

Resigned to remaining aboard ship, Quincy saw to it that his division was attending to their duties, then watched Gerard and Wainwright disembark at the head of a detachment of Lanes. The other ships sent out parties as well, including marines from the *Westfield* and *Clifton*. Becker joined Quincy to watch the force of about one hundred and fifty assemble at the wharf where the *Lane* was docked, then march off up the street.

"Where are they going?" Becker asked.

Quincy handed him his glass. "To the Custom House. That two-story brick, about five blocks up on the corner. See it?"

"Yes. There's quite a crowd of people there. I assume the old fellow at the door is the mayor?"

"Mayor pro-tem. The city government skedaddled with the army. Only loyal parties left in the town."

Becker silently handed Quincy his glass, and walked away without another word. Quincy gazed after him for a moment, then opened the glass and watched through it as the mayor made a few remarks and then handed Commander Wainwright a bunch of keys. The marines stationed themselves around the Custom House, and Wainwright went inside with a color guard, of whom Gerard appeared to be in command, to raise the flag from a pole on the second-story balcony. They remained there for half an hour, then took down the flag and withdrew, unaccosted by the crowd with the exception of a couple of dozen ladies and children who decorated the rifles of the marines with flowers. At the wharf, the escort broke up to return to the various ships. Quincy watched Gerard come aboard, a poppy thrust through a buttonhole of his coat.

"Enjoyed yourself, did you?" Quincy asked.

Gerard's grin flickered. "Galveston greets us with open arms. All the money has gone to the mainland, leaving the poor, honest folk in charge of the town."

"That's a change," Quincy said. "Don't suppose it can last."

"Who knows?" Gerard said. "But for now it's a free city. Cheer up. So I missed by a few days. We'll have supper in Galveston soon enough."

Quincy gazed out at the city. Its houses were handsome, its places of business well built. Its wide streets were lined with gas-lamps that had not been lit since their arrival. A prosperous town, until the money had departed. He could understand why it had been compared to New Orleans, though to his mind they were nothing alike. Galveston was bright and new, swept by sea breezes, full of promise. New Orleans was haunted by centuries of legend, deeds noble and dire, like layers upon layers of paint on a windowsill, softening its edges though the window's view remained unchanged.

He was curious to visit Galveston, but that would have to wait. He dragged his gaze away from the interesting city, and returned his attention to his duties.

Jamie arrived in Houston weary, dazed, and hungry. He had taken the stage for the sake of expediency, reaching the city late on Friday afternoon, and he hastened to headquarters, hoping to catch Colonel Debray before the day's business was concluded. The place was noticeably quieter than it had been on his last visit. He found the Roman-nosed adjutant's clerk with a much smaller pile of papers on his desk and an empty waiting room.

"Colonel Debray?" Jamie asked, reaching into his coat. "I have a letter from him—"

"Colonel Debray is at Virginia Point," the clerk replied, continuing to write. "Would you like to see Major Adams?"

Jamie sighed. "No. Thank you."

At Virginia Point. That implied preparation for an attack on Galveston, or that there had already been one. When he had visited Fort Hébert at the north end of the railroad bridge he had seen that it was the army's main defensive position, a larger earthwork with a greater concentration of guns than at any point on the island itself. He assumed this was for the protection of the bridge, Galveston's only connection to the mainland now that the bay was controlled by the Federal navy.

The clerk appeared to have forgotten his existence, and Jamie decided against trying to get more current information from him. Better to go down to Virginia Point himself in the morning, assuming the trains were still running.

He left headquarters and sought out the train depot, where luck favored him. The trains were not crossing the bridge, he was told by a tired brakeman, but they were running as far as Virginia Point. With a ticket for the next day in his pocket, Jamie walked to the Capitol Hotel on the off chance that Emma and May were there, though he did not expect to find them. Emma had written him a letter about the ball May had insisted on hosting and her subsequent collapse. If he knew anything at all about Aunt May, she would have remained in Galveston, enjoying her indisposition for as long as possible.

That was uncharitable, he told himself, though not necessarily untrue. His gut instinct, which he trusted, told him Emma was still in Galveston, or had been until the Yankees' arrival. Tomorrow he would learn more.

The Capitol Hotel's bright lights welcomed him. At the desk he inquired whether Mrs. Asterly had returned to town, or whether Miss Russell had possibly come on her own. The last caused the clerk to raise an eyebrow. He made no comment, merely turning over the pages of the register. "Mrs. Asterly does not appear to have returned, sir."

"Are you certain?" Jamie asked, peering at the book upside down, trying to spot Aunt May's signature.

"She was last here in August?"

"The end of July."

"Her name does not appear since then."

"What about Mr. Lawford? Albert Lawford?"

"Lawford," said the clerk, frowning as he flipped back through the register. "That does sound familiar. Let me see."

"Pardon me," said a woman's voice behind Jamie. He turned, and saw a familiar face smiling at him, framed by a bonnet trimmed with lilies and roses. "Is it Mr. Russell?" she said.

"Yes," he said, bowing. "How do you do, Mrs. Hawkland?"

"Very well, thank you. I heard you enquiring for Mr. Lawford. He is indeed staying here."

"Suite seven," the clerk supplied, tapping a finger on the register. "He arrived two days ago."

"Seven," Jamie said, nodding. "Thank you."

He stepped away from the desk, and Mrs. Hawkland went with him, her satin cloak gently swishing against her skirts. "He is not here at present," she told him.

"Oh." Jamie stopped.

"He is attending to some business," she added. "He expected to return rather late this evening, or so he told me."

"Do you happen to know whether he is traveling alone?"

"I believe so."

"Oh."

Standing in the center of the hotel lobby, Jamie tried to decide what to do. Weariness washed over him, potent enough that he couldn't think well.

"Would you like to have supper with me?" Mrs. Hawkland asked, tilting her head to look at him. "You seem rather tired. Perhaps Mr. Lawford will have returned by the time we are finished."

Jamie looked at his travel-weary clothes and the valise he gripped in one hand. He must present a pretty sad picture.

"That's kind of you," he said. "I don't want to intrude—"

"No, please, I would enjoy your company," said Mrs. Hawkland. "Otherwise I must eat alone. I had planned to be served in my suite, but if you object to supping in private, the dining room is open."

Momma would have frowned on his sitting with a lady in private, but he was hardly any threat to Mrs. Hawkland, who was just being kind. May would certainly have pooh-poohed any suggestion of impropriety, had she been the one issuing the invitation.

He smiled. "Private is fine. Thank you, ma'am."

She returned the smile and led him toward the stairs. Her suite was at the corner of the building, and the sitting room had views in two directions. She removed her bonnet and cloak, revealing a handsome gown that appeared to be black but shone deep red when the light hit it a certain way. Mrs. Hawkland invited him to sit on the sofa and he did so, watching the sunset cast an orange glow on the square outside while his hostess summoned a hotel servant and gave orders for their supper. The servant paused to draw the curtains and light the oil lamps on the mantel before leaving.

"Do you not bring your own servants with you?" Jamie asked.

"No, I prefer not to," said Mrs. Hawkland, settling into a chair. "It makes traveling so much more cumbersome."

True, but an odd sentiment for a lady, he thought. Aunt May would not dream of traveling without at least her maid. Emma would probably agree with Mrs. Hawkland, though.

Dredging his tired brain for conversation, he said, "Will you tell me about Mr. Hawkland? I don't know anything about him."

"He is a planter," she said, smiling. "A very kind and generous man. I am his second wife."

"Oh," Jamie said. "Have you any children?"

"We have not yet been blessed with children," she said, a hint of unhappiness shadowing her face, "but we still hope to be. My husband desires a son very much."

"Has he children from his first marriage?"

"No. His wife died in childbirth, and the baby did not survive."

"That's very sad," Jamie said.

"Yes."

They sat in silence for a moment, then Mrs. Hawkland sat up, and put on a bright smile. "Tell me what brings you to Houston," she said. "I had thought you were fixed in Marshall."

"I was," Jamie said, "but my aunt and my sister are in Galveston."

Mrs. Hawkland was a sympathetic listener, and he soon found himself explaining Emma and Aunt May's predicament. She nodded when he spoke of the city's evacuation. "There have been hordes of refugees," she said. "All of the hotels are full."

"Are they?" That might present a problem, Jamie thought. Perhaps Lawford would put him up for the night.

A knock interrupted them. It proved to be a waiter bringing their supper of sliced ham and roasted potatoes, with fresh oysters and hot, buttered bread, all of which he set on a small table by the window. Mrs. Hawkland had ordered a bottle of champagne as well. Jamie watched the bubbles rise in the glass the waiter poured for him.

"You don't mind, do you?" said Mrs. Hawkland. "I am very fond of champagne."

"No." Jamie shook his head. "I like it, too." When it isn't being thrown at me, he thought, remembering General Sibley in one of his fouler moods.

"To the Confederacy," she said, raising her glass.

Jamie raised his also, and sipped at the effervescent wine. The supper was excellent. At first he tried to eat slowly, but his hunger awoke with a vengeance, and Mrs. Hawkland gave him the opportunity to slake it by chatting about Houston, refugees, disrupted train schedules and so on. She paused to eat an oyster, daintily tipping the shell to her lips, then smiled.

"I am on the point of returning to New Orleans," she said. "I will probably be asked a great many impertinent questions by the Federals when I arrive."

"Is it safe for you to go there? Would it not be better to stay away?"

She shrugged, causing the lamplight to cast red glints from the rosettes adorning her dress. "I have a small business matter to attend to. It will actually be more difficult for me to return home, I expect. There have been Federal boats patrolling the river, and bands of guerrillas roaming the banks."

"They would not invade your home, would they? Your husband should be able to protect you."

She gazed at him, a slow smile curving her lips. "Yes, he should." She tilted her head and looked at him, long lashes veiling her eyes. "Perhaps I will change my mind. I have not been home in a long while. I just have one or two things to settle first."

Jamie ate a last bite of ham, then sat back and sighed with satisfaction. "Ma'am, you know how to choose an excellent supper."

"It begins with choosing an excellent hotel. Shall we move to the sofa? It is getting chilly by the window. Bring the champagne, please." She rose, taking her glass, moved across the room.

Jamie hesitated. Having supper was one thing; champagne on the sofa was something else. Was she teasing him? He carried the wine cooler to the low table in front of the sofa and poured for her, then went back to the supper table for his own glass, buying time to think.

When he turned she was seated primly at one end of the sofa. He decided he was getting too suspicious—blame it on Major Owens. Mrs. Hawkland was a lady, after all. He stepped to the far end of the sofa and sat down.

"Do you ever get homesick, Lieutenant?" she asked.

Jamie gave a low laugh. "Oh, yes."

"Maybe you have a sweetheart back in San Antonio."

He looked at her, trying to discern what had prompted that suggestion. "No," he said.

"I am surprised." She sipped her champagne. "I would have thought you must have one."

"Sometimes it's easier not to."

"Oh," she said, one pretty, dark eyebrow rising briefly. "I hope that does not mean you have been hurt."

"No." Jamie turned his glass in his fingers, then took a sip of wine. It was starting to get warm. He added to it from the chilled bottle, and watched the fresh bubbles spit and dance.

"I would think any girl would be proud to be your sweetheart," she said softly.

This was perhaps the strangest conversation he had ever had. Maybe the champagne had addled his head. He took another swallow, feeling it explode inside his mouth, then set the glass on the table before turning to look at her.

"I don't want to be the cause of someone else getting hurt," he said. She looked bewildered, so he added, "My sister's fiancé was killed in New Mexico. In a battle."

Her lips formed a silent O and her eyes widened. "I'm sorry," she murmured.

Jamie acknowledged it with a nod, and glanced down at his hands. Her dress, which was quite wide, fell in soft folds over the sofa and brushed the floor near his boots. She had a pretty waist. Even as he thought it, she moved nearer, and he glanced up, feeling his heart start to thump.

"I know what it's like to be disappointed," she said, "but at least friends can comfort each other." With a sad little smile, she laid her head on his shoulder.

Taken unawares, he was not sure what to do, so he held still. Mrs. Hawkland sighed, then uttered a cry of dismay.

"Oh! I have spilled wine on your coat," she said, jumping up. "I am so sorry! Here, let me have it, I can stop it staining." She put her glass on the table and held out her hands.

"It's all right," Jamie began.

"No, please—it is very simple to stop the stain, but it must be done quickly."

Having heard similar words from Momma before, he shrugged out of his coat and gave it over to Mrs. Hawkland. She removed the napkin from around the champagne bottle and dipped it in the icy water of the cooler, then dabbed at the wine.

"How stupid of me! Do forgive me," she said. "I do not know when I have been so clumsy."

"If you knew what that coat had been through you wouldn't trouble yourself over it."

"But it's the only one you have with you, is it not? There, that should do. No, let it dry before you put it on." She got up to hang the coat over the back of a chair, then returned to the sofa, smiling ruefully as she sat down.

"I do apologize," she said, a pretty blush raising color to her cheeks.

"It's nothing, really."

"How kind you are."

She laid a hand on his arm and squeezed it gently. Jamie realized he must be tipsy, because her touch inspired an unaccustomed reaction in his body. She could not want what he thought she wanted, could she? Because she was a lady—a *married* lady . . .

He became almost painfully aware of her: large brown eyes, the softness of her hair, a faint scent of roses. She was very close, and he tried not to breathe faster, though his heart felt like it was being squeezed. She was smiling still, a soft, lovely smile that widened a little as her lips parted to show pearly teeth. Yes, she definitely smelled of roses, and also something earthier. There was something he ought to remember, but it vanished as she kissed him.

Sweet, soft, wine-honey kiss. Jamie drew back as it ended and opened his eyes, trying to frame a question but it was difficult when she kept smiling and gazing at him with those beautiful, dark eyes.

The second kiss drove away all conscious thought. He felt her arms slide around his neck and he ran a hand down her back to that trim little waist, the fabric of her dress so silky-soft he feared his rough hands would damage it, and then he stopped thinking anything at all.

20

---•◆•---

J. W. Moore, Mayor pro tem., started for Virginia Point, to communicate to the confederate military authorities what had been done here. . . . Colonel Debray informed him that no communication whatever would be allowed with Galveston: no provisions, no letters or papers would be permitted to pass the lines. No persons coming from Galveston would be permitted to return.

—F. Flake, Esq., *Galveston News*

Jamie woke suddenly, sensing he had overslept. The soft bed must be to blame, he thought, fighting through the haze of drowsiness. The room was dark—good drapes—and the bed was very warm. He turned his head, and the last shrouds of sleep abruptly vanished.

Oh, God.

She lay with her dark hair spilled across the pillows, her bosom rising beneath the sheet with each breath, deep in sleep, or so it appeared. Jamie looked up at the ceiling, fighting down panic, though part of him wanted to wake her, wanted to forget the world in her soft, scented embrace.

Oh, my God.

Slowly, cautiously, he slid out of the bed. From the bright edges of light seeping around the drapes, it appeared to be well into morning. He stood gazing at her, his body suggesting he return to the bed. It had not been a dream. There she was, real as anything, naked beneath the sheet. Mrs. Hawkland.

He turned away, determining with a swift glance that none of his clothes were in the room. Moving to the sitting room door, he took a cautious look before going in. No one there; drapes closed, though thinner and letting in more light. He winced at the room's disarray—evidence of his debauch. He found his trousers and extracted his watch. If he hurried, he could still catch the train. Scrambling into his clothes as quietly as he could, he glanced now and then at the door to the bedroom, fearing, hoping.

Maybe he should leave her a note? But if he stopped long enough to write he might miss the train, and besides, what on earth would he say?

"Good morning."

She stood in the doorway, dressing gown wrapped around her, holding it closed with crossed arms. Jamie swallowed.

"I have to go."

She gave a small smile and nodded. "I just wanted to—to thank you."

He closed his eyes. He could feel his face heating up, burning with shame, with desire.

"Would you be surprised if I told you I don't usually do this?" she asked. "That I've never done this before?"

He looked at her, unable to find a single thing to say. She gave a soft laugh.

"Never mind. I don't know why I told you that. You certainly don't have any reason to believe it." She drew herself up and met his gaze. "We'll just say good-bye."

Yes, that was best. Jamie nodded. "Good-bye," he said, meaning it kindly, and filled with relief.

He walked to the door, where he'd left his valise and his hat. Picking them up, he opened the door quietly, peering out to see if anyone was in the hall.

It was empty. He stepped out and pulled the door shut behind him. "Good luck," he heard her say softly, just before it closed.

Anxious not to be seen near her door, he strode down the hall and took the stairs two at a time. His mouth was dry and his head ached a bit from the wine. As he passed the hotel desk he felt his face begin to burn again, but a glance that way told him a different clerk was on duty.

"Jamie?"

Nearly tripping, he stopped and turned. Mr. Lawford hurried toward him from the dining room.

"I thought so! I didn't know you were coming to Houston."

"Just leaving, actually," Jamie managed to say.

"Do you have time for breakfast?"

"No, I—no. Thank you, but I must catch the train." Remembering, somewhat late, his reason for doing so, he asked, "My aunt and my sister are still in Galveston?"

Lawford's face went grave. "Yes," he said. "I should tell you. . . ." He frowned. "I'll come with you."

Jamie's feelings were too much in a jumble for him to compose a protest, so he let Mr. Lawford accompany him to the street. He had intended to walk to the depot, but Lawford summoned a cabriolet, and bid the driver to hurry.

Leaning back in the cab, Jamie fought a desire to close his eyes. Mr. Lawford wanted to talk to him. He turned his head to look at the older man, and saw that he was frowning. Lawford noticed his gaze and shifted to face him.

"Your sister remained in Galveston to take care of your aunt. She is very ill, James." His frown deepened into grief.

Surprised, Jamie said, "Emma wrote to me. She had some kind of fever?"

Lawford shook his head. "She is dying," he said.

In a state of numbness, Jamie listened to Lawford's quiet explanation. This made matters more complicated, he thought, rubbing a hand over his unshaven jaw. This would require thought, which would require him to straighten out his distracted brain.

"Thank you for telling me," he said.

"Do you still intend to take the train? It will not go into the city."

"I am only going to Virginia Point, for now at least. I'm going to serve on Colonel Debray's staff for a short while."

"Oh? Tell the colonel I would be happy to help him in any way. I am talking with the owner of a steamer about selling it to the government. I understand a boat is needed to patrol the upper bay."

Jamie nodded agreement. The cab was slowing; they had reached the depot.

"If you do get to see them," Lawford said, then hesitated. He appeared to struggle with his feelings. "Tell them I think of them every day. Tell them I will see them as soon as I can."

"All right."

"You can write to me at the hotel," Lawford added. "They will hold letters for me."

"I will," Jamie told him, climbing down.

"I am glad I saw you," Lawford said, offering his hand.

Jamie shook it, saying, "Thank you for the ride."

"My pleasure. Go on, best hurry."

Jamie went straight to the platform and boarded the train, choosing a seat at the back of the single passenger car, which was largely empty. He wondered whether Lawford would see Mrs. Hawkland at the hotel, and if so what she would tell him. Uncomfortable with that subject, he tried to figure out what to do about Emma, but his thoughts kept drifting back to Mrs. Hawkland.

Adultery. Add that to the list of my sins.

He knew next to nothing about her husband. Would Hawkland find out, and want to kill him?

"Oh, what have I done?" he moaned.

An officer seated at the front of the car turned to look at him. For a heartbeat, Jamie thought it was Owens, then realized it was not. Just a stranger. Just someone staring at him, wondering if he was an idiot. Well, he was, he decided. He definitely was. He covered his face with his hat, leaned back, and tried to sleep.

Life in Galveston had become desolate. As October wore on Emma's days seemed to run together in an endless pattern of caring for May, keeping the household going, and hoping for a miracle. Gloom hung over the city. Too many houses were empty. All the main businesses were closed. In the market, the citizens paid shocking prices for what little food could be had. Always their eyes strayed toward the wharves and the silent menace of the Federal ships. They received no mail, of course, and the Yankee commander had ordered the citizens to show no lights at night, fearing they would communicate with the mainland.

To her surprise, Emma found that she had a supporter in Mr. Strythe, who had been unable to move his large collection of valuable musical instruments during the evacuation, and so had remained behind to protect them. He came over daily to visit, gossiping with Aunt May, sometimes bringing his violin to play for her, and continuing to instruct Emma on the piano. Emma thought it ridiculous to be studying music at such a time, but May begged her to continue her lessons, and Mr. Strythe confided to her that it pleased him to feel of use. He would not accept money, so she paid him in butter and eggs.

May had improved gradually since her collapse in the sitting room, but was still too weak to get out of bed. Emma did what she could to amuse her, saw to it she was comfortable, bullied her into eating and generally devoted herself to her care. Daisy slept in May's room at night, while Rupert occupied the slave quarters out back and kept watch over the kitchen and the animals.

Late one evening, as Emma sat in the parlor yawning over the pages of *Silas Marner*, she thought she heard a scratch at the front door. Frowning, she set the book aside. She had only a single candle to read by, which she picked up and carried into the hall. She stood listening, wondering if she had imagined the noise, when a soft, almost inaudible knock fell on the door. A tingle crawled across the back of her neck. She ignored it; anyone who wished to do mischief would be unlikely to knock.

"Who is there?" she said, keeping her voice low so as not to wake May.

"Emma, it's me. Let me in."

"Jamie!"

Emma set down the candle and hastened to draw the bolt. Jamie stepped in and pushed the door shut at once. He was dressed in civilian clothes—rather baggy and decrepit ones—and wore a misshapen hat that rode low on his brow.

"What are you doing here?" she said in a half-whisper.

"Shh," Jamie said, glancing toward the stairs.

Emma picked up the candle and drew him into the parlor. She sat down on the sofa and Jamie took a chair.

"How did you get into town?"

"Walked across the bridge," he said. "We've got someone in town most every night. I would have come sooner, except . . ."

A pained look crossed his face, then was gone. He looked up at her, eyes seeming strained, shadows cut in his cheeks by the candlelight.

"Mr. Lawford told me about May," he said softly. "He asked me to tell you both he's thinking of you." He shifted, knotting his fingers. "I have been trying to think what to do, Emma. I want to get you and May out of here."

"She can't be moved," Emma said, shaking her head.

"Is there not a hospital that could care for her?"

"It is overcrowded already. People are beginning to fall ill. I would not want to take her there, Jamie, she's too frail. Dr. Fisher visits us now and then. There is not really much he can do," she said, dropping her voice to a whisper.

Jamie pressed his lips together. "Does she know?"

"No," Emma said, "though I think she may suspect. She does not speak about getting well."

He was silent for a moment. Emma watched him, thinking he looked careworn. She thought of their argument on the beach, and felt half-inclined to offer him an apology—he certainly had been right about Galveston—but she didn't want to remind him of that day. He had been so angry.

"I've brought you some things," he said, rummaging the pockets of his dreadful clothes to produce several packages: coffee, sugar, dried peas, dried apples, dried cherries. Tears sprang to Emma's eyes as he put them in her hands. "It's not much," he said.

"It's a fortune," she told him. "Oh, Jamie, thank you!"

"I only wish I could do more," he said. "Is there anything you need?"

"Laudanum, for May," Emma said.

"I should be able to get some. What else?"

"Tea? Oh, I hate to ask you to bring anything! What if you were caught?"

"I won't be." He flashed her a grin, the first happy look she had seen from him. "Make a list, and next time I'll pick it up."

"Jamie, please be careful!"

"I will, don't worry. I'm here for you, Emma," he said. "As long as you need me I will be here."

She felt tears threatening again and brushed them aside. "You wouldn't have to do this if I hadn't been so stubborn," she said. "I should have gone home, like you wanted."

"Then May would have been here all alone," he said.

She sniffed, and fumbled in her pocket for her handkerchief. "She wouldn't have made herself so sick, fussing over that ball—"

"Emma, hush. That's water under the bridge." Jamie glanced down at his hands. "I've done some pretty stupid things lately myself. We just have to go on and do the best we can."

She looked up at her brother, relieved and also concerned. The haunted look had come back into his eyes. He was hurting, she could tell, and she wanted to comfort him but didn't know how.

"I'd better go," he said, watching her. "Got to get back before it starts getting light."

"Can you wait while I write a note for Momma?"

"Sure."

She led him into the sitting room, where she scribbled a brief letter. "I haven't told them anything except that she's too ill to move," she said. "Do you think I should?"

"No, better to tell them in person. I'll do it, if I get the chance."

"Poor Momma." She blotted the page, then folded it and handed it to Jamie.

"Next time I come I'll bring one back for you," he said as they went into the hall. "We did finally hear from Matt, by the way. He got nicked at Sharpsburg, but he's all right."

"Oh, thank goodness! Thank you for letting me know."

Emma set the candle down on the hall table while she unbolted the door. She and Jamie stood looking at each other, then he reached for her, a quick, tight hug.

"Good-bye," he whispered. "I'll come back in a week or so."

"Be careful," she told him.

"I will."

He picked up his hat, put it on and slipped quietly out. Emma shut the door to a crack and watched him shamble down to the street, where he turned west. She bolted the door, snatched up her candle and hurried upstairs to her own room where she opened the window and stepped out on the balcony, shivering a little as she watched her brother out of sight.

By mid-November, tempers aboard the *Lane* were getting edgy. It had been nearly a month since the *Rhode Island* had last delivered supplies to the fleet, and provisions were beginning to run low. Some seafood, at least, could be caught in the bay, but little could be bought. Most of Galveston's fishermen had left for the mainland during the evacuation, taking their nets with them.

At last the paymaster determined to visit the city market in hope of supplementing the salt beef and hard bread that was all the food left on the *Lane*. He invited Quincy to accompany him, and Quincy had no trouble getting Wainwright's permission to go and seek provisions for the Wardroom Mess.

The morning was cool and cloudy, threatening rain. Winter had set in; a tropical winter, but still uncomfortable particularly aboard ship, where it was constantly damp. Quincy wore his overcoat and kept a doubtful eye on the sky as he waited for Richardson. The lanky paymaster appeared with four landsmen in tow.

"Honor guard?" Quincy asked as they left the ship.

"Onion heavers," said Richardson. "To carry back our spoils."

"You're an optimist," Quincy told him. "The town is not much better off than we are."

The few Galvestonians who were out paid them little attention. The sailors had not been granted liberty, but the fleet's officers were frequent visitors to town and had ceased to be remarkable. Commander Wainwright had established cordial relations with the temporary government, and had expressed approval of the citizens' conduct. Galveston's residents were modest and cooperative. To Quincy, they appeared also to be rather distressed.

The offerings in Market Street were slim. Quincy picked over some withered yams, most of which appeared to be moldy, while Richardson haggled with a vendor over two bushels of cattails harvested from the island's bayous. To add to the pleasure of their expedition it commenced to drizzle. Quincy turned up the collar of his coat, and stepped aside to make room for a lady and her negro servant who ducked under the vegetable-seller's awning to avoid the shower. Moving on to the neighboring butcher's cart, he peered doubtfully at some sausages.

"No fresh beef?" he asked.

"No," said the stout, grizzled man behind the cart.

"Will there be some tomorrow?"

"No."

Quincy frowned. "Why not?" he asked, careful to keep his voice polite. There were plenty of cattle on the island, he knew. There should be beef in the market.

"Perhaps," said the lady beside him, "it is because your ships persist in firing on the butchers while they are trying to do their work."

Quincy turned to face her, discovering she was younger than he'd thought, tall and dark-haired, with black eyes and skin a bit browned by the sun. The rain dripped off the front of her bonnet, which was simple but on closer examination quite stylish. Quincy concluded she was a lady of means, an unusual sight in Galveston. Behind her stood the watchful negro, who looked capable of cracking the skull of anyone who troubled his mistress.

"We are under orders to fire at any lights we see on shore," Quincy told her apologetically.

"So I have heard," she said. "And the butchers are also aware. Can you wonder at it that they are no longer willing to work?"

Quincy looked from her to the butcher, who gave a single nod and crossed his arms. Drawing a breath, Quincy strove for patience. "Commander Renshaw has prohibited any lights on the island at night—"

"Yes, yes, because you don't want us to signal to the mainland," said the young lady, unimpressed. "Has it occurred to your commander that the butchers work in the same place every morning, at the same time every morning, and that they need their lanterns in order to see what they are doing? Has it occurred to him that perhaps the ships could refrain from firing on that place at that time?"

Her eyes sparkled with indignation, and Quincy involuntarily drew back. He felt himself reddening, for as the butchers worked west of town, past the cemetery, it was the *Harriet Lane* that had fired on them, being the westernmost of the ships in the harbor.

"I will speak to my captain about it."

"I hope you will," she said, and turned away to look at the yams.

Quincy watched her, curious to know why such a forthright young lady had remained on the island. Her class had largely deserted Galveston. He had no doubt she despised the Union occupation—that had been clear in the way she looked at him. What was she doing here, picking over wasted vegetables in the rain when she should have been dining on oysters in Houston?

"Excuse me, ma'am," he said. She turned a questioning gaze on him, and he gave her a self-conscious smile. "I was just wondering—well, it seems odd that a lady like yourself chose to remain in Galveston."

"I am caring for my aunt, who is ill and cannot be moved," she said, rather coldly.

"Oh. I see. Beg pardon."

She directed a frank look at him, then glanced at the sky and stepped out, crossing the street with her servant behind her. Quincy watched her go, fascinated.

"Eyebrows singed, mate?" said Richardson, rejoining him after paying for the cattails. "What a spitfire!"

"What a corker," Quincy said, grinning.

"Careful, lad. Southern belles are dangerous."

"Don't I know it," Quincy murmured, thinking of Mrs. Hawkland. He smiled at himself, then grew thoughtful. This young lady had dismissed him pretty quick. Obviously, to her his charms were overshadowed by his blue coat. Maybe nothing he could do would change that, but he resolved at least to prove to her that he was not the heartless conqueror she seemed to think. He would speak to Mr. Lea, and perhaps to the captain. One of them might be willing to address the question of the butchers with Renshaw. He glanced over his shoulder at her once more, then followed Richardson down the market street.

21

Magruder entered at once into the scheme, and commenced preparations to attack Galveston.
—William L. Davidson, 5th TX Mounted Rifles

"He is here," said Colonel Debray from the doorway. "Come and look."

Jamie set down his pen and joined the colonel in his office, where the drapes had been pulled back from the window. They had been expecting General Magruder, who was to be the new commander of the Trans-Mississippi Department, for several days. General Hébert, who seemed incapable of doing anything beyond wringing his hands, was finally being replaced.

It was late in the afternoon on a cold November day, and the sky over Houston was overcast. In the street below a carriage had pulled up before headquarters, followed by a wagon from which two orderlies were already unloading boxes of files. The carriage—which had to be Magruder's private vehicle—was elegantly appointed and drawn by a matched team of black horses. The man who stepped out of it was tall, dark-haired, and wore immaculately trimmed mustache and side-whiskers, and a handsome dress uniform with plumed hat. He walked into the building attended by two equally beautiful aides.

"Whew!" Jamie said. "Did you see how the shine on those boots repelled the mud?"

Debray chuckled. "I have heard that the general is very concerned about appearances."

"I'd better stay out of sight, then," Jamie said. "My old outfit will be put to shame in front of all that."

"Mais non," Debray protested. "The general must accustom himself. My uniform is not up to his standards either, I am sure."

"I can't agree with that, sir. You look first rate," Jamie said, indicating the colonel's well-cut gray coat, its sleeves ornamented with triple-loops of gold braid.

"Ah, but no tassels," said Debray mournfully. "No bullion! I can only hope the general will not be too disappointed."

Jamie smiled. He enjoyed Debray's dry humor, and was grateful for the warm welcome his former instructor had given him. He had settled in well in Houston, making himself useful at headquarters. Staff-work had its advantages, in this case including sleeping under a roof. Jamie occasionally felt a pang of guilt at the thought of the battery shivering in camp up at Marshall, but he lost no sleep over it.

Debray picked up his hat, tucked it under his arm, and said, "Are you coming?"

Jamie hesitated, then decided he ought to join the colonel in welcoming the new department commander. Debray seemed to want him along. He followed the colonel downstairs, grateful to his former instructor for remembering him and offering him the means to contact Emma. Even though he hadn't been able to get his sister to safety, he had at least seen her a couple of times, and was planning to go into Galveston again the next time Debray sent him to Virginia Point.

Sayers had been more than generous, too. The battery, still at Marshall, was getting conflicting orders about where it should go and to whom it should report. Sayers had kept Jamie posted and told him not to hurry back; once their destination was certain he would inform Jamie. When he'd realized he was going to be in Houston longer than he'd expected, Jamie had arranged for Cocoa to be brought down, braving the office of A and M Transport. A week after her arrival he'd received a scolding letter from Mr. Lawford, enclosing a bank draft in the amount he had paid for her transportation. He'd been unable to avoid meeting Lawford a couple of times since then, but had managed to stay clear of the Capitol Hotel. Lawford had not mentioned Mrs. Hawkland, and Jamie hadn't dared to inquire after her.

They reached the ground floor hall and found the new general there, eyeing Jamie's favorite clerk, whose name was Corporal Dunstan. Dunstan appeared to have come out to greet the entourage, and seemed unimpressed by Magruder's grandeur.

"General," said Debray, stepping forward. "Welcome to Houston. I am Colonel Debray, in command of the Houston subdistrict."

Magruder gazed at him for a moment, seemed to conclude he was worthy, and removed a pristine white glove in order to shake Debray's hand. "A pleasure to meet you, Colonel," he said with a pronounced lisp. "May I present my aides-de-camp, Lieutenant Magruder and Lieutenant Stanard."

Debray greeted them and introduced Jamie, who made his bow extra crisp in the futile hope of making up for his lack of gloss. The general's ADC's seemed unmoved and inclined to dismiss him, which was fine with Jamie. He shot a curious glance at Lieutenant Magruder, in whom he detected a family resemblance, and who wore artillery red trim to his dress uniform. Stanard's uniform denoted cavalry.

"Will you be going on to San Antonio, General?" Debray inquired.

"No," said Magruder. "I will operate from here. It is nearer the area of most concern. I do not know why Hébert did not move the department headquarters here long ago. You can accommodate me, I hope?"

"Of course," said Debray. "We have an office prepared for you. Dunstan, will you show the general's men where to bring his papers?"

"Already have, sir," replied Dunstan in his usual flat tone.

"Very good," Debray said. "If you will follow me, General?"

Jamie fell in behind the general's ADC's as they toured the

suite of offices that had been readied for the commander. Magruder asked Debray numerous questions about the availability of men and matériel in the department, and in less than half an hour rose considerably in Jamie's esteem. It was evident that this commander, unlike Hébert, had no intention of giving up the coast without a fight.

"What about light artillery?" Magruder asked, gazing out a window of the spacious office that had been allotted to him. "Have you any available besides what is already at Fort Hébert?"

"There is the Valverde Battery," Debray said, looking at Jamie. "That's Russell's unit," he added.

"Oh?" Magruder turned to Jamie. "What are they, horse artillery?"

"Mounted," Jamie said. "A six-pounder battery, but with one mountain howitzer."

"Hah. Better replace that," said Magruder.

Jamie bristled. "It would have been done, sir, but for two circumstances," he said. "First, there are no replacements available in the department, and second, the cannon are trophies captured by the Sibley Brigade."

"Are they? Yes, I heard something about that," said Magruder.

"Lieutenant Russell assisted in their capture," Debray added quietly, nodding in Jamie's direction.

Magruder fixed Jamie with a measuring gaze, which Jamie returned. At last the general gave a slight nod. "Well, we had better have them," he said. "Where are they now?"

"At Marshall," Jamie said. "I understand they are to report to General Holmes in Louisiana."

"That won't do. Can't let them leave the department. We'll send for them," said Magruder. "Make a note of it, George."

Lieutenant Magruder took a slim notebook of sleek, black leather from his pocket, glanced at Jamie, and scratched a few words. "Velarde?" he asked.

"Valverde," Jamie told him.

"Very good," said the general. "Now, Debray, I hope you will join me for dinner. My boys here and I have not had more than a mouthful since breakfast. Where is the best table in town?"

"That would be the Capitol Hotel," Debray replied.

"We are putting up there, I believe?" Magruder glanced at his son, who nodded. "Yes. Can you come along now, and we'll leave the flunkeys to attend to all this?" He gestured to Corporal Dunstan, who had just come in with a box of files, which he deposited unceremoniously on the floor.

"I would be happy to join you," said Debray with a courteous bow.

"And your aide, too," Magruder added, nodding at Jamie.

"I should probably stay," Jamie said, glancing at Debray. "I've got a report to finish—"

"Finish it tomorrow," said the general with a wave of dismissal. "I want to hear more about this battery of yours. It may be the key to our recapture of Galveston."

No words could have done more to win Jamie's approval. Abandoning both modesty and caution, he said, "Thank you, General. I would be honored to accompany you."

On the first of December, Aunt May declared herself well enough to come down to the sitting room once more, and was carried down by Rupert and established on her chaise with great ceremony. In celebration of this event, Mr. Strythe was invited to sup with her and Emma, and over scallion soup and biscuits he kept May entertained with descriptions of his recent fishing expeditions. These had become a regular habit with him, by which means he had kept both his own and Aunt May's table supplied with fresh redfish and flounder. He also kept a weather eye on the activities of the Federals, the alien population of the town (who were largely in sympathy with their captors), and the occasional scout from Virginia Point. Emma let him rattle on, knowing he amused her aunt and curious herself for any word of changes in the town.

"You heard, of course, that a German was shot the other

night," he said to May in a tone of suppressed excitement.

"I heard someone was shot," May replied.

"It was a fellow who has been hanging about the wharves. He went into town and encountered an expedition that had been sent from Eagle Grove to arrest some merchants. Apparently he was trying to nose out their business, but they detected him and when he ran they shot him."

"Dear me."

"It ruined their plans, of course, for someone began to ring the fire bell and then the ships all lit signals, so the expedition was forced to retire."

"I wonder what those signal lanterns mean," Emma said, preparing to savor the last bite of her biscuit. Daisy had learned to make them fairly well. "I wonder how one deciphers them."

"They have a code book," said Mr. Strythe. "Every ship has a copy."

"I heard the bell," said May. "I did not see the signals. Are they very pretty?"

Emma glanced at Mr. Strythe. "Not pretty, especially," she said. "I don't care to see them, myself, for they always make me think something dreadful is about to happen."

May sighed. She looked tired, but Emma knew she would resist an attempt to put an end to her evening so soon. She smiled, therefore, and stood up.

"We have a treat for you, May, dear. Shall we, Mr. Strythe?"

"By all means," he said, rising and going to the piano, upon which lay his violin case. "Miss Russell has progressed very well with her lessons, Mrs. Asterly. We thought it time you heard her accomplishments."

"Oh!" cried May, clapping her hands. "A concert, how delightful! But I cannot see you!"

Rupert was sent for to correct this problem, which he did by lifting the foot of the chaise, taking great care to be gentle, and swinging it about so that May had a view of the piano at the back of the room. "Thank you, Rupert," said May. "Would you ask Daisy to make coffee?"

"Yes, ma'am," he said as he departed.

While Mr. Strythe tuned his violin Emma glanced over her shoulder at her aunt. "I have been learning some popular airs," she said, "and since I can't sing a note Mr. Strythe will play the melodies."

"Charming!" May smiled.

Emma took her place at the instrument and struck the first chords of "Bonnie Blue Flag." She managed fairly well, as the accompaniments Mr. Strythe had arranged for her were simple. Her instructor played with vigor and concluded with a flourish, and Aunt May applauded. They followed with "Yellow Rose of Texas," and were just beginning Mr. Washburn's new song, "The Vacant Chair," when the sound of cannon fire interrupted their performance.

Mr. Strythe hastened to the window, violin and bow clutched in one hand while he moved the drape with the other. "It is the ships," he said. "They are firing at the wharf. Dear heaven, they are firing into the city!"

He flinched away from the window as a whistling shriek came toward them in a rising crescendo. A second later the sound fell off, punctuated by a dull thud. More followed, sounds Emma had never heard before. In moments the windows fairly rattled with explosions, and in between the frantic ringing of the fire bell a few blocks away.

"I want to see what is happening," Emma said, starting for the door.

"No, Emma!" shrieked May. "Don't go up!"

Emma dropped to her knees beside the chaise and put her arms around her aunt to soothe her. "I will be as safe upstairs as I am—"

Something crashed through the front wall, sending wood and plaster flying. Emma hugged Aunt May and buried her own face in the cushions, then when the thumping of the projectile ceased, looked over her shoulder. A round ball of iron, smaller than her fist, lay beneath the piano.

"It is a shell!" cried Mr. Strythe. "It will burst!"

"No, it isn't," Emma said firmly. "Let me go, May. It is safe."

"Safe?" said Mr. Strythe, his voice rising in panic. "It is not safe!" As if to prove him right, the cannonade outside increased in fury. "We must hide in the well! *There* we can be safe! Come, hurry!"

He ran out of the room on the words, down the hall toward the back of the house, still carrying his violin. Emma pulled free of May's feeble grasp and struggled to her feet.

"I cannot take my aunt into the well!" she called after him. "Mr. Strythe!"

"Never mind, dear," said Aunt May from her couch. "If he wants to go in the well I am sure he is welcome."

"Idiot!" Emma spat down the hall. She returned to May's side and took her hands. "Are you all right?"

"Yes, I believe so, only—" she winced as something very large thumped its way down the street outside like a running giant. "Only don't go upstairs, please!"

"I won't," Emma told her, smoothing a curl of her aunt's hair that had slipped from beneath her lace cap. May's eyes were wide with fright. Emma tried to soothe her with murmured words of comfort while the barrage continued outside.

"Miss, you all right?" Rupert said, appearing in the doorway. "That Mr. Strythe gone and climbed down the well!"

"Leave him there, Rupert," Emma said. "Thank you. Is Daisy unhurt?"

"She in the kitchen," said Rupert. "Won't come in the house."

"All right. You might want to go into the root cellar."

"No, Miss. I can't hear you down there if you call. I'll stay in the pantry."

"Very well. Thank you, Rupert." Emma looked at May. "Do you want to be carried to the cellar?"

"No," May said. "But you should go down."

"I am staying with you," Emma said, raising her voice over the sound of a passing shell.

"It doesn't matter if I am hurt," May said, "but you should be where you are safe."

"I will not leave you," Emma said, hugging her tightly. Her heart was pounding, but she continued by her aunt. There was really nothing else to do; the house was built of wood, not stone or brick. Any projectile that struck it would have little trouble piercing straight through. The root cellar might indeed be safer, but she was not about to go there without May, and she feared that trying to move her aunt would distress her even more.

"You do not deserve this," May said in a small voice. "On top of the burden I have been to you."

"Hush! You have showered me with kindness."

"You should have been home with your family weeks ago—"

"May, I am not going to argue with you now."

"—instead of being stuck here caring for a dying woman."

Emma raised her head to look at her. Tears trembled on May's eyelashes.

"Who said you were dying?" Emma demanded.

"No one. No one has to say it. I know."

"Rubbish," Emma told her, dabbing at May's tears with her handkerchief. She had to blink a few times to keep her own eyes from watering.

"You have been so good to me," May said. "I want you to have the piano."

"May, if you persist in talking like this we shall be at odds."

"Be sure to tell Albert, in case I don't see him again."

Emma gripped her hands, commanding her attention. "You will see him again," she said, holding May's gaze. "Did he not promise to return?"

"Yes, but I do not know if I can wait," said May, sighing. "I am so tired."

More frightened by these words than by the roar of the bombardment, Emma took her aunt's face in her hands. "You have to get better, May," she said. "You have to come to San Antonio with me." Feeling herself about to lose her composure, she gripped her aunt in a hug. "Momma wants to see you," she said in a shaking voice, wiping at her eyes with the back of a hand.

"Take her my love, dearest," May murmured.

It was too much. Emma felt tears slipping down her cheeks, and had no more will to fight them. She clung to her aunt, sobbing now and then, feeling May's frail body tremble in her arms as she, too, wept. They remained thus for several minutes, until Emma, exhausted by emotion, at last raised her head.

"I wish whoever is ringing that bell would stop," she said, sniffing as she groped for her kerchief.

"At least we can hear the bell," said May with a little laugh.

Emma looked at her. It was true; the cannonade had ceased, leaving only the fire bell clanging away. Even as they gazed at each other it stopped. Emma stayed still, listening.

"Oh, is it—can it be over?" May asked in a whisper.

Emma got up and walked to the window, cautiously looking out between the drapes. All was still. She glanced at the hole made in the wall by the shot, which had missed the window by only a few inches. Cold air came through it, stirring the drapes.

"I believe it is over," she said, returning to her aunt. May reached for her and Emma knelt to hug her. "Let me fetch Rupert to put something over that hole. Do you want him to take you upstairs?"

"Not yet. Let me rest a little." She closed her eyes. Emma watched her until satisfied that her breathing was steady, then stepped into the hall.

"Rupert?" she called.

He came at once, saying, "Coffee's burnt. Daisy still won't come in."

"All right," Emma said. "I will talk to her, but first look at this, please." She showed him the place where the wall was punched through. "Can you put something over it?"

"Let me get some wood," he said, nodding. "I'll be right back."
He left the room, and Emma walked back to the chaise. "I'm
going to check on Daisy," she told May.

"Very well," her aunt said in a sleepy voice. "What's that
squawking? Are the chickens upset?"

Emma paused to listen, then struggled to keep from laughing.
"Maybe Daisy and the wall should wait," she said, reaching for
her shawl. "I think Mr. Strythe is in need of assistance."

"It will not happen again," said the Federal commander.

Jamie watched him, trying to read past the somewhat bom-
bastic demeanor with which Commodore Renshaw addressed
the Confederate delegation. The party—a select group led by
Major Watkins of Magruder's personal staff—had been sent by
the general to demand an explanation for the bombardment of
Galveston that had taken place the previous evening. Jamie had
requested to go along, largely in the hope that he would be able
to snatch a visit with Emma afterward. To his dismay the delegation included Major Owens, who had returned to Houston in
advance of his newly promoted commander, General Scurry. No
doubt Owens's style suited Magruder exactly, Jamie thought,
eyeing the crisp gray and glinting gold of what appeared to be
a new uniform.

Being the junior member of the delegation, Jamie had accepted
the subordinate role of flag-bearer, and now held the white truce
flag furled as he sat with the others in Renshaw's quarters aboard
the flagship *Westfield*. Renshaw stood before them, hands clasped
behind his back, his large mustache draping down on either side
of his mouth like two woolly caterpillars as he responded to General Magruder's written request for an explanation.

"The ships fired in response to an altercation between a sentry
on the wharf and one Thomas Barnett, a citizen of the town,"
Renshaw continued. "It was the exchange of fire between those
two that prompted Commander Laws and Captain Guest to take
part."

"A misunderstanding, then," said Major Watkins, tapping a gloved finger on his thigh.

Renshaw bowed. "I was at Pelican Spit when the firing commenced, and I immediately got into a yawl and went to the *Clifton* to question Commander Laws. I told him then that he should not have opened fire upon the city unless he had been attacked directly, and I have issued orders to the same effect to the fleet. There should be no more such unfortunate incidents. Please assure General Magruder that in no circumstances shall my ships fire upon the innocent women and children of the town."

Major Watkins looked at the others of the delegation. "Your explanation is satisfactory, Commodore," he said. He looked to the city's mayor pro-tempore, who had met the delegation in town and accompanied them to the ship. The mayor nodded agreement. Watkins stood, signaling the end of the conference, and after much hand-shaking and cordial formality, the mayor and the Confederate officers were escorted back to the launch that had brought them aboard. Jamie glanced around him as they passed up to the deck, partly out of curiosity as he had never before been aboard a ship. Apart from the six well-kept heavy guns, he saw nothing that might be useful for Magruder to know about the enemy flagship.

The Federals escorted them to the wharf, from which the delegation turned their steps back toward the town. Once they were past their own sentries the mayor extended an invitation to the others to dine with him at the Tremont House. Major Watkins accepted, and Jamie, gripping the staff of his truce flag, leaned forward to speak quietly in the major's ear.

"May I join you there in half an hour, sir?" he asked. "I would like to visit an invalid relative who lives in the city."

"By all means," said the major. "Take an hour, if you like."

"Thank you, sir," Jamie said. Looking up, he saw Owens watching him. They had exchanged few words today, none about their last encounter. Owens seemed satisfied to gloat in silence.

As Aunt May lived on Tremont Street, Jamie accompanied the party to the hotel before continuing south toward her house. During the bombardment the Tremont House had been struck by a shot that had passed straight through it, and numerous buildings nearby had been hit. Grapeshot and shrapnel lay in the streets, and Jamie saw an unexploded shell beneath an oleander in the elegant garden of a private home.

He took leave of the party at the hotel door, promising to return within the hour. Owens also remained outside, taking out a packet of tobacco and commencing to roll a cigarillo.

"Say hello to your aunt for me, Russell," he said.

Jamie looked at him, frowning. "I did not know you were acquainted," he said.

"Oh, yes. I met her at that little party she threw. Sorry to hear she's still ill."

"Thank you," Jamie said stiffly, and returned the few paces down Avenue C to Tremont Street. As he turned the corner he glanced back, and saw Owens leaning against the hotel beside the doors, evidently enjoying his smoke.

The walk to Aunt May's house was not far. He found Emma in the sitting room, coaxing May to drink some broth. When Rupert showed him in May pushed the cup away and reached for him, crying, "Jamie!"

"How did you get here in broad daylight?" Emma demanded, setting the broth aside.

"Official delegation," he said, hefting the truce flag before leaning it against the wall. He hugged his aunt, then sat down and gave them a quick explanation of the delegation's purpose in town. "Were you troubled by the guns?" he asked.

Emma waved a hand toward the front wall. "What do you think? Of course, all you can see is Rupert's patch. You must examine it from the outside to get the full effect."

"I didn't even notice as I came in," Jamie confessed, looking at the foot-wide square of rough wood nailed onto the wall.

"And here is what made it," Emma added, handing him a sphere of lead.

"Grapeshot," he said, hefting it. "You were lucky."

"Lucky!" cried May. "It was dreadful! Have you ever been through a bombardment?"

"Yes—May," Emma said, laying a hand on her arm. "He has."

"Well, then you must know that I was in fear of my life!"

Jamie took her hand and squeezed it. "The Federal commander has given his word that it will not happen again," he said. "It was a mistake. Two men fired at each other on the wharf, and the ships thought they were being attacked."

"If that is all it requires I have no doubt they will next burn the town around our ears!" May declared. "People are forever being shot at, or abducted! Galveston is no longer a civilized place!" She picked up her fan, which lay in her lap, and fluttered it with indignation.

Jamie pressed his lips together to keep from laughing, and glanced at Emma, whose eyes were sparkling. "Well, you know, May," he said with a little cough, "we have been trying to talk you into coming away."

She sighed. "I know. You are such dears. But I fear I cannot face the journey, although perhaps—" She looked at Emma, frowning a little with concern. "Perhaps I should make the effort."

"Let us see what Dr. Fisher has to say," Emma said gently.

Jamie stayed with them half an hour, exchanging news and accepting messages for Mr. Lawford and the family. He had brought letters, one from Daniel that Momma had sent along to him, and several from Momma and Poppa. He was highly entertained by the saga of the music teacher in the well, and tried to remember something funny to tell them in exchange, but all he could think of was his embarrassment over Mrs. Hawkland and that was not a story he had chosen to share with anyone, besides being unfit for the ears of two virtuous ladies. The thought sobered him, and he sat silently for a moment, letting May's chatter wash over him. He might have debased himself, he thought grimly, but at least he could make certain his family never knew of it. He had learned from a chance comment of Mr. Lawford's that Mrs. Hawkland had left Houston a week after their unexpected liaison, and he sincerely hoped she would not return.

"Lawford sends his love," he told May. "He asked me to tell you he will come back soon. He has been helping us make arrangements for the brigade to come down."

"Thank you, dear," May said, giving him a pretty smile. "Give him my love in return."

"Oh, and Major Owens asked me to tell you hello."

"Owens?" May frowned in confusion.

"The man who came to the ball without an invitation," Emma said, and Jamie heard an edge to her voice. He glanced at her, surprised. Owens had given him the impression he was acquainted with May.

"Oh, yes," May said, "now I remember. What a charming young man."

Emma picked up a pillow and plumped it. "Not entirely."

"What do you mean, dear? I thought he was very gallant—"

"I hope the brigade will arrive soon," Emma said, tucking the pillow behind May's shoulders. "There are rumors of Federal troops coming to occupy the town."

"There have been rumors since October," May said crossly. "I don't believe it."

Jamie looked from Emma to his aunt. "Don't worry, May," he said. "Magruder's determined to recapture the island. Be patient just a little longer." He glanced at the mantel clock. "I'm afraid I must go," he added.

"Come and kiss me, then," May demanded, holding out her arms. Jamie obeyed, then retrieved his flag.

"I will go with you to the gate," Emma said.

Once outside, Jamie reached into his pocket for a small vial, which he gave to Emma. "I'll bring more next time. I can't always get it in Houston. Too many sick refugees."

"Thank you," Emma said. "This will help."

Jamie searched her face. "Are you all right, Emma?"

She flashed a smile, which was gone again too quickly. "Just tired. I get cross, sometimes, you know that."

"Did Owens offend you?"

She shrugged. "He was a bit too familiar, that is all. Aunt May assures me that it is poor taste on my part to dislike him."

"If he troubles you—"

"He has not been near us again. May had almost forgotten him."

Jamie frowned. He shouldn't have mentioned Owens at all. "Well. You'll have Lawford with you again soon." He started down the path to the street.

"Will we, Jamie?"

The concern in her voice made him turn. "Yes, he intends to come."

Emma licked her lips. "Tell him to come soon," she said, then turned and ran back in the house.

22

How many gallant souls that greet the new born year, will live to bid it good bye? What is to be the fate of our own loved South this year? What bloody battles will be fought and on whose banner will victory perch? Will this year close the war, and what will be the result? These questions naturally crowd upon our mind, as we float on Galveston Bay, as the new year is born.
—William L. Davidson, 5th TX Mounted Volunteers

Emma woke, thinking she had heard a knock at her door. She sat up and listened, and three soft taps sounded again. Getting up, she stepped into her slippers, put on her wrapper and went to the door, opening it a crack.

Rupert stood in the hallway, carrying a candle. "Excuse me, Miss," he said in a whisper. "Mr. Lawford is downstairs."

"He is?" Emma caught herself, and whispered, "Thank you! Let me get my candle."

She fetched it from the bedside table and lit it from Rupert's, then followed him downstairs to the parlor, where Mr. Lawford waited. When he saw her, he stood up, smiling wearily.

"Thank you for coming," Emma said, embracing him. "Was it difficult crossing the bridge?"

"I came in with a party of scouts," he told her. "That is why I am here so late, and have disturbed your rest."

"That doesn't matter," Emma told him.

"How is May?"

"Tired," she said. "She has been a little better, but is still too weak to walk."

A flicker of pain crossed his face. "Has Dr. Fisher been helpful?"

"As much as he can be. He does not think it advisable that she be moved."

Mr. Lawford nodded, his brow creased in a frown. A sound from upstairs caught Emma's attention. She glanced through the doorway to the hall and saw Daisy descending the stairs.

"Miz May said to come see if it was your brother, Miss," she said.

"She is awake?" Emma turned to Mr. Lawford. "Go on up, she will want to see you."

"I was going to wait until morning—"

"Go now," Emma said, giving him a little push. She watched him climb the stairs, his way lit by Daisy. Smiling, she went back for her own candlestick. Rupert followed her.

"All finished here, Miss?" he asked.

"Yes. Did Mr. Lawford bring a bag?"

"Yes, Miss. I took it up to his room."

"Thank you."

"Good to see Mr. Lawford back again," he said, moving to put out the lights in the parlor.

Emma watched him, glad for his loyalty, curious to know what had inspired it. She had become accustomed to the slaves, but still wondered from time to time what they thought about their situation. She could not imagine that even Rupert was completely content.

"Rupert, have you been with my aunt a long time?" she asked.

"Since she come to Texas," he said. He looked up at her, then doused the last candle in the branch and picked up his candlestick, adding, "Best thing ever happened to me, when Miz May bought me."

"Where were you before?" Emma asked.

"On a plantation up by Rusk. I was put up for sale after I got in a fight."

"Oh."

"Best thing ever happened to me," he repeated. "Miz May is a good lady."

Emma smiled, and said softly, "Sometimes I think Daisy doesn't think so."

"Daisy she been through some hard times. I think she lost her faith, a while back."

"But you haven't," Emma said. She knew he attended services at a negro church every Sunday.

"No, Miss. I put my trust in God. Back on that plantation, pulling cotton every day, I prayed to Him to lift me up. Well, here I am. Never pull cotton again. Miz May is good to me, so I'm good to her, too."

Emma stood watching him, the light from their two candles setting shadows dancing around his dark face. What did he pray for now, she wondered? Freedom, no doubt. He returned her gaze steadily, quietly.

Patience, she decided. Patience was the difference between him and Daisy.

"Thank you, Rupert," she said softly. "Good night."

"Good night, Miss." He nodded, and Emma watched him go back outside, through the cold night, to his quarters.

Jamie stepped off the train at Virginia Point and immediately shivered. The sun was setting over the swamps, and already the damp was rising, a cold that struck straight to the bone. Pausing to button his overcoat, he hefted the two satchels he had brought and walked down to the new camp where his former regiment, the 4th Texas Mounted Volunteers, had recently been settled. Rows of tents seemed to huddle together between stands of grass. The air had an unpleasant salt tang, and the ground was a bit too swampy for his liking. He was glad he wasn't camped here, though before long he could be. Magruder's plans were coming together.

Jamie located headquarters by the sight of a Sibley tent with stovepipe fiercely chugging, and since he knew Colonel Reily was in Houston having dinner with Magruder and Debray, he pulled open the flap and entered without ceremony.

"Hallo," he said, unshouldering his burdens. "Merry Christmas."

"Russell!" Ellsberry Lane jumped up from a chair by the stove and grabbed Jamie in a bear hug, pounding his back.

"Easy, there," Jamie said, holding his satchels out to one side. "You don't want to break these. Emergency medical supplies."

"Oho!" Lane relieved him of one of the bags and began unbuckling the straps.

"Not that one, it's for my family," Jamie said, trading bags. "Here."

The tent's second occupant, Lieutenant Wooster, came forward and offered a hand. "Good to see you again," he said.

"Howdy, Wooster. How's the quartermaster corps?"

Wooster shrugged and indicated their surroundings. "You can imagine. The surgeons are pestering me to build them a hospital that will stay dry, but without about a ton of rock, there's not much I can do."

"Lot of men sick?" Jamie asked.

"Not yet, but it won't be long in this place."

Lane, who had liberated a bottle from the satchel, let out a low whistle. "Straight from Kentucky," he said. "How'd you manage that?"

"Connections," Jamie said, grinning.

"May I?" Lane said, hefting the bottle.

"Of course. It's for you and John, unless you finish it before he gets back."

"May he rot in Houston," Lane said cheerily. "I bet he's feasting on champagne and oysters right now, the lucky dog."

"That's what comes of being the colonel's son," Wooster said.

Jamie, momentarily distracted by the mention of champagne and oysters, brought his attention back to the present. He set his second satchel near the door and went to stand by the stove.

"Going to be bitter," he said. "Don't suppose you can lend me a horse? Cocoa's back in town."

Lane looked up at him. "Are you crossing the bridge?"

"Yes. I have an errand to run."

"Got time for a toast?" Lane said, picking up a couple of cups from his desk. "It'll keep the chill off."

"A small one," Jamie said.

"How about you, Wooster? Care to join us?"

"Thanks, but I'd better get back," said the quartermaster, picking up an overcoat from the back of a chair. "I've got to finish getting ready for the morning. The colonel bought new socks for the men, and he wants them issued Christmas day."

"Have your sergeant do it," Jamie said, grinning.

"Hm. That's a thought." Wooster, who had been Jamie's quartermaster sergeant, gave him a wry smile. Shrugging into his coat, he went out, saying, "Merry Christmas."

"Merry Christmas," Lane called after him.

"Merry Christmas." Jamie watched him go, then turned to Lane. "You've got something hanging off your lip," he said.

"A little respect, if you please. That's two square inches of flesh that are warmer than they would have been. Come, sit." Lane poured a finger of bourbon into each cup, handed one to Jamie, and raised his. "We were hereabouts last Christmas, weren't we?" he said, grinning. "Drinking in a tent?"

"Here's to Christmas at home," Jamie said. He took a swig of the liquor and let it slide down his throat, feeling the fire blossom after it. "How's Mollie?" he said when he could speak.

"Very well, when I saw her last. I wish she would write more often. Three or four letters a day, at least. Here's to her," he said, raising his cup. "Oh my, yes. Jamie, you know the way to a soldier's heart. How is Sayers?"

"Getting annoyed. Conflicting orders. We tried to get the battery down here, but Holmes trumped us. Sayers had them halfway to Gerard, then got orders to return to Marshall."

Lane laughed. "The brigade is in the same fix. We keep getting orders to move, but the truth is, we can't afford to. No transportation, no credit, and no arms even if we managed to get to Richmond, or Vicksburg, or Bayou Teche—"

"That bad?" Jamie said.

Lane nodded, smiling wryly. "Everyone wants us, but no one wants to pay to move and equip us."

"You're staying right here for now. Magruder needs you."

"I am hearing that Holmes will overrule him."

"Oh, Holmes will get you eventually, but we've got a job for you first."

Lane leaned toward him, interested. "You have some news?"

Jamie nodded. "We'll be moving onto the island in the next few days."

"Wonderful. I'll have the men start making bows and arrows."

"Magruder has about twelve hundred stand of arms."

Lane's eyebrows rose. "Enough for the 4th and a couple hundred left over for Green's fellows."

Jamie grinned. "I think they may be divided a bit differently. We need to arm some sharpshooters."

"That's what the 4th are," Lane protested. "Sharpshooters, every one!"

"It's not my decision," Jamie said, raising his hands.

"I keep forgetting. More?" Lane picked up the bottle, and Jamie accepted another splash. "Well, if you're out running errands Christmas Eve for Magruder—I assume it's Magruder?"

"Debray, officially, but yes."

"Then something interesting must be in the wind. What does he have you up to?"

"We're getting together a small surprise for the Federals."

"You're very secretive."

"Well, the orders won't go out until tomorrow, but for you, Ells—" Jamie smiled. "We're preparing for a two-pronged attack. Land and water."

Lane guffawed. "With what, coal-tenders?"

"Just about. Cottonclad packets."

"Lord."

"Equipped with cannon, and stuffed with sharpshooters."

A slow smile spread on Lane's face. "You begin to interest me," he said.

"To coordinate with artillery in town. Magruder wants that big navy gun put on a rail carriage."

"That will be a sight to see!" Lane said, laughing.

"It won't be so amusing when the ships open fire."

Lane cocked his head to look at him. "Not afraid, are you, Jamie?"

"My sister is in the city."

Lane's jaw dropped. "Why haven't you brought her out?" he demanded.

"She's tending my aunt, who's very ill."

"I am sorry," Lane said in a sober voice. "Can I do anything? We have a little transportation—"

Jamie shook his head. "I'm going in tonight to see them. I'll try one more time to get them to move." He glanced at Lane, then swirled the bourbon in his cup. "It will probably make my aunt worse, you see."

Lane was silent. Jamie looked up to find his friend watching him. "I'll get you that horse," Lane said.

"Thanks."

"Are you all right? You look—tired."

Jamie sighed, and rubbed the bridge of his nose. "Penance for my sins," he said.

"You sound like a Mexican."

"Mm." Jamie finished the liquor in his cup, and set it down. "Have you ever . . ."

"What?"

Jamie shook his head. "I was just wondering if you'd ever done something you're ashamed of." He looked up to find Lane

324 ◆ P. G. Nagle

wearing a puzzled smile. "I keep making mistakes. Someday I'm afraid I'll make one bad enough that somebody gets hurt, or killed."

"We all make mistakes."

"Mine have been pretty spectacular lately."

Lane gazed at him for a moment, then picked up the cup Jamie had put down and poured more bourbon into it. Holding it out, he said, "Tell me."

Looking at the cup, and the friend's hand that held it, Jamie was tempted. Instead he shook his head. He did not care to disillusion Lane, who was happy in his new marriage. Besides, he could not consider himself at liberty to divulge a secret that was not solely his. Maybe Mrs. Hawkland regretted their indiscretion as much as he did. Certainly she didn't deserve that he should discuss it, even with a trusted friend.

"I'd better be going," he said instead. "Thanks, though."

Lane gazed at him a second, then set the cup on the desk. "All right. If you change your mind, I'll be here."

"I know," Jamie said. "And I'm glad." He smiled, and went to pick up his satchel. "So, how about that horse?"

"Good night, Mr. Strythe," Emma called from the doorway. "Merry Christmas!"

Mr. Strythe waved over his shoulder on his way to his house. Though it had taken some days for him to recover from his adventure in the well, he had resumed friendly relations with the Asterly household, and had spent Christmas Eve entertaining Aunt May with carols. Emma had accompanied him on the guitar, and both May and Mr. Lawford had joined in, singing all the old holiday tunes and a few patriotic airs for good measure.

Emma glanced up at the sky. It was chilly, with only the tiniest sliver of moon. Closing the door, she returned to the parlor where Aunt May sat talking quietly with Mr. Lawford, and began to tidy the scatter of cups and plates. She had marked the occasion by showing Daisy how to make eggnog from Grandmother's recipe—May had pronounced it perfect—and by baking a small cake with the last handful of raisins from a packet Jamie had brought them. She had set aside a slice for him, hoping he might be able to visit for Christmas, but that hope was fading now as midnight approached. With a sigh, she put the dish on the mantelpiece, and began collecting eggnog cups.

Daisy came in with a tray. "I'm sorry, Miss," she said. "You should've left that for me."

"It's just habit," Emma told her, putting her dishes on the tray. "At home I'm in charge of the kitchen." She smiled, but Daisy was too busy clearing up to notice.

"You should be at home, dear," Aunt May said from the sofa. "Won't you let Albert escort you?"

"Not if you can't come along. We've discussed this," she added.

"But Albert is here now," May said. "He can take care of me."

Emma smiled at the thought of Mr. Lawford simultaneously caring for May and escorting her home. "It would be dangerous for him to stay," she said, glancing at him.

"I don't mind the risk," he said. "I can keep out of sight."

"And who will go to the market?" Emma demanded.

"No one, I hope," said a voice behind her.

She turned to see her brother in the doorway, wearing a heavy coat and a grin. "Merry Christmas," he said.

Emma smiled and beckoned him into the parlor, where May greeted him with a small squeak. "I knew you would come!" she cried, while Emma fetched the cake she had saved.

"Aha! Here, these are presents for you all," Jamie said.

The leather bag he gave her was heavy, and proved to contain a bottle of rum, more laudanum (which she quietly pocketed), and a variety of edible treats. Emma handed them out according to his directions, piling most of them in May's lap, while Jamie gobbled the cake.

"I meant it about the market," he said. "Don't go there for a few days. Do you have enough in the pantry?"

"That and the garden, yes," Emma said. "Why?"

"You should stay away from the bay side as much as you can. Sometime soon there will be some activity."

"Ah," said Mr. Lawford. "Can you tell us?"

Jamie shook his head. "I do need to talk to you, though, sir. Do you have access to any cotton at the moment?"

"Mrs. Hawkland left a shipment in my hands, yes. What do you need it for?"

Emma saw a moment's hesitation on Jamie's face, then he said, "Where is it?"

"At my warehouse in Houston."

"We'll talk."

Christmas dawned cold and gray, and Quincy shivered as he came on deck. The ship's schedule was light, consisting mainly of a short service read by Mr. Lea. The crew wore their best uniforms in honor of the day, and stood at attention with the enticing scents of roasting meat to torment them. The Christmas feast would not be extraordinary, but at least there would be some cheer. Admiral Farragut had at last sent supplies and a precious delivery of mail from New Orleans. The *Lane*'s officers had supplemented the men's Christmas dinner with fresh beef purchased on the island and a couple of dozen wild geese. Quincy had gone out with one of the hunting parties that had landed on Pelican Island, scouring the small island under the *Westfield*'s protective guns. They had bagged numerous ducks along with several of the big sandhill cranes, enough to make the officers' table appropriately crowded with delectables.

Quincy had obtained permission to go ashore after the service, and he calculated he had just enough time to complete his errand and return for dinner. He summoned Isaiah to accompany him, armed with a musket and pistol from the ship's armory. Quincy carried a game bag over one shoulder, containing two of the ducks he had shot.

As they started for shore, Quincy glanced eastward. A troop

transport was unloading three companies of Massachusetts volunteers on Kuhn's Wharf, toward the east end of the island. The arrival of the advance guard of infantry was a mixed joy; the rest of the regiment was missing, somewhere in transit from New York. The other transports were expected to arrive soon, after which Quincy hoped the *Lane* would be free to go out to the gulf. At least the ship that had made it to Galveston had brought the regiment's commander and headquarters staff.

Once on shore, Quincy took Isaiah with him to Market Street. Most of the stalls were closed, but a skinny boy waited at one booth—a butcher's—with a paper-wrapped parcel for which Quincy paid him. The boy nodded his thanks and dashed off, no doubt to his Christmas dinner.

"Isaiah," Quincy said with awkward courtesy, "would you object to carrying this for me?"

Isaiah's mouth quirked up in a wry grin, but he answered seriously. "No, sir. I don't mind." He accepted the parcel and followed Quincy up the street, westward.

It had taken Quincy some time to find out the name and address of a certain young lady he had seen in the market. The butcher's boy had been helpful, and Quincy had paid him well for his services. There was no longer any shortage of fresh beef, Commander Renshaw having relented and allowed the butchers their lanterns some time since, but Quincy still wished to make this gesture. Call it a Christmas gift, an act of goodwill which, since he could not be with his own family, he would direct to a stranger's.

The day was quiet, with sea breezes blowing chill off the gulf and the occasional sad cry of a gull. Quincy saw almost no one on the street, which was just as well. Those who did pass took one look at Isaiah and hastened by. Quincy liked that, he decided. All his musings had not led him to a solution for the contraband problem, but he knew that he liked Isaiah, thought him trustworthy, and wished him well.

The house he arrived at was pretty, though Quincy could see

where it had been damaged by some large projectile, probably in the unfortunate bombardment a few weeks ago. He stood at the gate, his courage faltering a little. He glanced at Isaiah, who was watching him curiously.

Clearing his throat, Quincy opened the gate and stepped into the yard. With Isaiah behind him he approached the house and knocked on the door. It was opened by a large negro, the same he had seen in the market with the young lady, who directed a suspicious look toward Quincy, then a surprised one toward Isaiah. Faint conversation came from somewhere within the house; a clink of glass suggested the family was at dinner.

"Good day," Quincy said to him. "I have a gift for Miss Russell and her aunt." He gestured to Isaiah, who brought the parcel forward and gave it to the servant while Quincy opened his game bag and removed the ducks. These he laid across the parcel saying, "A beef roast, and some birds, with my compliments and best wishes for a merry Christmas."

"If you'll wait here, sir, I'll check if Miss Russell will see you," said the servant in a deep voice.

Quincy shook his head. "Don't disturb her. She is not expecting my visit. Just give her the gift, please."

"Who do I say it's from?"

"Acting Master Wheat," Quincy said, though his name would mean nothing to her. The servant had recognized him, he was certain, and would tell his mistress who had brought the gift.

"Thank you, sir," the man said.

Quincy made a slight bow and turned away, passing down the steps and through the yard with Isaiah following. He heard the door close. So much for the hope, admittedly a faint one from the start, of glimpsing Miss Russell. He would have to pray for the chance of meeting her again in the market one day.

Smiling at himself, Quincy left the yard. A clump of pansies grew by the gatepost, spilling out toward the street. He glanced at the house, but could see no one watching. He bent down and plucked a single flower, violet and brown with a pale yellow eye. He would not send this one to Miss Keller. He would keep it instead, with the daisy she had sent to him, and the single, faded rose he still had.

Straightening, he saw Isaiah watching him. The sailor looked away, suddenly stone-faced.

"I know," Quincy said. "I'm hopeless. My brother always tells me so."

Isaiah shot him a cautious glance, then in response to Quincy's smile he grinned. Quincy laughed.

"Come on, let's get back to the ship."

"Commodore Smith, will your boats be ready on the twenty-seventh?" Magruder asked.

Smith, who had lively eyes in an otherwise stoic face, stroked his beard and said, "No, sir. The artillery hasn't arrived."

Magruder looked around at his staff officers. "And why not?"

Jamie, thankful that he didn't have to answer that question, exchanged a glance with Lawford beside him. Their part in the naval preparations—providing cotton with which to give the boats the appearance, as Magruder put it, of being protected—was done. Lawford had already concluded the transaction, and was at the meeting as a courtesy. He had been curious to meet General Magruder.

Commodore Smith, who was an old friend of Magruder's, had been placed in charge of the expedition by sea, or more properly down the length of Galveston Bay. This consisted of two impro-vised gunboats, the *Neptune* and *Bayou City*, and two smaller boats that would go along as tenders. Captain Lubbock and Cap-tain Wiler were not present at the meeting, being engaged in securing Mrs. Hawkland's cotton to their vessels, which lay at Harrisburg. Not only were the guns assigned to the boats late in arriving, but the effort to raise volunteers in Houston to go on the expedition had been a dismal failure. Houston, appealed to for aid in the rescue of Galveston, was resoundingly apathetic. Jamie would have thought at least the refugees would provide a few volunteers, but so far only a handful had come forward. Magruder was beginning to talk about using men from Sibley's Brigade.

The room was a bit chilly. Jamie got up to add a log to the fire. A knock fell on the door, and he went to it, stepping outside. A tall gentleman in a major's uniform stood there.

"Yes, sir?" said Jamie. "How may I help you?"

"I am looking for General Magruder. I was told he was in a meeting."

"Yes, he is. Would you like me to give him a message?"

"I would prefer to go in, if I may. The general and I are old friends."

Jamie looked at him, weighing the likelihood that this was true. As the major spoke quietly and seemed modest in his demeanor, he decided it probably was.

"May I tell him your name?"

"Albert Lea," said the major.

"One moment."

Jamie stepped into the room and walked to the general's chair, bending down to speak to him. "Pardon me, General. Major Albert Lea is here—"

"Lea!" cried Magruder. "Show him in, my boy, show him in!"

Jamie returned to the door and admitted Major Lea, who gave him a brief, friendly smile as he went in. Magruder welcomed him with open arms. Taking his own seat, Jamie leaned toward Lawford.

"Another old friend for the general's staff," he whispered.

"Your general's staff seems a trifle top-heavy," Lawford murmured back.

Jamie nodded. "At least this one's polite."

Emma carried a branch of candles, leading the way up the stairs. It was not very late, not near midnight, but though Aunt May had wished to stay up to greet the new year, she had become tired and finally asked to be put to bed. She had been rather quiet the past week, ever since Mr. Lawford had informed them of the Federal troops landing. It was beginning to look as if Galveston would not be recaptured after all.

Emma paused at the head of the stairs to light the steps for Rupert, who carried his mistress in his arms like a precious, fragile ornament. When he reached the top step she went down the hall and into May's bedroom, where Daisy was already waiting.

"I am so sorry to have spoiled your evening," May said to Emma as Daisy arranged the pillows for her comfort.

Emma sat on the edge of the bed and took her aunt's hand. Lines of strain marred her forehead, Emma noticed, and the skin beneath her eyes was bluish. "You haven't spoiled a thing. Has she, Mr. Lawford?"

"No. I was getting a bit tired of Strythe's conversation," he said.

"Poor man," said May, sighing. "He means well."

"Well, he got to play 'Auld Lang Syne,' even if it was a bit early," Emma said.

"Remember to open the champagne at midnight," May insisted. "I want you to bring me a glass, even if I am sleeping. I always greet the new year."

"Yes, ma'am," Emma said.

"And dearest, I've made a decision." May looked up, reaching past Emma with her free hand, which Mr. Lawford enfolded in his. "I want to leave Galveston," she said.

Emma caught her breath. "May—"

"Can you find us a carriage, Albert?"

Mr. Lawford came around Emma to kneel at the bedside. "I will find one," he pledged.

"I want to go tomorrow. New Year's Day is always a delightful time for an outing."

Emma cast a worried glance at Mr. Lawford. "Perhaps I should let you discuss this—"

"There is nothing to discuss. I have made up my mind. Daisy, you will pack bags for me and Miss Russell tonight, before going to bed. Pack your own things as well."

"Yes, Miz May," Daisy said.

"And Rupert? Where is Rupert?"

"Gone back downstairs," Emma said. "Shall I send him to you?"

"No, just tell him to pack up the ornaments in the parlor. And the crystal, if there is room, but if not we can leave it behind."

"I will see to all that," said Mr. Lawford. "But, May, there is, in fact, something I wish to discuss with you."

"I'll go find Rupert," Emma said, and slipped out before May could protest. She had a feeling she knew what Mr. Lawford wanted to discuss.

Leaving at last, she thought, standing alone in the upper hall. She had forgotten the candle branch in May's room, but the moonlight shining through the lace was bright enough she didn't need it. Stepping to the window, she pulled the curtains aside and tried to spot the moon, but as the house faced north and the roof of the veranda blocked her view, she could not see it without going outside. She was tempted, but decided not to.

Out there in the bay, the silent ships watched. She pulled the drapes closed against the irrational fear that some sailor had a telescope aimed at their window. She would be glad to leave, there was no doubt about that—as long as Aunt May would be able to stand the journey.

Glancing toward May's room, she heard Mr. Lawford speaking in an earnest, quiet voice. "Say yes, May," she whispered, then went downstairs to speak to Rupert.

Jamie rode easy in the saddle, letting Cocoa set her own pace and giving her a pat of encouragement now and then as she walked over the planking on the bridge across Galveston Bay. She was nervous, but so far she had behaved, trusting Jamie. Some of the artillery's mules had been less cooperative and had utterly refused to set foot on the bridge. Debray, overseeing the artillery, had finally intervened, ordering the men to bring their guns across by hand.

Everything was moving toward Galveston. Magruder had assembled the grandest collection of commanders Jamie had ever seen, many of them old friends: General Scurry, over his illness at last, was in command of the brigade; Colonel Reily and his son John were there with the 4th Texas; Colonel Pyron's men of the 2nd Texas were already on the island and had commenced marching eastward as soon as it was dark, with three guns to be placed at Fort Point. Colonel Cook, whom Jamie had met in Galveston in the summer, was to take five hundred of his own men to the harbor and storm the wharf where the Yankee soldiers were camped. Colonel Green and Colonel Bagby already had their sharpshooters from the 5th and the 7th, armed with Magruder's rifles and calling themselves "horse marines," on the cottonclads *Bayou City* and *Neptune*. Jamie smiled, remembering the moment when Colonel Green had stood before the two regiments and called for volunteers for a dangerous mission. Every man of them had stepped forward. They'd had to draw lots for the three hundred who would go aboard the cottonclads while the rest of the brigade came into the city. Now the horse marines waited aboard the steamers at Morgan's Point farther up Galveston Bay, ready to steam down at midnight when the ball was set to begin.

Magruder's large staff had transferred his headquarters into the home of Colonel Nichols in Galveston, but Magruder himself remained with the troops, his dear friend Major Lea at his side. In the few days since Lea's arrival Jamie had grown to like him. His quiet, calm manner presented a striking contrast to General Magruder's magnificence.

As they rode off the bridge onto the island, Jamie reined in beside Debray. "Well," Debray said, watching the artillery come off the bridge, "we may have trouble getting our guns into position without attracting notice."

Jamie nodded, and glanced eastward toward the city. The

moon was still high, nearly full. He could see the masts of the Federal ships quite clearly.

Debray had charge of twenty-one guns in all, including a large navy gun mounted on a railroad car and protected by cotton. Jamie had his doubts about this novel arrangement, but it was a pet project of Magruder's, so he and Debray merely followed the general's instructions and had it moved from the bridge to a switch track near the west end of town. The other guns were to be brought into the city and, as quietly as possible, up to the wharves.

A figure on horseback rode toward them. Jamie recognized his friend Lane, and greeted him.

"Colonel Debray, you've met Lieutenant Lane, haven't you? He's the brigade's AAG."

"Of course. Good evening, Lieutenant."

"Good evening, sir. Are your men all off the bridge?"

Debray glanced toward it. "Yes, they have just finished coming across."

"Good. You're to form in column for the march."

"We will do so at once."

Lane turned his horse, and called over his shoulder, "By the way, happy new year!"

Jamie checked his watch and saw that it was nearly midnight, the hour set for the attack to begin. The column had barely begun moving toward the city; they were late. He glanced northward up the bay, trying to spot the cottonclads and hoping that Green, who was in command of the water expedition, would remember to wait for the signal Magruder had designated—a single cannon's fire. Otherwise, he thought grimly, they might already be in trouble.

23

To Major Smith, in command of the Gunboat Expedition, and Colonel Green, in command of the land forces on board: I am off, and will make the attack as agreed, whether you come up or not. The Rangers of the Prairie send greetings to the Rangers of the Sea.

—John Bankhead Magruder

Quincy welcomed the new year on the deck of the *Harriet Lane*, stone sober at the end of the first watch. A bright moon was shining, just shy of full, scattering shards of light across the restless waters of the bay. A light haze of fog promised bone-chilling cold before dawn. Gerard, who would relieve him, joined him just before midnight, slapping at his arms for warmth.

"Happy new year," he said, as Quincy acknowledged him.

"Not quite," Quincy said, consulting his watch by moonlight.

"Near enough. Thinking about home?"

"More about getting under a blanket," Quincy said, but he looked toward the mainland nonetheless. Home was a long way off. He wondered where Nathaniel was, and whether he had stayed up to greet the new year. Feeling less than sleepy himself, he lingered on deck, chatting with Gerard past the first bell.

"If someone had told you a year ago that this is where you would spend New Year's Eve, would you have believed him?" Quincy asked.

"You mean aboard the *Harriet Lane*?"

"In Galveston Bay."

Gerard shrugged. "Probably not."

"I don't think I would have, either." Quincy leaned against the brass railing, feeling the cool of the metal through his coat. "In fact, if you had told me when we arrived here that we would still be here now, I would not have believed it."

"Well, it won't be much longer," Gerard said. "The rest of the troops will be here soon, and we can get back to blockading."

Quincy nodded. Once a force large enough to hold Galveston was landed, the fleet's presence would no longer be required in the bay. Gazing westward over the *Lane*'s bow, he wondered if they would next sail to Corpus Christi or even as far as Brownsville.

Movement caught his eye; dark shapes on the water to the northwest. "What's that?" he said, taking out his glass. He had trouble seeing well in the moonlight, but was able to make out the shapes. "Steamers!"

"Four of 'em," Gerard said, nodding as he looked through his own glass. He pulled out his watch. "Fetch the captain, will you Quincy?"

Heart pounding, Quincy ran below and rapped on the door of Wainwright's quarters. A loud thump from on deck startled him; the next moment he realized it was a signal rocket being launched. Gerard must have ordered it fired above the enemy boats, to show their position to the rest of the fleet.

By the time he returned to the deck with Commander Wainwright, the quartermaster was hanging white and red signal lanterns for "enemy in sight" and "make ready for action." Another rocket went off, arcing high over the bay, sparks reflecting in the water. It would have been beautiful, Quincy thought, but for its meaning.

"The enemy ships appear to be retreating, sir," Gerard said to the captain.

Quincy watched the fleeing Rebel steamers fade back into the darkness of the upper bay. Wainwright peered after them through his own glass. "Yes," he said. "They would like us to

follow, no doubt. I think we shall wait for them here instead.
Very good, Mr. Gerard. Weigh the anchor, and when you have
it secured, beat to quarters."

"Aye, sir, weigh anchor, then beat to quarters."

Quincy left the bridge to go to his post, just as Becker was
coming on deck. Quincy gave him a quick explanation.

"Blast," Becker said, his voice still bleary from sleep.

Signal lights responded from the other vessels and the *Lane*'s
crew made ready for action. A short while later, another signal
appeared out to the east, in Bolivar Channel.

"It's the *Westfield*," said Quincy, looking through his glass.
"Looks like she's aground."

"Again?" said Becker.

"She must have been trying to follow those steamers," Quincy
said.

As the *Clifton* moved away to assist the flagship, all the *Lane*'s
officers watched northward, trying to spot the Rebel boats again.
Standing at his post, Quincy waited, listening to the small
sounds of the ship creep back into the silence.

All was in readiness for a fight. The men waited at their posts,
shivering a bit now and then. Poor devils, Quincy thought, and
trained his glass northward once more.

"The ships are showing signal lights, sir," Jamie said, riding up
to Debray. "General Magruder is concerned that they have seen
us. He's changing our route of approach, to bring us into town
under better cover."

Debray sighed. "So much for attacking at midnight."

"We've missed that already."

Jamie passed along Magruder's instructions and helped Debray get the artillery moving. It took hours to bring the guns
into town by Magruder's circuitous route, but at last the batteries moved quietly northward toward the wharves and positioned
themselves behind buildings along the Strand, ready to move
forward. The artillery horses were sent back out of range of the

ships' heavy guns. Jamie had suggested that, remembering how badly the brigade's horses had been shot up at Valverde once the battle began. He was tempted to leave Cocoa with them, but he knew he would need her. As a staff officer, his duty during the battle would most likely be carrying messages.

Three guns had been sent all the way east to Fort Point, supported by six companies of infantry under Pyron. The storming party of five hundred men under Colonel Cook waited to attack the Yankee infantry dug in on Kuhn's Wharf. They had fortified themselves pretty well, holing up behind a makeshift wooden bulwark protecting the warehouse at the bay end of the wharf, and cutting down the land end to one plank. It would be hard to take.

Debray stood behind the Hendley Building, waiting for the order to move forward. Two of Captain Gonzales's six guns waited with him; the other sections stood behind neighboring structures. In the process of placing the guns, Jamie had encountered Lieutenant Sherman, of whose kindness Emma had told him. Farther west a second battery was strung out for more than a mile.

Debray assigned Jamie to supervise the hauling of three more guns up to the second floor of the Hendley Building—a daunting chore, but much easier than it had been to haul the Valverde guns up and down canyons by hand during the retreat from New Mexico. Jamie found it strange inside the warehouse, standing between guns that waited to be run out of open windows. They reminded him oddly of the navy guns he had seen aboard the Yankee flagship. He stepped to a window himself, and could see the signal lights still burning on the masts of the ships. In the opposite direction, Twentieth Street, Scurry waited in reserve behind the Custom House with men from the 4th and the 7th.

All was ready. Jamie wished the gun captains luck and hurried back down the stairs, out of the building, glad he would not be in that small space when the guns started firing.

Magruder stood with Debray and Major Lea, quietly discussing

battle plans. Jamie joined them, glancing at his watch. It was
nearly four o'clock.

"Ah, Russell," Magruder said. "You can find your way to headquarters, can't you?"

"I believe so, sir," Jamie said. "On Broadway, isn't it?"

"Yes. Major Lea has not been there yet. Will you guide him? I
want you to keep an eye on things from the roof of the Brown
house next door, Albert," Magruder said, turning to Lea. "It's
the best vantage point, I believe."

"I will gladly do so," said Lea. "But may I remain here until
you give your signal?"

"Of course," Magruder said, sounding pleased. Showman that
he was, the general planned to begin the attack personally by
firing one of Gonzales's guns. He consulted an ornate pocket
watch, then glanced up as a courier approached and swung
down from his saddle.

"Colonel Pyron's compliments, sir, and the guns are in place
at Fort Point," said the officer, saluting. Jamie started, recognizing the lazy drawl; it was Owens.

"Thank you, Major," said Magruder. He turned to Debray.
"Move the guns out. It is time to begin."

The night's stillness was pierced by a single explosion. In an
instant Quincy had his glass out and aimed eastward, toward
Kuhn's Wharf. The Rebel batteries on shore began to fire in earnest. Quincy picked out guns at three separate locations along
the wharves before Jewell tugged at his arm.

"Commander Lea's orders, sir," said the midshipman. "You
are to fire at the Rebel cannon."

"Thank you," Quincy told him, then called to his men, "Second Division, load with canister!"

Drifts of smoke, pale in the moonlight, rose above the
wharves. Rebels were advancing on Kuhn's Wharf with scaling
ladders. Quincy looked toward the Strand directly opposite the

Lane and detected movement between the buildings there as well. Rebel troops, and what looked like cannon; he confirmed it with his glass and ordered his gun captains to aim at those targets.

The Rebel guns responded, and soon they were in a fight as hot as any Quincy had seen. Shells shrieked overhead, and the deck was lit with the flash of the guns. Gerard's division brought their gun to bear on the wharves as well, and the toll on the city was harsh as the *Lane*'s guns sent shells and shot crashing into buildings. It was getting hard to target the Rebel guns. Glancing west, Quincy saw the moon sinking ahead of the bows, bloodred in the haze of cannon smoke. With the loss of moonlight, it would be nearly impossible to see the Rebels on shore well enough to aim at them.

"Aim on the enemy's muzzle flashes!" he instructed his gun captains.

He looked at his watch and saw that it was just past five o'clock. Another hour before the dawn would help them see their targets. Frustrated at the darkness, he looked back to the contest raging around Kuhn's Wharf, where the fight was hottest. Gerard's division fired continuously, and the *Owasco*, at the foot of Kuhn's Wharf, had her guns blazing away at less than two hundred yards. *Sachem* and *Corypheus* were firing, too. Near Pelican Spit, the *Clifton* appeared to be returning and would no doubt join the fray, or perhaps she would go in to take the men off the wharf. Quincy wished his own division could be of more use, but the angle was too extreme for his guns to help the troops on the wharf.

"Dawes," he called as the midshipman passed. "Take a message to Commander Lea. I am unable to bring my guns to bear on Kuhn's Wharf. If it is possible I request that he back the ship until we are closer."

"Unable to fire on Kuhn's Wharf, request to back the ship until closer," the lad repeated.

"Yes. Go."

Quincy returned his attention to the shore, scanning for any movement. His guns and those of the other ships continued to fire, sending shells hurtling into the city and illuminating the fine houses with ghastly, momentary brilliance. A fleeting concern for the citizens—and for one dark-haired lady in particular—passed through his mind before more immediate matters claimed his attention.

The first explosion brought Emma awake and out of her bed. Running to the window, she peeked out and saw lurid flashes of fire and smoke in the harbor. The ships were firing again; she knew the sounds now, of shells flying by and the low thud of the big guns, though she had not been able to see the contest before. Flashes of light split the night, much like an electrical storm, but there was smoke along with the thunder. There was also a crackling sound that was new. Perhaps it was the rifles of the troops the Federals had landed on Christmas Day. In quieter moments she could even hear screams of hysteria from the street; women and children fleeing south, out of town, to take what shelter they could find in the sand hills near the gulf shore. She had not heard screams during the first bombardment, but she knew that civilians had fled then as well. She thought there were fewer shells coming near the house this time. Most of the firing seemed to be directed toward the east end of town.

An urgent knock fell on her door. She caught up her wrapper and answered it, finding Mr. Lawford in the hall in his shirtsleeves, about to shrug into his coat.

"We must leave now," he said. "Do you need Daisy's help to dress?"

"No, but—I don't think we're in such danger—"

"May insists. I will go out to find a carriage or a cart."

"At this hour? And we have no horses—"

"I will drag it myself if I have to!" He pressed a hand to his brow, closing his eyes briefly. "I am sorry. May is terribly frightened."

Emma bit her lip. "Let me go and sit with her."

"After you have dressed. Please, Emma."

"All right."

She closed the door and scrambled into the clothes Daisy had laid out for her—the gray Zouave jacket and skirt—then hastened to May's bedroom. She found her aunt dressed, sitting up on the bed with Daisy putting her feet into walking boots. As she entered, May held out a trembling hand. Emma sat beside her and put her arms around her.

"It is worse than the first time," May said.

"It sounds worse up here," Emma told her. "The ships are not firing our way, though."

"Not yet," May said, and Emma felt a shiver run through her.

Daisy finished tying May's bootlaces and got to her feet. "Shall I fetch your cloak now, Miz May?" she said.

"Yes, and my bonnet. Emma, go and get your cloak. I am sure it is freezing outside."

"I left it in the hall."

"Hand me my jewelry box, dearest. It is on the dressing table."

Emma retrieved it, and as she returned she heard footsteps running up the stairs. Mr. Lawford came in, his hat in his hand.

"Mr. Strythe has a sulky," he said, out of breath. "And a donkey to pull it. He will share it with us, but we must go now."

"I am ready," said May, clasping the jewelry box tightly.

"How resourceful of Mr. Strythe," Emma remarked. "I would not have expected it of him."

"Never underestimate the ingenuity of a frightened man," said Mr. Lawford. "Shall I carry you, May, or do you want Rupert?"

For answer Aunt May held out her arms. Mr. Lawford gathered her up and carried her out. Emma smiled as she followed, collecting her cloak and hat on the way. Though he had not told her so, she suspected from their recent increase of tenderness that May had accepted Mr. Lawford's proposal at last.

"Oh! I'll be down in a moment," she called after them from the head of the stairs, and darted back to her room to fetch the spare bottle of laudanum. Tucking it in her pocket, she hurried downstairs and found the front door open. Mr. Lawford, with May in his arms cloaked and bonneted, was halfway to the sulky that stood waiting in the street, with Daisy close behind. Mr. Strythe was sitting in the vehicle, the reins in his hand.

The sulky was small, with room only for two. Mr. Lawford tenderly set May on the seat and stood back while Daisy laid a rug across May's lap.

"Have you thought where we are to go?" Emma said. Mr. Lawford's face was hard to see in the crazy flashes of light and darkness, but she thought he looked disconcerted. "We cannot go out to the sand hills!" she added.

"The convent," said Mr. Strythe. "The army has made a hospital there."

"Yes," said Mr. Lawford. "Excellent. Rupert, I shall return for the luggage. Guard the house until then."

"Yes, sir," said Rupert. He caught Emma's gaze and nodded, then turned and went into the house.

Jamie led Major Lea to the Brown house without any trouble, a large mansion on Broadway that he had admired during his first explorations of the city. The Browns had long since left for Houston, but someone had provided Magruder with a key with which Major Lea now unlocked the front door. They climbed the stairs to the attic and stepped out onto the high widow's walk. Lea took out a pair of field glasses and scanned the harbor.

Jamie took a deep breath of the sharp night air. The moon had sunk toward the gulf beyond the railroad bridge.

"I believe you walked down to the westernmost wharf," said Lea.

"Yes, I did," Jamie said.

"That is the *Harriet Lane* on the left, is it not?"

"Yes, sir."

The colonel slowly nodded. Jamie knew the *Harriet Lane* was the preferred target for the cottonclads. She was heavily armed and a fast ship; a great prize if she could be taken. It was luck, perhaps, that had put her at the western end of the bay where the horse marines would have a chance to get at her.

"I'd better get back," Jamie said. "Do you need anything, sir?"

"No, thank you," said the colonel. "Tell the general all is well." His frown belied his words; Jamie thought he looked troubled. If he had been better acquainted with Lea he might have spoken, but the major raised the field glasses again, leaving Jamie nothing to do but retire.

Mr. Strythe could not keep his horse to a walk. The poor frightened creature started at every explosion, and Emma feared he was not giving Aunt May the most comfortable ride. Emma and Daisy, walking beside the carriage with Mr. Lawford, had to run a few steps now and then to keep up. Fortunately the convent was not far, and soon the sulky stopped before the three-story building. A nun came out to greet them.

"I am Mother St. Pierre," she said. "Please come in out of the cold."

"I will wait here for you, Mr. Lawford," said Mr. Strythe. His voice sounded nervous, and Emma hoped he would not panic and leave.

Mr. Lawford carried May into the convent, with Emma and Daisy following. Inside, a large room had been prepared to receive the wounded from the battle. The mother superior led them through this and into a smaller chamber where two women sat on a cot, talking in low voices. There were three other beds in the room, and Mr. Lawford placed May upon one of them. Her face was drawn and very pale. Mr. Lawford glanced at Emma, and sat beside her.

"I should stay for a while, I think."

"Is she ill?" the mother superior asked Emma.

"Yes," Emma said. "We are sorry to trouble you—"

"I will fetch a doctor to her."

Emma followed her out into the large hall, saying, "You

needn't do that. Or rather, I would like a doctor to see her, but it isn't . . ." Impatient with herself, she stamped her foot, and the nun raised an eyebrow. Emma sighed, drew a deep breath. "She has cancer," she said in a low voice.

Mother St. Pierre's eyes filled with understanding. "Ah," she said. "You will want to talk to a doctor, yes."

"Yes, thank you."

The nun led her toward a small group of men—army surgeons, Emma supposed—at one end of the hall, but before they could reach them a commotion claimed the doctors' attention. Two soldiers came in bearing a stretcher, with nuns hovering around them. The mother superior hastened to the wounded man's side and directed the soldiers to lay him on a mattress. It was then Emma saw the blood that had seeped through the blanket covering his abdomen. Glancing at his face, she gasped.

"Lieutenant Sherman!"

She shoved past the nuns to reach him, wincing at the mass of blood. His brow was furrowed in pain. She found his hand and clasped it, and he opened his eyes.

"Miss Russell?" he murmured.

"Yes. Don't talk," Emma said.

"I thought you had left the island."

"No."

"Miss, you are very much in the way," said an army doctor. Emma changed her position, moving closer to the lieutenant's shoulder.

"Don't leave," he said.

"I won't." She squeezed his hand, not knowing what else to do.

The surgeons uncovered the wound, which made the young man wince. Emma was glad she was not in a position to see. Something smelled foul, though, and she knew that must be a bad sign.

"I'll fetch some laudanum," said one of the surgeons.

"I have some here, if it would help," Emma said.

"Yes." The doctor held out his hand, and Emma retrieved the small bottle from her pocket. "Open your mouth," he said to Lieutenant Sherman, and when he obeyed Emma was astonished to see the doctor pour a heavy dose straight into it. He handed the bottle back to her, gave her a somewhat disapproving glance, and took his fellow surgeons aside.

Emma watched the lieutenant anxiously. In a few moments he seemed to relax. She smoothed his hair away from his face, and he looked up at her, at first seeming not to know her.

"Oh, yes," he said, smiling wearily. "Thank you."

"For what?"

"For being here."

Emma bit her lip, then tried to smile in return. A few moments later his eyes fell shut again, and his grip on her hand loosened. She watched him sleep for a short while, then when she felt sure she would not disturb him she slid her hand from his and went to where the surgeons were standing.

"He is sleeping," she told them. They frowned at her for interrupting their conference, but she did not care. "What will you do?"

They exchanged looks, then the one who had administered the laudanum said, "There is nothing to be done except to see that he is comfortable."

Shocked, Emma stepped back. The doctors resumed their conversation, but quickly dispersed as another wounded man was carried in.

"I am sorry, child," said a gentle voice behind her. Emma turned to see the mother superior looking at her with pity. "He is a friend, yes?"

"Yes," Emma nodded. "A good friend." She swallowed, then looked at the nun. "I am going to see that my aunt is comfortable, and then if you wish I will help you." She gestured to the empty mattresses, and Mother St. Pierre nodded, smiling sadly.

"Bless you, child." She looked up as more casualties were brought in, and she and Emma went their separate ways.

Jamie stood with General Scurry by the foundry at the foot of Eighteenth Street, watching the assault on Kuhn's Wharf fall apart. Up close Scurry looked tired, but his eye was now well again and determined as ever. They watched in silence while the men under Colonel Cook, including some of Pyron's, floundered in the waist-deep water beneath the wharves. The scaling ladders they had brought were too short to reach the top of the wharf where the Yankees were fortified. Ladders floated in the water, abandoned, while the men retreated under heavy fire. Some never made it to shore. Jamie's gut was a heavy lump, and he couldn't help frowning as he watched the awful repulse of the troops—some former comrades, some new recruits, some militia who maybe had never expected to be in a real fight.

Owens rode up on a bay horse and tossed off a salute. "Cook says he'll try to regroup behind that press," he said, pointing to a large structure just to the south.

Scurry nodded. He tapped a hand against the side of his thigh, then turned to Jamie. "Can we get a gun out there and hit them with shrapnel?" he asked, pointing to the wharf two blocks west, where a handful of sharpshooters were sniping at the Yankees from behind a warehouse.

Jamie eyed the warships beyond the wharf, and the heavily fortified Yankee position. "We can try," he said, though he was doubtful of success.

"Tell Gonzales to send one of his guns out. And don't you go with them," Scurry warned, his gaze sharp in the half-dark. "You're needed here."

Jamie acknowledged this with a nod. His gaze crossed Owens's, and he saw sudden hostility in the major's face.

"Owens," Scurry said, watching Cook's dripping men struggle out of the water, "I want you to ride to headquarters . . ."

Jamie turned away and began to trot toward Gonzales's battery. He had not been this close to the fighting most of the night. He had come back by way of the Custom House to check on the 4th and the 7th. There he had found Lane with the rest, waiting in reserve, cringing as shells from the Yankee navy punched their way straight through the building. He hated the sound of those shells overhead, but he had been so busy he had scarcely had time to notice them.

Reaching Gonzales's position, he noted how different it looked than it had an hour or so earlier when Magruder had ceremoniously fired the first shot to signal the attack. Grapeshot scattered the ground along with shards of glass that flashed every time the guns fired. Bricks and scraps of wood flew as shells ate away at nearby buildings. Men lay on the ground, too—Gonzales was working with short crews. Jamie was glad he had left Cocoa in a shed a couple of blocks south of the Strand.

Gonzales looked up as Jamie arrived and quickly explained Scurry's orders. "We will try it," he said, his face impassive. He summoned the officer in charge of the nearest gun.

Jamie returned to Scurry, arriving in time to watch the gun deployed on the wharf. The crew got off one shot, then the Yankees on Kuhn's Wharf directed such a terrible fire on them that half the cannoneers fell at their posts, and the rest scrambled back to the shore with minié balls hurrying them along. Gonzales could not afford such losses, Jamie knew. The gun would be abandoned.

Owens returned, dismounted and reported to Scurry. "General Magruder concurs with you, sir. He authorizes you to begin withdrawing the troops."

Jamie winced. Defeated. He felt an impulse to protest, but with the sky growing lighter the Yankee ships were finding their targets with deadly accuracy, and their heavy guns far overpowered the Texans' field artillery. The losses were too great to continue. They would have to retreat.

"Thank you, Val," Scurry said quietly. "Take the word to Cook. Have him mass on the Strand. Russell, will you tell Gonzales to pull his guns back there as well, and shelter them behind the buildings? Thank you."

Jamie ran through the nightmare landscape again. A shell howled toward him and he dropped to the ground out of instinct. The round buried itself in the street ten yards past him, then exploded, sending up a geyser of dirt. Jamie stumbled to his feet, ears ringing, then brushed bits of glass from his trousers and hastened to Gonzales.

"General Scurry orders you to withdraw to safety," Jamie told him.

A flash of relief crossed the captain's face, and Jamie felt a tug of sympathy. If his own section had been in such a position . . . he thrust the thought aside, saw to it that Gonzales's battery knew where to go, then returned to the corner of the foundry where Scurry had been. The general was no longer there. Jamie peered along the street, trying to spot him or any of his staff. He glimpsed Owens, still in the saddle, to the east, and turned westward, picking his way through the rubble. The scene was chaotic, what with wreckage everywhere and the bombardment continuing overhead, but Jamie saw the beginnings of an orderly retreat.

An artilleryman—one of Gonzales's—ran across the street before him, heading south. A second later Jamie heard a thudding of hoofbeats and a cry of "Halt!" He saw Owens pursue the artilleryman down the street, and with a jolt of concern ran after them.

Owens drew his pistol. "Get back to the line or I'll shoot you down!" he shouted at the private.

"Owens, no!" Jamie yelled.

He was too late; Owens fired, shooting the private in the back. Jamie's heart lurched. He ran up and knelt by the man—just a boy, really, he saw as he turned him over—and he knew even then that he was dead.

Trembling with rage, Jamie stood and faced Owens. "He was going to fetch the horses!"

Owens looked sheepish for all of a second, then his face hardened. "He should have said so. He should have stopped on my order."

"He's been serving the guns for two hours! He didn't hear you!"

For a long moment Owens returned Jamie's gaze with eyes flat as steel. Finally he shrugged. "Casualty of war."

Outraged, Jamie drew his pistol and pointed it at Owens. "Major Owens, I am placing you under arrest. Dismount, please."

Owens laughed, then a sly look came into his eyes, a look Jamie knew well. "I would oblige you," he drawled, "but I think there is a gal in town who needs my assistance."

Jamie frowned, confused. A shell flew past, crashing into a house two blocks down, sending up a shower of splinters behind Owens's shoulder.

"It is Tremont Street, isn't it?" Owens said, then with a sneering laugh, he spurred his horse and galloped down the street.

Jamie stared after him. "Emma!" he whispered, then broke into a run.

At last the *Lane* began moving, her wheels working in reverse, taking her slowly back along the channel toward Kuhn's Wharf. Now the sky eastward was beginning to lighten, revealing wreckage in the water beneath the Union troops' bastion. Splintered wood, remnants of the barricade, and abandoned scaling ladders floated in the water along with the grimmer shapes of dead men.

Smoke from cannon and rifle hung in the air over the Strand. The Rebel guns that had been at the foot of the wharves had drawn back; one began lobbing shells from the safety of a nearby foundry, aiming them at the warehouse where the 42nd Massachusetts huddled. Quincy sent a few shots toward the Rebel guns from the howitzer, but the Dahlgren still couldn't be trained on the Confederate position. He stood at his station, anxious for a clear line of fire, wishing the *Lane* would move faster but knowing that it would be dangerous in the harbor's narrow channel. A strong ebb tide was flowing, pulling her eastward. In a few more minutes he would have a clear shot.

A blast to the west made him spin around. The Rebel steamers had returned. In the predawn he could see now that two were small boats, tenders perhaps. Two larger boats, their decks piled with bales of cotton, were approaching the *Lane* from the west, the lead ship firing her bow-gun.

"Second Division, starboard watch, man starboard guns!" Quincy shouted, anticipating the captain's command.

A second shell from the lead steamer plowed into the *Lane*'s hull with a sickening crunch, just aft of the port wheelhouse. Quincy's pulse was racing and he strove to keep his voice calm as he gave orders to return fire. The two steamboats made directly for the *Harriet Lane*.

"Mr. Briggs, run between them," he heard Wainwright order from the bridge. "We'll give them a taste of our broadsides."

Hearing this, Quincy called out orders to load. A rifle shot hissed across the deck from the leading steamer, and Quincy saw the pilot slump at the wheel.

More rifle shots followed; the cotton hid sharpshooters as well as the boat's machinery. Suddenly a hail of balls rattled toward the *Lane*, thunking into wood, ricocheting off metal, shrieking death around the deck. Quincy dropped flat to the deck, and his division cowered in their places, save for the few who sprawled on the deck and stained it with their blood.

She'll ram us, he thought, and braced himself against the impact. When it came it was less than he had imagined; a glancing blow only. Venturing to look, he saw the *Lane*'s bow catch at the enemy's port wheelhouse, tearing away some planking as the two ships passed. With a groaning creak, the *Lane*'s cathead sheared away. Quincy gasped as he watched the anchor splash into the water and the cable begin to run out.

Chaos erupted on the deck. Quincy heard Lea shouting, a midshipman flew past him to Becker, then a dozen men leaped to the anchor cable, trying to halt its deployment.

The rifles had slackened. "Man your guns!" Quincy yelled, getting to his feet.

The enemy ship backed her wheels, then turned to pass under the *Lane*'s stern. Quincy read her name painted on her wheelhouse—*Bayou City*. He scarcely had time to see it before cries of alarm warned him of the second ship's approach off the starboard bow.

Quincy shouted encouragement to his men, sorry they could not aim the guns lower. The steamboat's hull was out of reach, but he should be able to strike her machinery. "Aim at the wheel," he called.

The starboard Dahlgren blazed a shell that caught the turning steamer in the bow, sending lumber and cotton bales flying. The guns ran back on their slides with a crash. "Good! Again," Quincy cried.

This boat, emblazoned *Neptune* with U.S. MAIL PACKET still painted on her side, also tried to ram the *Lane*. Quincy saw that she would miss her aim; the ebbing tide and the boat's unwieldiness seemed to interfere, and she managed only a weak blow aft of the starboard wheel. Her crew threw out grappling irons but a handful of daring Lanes rushed forward to cut the ropes, and she slid away.

Rifles sang again. A cry of dismay drew Quincy's gaze to the bridge, where the captain had fallen. Quincy froze, then breathed again as Wainwright got to his feet, clinging to the rail.

Turning back to his division, Quincy ordered the second captains to fire on the *Neptune*. The shell disappeared into the cotton on her deck. As she backed away, Quincy saw that the blow had stove in her bows; water was rushing into the great hole. The Lanes set up a cheer, and Quincy watched her movement with a critical eye. She made for the flats, seeking shallow water before she sank.

"She's foundering," he called out, glancing toward the bridge.

Lea nodded acknowledgment, and answered, "Mind the starboard!"

Turning aft, Quincy saw that the *Bayou City* had come about and was steaming hard for the *Lane*. A glance forward at the men still struggling with the anchor told him the *Lane* had no hope of escaping. He shouted orders to his division, the men sweating as they served the guns, the sand on deck beneath their feet dark with blood. A shot from the port side howitzer crashed through the enemy's starboard wheelhouse, but she came on, her sharpshooters raking the deck. A scream drew his eye sternward; Gerard's face was a mass of blood, then he fell and his division scattered, seeking shelter from the shrieking bullets, pouring away below decks like water through scuppers. Fire glanced along Quincy's thigh and he cried out, losing his footing, striking his knee hard against the deck. The steamer loomed, then with a terrible, rolling crash she struck the port wheelhouse and lodged, the *Lane*'s wheel braces piercing her, making one chimeric beast of the two vessels. The deck tilted as the *Lane* heeled to starboard. Quincy scrambled to get to his feet.

"Lanes, to me!" he heard Lea's voice above the spit of rifle fire. "Repel boarders!"

A man—an officer—leapt onto the *Lane* from the enemy ship and began cutting away the boarding netting. Quincy moved to join the cluster of men rallying around Lea, but his right leg would not obey him and he fell painfully, and then men were streaming aboard from the enemy boat, slashing at the netting, pouring over the rails, backing Lea and his men aft. A powder boy stood in defiance of them, pistols blazing in both hands. The next moment he fell back, part of his hand carried away by a rifle shot.

Wainwright shouted encouragement from the bridge, leaning against the rail as he bid the Lanes never to surrender their ship. Then a ball struck him square in the forehead—Quincy saw the blood fly—and he dropped heavily to the bridge. Quincy cried out, but his voice was lost in the confusion of Rebels swarming the deck, beating back the futile resistance. Lea fell, wounded, and the fight seemed to go out of the Lanes. Leaderless, they would yield. Quincy struggled again to rise, trying to swallow to moisten a throat hoarse with shouting. He had got to one knee when Becker stepped forward and said loudly, "We surrender."

"No!" Quincy cried. "Becker, what are you doing?!"

A rifle muzzle against his chest stayed him from protesting further. Becker stood on the listing deck, facing the enemy leader.

"I am the senior officer on board," he declared in a calm voice. "We surrender."

Quincy pushed away the rifle and at last managed to stand. Ungentle hands seized both his arms. He stared at Becker, who after a brief glance refused to meet his gaze. Gasping, dizzy and half-mad with fury, Quincy sank to his knees, then fainted.

24

"Come on, girl," Jamie said to Cocoa, leaning low over her withers, urging her to run faster through the torn and debris-filled streets. The precious seconds it had taken him to get to her had been enough time for Owens to get out of sight. Men were falling back onto the Strand, barring his way with cannon and caissons; he dodged a block south to Mechanics Row and saw the major's bay flash past on Tremont Street ahead.

"Get up!" he shouted, and Cocoa sprang forward with a startled neigh. A shell struck a building ahead of him, raining bricks into the street. The mare shied, but Jamie held her together. A red rage had overcome him and he pushed her hard, no room in him for mercy, no attention for anything but Owens's threat. He would kill Owens before he let him touch Emma.

He turned onto Tremont Street, barely slowing, Cocoa's hooves throwing up clods of dirt. She jumped the railroad tracks for him and he glimpsed the big gun on its flatcar to the west. Two short blocks more and he was at May's house. Owens's bay stood in the yard, cropping the flowers in the garden and the front door was open. Jamie jumped Cocoa right over the fence; she landed scrambling and he flung himself off—nearly falling— and ran into the house.

Silence. No lights. The family couldn't have slept through the bombardment, could they? A wave of relief was followed by sick fear; what if Owens had put out the lights? Frowning, Jamie drew his pistol and quietly went up the stairs. As his head came level with the upper floor a shot crashed—blazing light and a tug at his hair—he heard his hat fall onto the stairs as he ducked, gasping, cringing against the bannister.

He took a few breaths, then swallowed and called out, "She's not here, Owens!"

A flash of motion at the head of the stairs; Jamie shot wildly as another ball hissed past him and crashed into the hall chandelier. The crystals that weren't shattered at once continued to tinkle together, a restless, worried sound. Jamie backed two steps down the stairs. He listened, hearing a board creak, a dull thud of artillery from out in the bay.

"Owens? Come on down, let's call it a truce. I won't fire. We're on the same side, if you recall. Owens?"

A scrape behind him; a memory flashed in his mind of Emma stepping through the window upstairs. From the balcony, an easy jump to the ground. He flung himself over the bannister as twin explosions filled the hall with sulphurous smoke. Deafened, bruised and unsure whether he'd been hit, Jamie slowly picked himself up. A face appeared before him through the smoke—Rupert's face, shouting something but Jamie's ears were ringing and he put out his hands to hold him off. He had dropped his pistol. He didn't remember firing it again, but there was a body lying in the hall, just inside the door, surrounded by glistening bits of glass in a slowly spreading puddle of blood. Owens.

Jamie walked over and squatted beside the major, thinking to turn him over. The quantity of blood on the floor changed his mind. Looking up, he saw Rupert standing over him, a shotgun in his hands.

Quincy woke to a hideous throbbing in his leg. He could barely think through the pain, but he saw that he still lay on the deck of the *Lane*. Rebels walked back and forth, stepping over the dead and wounded like they were so many sacks of meal. A few feet away Quincy saw Lea, bleeding from chest wounds, his riddled cap lying beside him. At first he thought the XO was dead, but a Rebel nudged him with his foot, and Lea stirred.

Quincy would have liked to go to his quarters and lie on his bunk, for he felt very cold. He did not have the strength to get up, though, and it really didn't matter. He watched idly as the Rebels moved about the ship. The firing had ceased, he noticed. That was good.

A sound of men coming up from below inspired him to try moving his head, but the result was a piercing pain so he stopped. The slow footsteps came toward him, also the clanking of chains. Perhaps the men had got control of the anchor at last. Then he saw feet moving past, sailors' feet, walking slowly, herded by Rebels. Looking up from the feet he saw chains dangling, shackles on dark wrists—the boys, the coal-heavers, all the negro sailors from the *Lane*—and Isaiah, looking down at him. Isaiah, gazing at him silently until a Rebel prodded him into moving on. Quincy closed his eyes, for the tears stung less so as they slid down his cheeks to the deck.

At last there were no more new patients. Emma went to the long tables where supplies and instruments had been placed, and chose the least bloody basin of water in which to wash her hands. She had taken off her jacket and rolled up the sleeves of her Garibaldi shirt, which she feared was now ruined, along with her skirt, from the bloodstains. For hours the wounded had come and she had worked hard, humbly obeying the surgeons, gritting her teeth while she helped hold down screaming men, carefully sponging burned and shredded flesh. Blood did not ordinarily disturb her; there was plenty of bloody work associated with the ranch, but it was different when the blood was a man's and the man looked at one pleading silently with pain in his eyes.

Lieutenant Sherman had died, about an hour after she had spoken with him and let him be given her laudanum. The rest of the laudanum was long gone, and many other soldiers had come and some died since she last saw her friend. Both armies had sent their wounded to the makeshift hospital, and the sisters had welcomed both, even after one of the Yankee ships had mistakenly fired on the convent.

Emma noticed sunlight streaming in through a row of clerestory windows. No one had yet bothered to put out the candles. Gazing at the room full of wounded, Emma thought she should help the nuns who were going around to them, making sure each was comfortable, bringing them water, clean bandages, kind words. First, though, she should see to her aunt. She had not been back to the little private room since she had gone to leave her jacket there, hours ago.

As she approached the room Mr. Lawford came out of it toward her. He looked so grieved and worried he seemed years older. Emma reached out a hand to him.

"I am sorry I haven't been back," she said. "I kept meaning to come, but we have been so busy. Is my aunt sleeping?"

Mr. Lawford's jaw quivered. "She is gone," he said.

It took her a moment to understand, and then she felt as if she'd been struck a blow to the chest. She gaped at him, trying for breath. Mr. Lawford gathered her into his arms, and she stood there in silence, too stunned to weep.

Jamie led the bay at a walk so that Owens's body, slung over the saddle, would not fall off. As he rode toward the hospital he tried to decide how to explain the incident. He was not to blame—no one was to blame except Owens—but he feared the army would not be inclined to lenience over the loss of an officer. Rupert would be their target, he thought, but he did not want Rupert to be punished. Rupert had saved his life. Would they understand? He thought if he could explain why it had happened, they would. He had tried to arrest Owens, and the man had lost his head, gone berserk. He knew it was true, but it sounded lame.

He reached the hospital and a soldier hurried out to the street to meet him. "Wounded?" the man said.

"Dead," Jamie told him.

The soldier nodded and held out a hand. "Thank you, sir. I'll see to him."

Jamie handed him the reins and watched him lead the horse away. That was all. No explanation needed. There had been a battle, after all.

Reminded of his duty, he turned Cocoa back toward the Strand to find Scurry. The guns had gone silent, and he urged the mare to a trot.

A haze of smoke hung over the harbor. He found Scurry back at his earlier position, watching Kuhn's Wharf. The guns had been brought forward again.

"There you are," Scurry said as Jamie approached him. "That was a close one." He pointed to Jamie's shoulder, and Jamie saw that his coat was blackened and torn by the path of a bullet. "Got your hat, too, I see. Where's Owens? I can't find him anywhere."

"He's dead," Jamie told him, dreading that Scurry would demand an explanation.

"Oh," Scurry said. "Damn. Well, then I need you to go to General Magruder. Tell him that I am about to negotiate these fellows' surrender." As he spoke, a party of Yankees came out of the barricade on the wharf. They carried a flag of truce and began to cross the single plank that connected the wharf to the shore.

"That's Captain Lubbock," Jamie said, recognizing the *Bayou City*'s owner among the party.

"It is indeed," Scurry said, flashing a grin. "He's demanded the navy's surrender. Our horse marines did a good job. The *Harriet Lane* is ours." The general's blue eyes glinted in triumph as he watched the Yankees approach. "Go on, tell the boss. Git."

"Yes, sir," Jamie said, and hurried back to his horse, his feelings a jumble of elation and dread. He was glad they had won the day, and he still feared to report Owens's death. Maybe it would just pass without question, he thought, riding toward headquarters. If he said nothing, maybe no one would ask about how Owens had died. Was that right, though? Was that an honorable thing to do?

At headquarters, he found General Magruder surrounded by a long-faced staff. Major Lea was there, apparently reporting on what he had observed from the roof of the Brown house. "It is difficult to see for the smoke," he said, "but I fear the *Harriet Lane* may have captured our ship."

"No, it didn't," Jamie said, joining the group of staff officers. "Pardon me, General, but General Scurry sent me to tell you that the *Bayou City* captured the *Harriet Lane*. He's negotiating the surrender of the Yankee infantry on Kuhn's Wharf."

Magruder's face lit with joy, and the room burst into excited conversation. Jamie was pulled into the center of it and pounded on the back.

"What else?" Magruder asked. "How was the *Lane* captured?"

"I don't know, sir," Jamie told him, "but Captain Lubbock has demanded the fleet's surrender, and he's with Scurry now. That's all I know."

"General," said Major Lea, his face grave, "if this is the case, then I request permission to look for my son. He is serving aboard the *Harriet Lane*."

The excited chatter ceased. "My God!" said Magruder. "Why didn't you tell me this?"

"It was not important that you should know," said the major quietly. "It would not have been right for such knowledge to influence the battle."

Magruder grasped his friend's hands. "Of course you may go," he said, frowning with concern. "Go with him, Lieutenant," he told Jamie.

"Yes, sir."

Glad to get away from the scene of celebration, Jamie accompanied the silent major to the wharves at the west end of town. There they found boats coming and going from the two ships, which appeared to be locked together out in the bay. They rode out in a launch and climbed aboard the *Lane*, where they found proof of the bitter fight that had raged there.

Jamie had to walk carefully to keep his footing, for the deck was slanted. Casualties lay scattered about, and Major Lea at once moved forward to kneel beside one of the fallen men, taking his hand. Jamie felt a wave of pity. It appeared Lea had found his son, and it appeared to Jamie that the son was in serious shape; he could see several wounds in the young man's chest.

"Father," he heard the man say. He stepped away to give them privacy, his throat tightening.

The major spoke a few quiet words with his son, then called on some of the soldiers standing around the deck to carry him below. Casting a haggard glance at Jamie, he said, "Can you find me an ambulance? I must take him to the hospital."

Jamie nodded. "I think so," he said. At worst, they could load him onto a caisson.

"Thank you," said Major Lea. "Wait for me, I won't be long."

"Yes, sir," Jamie said, and watched him follow his son below.

Emma trudged down the street beside Mr. Lawford, with Daisy following behind. Mr. Lawford carried May's jewelry box tucked under his arm, and Daisy carried her bonnet and cloak. Mother St. Pierre had agreed to keep her body at the convent until a funeral could be arranged. There would be many funerals in the next few days.

Emma hugged her cloak tighter about her. The sun was bright; not strong enough to defeat winter's chill, but it revealed the devastation of the night's bombardment. Broken glass lay everywhere. Many buildings had been struck by shells, and the closer they got to the bay the worse the destruction appeared. Bricks, timbers, and whole sections of wall lay in the streets, as if a cyclone had struck the city. As they neared the house, a tremendous explosion shook the ground beneath their feet and a cloud of fire and black smoke rose from the east, out in the bay near Pelican Spit. One of the Yankee ships had blown up, it appeared. They paused to watch the plume rise before continuing on. Emma should have been glad, she supposed, but she did not have such feelings in her at present.

May's house had not been hit again, Emma was thankful to see, though Mr. Strythe's house had two windows broken. She wondered where he was—still out among the sand hills, perhaps. She followed Mr. Lawford through the gate and walked up the path, only to find the front door locked. Mr. Lawford pounded on it, and in a moment Rupert opened the door.

"Careful, Miss," he said, holding the door for Emma. "The floor is damp."

Emma saw that this was so, and noticed a mop and bucket against the wall. Rupert picked them up and carried them into the back of the house, past the suitcases still waiting in a row behind the stairs. Emma took off her cloak and hat, hanging them on the coat stand, and looked at Mr. Lawford.

"I'm going to change clothes," she said.

He nodded, looking weary. "Come into the parlor when you have done so, please. We have some things to discuss."

Her feet seemed leaden as she climbed the stairs. Something glinted in the corner of a step—a fragment of glass. She picked it up and continued up to the second floor, where a chill wind was blowing through the open hall window. Frowning, she hastened to shut it, then went into her room which was dark with the curtains still closed. She left them that way and removed her bloodstained dress, resisting the urge to crawl into bed. She was tired, but she doubted she would be able to sleep. Too much had happened. Too much remained to be done. If she went to bed she would only lie awake, turning it all over in her mind, and anyway Mr. Lawford wanted to talk to her.

The wardrobe was empty except for the dress she had worn the day she had arrived in Galveston. Daisy had packed her new clothes, except for those she had just removed. Not caring to go downstairs for her suitcase, or to wait while Daisy brought it up, she put on the old dress. She had been proud of it once, but now it seemed positively dowdy. How jaded she had become.

She found Mr. Lawford in the parlor. May's jewelry box sat before him, sharing the table with a coffee tray. Emma sat down and watched him pour, too numb to think of comforting words. She accepted a cup from him and sipped cautiously at the hot liquid. When she glanced up, she saw Mr. Lawford watching her.

"Emma, I have some things to tell you about your aunt's estate. May I do so now?"

Emma nodded. They would have to arrange for a funeral. She supposed all of May's Houston acquaintances must be invited, and wondered how they would ever manage to contact her Galveston friends, who were scattered all over Texas by now. Newspaper announcements, perhaps. The very thought made her weary.

"I am her executor, along with her banker in Houston," Mr. Lawford said. "It will take some time to divide her assets among her heirs—" he gestured toward the jewelry box, then to the house, "—but there are some things she left exclusively to you. She asked me to tell you they are a token of her gratitude for the sacrifices you have made for her sake."

Emma frowned. "Please forgive me, I am very stupid this

morning. Do you mean to say that I stand to inherit from my aunt?"

"All of her siblings, nieces and nephews are heirs to her estate," Mr. Lawford told her. "That means the Westons and the Gearys as well as your family. None of you will receive a fortune, but it will still be a substantial amount."

"But what about you?" Emma said, unhappy that he would be obliged to divide May's estate among so many strangers, some of whom had never even met her.

"She has left me some—mementos," he said. "I am in no need of more. This is not what I wished to tell you."

Emma put down her cup. She felt upset, but waited for him to continue. He sighed, his fingers knitted together and resting in his lap.

"May has left you the piano. I will have it delivered to your home in San Antonio, or wherever you wish. She has also left you her slaves."

"What?"

"Rupert and Daisy. They are yours now."

Emma stared at him, having trouble grasping the import of his words. Poppa had never thought much of slaves. Once or twice he and Momma had discussed whether to buy one for the ranch, but Poppa always said a slave would be more trouble than he was worth. Now they would have two. Emma tried to picture Daisy at the ranch, and could not do so.

"She didn't want them to be sold," Mr. Lawford explained. "And she wanted to give you something special for staying with her—taking care of her—for being here . . ."

He put his head in his hands. Emma saw his shoulders begin to shake, and got up to walk to the window. With two fingers she pushed aside the lace, peering out blindly at the street marred with wreckage.

Rupert and Daisy belonged to her. She had trouble believing that she now owned two human beings. Two slaves, rather. They were not considered human beings, though she had trouble believing that men and women who spoke and dressed—and in Rupert's case worshiped—like Christians were not human. What would she do?

A sound behind her drew her attention. She turned to see Mr. Lawford leaving the room, hurrying up the stairs. He had left the jewelry box behind. Emma moved to the table and picked it up. She would keep it safe until she could give it back to him.

As she stepped into the hall she saw Daisy standing beside the packed suitcases. Their eyes met, and Emma saw that the slave was weeping. Before she could speak, Daisy turned and ran out the back door. Emma followed a few steps down the hall and watched her disappear into the kitchen. When she turned, she found Rupert watching her. He was holding a dustpan and broom. Evidently a glass had been broken, for the dustpan was full of shards.

"New Year's Day," he said.

"I beg your pardon?"

"It be New Year's Day. Daisy was going to go to the Yankees on this day, 'cause they say she be free. But now the Yankees gone."

Emma drew a breath. "And were you going to go to the Yankees as well?"

Rupert shrugged, his eyes half-hooded, making him look sleepy, but Emma knew he was not. "Well, you are right," she said. "They are gone."

"You have more brothers, Miss?"

"What?"

"I was thinking you had more brothers than just Mr. James," he said, coming forward. "Is that right?"

"Yes, I have three others."

Rupert nodded. "That's what she's troubled about."

Emma looked after Daisy, the implication dawning on her. "My brothers would never bother her!" she said. At least, she did not think so. "I know they would not," she repeated, but uncertainty drained her indignation. After all, she did not know everything about her brothers. Matthew in particular was rather wild. Who knew what he might be capable of?

Unable to cope with such ugly thoughts, she brushed past Rupert, heading for the stairs. She began to go up, but her legs shook beneath her and she sank down upon the third step with the jewel box in her lap, and closed her eyes. She really ought to rest. She was becoming quite overwhelmed. A shiver of distress ran through her, leaving her close to tears. She drew an unsteady breath, then opened her eyes.

Something glinted on the step beside her. Reaching for it, she found it was a crystal drop, chipped a little on one edge. It was like the fragment she had found earlier on the stairs, and like the shards in Rupert's dustpan. Fine crystal, not just glass. She looked up, and saw the hall chandelier in ruins.

"Rupert?" she called.

The sound of sweeping down the hall stopped. Rupert came toward her, and when she held up the crystal and nodded toward the chandelier, fear came into his eyes.

"What happened?" she said softly.

Quincy came to consciousness with an uncomfortable weight on his chest. He opened his eyes to see the frightened face of the ship's cat, Fitz, who was standing on him. The cat yowled a question. Quincy reached up to stroke him.

He was lying against the bulkhead, down in the hold. Dr. Penrose, moving among the other wounded, noticed that he was awake and came over to check the tightness of a bandage wrapped around his thigh. Quincy tried to speak, but wound up coughing instead.

"Tired?" said Penrose. He held Quincy's chin and peered at his face.

"Yes," Quincy said, his voice a croak.

"You lost a good deal of blood, but don't worry. You won't lose the leg." Penrose gave him a small smile, patted his shoulder, and moved on.

Quincy gazed after him. In the dim light that filtered down into the hold, he saw that there were about a dozen others there, all wounded. He watched Penrose kneel beside a mattress someone had brought in and realized the man lying on it was Lea. The XO looked ghostly pale. Penrose was speaking to him, asking if he wanted anything.

"No," Lea said. "My father is here."

Penrose stayed with him a little while, speaking in quiet tones, then moved on to where another man lay with his head propped up on a blanket, his face an unrecognizable, bloody mess. Quincy looked at his frock coat and realized he was an officer. He was Gerard.

Quincy squeezed his eyes shut, unable to bear any more, but the sight of Gerard's face had reminded him of the fight, of all the terror and confusion and of Becker. Becker had betrayed them. They could have fought on—might have won free. Becker had given them up.

Why, he wondered, angry tears starting again. *Why?*

Then he suddenly knew. It was the slaves. Lincoln's proclamation. Becker had been distant ever since they had learned of it. Becker, who had come to Annapolis from South Carolina.

It was late. Jamie gazed at the half-empty bottle of brandy on the table between him and Ellsberry Lane. The Federal navy had fled the bay, and Galveston was back in Confederate hands. All over town the army was celebrating, something the brigade knew very well how to do. This meeting was not exactly of a celebratory nature, however, which was why Jamie had sought out a private parlor at the Island City Hotel.

He picked up the bottle and poured himself another half-glass, swirling it around, enjoying the glints of candlelight off the golden liquor. Taking a swallow he wondered why, after all that had occurred in the last day and night without sleep, and after all the brandy he'd consumed in the last hour, he was still conscious, not to mention sober.

He set the glass down and looked at his friend, who was watching him, wearing just a hint of a frown. "So," Jamie said. "What do you recommend?"

Lane sighed, folding his arms across his chest. "It's a difficult question."

Jamie nodded. "I don't want the slave to be punished."

Lane's frown deepened as he stared at the candle between them. "Right now," he said slowly, "the army believes that Owens is a war hero." He looked up at Jamie. "It would be a shame for his family to have to learn it was otherwise."

"Oh," Jamie said. After a moment he added, "I hadn't considered that."

"Board of inquiry, nasty scandal—the press would be bound to get hold of it. Let it pass, James," Lane said softly. "He's a casualty of war."

Jamie closed his eyes. "The strange thing is," he said in a rough voice, "I think Owens actually liked me. He seemed to always want me to be more like him."

"Thank God you're not."

Jamie let out a bitter laugh. "Wouldn't I be a better soldier if I were?"

"No."

"But—" Jamie took a large swallow of brandy and waited for the fire to fade out of his mouth. "He was never afraid."

"Who says that's a trait of a good soldier? I'd be more concerned if you stopped being afraid." Lane leaned toward him across the table. "We're human beings, James. War is an awful thing. We use it because we don't have a better tool. Anyone who actually enjoys it—that's the man who worries me."

Jamie leaned back in his chair, gazing at Lane. He felt as if a tremendous hand had been squeezing him and had suddenly let go, allowing him to breathe again.

"Thank you," he said.

Lane smiled softly, and nodded. "You're welcome."

———

Emma sat on the parlor sofa, a book in her lap, her eyes gazing blindly at the same page she'd had open for an hour or more. Candles glowed on the mantel and on the tables; she wanted the light to be seen from outside. Mr. Lawford had long since gone to bed, almost immediately after they had shared a silent supper. He was crushed, poor man. She wished she knew how to help him. For herself, she felt mostly numbness.

A sound outside caught her attention, the clack of one hoof against another. A tired horse might walk so. She raised her head and stared at the window, listening. In a moment she heard the slide and soft thump of someone dismounting, then the creak of the gate. Setting the book aside, she rose and hurried to peek out between the curtains. There was enough moonlight that she could see it was Jamie—she knew him by his walk and by the battered old hat he always wore. She hurried to the front door and opened it before he could knock. He looked about as worn out as she felt.

"Come in," she said softly, leading him to the parlor.

"Is Aunt May asleep?" he asked in a half-whisper.

Emma sat down and waited for Jamie to take a chair before answering. "She's dead, Jamie."

He winced, then closed his eyes. "I'm sorry," he said.

"Yes, so am I."

"I'm sorry I wasn't here . . . I did come by, but you were gone—"

"We went to the convent when the fighting began," Emma told him. "That's where May died. Quite peacefully, with Mr. Lawford beside her."

"Oh. That's—good. Was she awake?"

"I don't know. I was helping the sisters with the wounded."

Jamie's eyes came up sharply at that, then his gaze softened. "You didn't have to do that."

"Well, I could hardly stand by doing nothing." Emma sighed, the reminder of the dreadful work increasing her sense of weariness. "I saw two or three of your friends. They asked to be remembered to you. I'm afraid I've forgotten their names."

"I'll visit them tomorrow."

Emma watched him get lost in his thoughts, elbows on his knees, hands clasped together and his eyes far away. She drew a breath. Now was her chance to speak to him. She had sent Rupert and Daisy to bed on purpose for this opportunity, but she was a little afraid to begin.

"Jamie?" she said quietly. "Tell me . . . was it Major Owens?"

His head shot up at that. "What did Rupert tell you?"

"Everything."

Jamie's jaw worked. He picked up a seashell that was lying on the table, turned it over in his hands, then put it down. At last he said, "Have you mentioned it to anyone? Mr. Lawford?"

"No," Emma said.

"Don't." His eyes were hard now. After a moment he looked away. "He's a casualty of war, Emma," he said in a low, strangled voice.

Emma nodded, then licked her lips. "Jamie? Can you forgive me?" she said, nearly whispering.

He frowned. His gaze wandered toward her, but never met hers.

"When you first came home—I was cruel," Emma said, the words starting to tumble out. "I'm sorry for it. I was just so angry, and I didn't understand what you had been through. Probably I still don't, but now I think I have an inkling."

He looked up at her then, his eyes a well of sorrow. "Oh, Em!" he whispered, and flung himself onto the sofa and into her arms.

She held him tight, so tight, and felt his sobs shuddering through her. "I'm sorry, Jamie," she said. "I'm so sorry. I didn't know how horrible it was. I wish you had never gone."

He pulled back to look at her. She dabbed at his face with her handkerchief, but he caught her hand and just squeezed it. She thought he looked better, a little.

"You know," she said, "I think maybe Stephen was the lucky one."

Jamie sighed, saying nothing, saying everything with his eyes. He forgave her, she saw, and also he needed her, which was a comfort. He needed her to know, to understand. She would have to keep working at it. It was a great compliment, to be needed like that. He closed his eyes, leaning his head on her shoulder, and Emma smiled softly as she stroked his hair.

25

The Confederates lost some gallant men at Galveston, but it takes blood to make a war history, and if no towering monument mutely proclaims their fame, while the surf foams on the historic strand the grand old ocean shall call to memory their gallant deeds and glorious death.
—W. P. Laughter, 2nd TX Cavalry

Emma walked toward the cemetery with Jamie and Mr. Lawford, carrying a bunch of flowers—winter mums, and some pansies— that she had picked from May's garden that morning. The men being buried were Commander Jonathan Wainwright and Lieutenant Edward Lea, Federal navy officers from the *Harriet Lane*, neither of whom she knew. The flowers she had brought and which she would leave on their grave were not really for them. They were for May, and for Lieutenant Sherman. They were for Stephen.

May's funeral would come later, up in Houston, where she would be buried with Mr. Asterly. Mr. Lawford was already making arrangements, and Emma and Jamie would be going with him to the Capitol Hotel in a day or two. Jamie would travel on to rejoin his battery, Emma would attend the funeral and then return home. She wished Jamie could escort her, but he had already told her he didn't dare delay any more, and she did have Daisy.

Emma sighed. She did not know what she was going to do with Daisy. Neither she nor Momma needed a lady's maid, but

Aunt May had not wanted her sold and Emma didn't want to go against her wishes. She didn't much like the thought of selling her anyway, but what would she do with her? Rupert was looking forward to seeing the ranch, and Emma thought he would be a big help there. Daisy remained silent, which boded ill. Emma suspected Momma would not like Daisy's manners.

They arrived at the cemetery to find it already crowded. Hundreds of people had come to the funeral, mostly soldiers and sailors. The prisoners from the *Harriet Lane* had asked permission to be present, and General Magruder had granted it. They stood together under guard to watch their commanders be buried, many of them openly weeping. As Emma and her family walked past them she paused, seeing a familiar face.

The sailor—an officer, by his coat, though she did not understand the Federal insignia—stood grim and silent, supporting himself on a crutch. One leg was bandaged, and he looked rather pale. Emma stepped toward him and he looked at her, startled recognition in his face. She gazed at him for a moment, knowing that she was supposed to hate him but unable to summon anything like that feeling. She pitied him, she decided.

The men beside him were becoming curious. The officer noticed, and removed his hat, bowing slightly to Emma. "Ma'am?" he said, looking uncertain.

"Thank you for the beef, and the ducks," she told him.

A half-smile flickered, then was gone. He bowed again, formally. Emma gave him a sad smile, then moved on. Wheat, she remembered, Rupert had said his name was Wheat.

Mr. Lawford found a place from which they could see the ceremony. Commander Wainwright being a Mason, the funeral included full Masonic rites, which consisted of mysterious gestures and commendations to God, each repeated thrice. The two bodies were placed in one grave, far from either man's home, but near the sea that had shaped their lives.

"That's Edward Lea's father," Jamie murmured to Emma as a

tall man stepped up to read from a prayer book. "He's on Ma-gruder's staff. That prayer book was his son's."

. It made as much sense as anything had in the last two days. Emma was tired of conundrums. She did not want to think about such things. She was content to watch and listen.

Major Lea looked aggrieved as he read the burial service, though his voice was strong and clear. Emma felt in sympathy with him. She thought of Stephen, how angry she had been, how heartbroken. She still loved him, would always love him, but the sorrow had softened. Oddly, though she now had more losses to grieve for, her pain was somehow lessened. The panic she had felt was gone. She thought perhaps it was because she now knew better who she was; she had done as Momma had wished and learned from Aunt May what it was to be a lady, but the knowledge had not changed her. If anything, it had strength-ened her resolve. Galveston was a beautiful place, and she would always have fond memories of her time here, though there would be painful ones as well. Now it was time to go home, back to the ranch where she belonged, and where she hoped to find peace.

Major Lea closed the small prayer book and looked up to address the assembled soldiers, sailors, and civilians. "Allow one so sorely tried in this his willing sacrifice to beseech you," he said, "to believe that while we defend our rights with our strong arms and honest hearts, those we meet in battle may also have hearts as brave and honest as our own." He paused, blinked a few times, then continued. "We have buried two brave and hon-est gentlemen. Peace to their ashes; tread lightly over their graves. Amen."

"Amen," Emma whispered, feeling tears slide down her cheeks. She let them fall, glad to be free of them. She had held them inside far too long.

Epilogue

Galveston, Texas
January 2, 1863

Dear Mother and Father,

    I write to inform you that I am a prisoner of war. Our ship was taken yesterday and the island of Galveston recaptured by the Rebels. I am wounded in the right thigh, not dangerously but it will be some time before I am well. We are being treated decently and have been told we will be paroled, but I do not count on it being soon in my case as the officers will not be exchanged except in a pretty hard bargain. Acting Master Becker has been paroled already—they set him free almost at once, a reward no doubt for his betrayal of us. I have heard that he went out in a boat to the *Clifton* with the Rebel officers, and told them the *Lane*'s crew had all been killed save for 5 or 6 men. This was a black lie, and was the cause of the *Clifton*'s departing the bay and our loss of the battle. If the *Clifton* had come to our aid, we would be free now and the island still ours.

    Our captain and executive officer were both killed. We were permitted to attend the funeral today, where the service was performed by Lieutenant Lea's father who is a major in the Rebel army. He seemed sad to lose his son, but not regretful of the insurrection that had caused his death.

    Our infantry who were captured in the fight are very bitter against the Navy—they say that Renshaw promised to take them up from the wharf if the fighting went badly, but the *Clifton* and *Owasco* both steamed past without answering their hail. Renshaw has paid for his sins. He blew himself up in destroying the *Westfield*, which has spared the Navy the expense of conducting a court-martial for his bungling of the battle.

I do not know when I will be home. Will try to write again if I am permitted. We are to be moved inland so do not send to Galveston. Please inform Nathaniel of my capture, and tell my friends not to worry, that I am on the way to being well again. Their thoughts and prayers are treasured by

Your son,
Quincy

Author's Note

While this novel is based upon actual events, it is a work of fiction. Any inaccuracies or errors are solely mine. In some cases I have given to fictional characters the actions and positions held by real people. For example, Jamie commands a section in the Valverde Battery, a real unit with a proud history. All the men in his imaginary section are fictional. In actuality the third section commander of the battery was Lieutenant William Smith. Another example is Frank Becker, who takes the place of the *Harriet Lane*'s real Acting Master J. A. Hannum, and plays his part in the Battle of Galveston.

Fictional characters in this novel include the Russell family (Jamie, Emma, Momma [Eva], Poppa [Earl], Gabe, Matthew, Susan, and Daniel), Val Owens, May Asterly, Albert Lawford, Rupert, Daisy, Quincy and Nathaniel Wheat, Robert Gerard, Gordon Hinks, Isaiah, William, Colonel and Mrs. Hawkland, and various minor characters.

Many characters, major and minor, represented in this book are real people. For any errors I may have made with respect to them, I humbly apologize. This work is intended as a tribute to their memory and to their gallantry.

In *Galveston*, the encounter between the *Harriet Lane* and the Confederate vessels *Webb* and *Music* is fictional, although they were all in the vicinity at that time and such a clash could have occurred. Likewise, the *Lane*'s encounter with a blockade runner is fictional, though she was indeed blockading at that time.

While the Hawklands and their plantation home, Rosehall, are fictional, the plantations of Belle View and Angola are real. This area, the confluence of the Mississippi and Red Rivers, was an important location throughout the war, particularly for Confederate communications, transportation, and trade.

The *Harriet Lane* was converted to a blockade runner by the Confederates, but was never able to leave Galveston Bay due to the Federal blockade. Years later she was renamed the *Elliot Ritchie*, and was eventually lost at sea.

The Battle of Galveston restored the island and its harbor to Confederate control and dealt a severe blow to the confidence of the Federal Navy, who never attempted its recapture.

For more information about Civil War events west of the Mississippi, please visit *www.pgnagle.com.*

Suggested Reading

This short bibliography represents a selection of references which the author recommends to readers wishing to learn more about the Battle of Galveston.

Cotham, Edward T., Jr., *Battle on the Bay: The Civil War Struggle for Galveston*, University of Texas Press, Austin, 1998.

Frazier, Donald S., *Cottonclads!: The Battle of Galveston and the Defense of the Texas Coast*, McWhiney Foundation Press, Abilene, 1998.

Josephy, Alvin M., Jr., *The Civil War in the American West*, Alfred A. Knopf, New York, 1991.

McPherson, James M., and Patricia R. McPherson, eds., *Lamson of the Gettysburg, The Civil War Letters of Roswell H. Lamson, U.S. Navy*, Oxford University Press, New York, 1997.

Mahan, A. T., *The Navy in the Civil War: The Gulf and Inland Waters*, Charles Scribner's Sons, New York, 1881–1883 (facsimile edition, The Archive Society, 1992).

Soley, J. Russell, *The Navy in the Civil War: The Blockade and the Cruisers*, Jack Brussel, New York, 1881–1883 (facsimile edition).

Williams, Edward B., ed., *Rebel Brothers: The Civil War Letters of the Truehearts*, Texas A & M University Press, College Station, 1995.

About the Author

A native and lifelong resident of New Mexico, P. G. Nagle has a special love of the outdoors, particularly New Mexico's wilds, where many of her stories are born. Her recent historical novel, *Glorieta Pass*, and its sequel, *The Guns of Valverde*, are set during the New Mexico Campaign of the Civil War.

Nagle's work has appeared in *The Magazine of Fantasy & Science Fiction* and in several anthologies, including collections honoring New Mexico writers Jack Williamson, who lives in Portales, New Mexico, and the late Roger Zelazny, who lived in Santa Fe. Her short story "Coyote Ugly" was honored as a finalist for the Theodore Sturgeon Award, and *Glorieta Pass* was a finalist for the Zia Award.